The midnight adventure in the 1965 Plymouth Valiant started normally enough. The four of us were in Dante's Bar, marking the end of Spring Semester. I had no way of knowing it would be the last normal day of my life…

…when the smell of Jack Daniel's woke me it took me awhile to be amazed that the three of them were still at it, drinking like demons and driving the Valiant in the darkness…

Nattie wasn't sleeping but she was quiet, listening to Adams and Daniel O'Neill going back and forth, talking mostly nonsense in that way they had of assigning a great deal of importance to frivolous or silly discourse.

I tried hard not to listen, not to think, not to wonder. A deformed piece of time and space had just spilled out across the prairie, escaping from a dark little midnight crevice. It swallowed us up and nothing was the same. Something skewed; something else twisted. A macabre tilt in the darkness out in the middle of our midnight nowhere.

I float in the Valiant like a madman

Midnight Valiant

A Parable

Bobby Haas

First Edition

Cover Design by Mark Harris

*   Thanks to Dz, Coly, and O'Rourke
for generous
assistance with gestation, and

Thanks to Harry for seeing it, and seeing it through, and

Thanks to the Professor, who rapped
commas with a red pen like
knuckles with a ruler, and

Thanks to vV, who cried
when first she read it, and

Profound thanks to my daughters,
who both understood it
with shockingly keen insight

This Book is Dedicated to

Sarah Bug
and
Ali Kat

the Sweetness of my Heart

Midnight Valiant

Book One

Life's but a sweeping moment, a stone stairway
That reaches up and out toward the stars
And then explodes in fire: it is a tale
Told by a madman, full of dust and chaos,
Signifying God.

From *The Plagiarist*
- by John Gophe

Introitus
(Requiem Aeternam)

My Passion is the sound of prairie cicadas. My Crown of Thorns is the memory of Becky Dreiling's farm. My resurrection is my penance – sweeping sacred dust into careful piles of daily devotion. But no more.

It is finished.

I celebrate Calvary and sing Gethsemane. I work the beads to no avail: all redemptive swirls of Confessional incense now stain instead of cleanse my soul.

Nevertheless, I refuse to renounce the Sacraments.

Likewise, Christ did not escape. But what if he had? What if he had lived on in Lazarus? What if he had transformed his body, and transferred his soul, and lived long on the soil that was forbidden to him? What then?

***

Cicadas buzz incessantly, loud and long in the hot Kansas summer. They buzz high up in the few trees providing little shade against blistering sun and ceaseless wind. Cicadas are crunchy bugs the size of your thumb and they buzz and they buzz and they buzz. When the prairie afternoons turn hot and still, it begins: they buzz and they buzz. In the small towns of north-central Kansas, towns on the High Plains where farmers harvest sunflowers and winter wheat, cicadas buzz and the children of immigrants do not call them by their correct name. No one calls them cicadas. Everyone calls them by their true name: "Goddam Locusts."

They buzz and they buzz, ceaseless like the hot wind, and their name is always the same. It doesn't matter what you call them, it doesn't matter how their name is said, they just buzz and they buzz and they buzz. Goddam Locusts.

3

***

And so it is with me. My stomach buzzes and buzzes because no one will correctly say my name. I sit a silent vigil, waiting with reverence for the end of my stomach buzz: no more subdued or stammered murmurs of correction; no more repeated mumble: "Rhymes with Off, not with Oaf."

It doesn't matter what my name rhymes with. It doesn't matter anymore how it is said, or by whom. Rhymes with cauldron. Rhymes with stove. Rhymes with Eucharist or Sinclair. Doesn't matter. Until I grasp this, I will continue tumbling down into the choking chaos. It is the precise moment when the buzzing Kansas locusts bless me with Extreme Unction that I notice the tiniest crumbling of dust.

That's how it was at Becky Dreiling's farm, when the stones and mortar of the *stairway to the stars* came crashing down and filled the barn with choking dust: that first Catacomb crumble was small and subtle. A slight shift, a speck, a tiny tremor and then settled and still and, if you weren't paying attention, you might have thought that was all. Like an aftershock when it's all over, a herald of the end.

Would that it had been so.

In any event, clearly, that early crumble of dust was when it began.

***

It's this curiosity about the chronology which adds to the difficulty of knowing the story. The story itself is confused about time. My story is confused about time and so my name, in a strange sort of way, is confused, is lost about time. As if only through immigration and migration and movement are we connected to the fabric of time.

Your grandfather's name when he arrived on these shores doesn't always stay your name. Your grandfather's name is no longer your name because somewhere along the line it wasn't protected. A careless immigration clerk. An overworked second grade teacher. Somebody takes it because you neglected to protect it. You didn't defend it.

I remember my Grandfather saying our name, long ago when I was little. The way he said it sounded like a British person saying laugh. "Lough." But then they would just say "Loaf" so that doesn't matter too.

It's just a name, after all. Just my name. It's okay, whatever they want to call me.

It's not as if it's a name like Dreiling; a name filled with the hope of the Trinity and the terror of the Triple Goddess. Mother and Maiden, Holy Ghost, Father, Son and Crone. Two great movements and forces hurtling toward each other, crashing into conflict.

I don't care all that much for conflict, if you really want to know. I'd rather just get along, whenever that's possible.

Instead of making a scene and taking a stand, I'd clasp and shake the hand of any man. I'd shake the hand of Adolph Hitler if he offered it.

That's a shameful plagiarism, and one bastardized to boot.

But of course I've never been above stealing and molding and creating into my own. Throw whatever's handy into the pot, give it a good name and bask in the glow of my newest stew. A pathetic lack of original substance and a pitiful clinging to meaningless form.

***

I was that way before I went to Becky Dreiling's farm. I am that way still, so clearly it's difficult to remember where I am and if I really ever left the farm at all.

Perhaps I never did. The voice of the farm is with me always, chattering like the incessant winds blowing ceaselessly across the Great Plains prairie. A voice filling my ears constantly, whispering sometimes, screaming always "no escape, no escape."

The wind from the prairie can comfort even as it terrorizes; it can excite even as it blows, constant and mundane and always. The prairie wind has the same voice every day and every year and forever – hot and sticky in summer, frigid and piercing in winter. But always the same voice; the voice of the prairie, expansive and forever. I've left that voice because I've left the prairie. But the voice of the farm is different. The wind from Becky Dreiling's farm fills my ears and snares my soul and haunts me always.

It never leaves me.

I might have thought once that wind is wind and nothing in the one is different than the other. I now know the difference is as real as that between sandpaper and soft skin, or true friends and empty nights. Or between the sound of your car and the sound of any old car. If you pay attention the differences are breathtaking.

Like you can hear the difference in the engine of some old dusty and distant four-door sedan. You know the many sounds the engine makes, so you know when its sounds are different. The sound of a comfortable engine doggedly driving you forever across the prairie, taking you far away and turning you into a speck on the horizon; the sound it makes when you get there and the sound it makes when you turn it off.

Pick any old car, and if you've grown up with it, or it's grown old with you, you can hear the difference. Differences of laughter in the back seat, or sounds of cussing and drinking, rollicking back from the front seat. The sounds that make the engine unique so you know the car when you hear it coming, or when it's taking you away.

Doesn't matter what kind of car, as long as it's old, and reliable, and holds some part of your life. A baby-blue Rambler parked down the street when you were a kid; a drab olive green Dodge Dart your uncle drove.

Even a faded tan 1965 Plymouth Valiant.

***

The wind from the farm was like that, blowing always, sometimes filling your ears with only one voice, and other times you could hear distinctly the several voices blending into the one. Sometimes just the farm voice, sometimes the voices of those left behind, calling me always. Clawing and grabbing at me to stay behind still. I cover my ears and try to block them out. Clumsy, I tip the crystal tumbler and spill most of the ice. And the wind is relentless, and it blows in my head always.

The wind voices of Becky Dreiling and Nattie Sinclair, so soft and pretty and smiling, both of them. Women I loved who never loved me; women I would have touched with thousands of caresses but never did; women into where you fell deep and never got out; women mysterious and dangerous and fine.

Lance O'Neill not calling but in the wind all the same and at the farm even still. Not a father not an uncle not a husband not a friend. Lance O'Neill not calling but cussing and winking and watching me always.

The voices of Nattie Sinclair and Adams raging also in the wind. Their single voice beautiful and clean before the farm, when they were first falling in love; their terrifying voice afterwards.

Daniel O'Neill's voice perhaps the loudest – I can feel his soul clutching its way out of the wind. I can see him as I cover my ears and scream over the wind. I see his eyes. I see his face; I admire its strength and love its softness. I can see that scruff, neither whiskers nor beard. The jeans and work boots. Jet-black long hair. A face Celtic, chiseled, and clean.

***

I drink now because I can't stop the farm wind. I drink now in a desperate hope of hearing again the prairie wind, if only for a moment of reprieve, a moment of release, a moment to take me away. I drink now because I didn't drink then.

"Dag!"

The little whiskey left in the bottom of the glass has eaten the last of the ice. The cool dilution tastes like a tease.

And so forget you, Daniel O'Neill, forget you all and forget the fresh ice. I pour the glass full brown gold and empty it.

I know that was one of the better than fine rules and I just broke it.

"Lots of ice, a little Jack, and pour it often."

Platitudes now plagiarized.

Haas

I haven't yet drunk enough Jack Daniel's to bring whiskey tears. Jack Daniel's was Daniel O'Neill's whiskey. He brought it to us in college; he brought it with him from Kansas. He drank it in defiance of the Frat Boys' gin and the Jocks' scotch. He drank Jack Daniel's whiskey because it was his. He drank it because no one else did. I couldn't drink it with him when I knew him, but I drink it without him now.

Daniel O'Neill's life was one long tack strip of talismans: Jack Daniel's whiskey and 1965 Plymouth Valiants, midnight drives and burning alone.

I know that when morning brings a clear head and shines its light through the monsters of this bottle, I know I'll remember Becky Dreiling's farm is dead. I know that, while holding my hangover and sucking sodas for dry mouth, I might spend tomorrow's Sunday in the Valiant of my mind, slamming the doors and driving toward its tomb, plowed up and buried six feet beneath the hot dusty nowhere.

Driving with all four windows rolled down, hot dry air thundering around the car battering steadily through the infinite grassland Prairie. Driving long and distant with the sound of laughter in the engine, the sound of silly in the adventure. Driving all afternoon through burning white sun away from middle of nowhere exploding orange sunsets. And then nightfall. Darkness. Driving and celebrating the exhilaration and the terror as he turns off the headlights in the new-moon darkness. Everything else in the universe disappears except for the screaming wind and the utter blackness. Desperate, mindless. Driving the Valiant in the midnight darkness.

But tonight, a ridiculous dribble of Jack Daniel's staining my shirt, I remember a kitchen sink stained with old coffee and a kitchen floor stained with caked yellow mud from a farm long ago. Tonight I cannot stop the wind. I cannot silence the cry.

I have attempted, over the years, to plug that plea with everything imaginable, anything possible. I sand wood and sweep sawdust. I eat and drink.

I watch the outside through my window. I never laugh and seldom speak.

I sleep (perchance to dream.

That does not count as a plagiarism, as I do not take it for my own. I have no use for that dithering little whine and murderous self-indulgence. Do it or don't do it, decide and move on).

"A man who doesn't pee in his own backyard
Has no idea where in the hell he lives."
- Lance O'Neill

Chapter 1

The honky tonk outside of Dodge City erupted in hoots and hollers as the local band hit the first notes of Hank Williams' *Jambalaya*. A few real cowboys and a lot of gussied-up Saturday-nighters grabbed their gals unprodded and headed to the oak parquet dance floor.

"Goodbye Joe," Lance O'Neill mouthed along. He sat alone at a small table off in a dark corner, slouched against the busted terminal of a video poker machine. "Me gotta go."

Christ almighty, his leg hurt. Like a son of a bitch. Both he and this dive reeked of cigarettes and beer, and his goddamn leg hurt. He closed his eyes and used the technique to fight off images of the jungle and so to calm the pain. He inhaled slowly through the fire and exploding terror and he exhaled slowly to silence the screams. Slowly in, slowly out. Blue in, red out. Flowers in, fire out. Think Van Morrison: You breathe in you breathe out, you breathe in you breathe out, you breathe in you breathe out, you breathe in you breathe out. Becky in, Danny out.

"Shit," he said aloud, and he began again with the technique. Danny was the reason for the technique. He couldn't be part of the technique.

Danny's face, framed in fire, glowed like the face of a scream.

And his goddamn leg throbbed. Focus. Again. Breathe. Budweiser in, dysentery out. Long, aimless driving the pickup in, long, aimless slogging through jungle out. Musk perfume in, blood and gunpowder out. Laughter in, terror...

"Another beer, Hon?" Her hand touched his and then both wrapped around the top of the glass longneck. Lance opened his

11

eyes and followed her arm up to her smile. He held onto the bottle for just a moment, just long enough to get the rush. The rush of the waitress smile. You could feel like shit, or feel invisible, or feel nothing at all except the throb and scream of your goddamn missing leg but the rare, right kind of waitress smile gave you that last gasp of maybe just one more day. Not the common "need a beer hope you tip well" smile, but the "you look like shit and I'm just a waitress" smile. The smile that softened the edge, lit the blackness and cooled the rage.

"Thanks, Doll," Lance O'Neill said. "Dig me up a cold one."

She winked like a sister and patted his hand, took the bottle and then turned and moved across the edge of the dance floor toward the bar. Lance watched her go and he imagined her life – a couple of kids, junior high age, probably, whom her mom watches when she works a couple of shifts slinging drinks for vacation money; a string of infrequent and mostly lousy boyfriends, one guy she fell for hard and still thinks about; a class every now and then at the community college; a Chiefs or Royals T-shirt she sleeps in because she usually sleeps alone. Those rare nights she slips on her champagne pink silk sheer are the nights when she gives much more than she gets with men who don't understand her and don't care enough to try. She knows she deserves more and one day she'll make it happen. One day her real life will begin.

She returned to his table with only one beer on her tray and a warmer smile and fresh gloss on her lips.

"That's one-seventy-five, Hon," she said. "Sorry, but it's after nine; price goes up when the band comes on."

"That's all right."

"Lots of people get mad. Guys, mostly. Tips go down first hour or so after the band comes on."

"You got to make a living, same as the band."

"Years ago, I dated the bass player. We went to high school. He used to be nicer. A lot nicer. Sweeter, even. Now he thinks he should be in Nashville."

"Guess nearly everybody thinks they should be somewhere else." Lance nudged the stack of bills across the small round table toward the waitress.

She smiled again, nervous. Her finger drew a slow circle in the water sweating off his bottle of beer. Finally she asked, "Do you ever braid your hair? It's beautiful. I bet Charlene, the bartender, that you're Indian, or at least part. Half at least."

"What did Charlene think?"

"Nothing, just not Indian."

"How much the bet?"

"Not very much. In fun, mostly."

"Good. I'm not."

"Indian?"

"Not even half. Not even a little. Irish, all the way through."

"No. Really? With your dark hair? Irish have red hair."

"Not the black Irish. Not me."

"Wow. I thought sure Indian. On account of your hair, and the jewelry. The earrings and, uh, well, I guess it's not called a necklace for a man, but you know. Most men around here don't have earrings, or much jewelry at all except belt buckles and goddamn wedding rings."

"Well," Lance said, reaching for the bottle of beer, "mostly I'm from somewhere else."

"Sometimes I wish I was. Some day I will be."

Not tonight, though, Lance thought, and then he thought a moment about her champagne pink silk nightgown. "Not tonight," he said aloud.

"Yeah, not tonight. I gotta go."

"Thanks for the beer. Don't forget me sitting back here."

"I won't," the woman smiled again.

Lance figured not.

And then, even though it violated every part of the technique, Lance O'Neill reached into the inside breast pocket of his beat-up khaki army jacket and pulled out a stuffed, crumpled envelope. He wiped the table in front of him clean with his sleeve and then he polished it with a napkin. He set the envelope down. He reached into the outer pocket on the same breast side and pulled out a soft leather pouch holding his fixings. He peeled off a rolling paper and sprinkled an even layer of long-cut tobacco into the crease. He massaged the tobacco inside the paper until both edges of paper were clean against each other and then he quickly turned the front edge over and into the back. He licked the gummed edge and ran his finger over the seam and then pinched off both ends of loose tobacco with his fingernails. He tamped the cigarette several times against his thumbnail. He looked at his brother's Zippo for a long time before popping the lid and striking the wheel. He touched the blue flame to the end of the cigarette and felt the calm of the nicotine, and then he listened to and let echo the metallic sound of the lighter – its lid snapping closed with clarity and finality.

Lance smoked for awhile and then put the cigarette down in the amber glass ashtray and picked up and opened the envelope. He removed the bundle of worn papers – torn scraps and folded notebook leaves, a bar napkin or two all crumpled and faded, some stained, and he began to look at them, one at a time. And then he breathed in and breathed out and breathed in and breathed out, and he let the memories and the laughter come back.

Danny, Becky, Lance. Danny, Becky, Lance. Every paper, every scrap, Danny, Becky, Lance underlined across the top. Danny, Becky, Lance always with the circled bid first, and then the meld, and then the points in the tricks, and then the totals. Three running columns, a yin-yang next to the score when Danny won, a pentagram for Becky's victories and a peace symbol scrawled next to each number if Lance won. A smiley face but with a frown instead when you went set. Danny always keeping score, Becky always dealing the three-handed way like her dad and uncles did, and Lance breathing it all in and breathing it all out.

Lance picked up and re-lit his cigarette. "Goddamn," he said and then, in one long swallow, he drained the beer from the bottle. He removed the broken-down deck of pinochle cards from the envelope and slipped them methodically from hand to hand feeling the edges on his fingertips and listening to the laughter fluttering through them.

"Goddamn," he said again.

The waitress returned, this time balancing a tray filled with drinks, mostly cocktails but some beer also, and she set a bottle on the table in front of him.

"This one's on me."

Lance regarded her a moment. "Ever wonder why one-legged men don't play three-handed pinochle?" He knew he was getting intoxicated. He kept his gaze fixed on her. The waitress glanced nervously down to the legs of his bar stool.

"Does it hurt?" she finally asked.

"Which part?"

"I gotta deliver these," she said. She looked down again, and then she left.

"Leg hurts sometimes," Lance said after her. "Pinochle hurts always."

Lance carefully repacked the envelope and worked on the fresh bottle of beer. He sat through the night and drank several more, and then he said "goddamn" and got up and clumped heavily across the edge of the dance floor and limped out the front door of the bar.

***

Lance usually parked the pickup facing east so the morning sun would hit and wake him early. It did. Somehow his leg got wrapped around the gearshift lever sticking up from the floorboard, and the wooden peg got wedged awkwardly and painfully between the seat back and the rear window. Lance mumbled "shit" and rubbed his jaw, feeling the stubble as if checking a calendar. Suddenly he clutched in agony as a muscle spasm gripped the back of his leg, in the thigh above the wood. He rubbed the hardened muscle and worked to visualize it as smooth and flowing and fine rather than as the quivering mass of grotesque that caused his fingers to flinch. He worked slowly, trying to relax the muscle, trying to stretch it, trying to visualize its release, imagining it attached to ligament and bone instead of ending in a gnarled stump of nothing and carved wood.

He slowly untangled himself and then he fumbled for the door handle and spilled outside to pee in the early morning cold. Sure as hell he was parked out in the middle of Kansas nowhere. First he remembered the waitress and the honky tonk, and then he remembered he didn't go home with her. Somehow he found his way out of Dodge City and had driven himself back out into the country. Back to the middle of nowhere, back to the land of yellow stone fence posts encircling yellow stone churches with steeples made of the yellow limestone rising from endless expanses of yellow dirt. He thought of home. The only things in Monterey yellow like this yellow were the yellow oxalis that bloomed in spring along the beach rocks amid the succulent cacti.

He thought of waking up along the wharfs of the bay on similar autumn mornings, lounging among the rocks and concrete pylons beneath the deserted canneries. Or perhaps up top on the last rough timber wharf. Once the sun hit the gulls their chatter drowned out the water swelling and sloshing against the rocks; sea lions barking and hollering out by the buoys; the flap of pigeon wings. Mornings as noisy and alive and full of promise as this morning was still and faceless and lost.

Just as the endless empty expanse of Kansas dust prairie was once a magnificent inland sea, transformed over eons into desolation, the deserted canneries were transforming back into hustles of commerce aimed now at tourists instead of sardines. He left just as the renovation began. He left hoping the over-harvesting of retirees would lead also to their disappearance, just like the sardines. Years before, when he and Danny left for Berkeley, he dreamed of coming home triumphant and watching the giant purse seines once more unload tons of slippery silver sardines. As if the return of the Brothers O'Neill could refill the oceans with fish like so many screaming fans on a football Friday night. The Brothers O'Neill – State Finals. The Brothers O'Neill – Fishers of Men. The two of them, together, winking and laughing, striding tall through it all like true Princes of Ireland.

Lance had waited a year after high school, working at the wharves and at a fisherman's bar, until his brother's graduation.

Sure he could get a year under his belt and scope the place out, but what the hell. Why break up the brothers in their prime?

"You can look after each other that way." Both believed their mother was touched by the angels.

Their father saw it differently. "He needs to get his goddamn ass out of the house and into college. Danny'll be fine for a year without him. No damn reason to hang around here, bumming at the wharfs, begging those S.S. Nazis to come pick him up."

"Selective Service aren't Nazis, Pop."

"Anyone who sends boys to die in the jungle for politics is a Nazi."

"Geo politics, Pop. It's about stopping the Chinese there, now, rather than at the Bay Bridge tomorrow."

"Bullshit. It's about somebody else's war. We've got no business there. No business sending 200,000 of our boys off to die in a goddamn jungle."

"Some things are worth fighting for, Pop. Patriotism, for one thing."

"Screaming in the jungle when your face is blown off is not patriotism. Is that worth dying for?"

"Freedom's worth dying for," Lance said. "You ought to love this country more, Pop. It's been pretty good to us."

"I love this country just fine." His father's eyes blazed, then softened as they shifted toward Danny. "It took us in, gave us an American-born son. America isn't the government," he told Lance. "You should have paid better attention in school. America is us."

"Well, it doesn't matter, Pop. We're not talking America, here." He laughed and nodded toward his brother. "We're talking the American Boy."

Lance enjoyed knowing he could steer his father's attention by driving his father's favorite subject.

"We're talking your ass in college where it belongs and your grades up so's to keep your goddamn deferment. That's what we're talking about."

Danny gave Lance the look even before Lance formed the thought. Don't say it, Danny's eyes insisted, almost demanded, almost mean. Don't say a thing. Lance smiled at his brother, pretending to reassure.

"Sure to say, Danny Boy will no doubt be fine; boy's a marvel, boy's a wonder." Lance winked at his brother. Danny shook his head – what's the point?

"Thing is, Pop, you might need help around here, stashing all the boy's football trophies, record books and cheerleader panties. Promises to be a senior year for the ages."

"Won't happen without you throwing' it up," Danny chimed in. "You've got the cannon and you've got the touch, Big Brother. Kilpatrick's got shit for an arm, and he's easy to blitz, because he's got rocks for feet. We'll be a running team, Smitty will be the hero with the huge numbers, and I'll spend the season throwing downfield blocks. My numbers will fall, you wait and see. Kilpatrick's not anywhere near the quarterback Lance is. Nobody is, Pop."

"Kilpatrick's fine. He's only a junior, for chrissakes. Give him a year, he'll be fine."

"Boy here doesn't have a year, Pop. Boy needs his numbers now. This is his shot."

"Goddamn," their father said.

"I won't ever get the stats without Number 9 here putting it up," Danny said. "Nobody throws like the Brother O'Neill. Sure as hell not Kilpatrick. You know that, Pop. Shoulda heard what Richter said about Lance, end of season meeting."

"Coach Richter's a damn fine man. A damn fine coach."

"Lance O'Neill is a damn fine quarterback," Danny said, feeling fine about pushing his father.

"Lance was a good ballplayer, no question. Showed up for every game."

"Gee, thanks Pop," Lance said. "Means a ton."

"Goddamn interception in the championship."

"That's bullshit, Dad." Danny's eyes blazed. "Lance holds half the records for the whole goddamn high school. Yards in a season. Yards in a game. Touchdowns in a game. Yards rushing in a single game, for chrissakes. Three hundred eighty-three yards for a quarterback? Jesus, Pop."

"Who caught all of those touchdowns? You caught four of the five." The old man's eyes softened a little, just for a moment. "The Brothers O'Neill," he said, smiling at them both. "They'll talk about that game for years."

"In most houses, Pop," Lance said. "In most houses they probably will."

"They'll talk about Lance O'Neill in any house that knows anything at all about football," Danny said.

"They'll talk about the Brothers O'Neill," their father said. "And don't forget," he said, nodding to his younger son, "you've still got an entire year coming up."

"Kilpatrick's got shit for an arm, Pop," Danny said.

"Jesus H," Lance said. "I'm going out for some air."

So without welcome or why, Lance stayed the extra year, watching the numbers and waiting for Danny. Sometimes at the house but mostly not, Lance waited for his brother to set the records, warm the old man's heart and get the hell out.

They drove to Berkeley in April for the demonstrations, but since they still lived at home Danny said leaving San Francisco and driving back to Monterey made him feel like a dilettante, like a poser. Lance had to twist some serious arm to get his brother to leave the campus and go back home.

"Graduating high school is bullshit, it's manipulative, it's about nothing more than making us all good little rule-following citizens, making sure we all conform, making sure we all get our foreheads stamped and become obedient little cogs in the military fucking industrial complex. It won't change until we stand up to it," Danny's eyes sang with the lilt of his passion. Lance listened with some mix of pride and incredulity. "I'm going to stand up to it," Danny said. "I'm going to make a stand, right here, right now. I'm not going home, and I'm not going to graduate."

Lance laughed, feeling for just a moment like a father watching a child slip and fall in the waves. "You sure as hell are not staying here, and you sure as hell are going to graduate," he told his brother. "You've got six weeks left; we're going to Berkeley as soon after that as we can get packed, and I'm here to tell you they won't want some knucklehead who dropped out of school at the end of his senior year.

"We're going home," Lance said, and they did.

Within weeks of Danny's graduation, they were back on the road, arguing about their father and heading to Berkeley for good.

"He just gets excited, goes overboard sometimes," Danny told his brother. "He doesn't know how to show it."

"Seems to show it pretty clearly when it comes to receivers and second-borns."

"It's not that way," Danny said. "Really it's not."

"I'll tell you what it's not," Lance said, winking at his brother. "It's not anything about you and me, so don't worry about it. Our deal is not his deal. No doubt he'll cry at my funeral, so I've got that going for me."

"Yeah," Danny said, smiling back with mischief. "But sure as hell he won't let 'em play *Danny Boy*."

They both laughed, and relaxed in the ride.

"Far out," Danny said after a while. "Berkeley, you know?"

"Berkeley," Lance said. "Far fucking out."

"It ain't seen nothing 'til it's seen the Brothers O'Neill."

"You got that right, Danny Boy," Lance said, winking and laughing from down deep. "You sure as hell got that one right."

The brothers O'Neill didn't exactly burn the place down, but Danny especially was determined not to miss out on any more of what he called the tilting shift of the planet.

From the moment they arrived at Berkeley, Danny jumped into the summer of love and nearly drowned, choking on serious, sputtering self-righteousness. They laughed, partied, loved and protested through a semester and a half at the U Cal Berkeley Center of the Enlightenment, and then they met Becky Dreiling, a gorgeous and brilliant co-ed from Kansas.

And from there things moved very quickly and bad. As he shivered in the early morning of the Great Plains prairie, Lance O'Neill realized again that he never saw any of this coming.

When he left with his brother for Berkeley he dreamed of many things, so many things but he never caught even a glimpse of this. Never an inkling of how things turned out. Not Danny, nor his leg, nor being in country. Not Becky Dreiling, nor her boy, and sure as hell not middle of nowhere Kansas. Never in a million years, never in twenty guesses, never in a crystal ball.

He sure as hell never saw this coming.

Suddenly he remembered driving last night. He remembered a shift and then he remembered promising himself it was time for a change. A real change. Christ. He even remembered swearing on his brother. "For God's sake," he said out loud.

And yet. The truth is he didn't go home with the waitress and even in the sobriety of morning he remembered her as being somewhat pretty and very sweet. But he didn't let her take him home, and he knew finally that part was over. He shivered as he zipped himself up and he looked directly into the cold April dawn. And then he knew it was time to go home, and he knew that going home didn't mean California but meant going back for good to Becky Dreiling's farm. He got back into the truck, and as the engine sparked to life, he swallowed against the pressure at the back of his throat and behind his eyes.

***

It was later that same day while heading mostly back to the farm but taking the long way on country roads through nothing little towns that Lance O'Neill found the wood-burning cook stove. It sat desolate and out of the weather, abandoned behind the post office connected to a little antique store next to the filling station where he stopped to get seven dollars worth.

"Belonged to my Henry, before he passed," she told him. The heavy-set shopkeeper pushed her glasses gently up her nose and tamed some gray strands sticking wayward from her head. "Had several offers to sell it, over the years, but never did, somehow."

"How much will you take today?" Lance asked.

"Don't rightly know," the woman said. "It always worked good, but its two back legs are broke off. Its been sitting out there awhile. I guess you can tell that by the way it looks."

"It looks fine," Lance told her. "Or better, we could trade. What have you got needs fixing? I've got my own tools."

"Well," she began. "I can tell you, as I'm on the council and also the post-mistress, I can tell you the railing, porch and stairs of the post office are in bad shape, and since there's some insist we wait on federal money, we'll wait forever until someone falls through and breaks their neck. Clete over to the lumber yard's already said he'd put up for the boards, but I don't know the stove's worth all that."

"Stoves worth every bit of it to me," Lance said. "I'd need a place to stay a day or so."The woman eyed him carefully. "Don't even know for sure that stove works anymore. Been settin' there, like I say, for quite awhile."

"I'll have a look first. No moving parts though, so I'm guessing it's fine. At least nothing wrong I couldn't fix."

"It's got those two broke legs, like I told you."

"Doesn't matter."

The woman picked up a letter opener from atop a glass display case and ran the dull edge back and forth across her index finger. She rubbed the cast aluminum eagle on the handle.

"Ray Hermann's got a big old Victorian a few blocks over on Elm. He used to rent out rooms until the Interstate went through up north. Now next to nobody comes through so he don't anymore."

"I can't pay for a room," Lance said. "I can sleep in my truck, just need a place to park it. And a bathroom. Shower would be nice but not necessary."

The woman glanced quickly down at his one work boot. "How would you ever load it onto your truck?"

"Got a hand winch and bar extensions for the ladder rack. Have block and tackle as well. I've loaded heavier."

She considered a while. "Maybe you ought to just take it. It's sat there a long time. Henry loved it. Would give him pleasure knowing someone wanted it as bad as you seem to."

"I appreciate that," Lance said. "I really do. And I'd gladly accept, but for concern about walking up those post office steps to get at it. I'd hate to be the one to fall through and break my neck."

The woman said nothing for a time, and then finally "There's a small storeroom in the back of my shop. It's got a john and a slop sink, but no shower."

"Maybe I could just pull around, take some measurements for the steps and railing."

"Maybe," she said. "I'll call Clete when you're ready."

As Lance followed the directions outside of town to the lumber yard, he began planning where he'd put the stove in the barn, and he thought of sitting in front of it, blazing hot while snow swirled outside, talking quietly with Becky Dreiling. Perhaps drinking red wine like normal people and perhaps talking quietly with Becky Dreiling about maybe starting over and maybe starting for real.

***

Three winters back Lance decided the hell with farming. Deep down he knew Becky had already settled on leasing the rest of the north quarter to Leiker's boys. Leiker himself bought the entire herd right after her father died, and they worked out what Becky knew was a generous lease for 80 acres of pasture. She held on to the rest; Leiker said he'd happily send the boys around to check on things, so Becky Dreiling figured she'd farm a little milo and winter wheat. Leiker's boys had been helping her dad the last few years anyway, so the place was already running fine. And then out of nowhere Lance shows up looking like hell and saying he needs a place to settle down and maybe he'd give farming a try. Becky had already moved the cattle money into business in town so she wasn't dependent on cash from the crops. Becky was shocked enough to see him as well as increasingly concerned for his state of mind, so that she didn't care what he did around the place. He realized early on she was great at letting him wander, but rather than feel fortunate or lucky, Lance filed her understanding and compassion with all the rest that life threw him which he didn't deserve. He felt like a lucky son-of-a-bitch with the emphasis on son-of-a-bitch.

So throughout the years of dicking around, of driving off and then coming back, for Becky's sake Lance had always intended to put forth a decent effort to become a Kansas farmer. He knew that he could, if he set his mind to it. Most of his life had already been spent in endeavor not of his choosing anyway. What difference did it make? He had been a warrior. And then a wanderer. He was good at both; he could be good at farming. How the hell hard could it be? Lance figured the hardest part would be to keep the tractor running and cut a good deal with a combine crew in the fall. It would either rain or it wouldn't. Leiker had been cutting their small farm for years with his own crew, but Lance was sure he could get a better deal from one of the crews passing through on their way north. Leiker could keep his goddamned crews busy on his own land, which was enough sections for his own damn county. Leiker, a fourth generation Kansas farmer who bought a brand new Chevy pick-up every other year, had no respect for Lance, and Lance didn't give a shit.

But this godforsaken prairie had conspired against him at every turn. The first year Lance changed out milo for feed corn and then he watched the whole damn crop get all beat to hell and ruin by a mid-summer hailstorm. The next year he decided to seed both fields in winter wheat. After one of the wettest falls, which brought the wheat up well, the county had one of the driest years on record, and the wheat crop was forty-three percent of average.

By Halloween of Lance's second year on the farm, Becky had made the deal with Leiker. Lance was furious that Leiker swept in with his money, arrogance, and condescension. Lance didn't need his help, he didn't need his advice, and what with Leiker's insisting on paying over market on the lease, Lance sure as hell didn't need his pity. That was the first and only time Becky had shown any anger toward Lance since he arrived.

"He was good friends with my dad," she told him in measured tones. Her eyes blazed. "With this lease, Mr. Leiker chooses to honor my father. If you can't see the goodness in that then you're far enough gone you'll never make it back. Either accept it, or move on. It's none of your damn business, anyway."

By Thanksgiving Lance had emptied the barn of every last piece of anything remotely resembling a farm implement – old rusting discs, fence wire, bailing equipment and the like that he hauled up to the corner of the north forty and dumped all in a pile on the ground. Leiker's boys could pick it up or it could sit and rust and rot. Lance didn't give a shit one way or the other. The decent hand tools he hung in the mudroom at the back of the house for Becky's kitchen garden.

Only the many woodworking tools remained.

They were the old man's hobby and passion; relaxation from the fields. Lance kept them initially as a perverse stake in the old man's claim. They would ultimately become his connection to staying put and staying in touch.

Once everything was out, Lance started in, retooling the barn as his own. He finished off the hayloft and put in a cracked walnut bed frame and mattress, a couple overstuffed couches he found in town, and a mahogany frame rocking chair from the attic. He didn't ask Becky about the history of the chair or who used it before.

He dug a three-foot trench from inside the barn 50 feet away to the septic tank near the side of the house and laid together sections of clay drainpipe that had been stacked for years near the stock pump. He sweated a copper water line and built a bathroom.

He outfitted the barn as haphazardly as he lived his life. Lance O'Neill was a scavenger. His frequent trips away from the farm, especially in the early years, were no more mysterious nor meaningful than that. Rambling along in his old beat up pick-up truck from dinky town to dinky town, for days on end, looking to pick up the discarded pieces of other people's lives. An oak framed storage cabinet came from behind a hardware store; once he replaced the broken glass and missing hinges, it would be perfect. He found a set of metal shelves leaning against a schoolhouse somewhere. The bed frame came from an alley in a turn-of-the-century neighborhood off the main street in another unremarkable small town. Similar hours spent over unremarkable days picking up the pieces and repairing other people's cast-off pasts.

Before he decided to create the woodshop, he scavenged without reason or purpose, collecting whatever to use whenever for who knows why. Years ago, Lance had spent an entire fall and winter driving his truck throughout northern Oklahoma. Just driving, scavenging, repairing, and discarding along the way. He'd find something here, fix it up along the way to there, and sell enough of it somewhere else to keep his gas tank full, a bar stool warm and a few cans of food stowed in a wooden box in the bed of the truck.

He slept in the cab of the truck when he wasn't taking the waitress home. Sometimes they were ragged or ugly and sometimes they weren't, but they all had a shower and usually a bed for the night.

It was months of driving through cold and windy and raw.

The engine clattering its lifters along for miles and miles of desolate nowhere. White dust snow swirling furiously across the pastures and prairies and highway. The truck's heater had two settings – bitter cold or blowing hot air that filtered musty and pungent through torn seat upholstery. Most often, Lance said the hell with it, unfolded the rim of his navy wool Longshoreman's cap, pulling the thing well over his ears, flipped up the collar of his army jacket, and rolled the window down.

Deep within himself, Lance hoped the isolation and the penance would somehow be cleansing or invigorating, but it wasn't. It was just irritating, and then numbing, and then flat. And one day Lance realized, finally, that he couldn't give a shit. Not didn't give a shit, couldn't. Wasn't capable. He drove the rest of that day, letting it sink in, even crying for a full hour, and that night he turned his truck and found his way back to the farm. That wasn't his last trip away from the farm but it was the last one where he didn't know if he'd come back. He'd still take off once a month or every six weeks but he always found his way back to the farm.

He and Becky never spoke of where he'd been or when he would return. Certainly not why he went. Some bizarre unspoken agreement that their lives wouldn't be normal, couldn't be complete. As if the bill finally came due for the indiscretions of their past. All the wonderful free love be damned; build a mud castle leading to now. Who gives a shit? Whatever it was, they had both, over the years, settled into a resigned acceptance of the strangeness of their lives together.

When Lance found the wood-burning cook stove, he knew just like that it was time for a change.

Becky watched from the dining room window the day he pulled up with the huge wood-burning stove lashed in the back of his pick-up. Lance wasn't sure what would happen with Becky, or with their relationship, but he smiled to himself as he realized that, at least now, he had a wood-burning cook stove. His own hearth. A circle of home. He figured maybe he'd try a ritual, too. Clean the stove once a month when Becky oiled her mother's cast iron cauldron. They could do it together, and meet in the middle. Maybe that would help.

Becky came out into the yard carrying two bottles of beer, as Lance struggled to rig slider beams off the tailgate to unload the stove.

"Nice looking stove," she said, opening one of the bottles and setting it out of the way on the ground near the rear tire. "Need any help?"

"Nah, but thanks. Son of a bitch is so big, I just need to figure out how to let gravity do the work. How's everything been?"

"Fine. No real news. Spent all of Monday and most of yesterday in town on the committee. Nothing much to speak of over the weekend. Been real quiet, stayed real still." She sipped her beer. "You?"

"Same. Lots of driving. Meant to get back Sunday, but, you know."

"Yeah," she said. "Not really."

How could she know, when he didn't? How could she explain it, if he couldn't? Two cottonwoods, long ago as saplings leaning together to protect each other from the wind, now grown and gracefully brushing their leaves during those quiet midnights when a soft breeze carried fragrance from one to the other.

Then they were young and he and Becky filled each other and completed one another. Their roots stretched down and suckled together beneath the crisp sweet river of fate. They were for and with each other. But they were too smart, so much smarter than their fate. Part of the chosen generation. Who better but they to decide when to alter, what to alter, with whom and why?

Ten years ago, in 1968, that was enlightenment.

And then, enlightenment began to cripple and atrophy and started reeking of decay and bitterness. Empty. Who really gives a shit anymore, Lance thought as he let go the rigging rope tied to the bumper of his pick-up and stooped for his beer?

"Thanks, tastes fine." He took another long swallow and nearly emptied the thing.

"Listen, Beck, I know you didn't ask, but I've done a lot of thinking this time. And I'm thinking this barn, this woodshop may be the ticket, you know? It's gonna be mine, so maybe for the first time in almost forever, something will really be mine."

He caught the hurt build in her eyes, and immediately regretted his words.

"I don't mean it like that. But we both know this grotesque can't go on. I know I haven't helped it; I'll take the blame. We're both carrying around too many goddamned skeletons. Always have."

"That's all right," she said. "You don't need to explain. It's not like I've come here clean, or made any of this easy. For you or for me."

"It's not your fault, Beck, and maybe part of it's not even mine. Just life. Our lives, with all our choices. Our fate, I guess.

"People've had worse. But I tell you what, once you hit 30, you realize your life's gonna finish out pretty much whatever it is right then and there. I'm thinking if we're smart about it, really start paying attention, we may yet be able to salvage something. It doesn't have to stay this way. I'm thinking of starting off by staying around. I'm getting awfully bored with all of this on the road crap, driving aimlessly, searching for nothing. All these overwhelming issues that were so important five years ago, ten years ago, suddenly seem like someone else's ancient history. You know? Almost like who gives a shit anymore?"

"Well," Becky said, smiling and slipping her hand inside his shirt and running her fingernails softly across his chest, "I've got two years to go, two years to believe my life's still going to turn out like a dime store romance, filled with youthful mistakes leading to cosmic possibilities. Although," she giggled, as he unsnapped the top of her blue jeans and slipped his hand down along the small of her back, "this is beginning to feel kind of cosmic right now."

Lance O'Neill placed his other hand behind her shoulders and gently eased Becky down onto the wooden plank angling down to the ground from the back of his pick-up.

"You're a beautiful woman, Becky Dreiling," Lance murmured as he unbuttoned her shirt. "Always have been, inside and out."

She still had the tight and graceful body of a co-ed. Her breasts and belly formed tiny goose bumps from the cool April breeze, and he smelled long and slow from her neck down to the top of her panties. She raised herself up and he slipped off her sandals and blue jeans. She reached for the back of his neck and softly pulled him toward her lips; her breath nuzzled in his ear.

Lance held on for a moment; he struggled to relax and struggled to hang on to the moment. And then, finally, he closed his eyes and let go for the ride. He listened to her breath nuzzling and coming in to him. He imagined its sweetness into flowers and laughter and Christmas. He thought of Astral Weeks when they would listen over and over – *Beside You* – watching the vinyl spin around and around and around. Breathing in and breathing out. Into a cleansing that moved into him and through him and down deep inside of him. Lance squinted his mind and watched the mean and the humiliation and the rage well together deep inside his belly, swelling there into a swirling mass of white hot gas. He took pieces of the inferno, and slowly breathed them out. Her meadows and Calico dolls buzzing slowly in, his mortar explosions and face-ripped bleeding brother out.

Shut his mind off, turn his body down, and follow the cycle of breath, in and out, cleansing and replenishing. You breathe in you breathe out. You breathe in you breathe out. Calm quiet Kansas wind. Prairie grass. You breathe in you breathe out. You breathe in you breathe out.

A calm exchange of fresh air for foul, living breath for decay. A breeze to soften the fire, rain to moisten the earth.

And then he saw it, the guilt, the anger. The dominating power, the return. Suddenly his breath no longer dissipated as he exhaled but now circled back and melded with hers, entering him again and re-contaminating him. No longer a cycle, now a circle. Her meadows turned into mountain lakes, and then into one particular glacier-formed Colorado tarn lake filled with gold, and so lonely.

Naked at the shore, his body shivers and then abruptly calms. Rage and his tears drip into the black water leaving expanding rings of rape and remorse.

And then he knows the circle is unbreakable. The future can't flow in on its own, it will always be pushed by his past.

He felt her body, then, against his, and gratefully accepted at least that. He quietly closed his lips and stopped the breath of his soul.

"Welcome home, Lance O'Neill," she whispered.

"There are no heroes.
Only clever sons-a-bitches
Who never get caught."

- Lance O'Neill

Chapter 2

Lance stopped and pulled at the rusted nail hanging loose in the fence post rock. The head broke off in his hand, and the strand of barbwire sagged even more.

He kicked the post, and the limestone clanged against the tip of his wooden leg. The post rock was dull yellow like the dirt and the dried weeds it was planted in, and it stood in a long line of hundreds running the length of the landscape atop the flood ditch along the dirt road. Like sentinels to maddening serenity, along every road and cutting every farm, the post rock fenced up the county. Three and-a-half-foot soldiers, in endless single columns standing at weary attention. Lance wondered again what in the hell kind of people settled in a land so barren they had to dig rocks out of the ground to make fence posts? Hard-working my ass. Unhappy martyrs to the dour lives they live out to prove they love God. Immigrant peasants without expectations. The Cheyenne and the Arapahoe were at least smart enough to migrate through; these damn people unhitched their wagons, buttoned up their children, chiseled rocks into fence posts, and stayed put. They stayed put through oppressively hot dusty summers, and they stayed put through frigid blowing winters. Constant nothing and endless nowhere. Old World immigrants, Nineteenth Century immigrants. Hard working and serious immigrants who spoke with thick accents and kept to themselves. German peasants who moved near the steppes of Russia two centuries ago and then, a century later, when they decided to improve their lives, picked up and moved halfway across the world to this prairie wasteland out in the middle of North America. "Gee, looks desolate, just like home. Guess we'll stay here." And the sonovabitches did stay and are still here, growing sunflowers and winter wheat, raising cattle and Catholic Churches.

And beautiful women, Lance reminded himself. Beautiful women like Becky; archetypical Kansas farm girl. Muscular, lean and witty, quick to flash laughter and quicker yet to unflinching resolve. Great legs and strong cheekbones, tight blue jeans and endless optimism. Becky was that single moment when the prairie is washed in all its harvest glory; she shimmered constantly coupled in a seductive dance with life.

And he was seduced, and it wasn't her fault. Once you slip into a woman like that, you tumble and fall and begin to lose yourself, and she wraps you warm and soft in her veil and you fall further from yourself. It's safe, though, because she's there nurturing and holding you close within her, within her comforting secret of acceptance. You stop reaching as high or trying as hard and it's okay, she loves you the more; not for your weakness but for your splayed humanity – like God loving the pitiful in his children. And then, because one day you feel that love actually transform into the lap of God, you fuck up, you forget the rest of the world and you fuck up big time. Not something bad that can be fixed, not something mean that will be forgiven. Something evil that can't go away. Evil isn't the opposite of God, it's the opposite of life, and where one exists the other can't. And she doesn't understand that because it wasn't her fault. And when God turns away you lose the chance to pay for the fuck-up with your life. You pay with your brother's life, and you're sentenced to spend the rest of your days trudging across barren prairies, sweat pouring in your eyes, reminding you incessantly that you really fucked up.

Lance wiped his sleeve across his forehead and spit dust from his teeth into the nearest cow pie.

"Shit," he said out loud.

And then, like so many times before, the endless lines of fence post rock stopped looking like soldiers and turned again into gravestones, straight in a military line and forever seeking the horizon.

The heat was everywhere – rolling dry and dusty off the pastures and prairie. All clouds and moisture had burned out of the sky hours ago. Sweat poured from beneath his Ford Tractor baseball cap. The sweat dripped from his forehead; it mixed with the yellow dust there and stung his eyes.

He looked ahead along the line of posts. Most of the wire was loose or gone. It all needed work. The whole damn farm. Repairing just the fence would take a week. One year of the old man being sick and then dying and now the whole damned farm looked like shit.

Sure Lance could have worked the place the last year while the old bastard withered away, but he didn't want anyone, including himself, getting the idea he was staying around. Besides, why give the decaying son of a bitch the pleasure? Screw the narrow-minded little bastard. Let him die while his farm died around him.

And then the old man did die, and Lance thought maybe that would finally free up something in Becky, or maybe one more fucking death would free up something in him. Besides, he needed the work to break a sweat and build a callous. Lance thrived on physical exertion the way Becky thrived on watching acres of sunflowers or fields of wheat, and he sure as hell could use a recharge. He had decided to stay after all, in spite of all the shit that was there holding him, all the shit that was there driving him away, all the shit that was slowly suffocating him.

He picked up a rock and aimed at a cow pie plopped in the dirt near the fence. Suddenly, he cackled and stopped his arm in mid wind-up. He casually tossed the rock out into the pasture and broke into a hearty laugh.

"That's one hell of a good fresh one," he said aloud.

He looked back, squinted. He waited and then smiled again when he heard the distant sound of a firecracker. It popped in the heat like a locust beneath his boot.

Lance chuckled to himself, unhitched his belt, dropped his pants and held onto a post rock for support as he squatted over the fresh cow pie. He laughed out loud; he figured it would take the boys about ten minutes to reach him.

Lance wished he'd brought a newspaper.

***

The boys ran for cover. Pete counted down as they jumped into the little dry gully.

"Three, two, one."

They waited, then rolled on the ground and howled with delight.

"All right!" Daniel O'Neill yelled. "Splattered all over that rock. Direct hit!"

"Yeah," Pete conceded, "but I still say dry ones fly farther. And they spread out more."

"Baloney," the boy said. "Fresh ones are best. Dry ones don't splatter, and they don't stick."

"Well, they're my firecrackers too, so we have to do some dry ones. We only have ten matches left."

"We can catch up to Uncle Lance, and get some more," Daniel O'Neill said. "I wish we could sneak up on that bird and explode that fresh one. I'll bet we could splatter him."

"If we did a dry one, we could probably knock him off the post," Pete said.

"Yeah, but then he would just get up and fly away. If it was a fresh one, he would be splattered and all covered. Then we could catch him."

"Get real," Pete scowled. "Who's going to pick him up if he's all covered in fresh cow shit?"

"Well, if we had a box, we could put him in that with a stick, and then we'd have him."

"Well, we don't have a box, and we can't sneak up on him anyway, so the whole idea's pretty dumb. Let's do that dry one, and see if we can fly it over to that rock."

"Well," the boy said, "I just said if."

He picked up a flat, dry cow pie at his feet. It weighed almost nothing and was so dry that grass didn't even stick to the bottom. It looked like a cross section of a cut tree – circles going around and around toward the center. During their Easter break, the two boys had a big argument over whether or not you could read a cow pie like you could read the age of a tree by counting its rings. Daniel insisted the different rings in a cow pie were because of the different things the cow ate. The outside rings were from the grass in the pastures, and as the cows wandered lazily all day long, munching as they went, the rough pasture grass lined their stomachs. At night, when they got hay in the corral, it was sweeter and the cows like it better, so that hay went right to the middle of their stomachs. When it came out, the grass made the large outside rings, and the hay made the tight little inside rings.

"Bullshit," is what Pete said.

He claimed the rings were because when the poop dropped out of the cow's butt onto the ground, it plopped, not all at once, but plopped as it came down in a stream from the cow's butt, and that's why the rings.

"Just watch when they make one," Pete said. "You can see the rings when it plops onto the ground."

The boys agreed to let Daniel's mom settle the question. They found her in the kitchen with Uncle Lance. Both adults were still drinking coffee and were still sitting at the kitchen table.

Pete came crashing into the kitchen behind Daniel, chattering excitedly as the screen door slammed shut in the little mudroom leading into the back of the kitchen. Pete immediately shut up and shied against the wall when he saw Uncle Lance. The man scowled quickly at the boys, first at Daniel, then at Pete, then quickly back again at Daniel. Pete was scared shitless whenever Uncle Lance was around, and Daniel didn't blame him. Hell, Lance hardly ever spoke to Daniel, and he'd probably grunted only half a dozen words at Pete since last summer.

At first Uncle Lance didn't even want to hear the argument. He told the boys to get their asses out of the kitchen.

But his mother listened, first to Pete and then to him. She started laughing when he got to the part about the hay being in the middle of the stomach, and then she just laughed and laughed.

"What we need to do, Lance, is figure out how to package and sell the crazy ideas of little boys."

Still laughing, she stirred sugar into her coffee. "I always imagined you guys spent your days chasing rabbits, or looking for arrowheads, or doing something like what little boys in Life magazine do."

Lance lit a cigarette, got up from the table and walked to the window over the sink.

"Beck," he said, looking off through the glass, "maybe we could discuss cow biology and cow pie physics with Tonto and Tonto here some other time."

His mother just laughed. "Boys, if you've got nothing better to do than argue about cow pies, I've gotta believe I could dream up ways more productive for you to spend your time."

Pete backed toward the door. "She's right, Daniel. It's stupid. Let's go."

"Better'n that," Lance mumbled, "take these little shits down and throw their asses into military school. I don't think they concern themselves much with cow pies in military school."

Pete was out the door, and they never argued about the rings in cow pies again.

***

Daniel O'Neill looked at the rings in the pie he was now holding, and then flung it like a Frisbee, easily clearing the rock.

"Anyone can throw one that far," Pete said. "The trick is to blow one up that far."

"Let's try it," the boy said.

Uncle Lance said a lot of things about military school, and though the boy didn't really know what kind of school military school was, it didn't sound good. He wanted to stay just where he was.

Before Lance came it was just Daniel and his mother and the old man who died. When the boy was little, the old man was mean and did all the work. Then the old man got sort of crazy and his mom tried to do the work. And then Lance came, and then the old man died.

When Uncle Lance first came to the farm, the boy's mother cried all the time. Uncle Lance and the boy's mother talked a lot at night, but the boy could never get to where he could listen without getting caught.

Until Lance came, the boy didn't even know he had an uncle. He knew about Lance and his mother and father from a picture that sat on the mantel above the fireplace.

Daniel looked at the picture a lot, sometimes took it down from the mantel and held the rough-carved wooden frame.

His mother often looked at the picture with him and told him about his father, and how they had only just gotten married and this was the end of their honeymoon and how Lance was with them at the lake in Colorado for their honeymoon. She told him about their friendship, how things seemed different back then, how a lot of people didn't understand their friendship but how that didn't matter.

She told him that Lance and his father were best friends. He knew they went to the war together, when the boy was still in his mom's stomach. And he knew his father was killed and Lance wasn't, but his mom didn't know where Lance was.

And last year, after he showed up at the farm after all these years, his mother told him this man in the picture with his father was actually his uncle.

In the picture, the three of them are standing in front of the lake together, smiling with their arms around each other. Behind them, parked right on the shore of the lake, was his dad's brand new 1965 Plymouth Valiant, the car he'd bought after he'd married his mom to take them all on a grand honeymoon adventure traveling across the country.

The water in the background is dark blue, and some sailboats sit on the shore off to the side, tilting slightly into the sand. His mom is all suntanned and her flowered shirt doesn't have sleeves, and her neck and arms and chest are golden brown. Her long hair is lit by the sun, and she looks like a high school girl. Her new husband is young and strong. He's not wearing a shirt and his muscles are hard. He's wearing sunglasses and holding a can of beer in one hand with his other hand around his wife's waist. Uncle Lance is behind them both, one hand on his mom's shoulder and the other on her husband's shoulder, and they look like best friends – the two men look like best friends and all three of them look like best friends together.

The boy had looked at the picture of these two men all of his life, and he had imagined so much about them. He imagined the closeness of best friends and he often wished he was in the picture and that he was best friends with these two men. And then suddenly, out of nowhere, one of these mythical men was actually in his life – like a person from a vivid reoccurring dream the boy could not remember having.

Last year, right before school started and right after Uncle Lance came, the boy sat out in the barn with this suddenly new relative, and Uncle Lance drank whiskey out of a bottle.

"I'll tell you about the war," Uncle Lance said after a long silence and after a long spell of sitting. "It was simple. We left our homes here and got on a bus. We got to their camp and they trained us. They told us what to think and they taught us how to survive. They made us soldiers.

"Then they put us all on a big plane, crammed all us American soldiers, all our guns and all our stuff onto this big plane, and they sent us half way across the planet to Asia. On the way there they reminded us that we hated these Asians, and they told us these Asians hated us. They told us to kill these Asians, and they told us these Asians wanted to kill us."

Daniel O'Neill wasn't afraid of his uncle right then, but he was scared, and he stayed still. The barn was quiet; the man and the boy sat on the dirt floor with their backs against the workbench. Roy slept underneath, his paws outstretched on the cool dirt floor. The pigeons sitting in the rafters cooed softly.

"I killed a lot of Asians," Uncle Lance finally said, "and a lot of Asians tried to kill me. I hated Asians."

And then Uncle Lance took a long drink from the bottle and looked right at the boy. He started to talk, and then he looked away.

After a long time he said, "And then Asians killed my brother. Later I had to come home and tell your mother that my brother and her new husband got killed by Asians who none of us knew."

The boy held still, stayed tense. He realized, maybe only fully for the first time since Lance came back, that this strange man and brand new relative was a direct link to his father.

"My dad got killed a long time ago, when I wasn't even two," the boy said. "I'm ten now."

"I came back a long time ago," Uncle Lance said. "But I had to leave again. I had to leave for a long time."

"Why?"

Lance didn't answer. He lit a cigarette and smoked the whole thing.

"Where did you have to go? Back to another war?"

Lance flicked his cigarette toward the pile of tools at the other side of the barn. Finally he said "I had to go and learn that I didn't hate Asians anymore. I had to remember that I didn't even know any Asians. All I knew about Asians was what they knew about me – we were trying to kill each other.

"Except they didn't kill me. They killed my brother, and he shouldn't even have been there. And then I remembered who I really hated."

That was the only time Daniel O'Neill ever saw Uncle Lance almost cry, and then Uncle Lance threw the whiskey bottle at a stack of pipe leaning against the wall, and the boy jumped and cried out when the glass shattered. Commotion exploded inside the barn. The pigeons roosting in the rafters flapped immediately in noisy flight, wings and motion everywhere. Soft white feathers and pigeon shit fell from the rafters and filled the shaft of sunlight shining through the door up in the loft.

Roy came crashing out from beneath the workbench, knocking over a rusted shovel and barking wildly. The dirty yellow hair on the dog's shoulders and back stood straight up as he challenged the unseen hiding in the stack of black pipe. After a while the pigeons settled down a bit. They began circling in formation around the main beams inside the barn, their clumsy wings flapping against themselves on every down stroke. All the noise, the birds, and the barking made the boy think the wings were slapping his own head. Roy began chasing the falling feathers, barking at the birds, and then at the pipe, and again barking at and chasing the birds.

The whiskey soaked slowly into the hard packed dirt floor.

"And now," Uncle Lance said when it got quiet again, "I'll tell you something about whiskey. It doesn't matter if you drink the whole thing in one day or smash the bottle and let it soak into the dirt. You're still here and your brother isn't; you still have to look every day at a woman who doesn't have a husband anymore; you still remember the times before, when you and your brother and his wife were together, when you all loved each other and you were all together. And you sit and you wonder how many Asians are also sitting right now in a barn over in Asia, throwing bottles against walls and realizing they don't hate me anymore, either."

He looked at the boy hard again, and then, with slightly slurred speech, said, "And you don't know what the hell it was all about, but you know it was your fault."

The boy wanted to say something, but he couldn't think of anything. He thought maybe he should pick up the pieces of broken glass, but he didn't move.

He watched the pigeons settle back into the rafters, tucking their heads again sideways beneath their wings. He was surprised that he only counted three of them.

The pieces of glass from the broken whiskey bottle lay in the dirt right where the shaft of light hit the floor. He worried that Roy, now sniffing around the stack of pipe, might cut his paws. The boy again thought maybe he should go over and pick up the broken glass. But there were many pieces, some long and skinny, which he knew, had several cutting edges, and Roy stayed away because of the whiskey smell.

The boy wanted to do something, but he didn't move.

"Finally," Uncle Lance said, "it doesn't matter. It just soaks in." That's all he ever said and he never said anything about it again.

When the boy went in the barn the next day, the glass was cleaned up and the soaked-in whiskey looked like any old stain where something had been accidentally spilled and had just soaked in. After a few days the stain was gone altogether.

***

As he walked along the fence with Pete, saving matches for perfect cow pies, Daniel O'Neill wondered what Pete's wife would be like. He hoped the three of them would all be friends, like the picture on the fireplace of his mom and his father and Lance.

In the picture all three are happy, and his mom told the boy he's not in the picture anywhere. "Not even a twinkle," she said," in the eyes of that pretty young girl or those two handsome men."

And then Lance showed up, and after days and nights of his mom crying and talking with Lance, the boy learned this man was more than a friend; he was his father's brother, and Daniel O'Neill suddenly had an Uncle, a blood link to his dad.

And as the boy walked along, he realized this summer was already off to quite a start, what with the old man now dead and Lance staying and saying the farm needed work.

The boy had always played in the summers with Pete. During the last week of school they did nothing but make plans to fill their vacation.

But now Daniel O'Neill was beginning to hope he could help Uncle Lance fix up the farm, and he suddenly worried that Uncle Lance might think exploding cow pies with firecrackers was something only little kids did. Agreeing with Pete to blow up some dry ones made it seem to him that this was all really Pete's idea; it made him think he was just going along with the silly ideas of a little kid.

"Hey, c'mon," Pete said. "What's wrong? That was a great one. I knew we could explode it past that rock."

"Let's catch up to Uncle Lance," the boy said.

"We've still got five matches," Pete said. "Let's light some on the way."

Daniel O'Neill started walking, and Pete ran to catch up.

"Or, we could do some ant piles," Pete said. "I love it when they start running up the fuse while it's burning. Crazy little bastards, scurrying around, exploring. They've got no idea their whole world's about to explode."

"Okay," the boy said. "But I think we should catch up to Uncle Lance. Maybe he needs our help with these posts. Maybe we should be doing some work."

"What a weird guy," Pete said. "I mean, where'd he come from. First he's your dad's friend, and he got killed in the war, then all of a sudden he's your uncle, he's not killed in the war and he shows up here with only one leg. My mom says she doesn't even think your dad had a brother."

"Well how in the hell would your mom know?" the boy nearly screamed. "You guys didn't move here until second grade. Anyway, I never said he got killed in the war. I said my dad got killed in the war. He lost his leg, probably by being a war hero, something you wouldn't understand."

"Yeah, but that was years ago. Where's he been all this time, and how come he's suddenly your uncle?"

"My mom thought he was gone forever. She didn't want me to lose a dad and an uncle, so she told me they were best friends."

"It doesn't make any sense. I think it's weird. Why's he so mean? Is he going to stay in the house with you guys? Is he going to marry your Mom?"

"Why don't you just shut your face," the boy told his friend. "You don't know shit. Maybe it's better to have a best friend who's really your brother than just having a best friend. Did you ever think of that?"

"Jesus," Pete said. "What's the big deal? I was just asking."

"Well, why don't you ask about things you know about, stupid things like exploding cow pies? Only a little kid dork would blow up dry ones anyhow. Some people have to grow up, you know."

"Well, you don't have to yell at me. If you're too grown up to do it, I'll do the last five. If you're afraid precious Uncle Lance will think this is stupid, then don't do it."

"I'm not afraid of anything. But if I was in a war, maybe even a war hero, I don't think I'd be hanging around stupid little kids who blow up cow pies with firecrackers. I think I'd have better things to do with my time."

"Holy shit!" Pete cried. "Look at that one, by the fence. What the hell is that?"

The boys stooped over a fresh pie next to the fence. Right in the middle of the rings was a plop of something else, something that looked like shit but not like cow shit. It kind of crested on the center of the cow pie, making it look like a flying saucer instead of a flat Frisbee.

"I knew it!" the boy squealed. "That cow ate something really weird, and this is how it came out."

"Bullshit," Pete said, poking the pile with a stick. "This isn't cow shit, unless that cow was eating corn. There's no grass in it, and it sure doesn't smell like cow shit. Something else came and took a dump right on top of this cow pie. Look how they don't come together."

The boy grabbed a stick and poked. "Wow. Maybe a coyote. Do coyotes eat corn?"

"I guess they do, if they find it. But why would a coyote do that, especially right here in the open, right next to this fence. And it's fresh, so it happened just a little while ago. Coyotes are only out in the night."

"I wonder if Uncle Lance had to chase it away. I wonder where he is?"

"I don't think this was a coyote," Pete said. "It doesn't make any sense."

"It doesn't make any sense that anything would take a dump on top of a cow pie. Something weird is going on here."

"I'll say," Pete said. "Wanna blow it up?"

"No way," the boy said. "It might make something, or someone, really mad."

"What are you talking about? Who's going to get mad if we blow up their shit?"

"I don't know. But if it's not a coyote, it had to come from somewhere. What if it came from the ghost of that old lady nurse?"

"No way," Pete said. "One, she also only comes out at night. And two, she only hangs around her grave, up by the rock pile. And three, I don't think ghosts do stuff like this."

"How do you know?"

"Well, how would they do it? I mean, first you have to eat something. Then your stomach has to turn it into shit. How would a ghost do that? They don't even have stomachs."

"Yeah, well how would a ghost move that pile of rocks, and she did that last summer. Ghosts don't have muscles, either."

Pete didn't say anything, and both boys dropped their sticks.

"Let's get out of here," Pete said. They ran back along the fence, toward the house, for half a mile before stopping.

"Hang on," the boy called out, panting. "I've got to rest. Anyway, she's not going to chase us this far. If the Old Lady Nurse Ghost wanted to get us, she would have gotten us back there. Maybe she was just telling us to stop blowing up cow pies."

"Or maybe," Pete said, also panting, "she was trying to see how brave we are. Maybe she was trying to see if we were brave enough to blow that one up, too."

"Want to go back?" Daniel O'Neill asked.

"Do you?"

"Maybe. But maybe tomorrow. Then, if it's not there, we'll know it's from her. If it is, then maybe we can blow it up."

"Are you going to tell your mom?"

"Are you going to tell yours?"

"I don't know," Pete said. "She might tell us to stop blowing them up."

"My mom doesn't believe in the Old Lady Nurse Ghost. She says that's an old grave from a long time ago, and it's probably the grave of a dog or something. Maybe this would prove it to her."

"Yeah, but maybe she'd get scared, and tell us to stop blowing them up. I say we don't tell anyone."

"Okay. But now we should really be on the lookout for other signs. If the Old Lady Nurse Ghost is trying to contact us, we ought to pay better attention."

They climbed through the fence and cut across the corner of the pasture, climbing through the other side near the barn in the boy's yard.

Uncle Lance was in the yard, carrying tools out of the barn and stacking them against the steel round water trough.

The boys looked at each other, worry and excitement in their eyes.

"How'd you get back here before us?" Daniel O'Neill asked.

"Doubled back along the ridge. You guys run out of firecrackers?"

"No," Pete said. "Matches."

"Blow up any good ones?"

The boys exchanged glances again.

"Some," Pete said. "We left some others alone."

"Saving 'em for another day," the boy added.

Uncle Lance scowled at the boy, finding inner delight in scaring him.

"More'n likely you'll run out of ammo or interest long before you run out of cow pies. Don't leave the good ones for tomorrow, if you can splatter them today."

"We did do some good ones," Pete said. "I better get going on home."

Uncle Lance scowled again. "Stay on your toes, soldier. You never know when you'll find a good one just over the next ridge."

"See you tomorrow," Pete said as he hustled off to pick up his bike.

The boy watched him go, then inspected the pile of tools leaning against the tank and exposed in the sun. Most of them looked old, and splintery, and like they were falling apart. In the barn, hanging up, they seemed better, stronger. Not like they could do any work, the boy supposed, but like they belonged in the barn, hung neatly and ready for work, at least. Now they looked like a pile of junk, like a big pile of junk.

Everything used to seem so quiet around here, the boy thought to himself. He watched Uncle Lance drag a disc plow across the yard and deposit it near the pile.

"Whatcha doin'?"

"Organizing these tools. Some of this crap must be a hundred years old. We're going to have to replace some. That barn's a piece of crap, too. Don't know how it made it through last winter. Looks like your days of hay-sitting in the cool barn are over."

"Can I help you fix the farm?"

"Damn straight. But I'm not talking goofing off and getting in the way. I'm talking real work. No bullshit."

"I know," Daniel said. "I can work. I want to."

"It's one thing to be anxious and want to. It's another to be able. You're big enough. I guess we'll find out if you're tough enough."

"I am," the boy told his uncle. "You'll see."

Lance bit the inside of his lip and looked through the boy, looked way off through the distance.

"Uh huh," he said. "We'll see."

"Sometimes good things happen
Simply because it's a good life."
                                                    - Becky Dreiling

Chapter 3

His Grandfather was a sour old man, and the little boy was glad he was dead.

Not glad, really, because that seemed wrong, or at least not honorable, and anyway, nobody really knows if you are still around after you're dead, and if you are around, nobody really knows where you are exactly, and if you are not around anywhere at all then it would always be better to be alive, even if no one liked you when you were alive and you did not like anybody or anything.

The old man was dead, and Daniel O'Neill felt unchanged by it. He certainly did not laugh or smile about it but did not cry either, and he would still get Pete and go fishing if his mother allowed him.

It surprised him that they came so fast. He was afraid it would use up the whole day, but fifteen or twenty minutes after his mother made the phone call the long white car pulled slowly into the dirt and gravel driveway. The car carefully made tight turns, staying in the middle of the drive that meandered in a half circle in front of their gray and white farmhouse.

His mother cried at first, but afterwards, while they waited, she said very little; she smiled at him.

He sat next to her on the front porch step; he ran his hands along the rough wooden slats, alternately getting splinters in his skin and then pulling them out. Bees and locusts droned on in the hot, still air. He methodically threw the splinters at his new puppy Roy, who slept in the cool dirt beneath the porch.

He felt his mom's sadness, but she had to be sad because the old man was her father. For a moment, the boy wished he had a father;

then he wished his father had just died so he could feel sad for his father.

Daniel O'Neill's father was killed in the war, before the boy was born. Daniel O'Neill never knew his father. He imagined often that they played together, read books together, and fished together. When he looked at the picture of his father, he always imagined they were best friends.

He imagined that he curled up with his father in the big chair by the fireplace hearth and mantel made of smooth river rock. He sat with his father on these nights, safe in the arms of this strong man, and listened as his father told war stories and hunting stories. The one about the coyotes, or the cannons, or the bear.

The boy often fell asleep this way, imagining his father putting him to sleep telling magnificent imaginary stories.

He had known his father in this way ever since he could remember, ever since he was four or five, certainly, and maybe earlier. What the boy liked best in his life were these stories. Bedtime stories, lazy winter Sunday stories, all his father's stories where the boy learned about survival, and courage, and where he learned about honor.

He would never say so out loud, but the boy knew he would be sadder if the old man who died was his father's father, instead of his mom's.

The old man was not like a father, wasn't like a father even to his mother. The old man was like a big baby, or a crippled colt; Daniel O'Neill would not miss his grandfather.

The car was long and white, an ambulance, but quiet without its siren on and unhurried. After it parked in the partial shade of the elm tree by the road, the engine ran on for a moment before anyone got out. The two men were nice. They wore white clothes and black shoes and they spoke softly to his mother and one of them smiled at him.

He wanted to ask how many people died today and if they had all been old, but his mother told him to go in the backyard. She said why don't you call Pete or Rhonda and ride your bike.

He once read a story in Mrs. McCreedy's class, and they took that woman down the stairs in a long wicker basket. After they put the dead woman in, the basket wrapped around her body like a cocoon, the story said, and the name of the story was something about butterflies.

Daniel O'Neill wanted to see the wicker basket, and so he decided to go out back and wait a moment near the barn, then come quietly through the screen door and watch the back stairs from the kitchen door.

The farmhouse backyard hit Daniel like a furnace, just like it felt last summer inside the barn when he made a small wood fire in the dirt floor so he could melt that old bucket of lead army men. The backyard was quiet that day too, and just as hot. For a moment, Daniel felt like he was standing in that picture down at the library, the one where there's a tree swing out in the middle of a wheat field. You could see the heat there, too, and nothing moved. The bees working and droning around the marigolds just looked like wisps of a brush stroke, their buzz like constant, hot wind rustling through constant, dry grass.

As he surveyed the back yard, Daniel realized he could hear a chainsaw down by the creek.

Suddenly, the boy jolted when he looked toward the barn. He got goose bumps when he saw Uncle Lance's work boot and wooden leg sticking out of the cool, dark barn. Just the one work boot, sticking out of the big sliding doorway, and just the one wooden leg crossed atop of it.

Even though there was distance between them, Daniel O'Neill took a step or two back away from the barn. He doubted his uncle was sad about the old man; he doubted his uncle was ever anything but mad. And the little boy's fists tightened as he looked at the work boot and the wooden leg sticking out of the barn.

Daniel hated looking at that one work boot. He hated knowing his uncle was just inside the door, probably watching him, lounging there in the barn. Probably smoking a cigarette or maybe doing nothing at all. He hated rushing outside of a morning, hoping to find his uncle had left again somewhere in his pick-up. More than anything, though, Daniel O'Neill hated how much he wished his uncle would ask him inside the barn. His uncle never asked him anything. Never. He just told him, always in a mad way. Do this. Do that. Never please. Never thank you. Just do it. Not like his dad would. Daniel could do much more than his uncle realized, but he never got the chance. He didn't have to be so mean; they could be friends.

Sometimes Daniel just went in the barn himself when his uncle was in there, doing his stupid woodworking. If his uncle ever told him to get out, he would say it was his barn, and his mom's barn, too. But his uncle never said anything, usually pretended he didn't even know the boy was there. It was just a lot of yelling, and cussing, and that freaky leg clomping around, raising little dust storms all over the dirt floor.

Daniel didn't say much, either. He didn't know what to say, or how to ask any of the many questions he had: questions about his dad, questions about his mom, questions about the war. Mostly, the boy wanted to know why Uncle Lance didn't like him. He never asked any questions because he didn't know how to ask without sounding like a little kid, so he just stayed quiet and watched his uncle run the saws and cut the wood.

When Daniel went into the barn on his own terms, it was much better than when Uncle Lance told him to come in. Maybe it would be at dinner, or maybe when he came back from riding his bike, but Daniel really hated it whenever his uncle gave him that awful squinty-eyed look and told him he "needed some sanding done."

Daniel hadn't said anything all summer long to his mom about it, since she was so worried all the time about his grandfather. But a lot of his time this summer was getting used up sitting on a rickety stool in front of the belt or spindle sander, running piece after piece of wood through – every edge, every face. First every piece sanded with 100 grit, then 150 grit, then 220 grit, then 440 grit. Every piece, every edge, every face, making everything smooth. Piece after piece, hour after hour, until finally Daniel had emptied the "raw wood" box and filled the "sanded wood" box.

The boy seethed with anger when he did this job because his uncle wasn't doing anything with this wood – just making him sand it.

"Because I'm telling you to and because it isn't any of your goddamn business."

Some were little pieces, some were big. Some were curved and curly off the band saw or jig saw, some were straight, right off the table saw. Some were beveled or angled off the radial arm, but they were all just dumb pieces of wood.

Daniel fought the boredom of the sanding job by forcing himself to identify which power tool had cut each and every piece. This allowed him to remind himself that yes, he was certainly capable of offering much more help in the woodshop than being the "sanding boy," which is what his uncle called him after he'd drunk too much whiskey and beer, or when he just wanted to be mean for no reason.

"Where's Sanding Boy?" he'd bellow to his mother late at night back in the kitchen. "Don't think you can protect Sanding Boy forever."

And that's what Daniel O'Neill hated most of all – not being called Sanding Boy and not the one work boot and that freaky peg leg. He hated listening in silence while someone yelled at his mom.

And so he resolved, during that summer of his life after fifth grade, to either do the honorable thing and make Lance O'Neill into a nice person, or to kill him.

***

Lately, even before Uncle Lance came, the old man stayed out of the barn. He didn't even go outside much anymore, because he usually got lost when he did, like that time in the spring when the boy and his mom found the old man down by the pond, sitting in his underwear at the edge of the water.

At first his mom was mad and yelled at the old man about wandering into the pond and drowning. His legs and face were covered with dry yellow mud. His clothes were scattered all over and one of his work boots was in the pond.

He looked up at his daughter and just smiled. He didn't say why he was there or why his clothes were off, and then the boy's mom cried and helped him get up.

Daniel O'Neill gathered all the clothes and waded into the water for the boot. The old man leaned on the boy while his mother helped him get dressed. She didn't even put his socks on, just laced the boots lightly, even the wet one.

It took them a long time to get him back to the house, and the boy sat with his grandfather at the kitchen table while his mom filled the bathtub in the back room.

The old man pretended he didn't know who the boy was. He kept telling him to get his own ride home.

"Leave me alone to mine," the old man kept saying. "You go get your own ride. You must ask properly, and you do not. Ask properly. Who is the Valiant for? Who drives the Valiant? Who owns the Valiant and why? You must ask properly, and you do not."

He said it over and over, not even looking at the boy, and it made Daniel O'Neill mad that his grandfather was being so mean after he'd just helped him with his clothes and his boot.

When his mom came back into the kitchen, she said never mind and asked him to make some toast with strawberry jelly and take it upstairs to the attic bedroom that his grandfather insisted on moving into when Uncle Lance came. The old man yelled at Uncle Lance a lot, told him to get the hell off his farm.

"If you want to steal a farm, go steal somebody else's farm," he often said. "You get the hell off my farm now."

His mom just said, "Ben, it's all right. He's here to help out, he's here to fix some things."

He told Uncle Lance to fix the fence or cut the dead branches off of the elm tree.

The elm tree in the front yard didn't give as much shade as it used to, because it got that disease with the bugs, and many of the branches on one side were dead and bare.

The old man told Uncle Lance "Get your butt out of that barn and trim that tree out," but Uncle Lance didn't.

Ever since last Christmas, the boy's mom didn't call her father "Dad" anymore. She called him "Ben" and they almost never laughed together anymore, and they never played two-handed Rummy at night like before.

It seemed the old man got meaner and meaner since Christmas. He didn't do any work or planting in the spring, and he hardly ever called the boy by his name anymore. He was so mean and stubborn his mom almost had to take care of him all the time. He wasn't even nice to her; once he tried to throw a coffee cup at her, but it was a bad throw. It hit the ceiling and then landed on top of the pantry.

Last week, when his grandfather was so sick he couldn't even get out of bed, his mom sometimes asked the boy to go up and bring the soup bowl down to the kitchen, or take up some fresh ice for the water pitcher. He went up once and Uncle Lance was in the room. Daniel O'Neill heard his uncle tell the old man all the dead limbs were trimmed off the elm tree. His grandfather smiled like a little child when Uncle Lance said some new growth was already starting.

Daniel O'Neill didn't ask why his uncle lied to the old man.

Sometimes when Uncle Lance left for one of his trips into town that usually lasted for several days or sometimes a week or more, the boy would spend the hot part of the days out in the barn with his friend Pete. Lying in the hay shooting pigeons with their slingshots, or just lying in the hay doing nothing at all.

Summer was a good time because you could think more. Pete said that was because parents left you alone more and you didn't have to think about school or going to bed when you wanted to stay up. Also, they agreed that not wearing shoes was always better and summer was good for that, too.

His mother did not mind so it was okay, and he was happy he would not have to listen to the old man bitching about his bare feet, warning stupidly about broken bottles and stickers and bees. His feet were tough, and he had quit trying to explain to the old man. It was stupid. No matter how well he explained it, the old man still said the same things, the same stupid warnings.

Sometimes Daniel O'Neill's grandfather said silly things when Pete was around and the boys laughed, but mostly he said stupid things, and he was mean and smelled like cigars in the bathroom, and his whiskers scratched his face every night when the boy had to kiss the old man before bed.

The boy met Pete's Grandpa once when he came and visited from Illinois. He was fun. He laughed a lot and teased them. He went fishing with them. It was okay with them at the end of the day when Pete's Grandpa was tired and told the boys to clean the fish and then run along. He was nice, and they had all caught fish, and Pete's mom sent along a paper bag filled with ham sandwiches and potato chips and half a chocolate cake. The boys knew Pete's mom packed the special lunch because the Grandpa was visiting but they ate it just the same.

Pete thought the two old men might like to meet, but Daniel O'Neill said no and did not want to talk about it. He was afraid his grandfather might say something mean or stupid or make those ugly noises like that time when Rhonda came for lunch. Rhonda was polite and did not say anything, even when they were alone outside, but the boy still felt bad and did not play with Rhonda for a month.

Rhonda was nice. She was pretty and smart and when they were little kids they said they would get married, but the boy knew now that it would never work because she was already 11, and besides he and Pete were not getting married. When they turned 16 and could drive they were moving to Alaska to start a fishing business.

They would have a small boat, just big enough for the two of them, and they wouldn't hire anyone else, just do all the work themselves.

It would be fine because they would take off every Wednesday when the movie changes at the Main Street Theater. They'd go and see the old show in the morning, then go get a malt and a hamburger at the best malt shop in town, no matter the price, and come back and see the new show in the afternoon. They would sit in the cool theater slouched way down in their seats eating Tootsie Rolls and Milk Duds, sucking them until the last bit is melted and looking forward to watching the same movie all over again next week.

He used to worry about his mom being alone with the old man, but now Uncle Lance was here. He would miss his mother but would call her on the phone a lot. He would not miss his grandfather; he would like living in Alaska without him. Of course that part of it did not matter now.

Daniel O'Neill suddenly felt torn between seeing the wicker basket and staying out in the hot sun. He thought about going around front and crawling beneath the front porch, maybe finding spiders and mostly letting the afternoon pass him by. He could stay under the wooden porch for an hour or so, and then he could go into the kitchen and it would all be over and he could go fishing. He could look for crickets in the cracks between the dirt and the wall of the house; the biggest bass go crazy over those black crickets.

But then the boy wondered where the handles would be and how they would be strong enough to hold the old man. He decided on the basket and went into the kitchen and stood quietly by the pantry door.

He listened to the two men walking on the shiny oil-waxed sugar pine floor of the attic bedroom. They wore big black shoes with rubber soles, and the shoes squeaked as the boy imagined the men walking around the old man's bed. It sounded to him like fireflies circling closer and closer to a candle – not like the sound of fireflies but like the light of the squeaking.

The kitchen smelled hot and flowery; the outside followed him in through the screen of the back porch door.

They began coming down the stairs behind the pantry in the kitchen. Daniel O'Neill could see the white leg and black shoe of the first man, coming down backwards, slowly.

They were not using a wicker basket. They were bringing him down on a stretcher, slowly, and at an angle.

The boy watched, wondering why the old man beneath the white sheet did not slide off and bump down the stairs. Daniel O'Neill almost laughed when he thought of that, so he went out the back porch door and ran around the house to join his mother on the front porch. The men came outside, opened the back of the ambulance, and loaded the stretcher inside.

His mother had to sign a paper and then they got into the car and drove off. They did not say goodbye, and they did not turn on the siren, so it was quiet and stayed very still.

And now the old man was gone.

Neither spoke. The ambulance turned at the end of the road and drove away. The woman stepped closer to her son, put an arm around Daniel O'Neill's shoulders.

"I thought you were playing with Pete," she said, looking still at the bend in the road.

"I couldn't find him. I wanted to watch when they took him out. I thought it would be a wicker basket."

His mother held him closer. "I'm sorry you didn't know him before he got so old."

"I know. You said he was nicer then."

She nodded her head, remembering. "Nicer," she said.

She ran her fingers through her hair, gathered the long blond strands at the back of her neck. She slowly rolled her head from side to side.

"Nicer and softer." She smiled and looked down at her son. "He was so much softer."

"I'm sorry, Mom," the boy said. "I'm not glad, you know? But I won't have to listen anymore about wearing shoes, or be careful riding bikes. Or those noises."

His voice cracked against the pressure of tears building at the back of his throat.

"I hated those noises."

"He was old, Daniel. He was sick and he was very old."

The boy's confusion turned to anger.

"I liked him, and I'm sorry. It's just that, he wasn't like a Grandpa, and he was always saying those things. We won't have to be quiet anymore when he takes a nap. We won't have those smells. I'm not glad he's dead, though. But he never went fishing with me anyway, and I'll still go fishing. I'm just sorry."

The boy's shoulders quivered under his mother's arm. He pulled away from her and looked up at his mother.

"Do you know what I mean, Mom? He didn't like me anyway, and he never did anything with me, so it doesn't matter except that he's gone and he won't be around to say mean things, or make those noises or tell me to be quiet for the radio or whatever. I'm not glad though.

"I'm just sorry," the boy said again.

He took another step away from her. He clutched his arms across his chest and worried an ant with his big toe. His mother reached out and gave him another hug. She let out one sigh, smiled at the boy, and lightly swatted his behind.

"Why don't you get Pete and go play. Ask him to supper and I'll fry up a chicken. Or I could make Sloppy Joes."

The boy smiled too. "Thanks, Mom."

"And stay out of the creek," his mother called after him. "You can swim after we eat."

Daniel O'Neill ran and got his bike from the side of the barn, grabbed his fishing stuff off the bench and quickly tied the rod and reel onto the silver sissy bar rising over the back seat. He hung his canvas creel over the top, hopped on his stingray, and sped out of the barn into the hot sun.

He waved to his mom as he turned off the dirt driveway onto the road.

Then he circled again back into the driveway, popped a wheelie in front of his mom and rode off down the road to Pete's house.

"Sloppy Joes!" he called back over his shoulder.

The day still had some good fishing hours left, and if Pete was ready, they would have good luck before supper.

The boy hoped he could surprise his mother with a big bass, or a sweet channel cat. He would help her strip and bread it, and then he would sit on the stool next to the stove as she worked, and snitch the little pieces that bubbled and popped as they fried in the hot grease.

"She shouldn't have to think about making food tonight," Daniel O'Neill thought to himself. "I'll bring the supper home for her."

"Blame the Industrial Revolution.
No more stars, no midnight sky.
After hundreds of thousands of years,
Our species is lost – fallen head first
Out of our night-sky cradle."

- Danny O'Neill

Chapter 4

Becky Dreiling gripped the handle on her early morning cup of tea. She bore down against the muscle spasms of morning sickness; her body quivered along with the wave of heat that rose through her flesh and finally left through her scalp. She shivered and rubbed the goose bumps off her arms. Her shoulders and chest convulsed quickly, and then it passed. She closed her eyes and took a long, deep breath.

Becky closed her hands around the hot mug. She fished around in the steaming cup and pulled the string of the tea bag tightly around the spoon. She squeezed the water out.

"God," she said out loud. "I hate tea."

She took one sip, and before the hot, weak tea reached her stomach, she was off to the bathroom, kneeling on the floor and retching from her toes into the toilet. She felt it coming again. She tried to relax, tried to concentrate on softly flowing rivers, on leaves wafting gently to the ground, on letting her body release without effort.

She almost knocked her head on the uplifted seat as her body jolted against its own impulses. She crumpled onto her knees, clutching the soft t-shirt as she held her arms tight against her belly.

"Little bastard, you just can't make it easy, can you?"

The young woman rose from the floor and brushed her teeth. She looked at the hollow-eyed ghost in the mirror. She recognized the full lips and the blue eyes, but the rest of the corpse was a stranger. She moved the hair stuck to her sweating forehead. She reached for the flannel robe hanging on the painted hook screwed into the bathroom door and padded back to the kitchen, exhausted and hungry.

"Pop," she said fondly, and thankful to see him over the stove. "You ought to at least comb that gray age before you get up at five in the morning to baste eggs."

The man standing at the stove with his back to her chuckled. He pulled up his baggy trousers and fumbled a bit in trying to tuck his undershirt into the top of his pants.

"Don't concern yourself so much with how things look, girl."

He waved a metal spatula over his head – strong, gnarly fingers gripped the wooden handle; the man's big knuckles made a hard fist around the small utensil.

"And you, Baby, you sit your Momma and settle her down. Tell her how much you like them eggs your Grandpa makes. Tell her how healthy you're growing there in her belly. Keep on reminding her that it's these eggs making you big and strong." He looked over his shoulder and winked. "And you tell her if she gets any prettier while you're in there, well by golly she might start a busting up mirrors all over the house."

The man cut two large pats of butter from off a plate and tried to spread them over two pieces of toast. The knife and cold butter went right through the first piece, tearing a hole in the bread. He glanced again over his shoulder and then rubbed the butter around with his thick thumb.

"Take it out sooner, Pop. If you let it sit awhile, it's lots softer, and easier to spread."

"And Baby," the man said as he opened the lid on the skillet and splashed in some water from a glass, "you tell that Momma of yours she's a sight lucky to have come back here from California. We might not know books and bullshit fancy nonsense out here in the middle of Kansas, but by God we know something of cooking eggs in the morning and buttering toast."

He lifted the skillet lid and breathed deeply of the steam rising from the pan. With one motion he scooped the eggs on to the toast plate and brought it to the table. He carefully set the plate in front of his daughter.

"And Baby," he said, reaching for the girl's hand, "you take it a might easier on your Momma in the mornings."

The young woman cut the eggs quickly with the edge of her fork, mixing yolk and white, and then scooping with her toast.

"That's the way," he winked at her.

"I miss peppering them," she said, and when he raised a thick unruly eyebrow in her direction, she said, "Thanks, Pop. I don't know how you put up with me. Every night I lie there in that room and half expect you'll come in at midnight and tie my legs and throw me in the stock pond."

She coughed, almost choked on a bite as she laughed.

"Good Lord," she said. "Stock pond. Did you hear that? Doesn't take long for it all to come back, does it? Jesus, they'd love 'stock pond' at Berkeley."

"Not gonna calf tie and drown you," her father said. "You got my Grandbaby in there." His eyes twinkled as he sipped his coffee. "Be kinda like a chicken farmer taking a hammer to his incubator. No sense in destroying your future, even if the damn incubating machine's giving you hell. Best thing," he said, reaching out and stroking her long blond hair," is to put up with the infernal machine 'till them chicks hatch, then you can bust it up and shop for a new one."

She smiled broadly, took his hand and held it against her cheek.

"Or don't shop for a new one and get out of the business all together," he said.

"Why don't you make some eggs for yourself," she said. "Or I will. You know how it is, once I get everything that's not in there out, and once I get some of your eggs in, I'm fine. Sit here, Pop, let me make you some breakfast."

"Don't need it and no thanks. It'll just slow me down. Besides, I always gotta save room for dinner. Nothing like coming in at noon and seeing you frying chicken or breading chops. You look just like your Momma, God rest her soul. There's nothing makes me happier you're back home, Becky, then seeing you cooking like that, and remembering your Momma."

"I know, Pop. Sometimes I think I should have come back sooner. You've been alone so long. But you know how it is. Meant to at Thanksgiving. Meant to over Christmas. And then this happens, and Danny off to that goddamn war. Now seemed like the right time."

"Course it is. There's nothing wrong with needing some caring. That boy's doing good, and you ought to be proud.

"I'll say it again, Becky, I'm surprised. Didn't think I liked that son-of-a-bitch. By God, you show up last month, coming through here on your way to who the hell knows where, you tell me you're on your honeymoon, for God's sake, and he looked like one of those goddamned hippies. I about threw up. You'd gone and married a goddamned California hippie. But I was wrong about him, Becky. All that Mr. Dreiling this, and Mr. Dreiling that, even though I'm telling him the whole time my goddamned name's Ben, seems like he's poking fun, like some slick goddamned California hippie.

"But by God, I was wrong and I admit it. That boy's all right, by God, he's all right."

"Yeah, Daddy, but I wish you were right. I'd rather be newly wed to a goddamned California hippie than be a widow to some son-of-a-bitching war hero. There was lots of ways he could've gotten out of going. He went for spite, Pop, not honor."

"Don't know about that, and it's none of my business. All I know is he got called up and he went. You tell me he could have gotten out of going, but he didn't, and that's the whole point of it. All these goddamned kids now' days, what's in it for them, what's their angle. How can they get out of something they know damn good and well they ought to be doing. Like his brother, that son-of-a-bitch you and Danny came through here with. Now there's a snot-nosed son-of-a-bitching hippie. And on your honeymoon for God's sake. Free-loading son-of-a-bitching hippie."

"He went in the army too, Pop. Lance is awfully important to me. He's important to all of us."

"Important like my butt's a hole in the ground. Free-loading son-of-a-bitch, you mean."

Lance and Danny. California and school. The Colorado honeymoon camping by the lake. Light years away and lifetimes ago. As Becky Dreiling rubbed toast crumbs across the wooden tabletop, she wondered again what in God's name happened on that honeymoon by the Colorado lake. They were so perfect, weren't they, the three of them? So close. So right. What the hell was she thinking?

At the time she blamed her behavior on the war, on the fact that her so chic and silly sacred little manage a trois was threatened by bullshit establishment politics. The military fucking industrial beast breathing down on them. Oh my, they were so goddamned smart.

They were so hip. So cool. Real players in history's morally superior rebellion. Changing the world. Being like Jesus, peace and love and colorful clothes. What a joke. Turns out the rebellion didn't cleanse anything; it merely sacrificed innocents to chaos. It sure as hell did for her. She had sacrificed them both, lost them both, condemned them both to South East Asian hell. She still hadn't heard from either one of them, had no idea where they were or what was going on.

How insanely reckless of them.

How unforgivably careless of her.

Careless because they were all so amazingly irresponsible – breaking rules with self-satisfied arrogance and making up new ones with self-confident ignorance. Careless because they had the hubris to believe they could create their own dangerous reality. Danny enraged and betrayed by her love for Lance, Lance spiteful and lost because of her love for Danny. Both of them trapped by their love for each other.

So much for free love.

Who the hell did she think she was, setting brothers against each other and so losing them both to this obnoxious war. A war that now left her not only alone, but alone with a piece of both of them growing inside her. Alone in retreat to the home of her childhood. Defeated and alone.

Back to the womb, Becky Dreiling thought as she sat now in the early morning kitchen of her father. She watched the collection of copper pots dangling above the stove. She searched each one, looking for the comfortable reflections in the shiny surfaces, looking for that world beyond this one.

As a child, she sat at this same table with crayons spread out before her. Her mother baked, or cooked, or cleaned dishes, and the little girl drew pictures of the reflections in the pots. The wooden spoons or flower wallpaper and wooden doors waffling and shimmering in the pots looked like they were forever stuck in a distortion of amber repose. She believed those reflections led to a world of mysteries and magic, a world hidden just out of sight on the backside of the pots, like in the book where the little girl walks into the mirror.

She had been meaning to check her boxes in the attic and find those pictures, pictures she saved because she believed her mother that if she could get the drawings just right, she could find the magic on the other side.

Perhaps after the summer heat passed she would go up and look. Perhaps as the leaves changed and then fell, she would climb the steep, narrow stairs behind the kitchen pantry and sort through the old treasures stored in the attic.

Every spring she helped her mother pack heavy sweaters and cotton long johns and wool socks into the hard paper drums. Steel snap rings clamped the metal lids firmly to the top of the drums and kept attic moisture and moths at bay.

Becky Dreiling looked forward to spending entire afternoons in the attic, perched on a milk crate and fingering, smelling, and holding individual pieces of her family's legacy. She knew her crayon pictures would be childlike. She knew the colors and shapes, lovingly carried in her memories, didn't exist in the attic boxes. And she knew the initial flush of excitement, when she found the boxes and prepared to open them, would quickly fade with this disappointment.

But she smiled now into the pots just the same. She knew also the magic never really existed in the drawings, and not even in the awe and excitement of a little girl full of faith and determination.

"Just in me, keeping it here inside all these years, taking it to California with me," she said out loud.

"Damned if you'll take any good Ellis County anything out to a wasteland," her father said. "Them California bastards'd no more appreciate anything or anyone here at home than a goddamn hound dog with its nose stomped by a mule. Any of them things here you needed out there, you shoulda come back for them, not hauling out to goddamned California."

"Things in California are different, Pop, not like here. I don't say better, but different. Lance and Danny and I, we're awfully close, awfully special to each other. All three of us."

"California's a wasteland. Sounds like a goddamned commune to me."

"Sorta was, Pop. Was in a good way, you know? People living together, working together, caring about each other. Not so different than around here, really. You know, when we'd have those huge barbecues up by the pond, Aunt Ginny and all her kids, Uncle Roy and Uncle Chet, all their kids. Everybody being together, a big family. Momma always making those bean salads, coleslaw, and stuff none of us kids would eat. You and Uncle Chet arguing, Uncle Roy cooking meat over the fire pit. That's family, Pop."

"Out in California, a lot of us didn't have family around, so we kind of made one. You know? Sort of choosing your family – for holidays, for laughing together, for a shoulder to cry on."

"Bullshit. Goddamned commune's nothing like family. There's no blood."

"We made blood too, Pop."

"And so you did and good for you. And see there, that boy didn't fool around there, either. Had a job to do and did it. Could 'a run off but he didn't. Married you, by God. Big strong son-of-a-bitch too, that boy. Mrs. O'Neill, you've done fine."

"Well, Mr. Dreiling, don't be fooled too much by how things look. Those California Danny O'Neill genes may come back to bite us all in the ass one of these days. Sure giving me one hell of a run for it right now."

"And you're bucking up fine. It'll get better, Darling, it's gonna be fine. Your mother was the same way. Goddamn shame, though, that boy's gotta miss his own child coming. But hell, less than two years, you'll be so used to living here, you'll get that boy to stay too when he comes home to you. Roy nor Chet didn't do shit for having sons. Guess I didn't either, but that boy of yours'd make a hell of a Kansas farmer. Hell of a good place to raise little ones, too.

"I saw it in that boy. California or no, I could make a damn decent farmer out of him. Hell of a nice place for kids."

The man finished the last of his coffee, and pulled at the suspenders hanging loose over his shoulders.

Becky noticed his shoulders were smaller, perhaps, but only slightly, the bones maybe just a bit more visible through the white undershirt, but strong still, she could see, and square. The shirt barely covered the man's elbows. His forearms, like his hands, looked animated for all the different muscles that danced about as he gestured when he talked. She used to hang on those arms and giggle and poke the tight ball of his bicep. The arms were still covered with hot sun and hard work, though the hair on them was lighter – grayer, she supposed – but covering arms still capable of twisting iron and supporting dangling children.

"I'm not gonna live forever, Becky. This house ought to have family in it again. Hell of a nice place. Not California where those God dammed people drink whiskey with the Devil, by God, and thank the Good Lord for that. But this farm, I tell you what, it's one hell of a nice corner of God's backyard."

"That it is, Pop. That it is."

Becky Dreiling got up from the table and loosened her robe against the heat already in the kitchen. She took her plate from the table to the sink, and brought the coffee pot back.

The man put his large hand over his cup.

"Can't do it, Darlin', cattle are calling." He swallowed the last of his coffee and stood up. "And listen here, you quit this fool cleaning and organizing all around the house while I'm out. Put

65

your damn feet up. Drink lemonade. Watch butterflies. Shame you don't read those magazine romances, like your Mother. She could spend the day at 'em, and never tell you what the hell they were about that night. Passed the time though, God rest her soul. But you, you take it easy today. I'll see you noon."

"Take it any easier, and I'll calcify, Pop," she called after the man as he went out into the mudroom behind the kitchen to put on his boots and field clothes.

"Calcify or go crazy," she said to the slamming screen door, and to the kitchen now filling with silence spilling into an early morning sunrise.

She took her teacup and settled into the window seat on the north side of the dining room. Becky Dreiling cradled the hot cup in both hands and remembered how much she loved the dining room still. She remembered how much she loved being a little girl in this room.

She loved the long, double-pedestal oak table, hand-crafted years ago by her great grandfather. Once and always filled with centerpieces of dried flowers; now covered with paperwork, stacked bills and farm implement mail brochures.

She loved the window seat; its individually glazed windowpanes reached nearly to the top of the ten-foot ceiling. Most of the panes were original, made from old, imperfect glass. The low-tech waves and distortions in the glass came from a different time and from another world. Each pane reflected a slightly different view of the outside.

Heavy pinewood window frames anchored this gentle mosaic. The frames grew from the wooden bench of the window seat and secured the clear but changing light. The elegant, polished window frames contained and controlled this subtle dance.

The window frames reminded her of her father – strong heavily veined support enveloping light.

Her mother was the delicate white lace valance – completing the wood frames, softening the tops of the window frames, diffusing the light and interpreting it into shadows and shapes across the polished wood floor.

Each together creating a perfect balance. "Yin and yang," Becky said out loud. "Imagine that, the Age of Aquarius, right here in my childhood out in the middle of Kansas." She smiled, sipped her tea, and relaxed fully into the morning.

More than anything, Becky loved looking through the distorted windows at the huge cast iron cooking pot sitting out in the yard. The enormous black cauldron rested on three sharp cast iron legs. It was as big as a wheelbarrow. It set on flat stones in the ground at the front corner of the porch. It had been there, unmoved, all of her life so that the black pot had been there forever.

Mothers of grandmothers brought it with them across the prairie, so that the black pot belonged always to the daughters of the family. On every new moon, Becky and her mother cleaned and oiled the magnificent piece. Grandmothers of mothers had done the same – every new moon, every month for every year. Even when the new immigrants lived those first few years in sod houses, and the pot was actually providing meals over open fires, it was revered at the new moon. Probably especially then, Becky supposed.

Once, the new moon was on Christmas Eve, and there was a blizzard. Becky was ten or eleven and she was in awe of her mother and proud of herself because they bundled up, braved the storm, and honored the cauldron.

A grounding ritual, Becky realized now. Bringing yin balance into the incessant yang howl of the constant prairie wind. There were stories from the old days about how the ceaseless wind had driven some women back to St Louis; and how it had driven some women mad.

Women in Becky's family oiled and honored the cast iron cauldron.

An enormous source of earth-nurturing and sustenance. How wise, she thought, realizing with a twinge of embarrassment that these ancestral women had never been to Berkeley.

Becky looked past the black pot. The sky beyond the windows was now fully brushed onto the summer canvas of Kansas morning.

She shook her head in wonder at the colors and at the quiet anticipation filling the sky. She smiled, remembering her own mother sitting with her in this very seat, in this very spot, so many and every morning ago.

"Hear all that quiet in the dawn?" her Momma would say. "That's the Good Lord, yawning big and strong after His night's sleep. All that rose color coming off the grasses and weaving up into the sky is His sweet breath, waking up the world.

"The ancients called it "The rosy finger of dawn," but they were wrong. It's not the Good Lord's finger, Honey. All that color and softness is His first sweet breath of the day. Once He's over his yawn, His breath's going to clear up, business-like, because He's got all of us to look after, and He's got to be sharp."

The little girl would snuggle closer to her mother, hoping the day would stop right here and the dawn would never leave.

"I love this part of the mornings best," her Momma would say. "It's the only glimpse you ever get when the Good Lord is relaxed. We're on our own, for just these moments of every morning. Angels watching over us at night, Good Lord taking care of us during the day.

"Dawn is our time, Sugar. Not angels nor God, just us."

Becky Dreiling now sobbed and gasped along with the color of dawn. She gently stroked her stomach, still flat and hard, but waking slowly with its own heavenly yawn.

"Seems like it makes good sense right now, hey little baby?"

She fought tears as she stroked her belly without feeling it and rubbed around and around with a rhythm not yet a heartbeat but primal, not quite maternal but belonging.

"Oh, little baby, would that I could make your life as simple and sweet as the Lord's breath in Momma's wonder. As that sweet old man, knocking around in the barn, knows it should be.

"I've made a mess of things, little baby, I've made a mess of my life, and I'm afraid I've made a mess of your life, too."

She sat and let the tears go as the full morning came.

"Oh Lord," she said, near to choking between breaths. "What'll they say when your Daddies come home?"

As she sat in the window seat in the dining room soft with memories and the light of her mother, in this farm house built by grandfathers and held straight and strong by her father, Becky Dreiling felt very much as if she had wandered up to the stagnant north pond where the sick cows go when they're shunned by the herd.

The other cows, and sometimes the bull, will separate the sick cow from the herd and keep her away from the calves.

Maybe the sick cow has lost one eye, maybe a leg is bad, or a fence-torn sore won't heal. And the herd keeps her away.

Away from the calves, away from the grain, away from the sweet water.

The sick cow tries again and again to come back, tries to graze with the rest, but she's chased off, forced away.

Finally she settles on solitude and paces around the north pond. If one eye is bad, she turns the good eye to the foul water and paces the shore, blind outside her circle. If it's a bad leg that's made her an outcast, the pond's black mud sucks onto her hooves with each step, holding her, slowing her, bringing her down.

An open, festering wound draws flies, and its dripping puss stains her hide and creates her stench.

She paces for days around the pond – a machine wasted and used up, simply running itself out.

She will collapse, finally, exhausted and starved, food for the coyotes that snarl at magpies and crows. Her hide decays and reveals the worms and maggots. And then, finished off by carrion seekers and sun, she's finally just bleached bones, scattered like driftwood and melding back into the earth.

"Jesus, Becky, you morbid bitch," the woman said out loud. "Keep this kind of shit up, and this baby'll be born deformed just like that one at the lake, a hideous and wobbly big head. Won't make a bit of difference who the daddy is, neither one of them will want it. Lighten up and drink lemonade, for God's sake."

*"My life feels like hiding
In a candle-lit confessional
While reading a smuggled classic
Of Literary Impressionism."*

- John Gophe

Chapter 5

When I consider clearly, I realize I am incredibly incidental to the story, perhaps even pathetically so. I am like one of those children running and playing high above the sea on a grassy plateau. I am one of those many hoping to be one of the lucky few. I am hoping that the one older kid standing in the tall rye catches me before I tumble over the cliff of obscurity.

I've bumped through life in this fashion for as long as I can recall – a barely sentient mollusk clinging to the shore of a facade. This is no new revelation to me; it does not humble nor demean me. The truthful fear is that I've always been this way. I wandered through high school unnoticed, blending into the gray lockered walls. I avoided conflicts, always stepping out of the way during those frequent games of adolescent chicken where the pecking order scratched its way into crowded hallways between classes. Two roosters, flowing toward each other in a sea of admiring sycophants. They bump shoulders, glare each other down. Roosters barely beginning to sprout crowns, yet anxious to show the world, or at least a hallway filled with impressionable classmates, that they were developing formidable claws. Capable claws. Claws increasingly adept at grasping and holding hens. Hold and win the giggle, the budding cleavage, the willing admiration. All the strutting, all the stammering, all a calculated play for the hens.

Adolescent chicken. I never lost the game because I never played the game.

I never suffered the bruises of team sports, never reveled in the camaraderie. I never felt the adrenaline rush of yelling in the bleachers with friends during pep rallies.

In the senior yearbook, I wasn't voted Most Likely to Be Boring or Most Likely to Be Forgotten. I wasn't voted anything at all. Just my picture; no accolades or teasing in good fun. Just me.

I left high school carrying the only diploma available to me – a golden stamp of normalcy, the model student of mediocrity.

I spent the summer after graduation lying around the house, driving my mom crazy, going to movies, avoiding chores and responsibility, lying around the house.

I did get invited, inexplicably, to a senior camping trip. I think it was in July. Melinda Morrison called, and had to leave a message with my mom. I didn't call her back, and a week later Jake Patton called to ask if I was going.

I knew Jake Patton since first grade. We weren't friends, never had been, though always friendly enough, based, I guess, on nothing more than our tenure.

Jake Patton never called me, ever. So I wasn't all that sure whose voice was really on the other end.

"Patton, you moron," he emphasized. "From Velmont High. Hey, Gopher, it's only been six weeks since graduation."

"Right," I said. "Jake. How's it going? What's up?"

I began mumbling some question, a friendly inquiry about his summer. He cut me off.

"Listen, Gophe, Melinda made me call you. Are you going camping or not? It'll be fun and you'll have a great time. You're invited. Here's the deal. You remember Connie Roder? Well, she's a friend of Melinda's, and she likes you, she hopes that you'll go. So go. Be there.

"And listen, Gopher, I'm serious as a heart attack here. If Melinda asks you, make damn sure you tell her I invited you nice. Don't shit with me on this. You understand? Call Melinda. She's organizing the whole deal."

"Okay, Jake. Thanks for the call. I appreciate it."

"Right, Gopher. Later."

Connie Roder? A friend of Melinda's? Why would she like me? Is that Connie Roder from American Lit?

Melinda and Jake started going together in Junior High. Or maybe even sixth grade. A long time. Like I say, Jake was always friendly enough, but he was on the football team, and Melinda was a cheerleader, and they weren't my crowd. I didn't have a crowd. Who the heck was Connie Roder?

My mom started in. This was two phone calls in one week, and her radar clicked and clattered.

"Do I know Melinda Morrison? She sounded sweet. Did you call her? It would be great if you'd start seeing some of your high school friends again, Johnny. These are the best days of your life."

Was she kidding? Melinda Morrison was a peppy, self-centered, air-headed social butterfly; sweet she was not. Melinda Morrison had friends from high school, and she was obviously planning to take those friends camping and then keep them the rest of her life. The best days of my life were definitely yet to come, or would never arrive, and I had no friends from high school. Connie Roder?

"Right," I shrugged. I never RSVP'd to Melinda Morrison. I didn't know what to say. Eventually, the summer came to a close.

Jake Patton never called me again.

I don't know what Melinda Morrison and her friends from high school did after that summer. I've occasionally imagined that they stayed together forever, raised their children together, took all their camping vacations together, and probably went on to star in a movie about friends who stayed together forever.

I went away to college.

I went out of state to a small school on the Western Slope of Colorado. I'd always figured I'd go to the school right in my town, but my Dad said I was going out of state, so I did. He wasn't a great one for clichés, but when he found one he liked you heard it a lot. Since I was in eighth or ninth grade, "Get out from under the apron strings" popped up often when he talked about me. I wasn't as much like him as I wished I was, and I imagine he didn't see much of himself in me. I know this didn't make him love me any less, but it wasn't all that easy for him to like me much, either. It wasn't one of those things you talked about, but we both felt that way. He was my Dad and I was his kid, and he wanted me to go away to college, so I did.

I left home. I buckled myself into the freshman sleigh and I whisked off to a new and exciting chapter in my life. I arrived crammed in among thousands of novitiates who looked exactly, more or less, like me.

It was a campus rule that freshmen who had no family in town must spend the first year in a dormitory.

So I moved into a dorm: Drucker Hall. Just a bunch of us thrown together, like a summer camp but hardly any rules: the inmates running the asylum energized by hormones and first-time-away-from-home brand new. If you think about it, the similarities to kindergarten are striking. The first week of dorm life was one big party; a party where you get to dress however you like and leave or show up whenever you want to. I figured the forced socialization would do me some good, as long as I didn't run in to Melinda Morrison.

The first week of actual school impresses me now as one tediously long, incredibly boring wait in line. We were addressed by school officials, counselors, registrars, Greeks. We were told what would be expected of us. We were given orientation lectures designed to clarify the incredible amount of facts, services, expectations, opportunities and rules. We were welcomed to the college by the president, who recounted the grand tradition and notable history, as well as a glowing record of community service and fine reputation nationally as an institution of higher learning. We were encouraged to be proud yet humble, forthright yet relaxed, studious yet, as the president suggested with a wink, availing ourselves of the numerous opportunities for activity – a well-rounded college experience.

This was, after all, a unique time in our lives when, in accepting this supreme academic challenge and facing straightforward our responsibilities, we could afford to enjoy ourselves and ignore, if only slightly, the call from society.

It was funny listening to the college president talk that way. A grownup telling kids to be kind of wild and have fun, as if that was a good way to begin growing up.

A few rows in front of me a small flock of girls, probably all onetime cheerleaders and possibly part of Melinda Morrison's extended friends from high school, sat in a constant state of giggle, flipping their manes of candy-dyed hair and passing notes to one another. I appreciated their scorn for the lecture but clicked my tongue and raised an eyebrow at their style.

Directly in front of me a fellow sat taking notes.

Quite a bit of time during those first days was taken up by standing in line for a pink card, waiting on line for a yellow form, and queuing up early in the morning to lounge around all day for a computer-record-pull-registration-form. After a while, you get desensitized to the meaning of things, much like becoming accustomed to dorm food. Surprisingly few of us questioned what a computer-record-pull-registration-form was.

This mollifying tedium lasted most of the week, designed, I assume, to weed out the weak blood or stave off bouts of homesickness.

I never got a chance to get to know the fellow I'd been assigned to share a dorm room with, which was too bad because, in making dorm room assignments, the housing authorities were supposedly guided by a personal preference questionnaire, and thus I never got a chance to discover either how well I knew myself or how perceptive the housing authorities were. I made a joke once to my first roommate that roommate assignments were part of a covert graduate sociology department experiment designed to test the limits of human endurance.

He didn't get it, at least he didn't laugh. Alan Whatever-His-Name-Was looked 12 years old, maybe. He had a terrible case of acne. He was very quiet, even more than me.

Alan was gone after the first week. Disappeared. I returned from breakfast that first Saturday and his half of our shoebox was empty, cleaned out. A sardine, I think, who squished to the edge of the can and popped out over the side, to go back, probably, and run the family filling station forever and for a good part of the rest of his life.

The next day Cib Adams moved in.

I was laid back, propped against the wall in bed, playing my harmonica poorly with not a thing to do until dinner except join the Get To Know Your Neighbor Fifth Floor Drucker Hall party or, more likely, masturbate, when he pushed open the door and walked in, slinging his duffel bag ahead of him. He noticed me the way you might eye an overstuffed chair that's always been around, comfortable and unremarkable.

"Howdy Dude." He extended his right hand warmly, flung his cowboy hat on the empty bed with his left.

"Cib Carkus Adams. Got here late, just this morning. They assigned me up here to you. Guess we're bunkies. Hope you can stand me. Usually I fart only in the bathroom and fuck only in bed. You're welcome to kick my ass when I transgress on either point. How the hell's the food?"

I laid my harp down deliberately and just watched him.

"Whooee!" he squealed. He had all the charm and decoration of a good old boy from Texas or Tennessee. His lack of a drawl made him no less animated. He was big, and he looked strong. His face was burned red by sun and wind. The sleeves of his T-shirt rolled up, right below the shoulder. He looked like he had just stepped out of American Farm Boy magazine or something.

He sat down on the other bed and tested the springs.

"Man! You've got some lovely ladies strutting around this place."

He grinned, and the sun wrinkles went out of his face, softened around his eyes. For a moment, he looked like a little kid, but for just that same moment, his eyes went flat, like exhausted.

"Fantastic." He winked at me.

"The ladies are filling the hall down the way, a corral of them. Gorgeous puntang waiting to be tried. Why the hell you in here blowing the blues by yourself? You need to get down there and audition some conductors."

He laughed out loud, a deep laugh that vibrated into a familiar and uncomfortable buzz deep down in my stomach.

"Where you from, Cib?"

I felt foolish for my attempt at parlor small talk, foolish because I lacked his natural, easy-going nature. I didn't feel intimidated, exactly, yet I could see a certain amount of control lying at the foot of my bed, barely beyond my reach. I felt foolish because I was already here, and he was so much more at home. I felt foolish because I didn't really know what to say. I felt foolish because I didn't know whether or not I believed his name was Cib.

"Outside of Denver, over on the other side of the mountains."

The turn in conversation didn't slow him at all. "Best goddamned city in the country. A mile high in quality. Cheap beer, easy women, Broncos, blizzards and sunshine."

He walked to the bathroom, grabbing his hat off the bed.

"Decided to come here to school. Women all cried, opposing linebackers rejoiced. I kissed the babes and had a final beer with the boys, climbed on a bus and here I am. Might just stay forever."

He giggled and shut the door.

***

I felt some jealousy as Adams and I mingled with the crowd at the end of the hall at the get-to-know-your-neighbor party. Adams introduced himself all around, indiscriminately to both sexes. I felt very much the newcomer, and was hesitant to feel taken under his confident wing. Many of the people he was talking and joking with were the same people I had already passed often in the dorm, back and forth to the showers, or to the cafeteria. I had never mustered more than a simple "How's it going?"

These same people had made no real overtures to me, and I couldn't tell whether or not they were also uncomfortable being brought together by this burly extrovert. Nonetheless, I was hesitant to feel incapable of comfortably socializing without him.

I tried, for that reason, to steer clear of him and mingle on my own. Undaunted by my indifference, he continued to appear with one new friend after another, introducing me as his "number one buddy," his "partner in campus crime," or, most embarrassingly, as his "mentor in pleasuring female anatomy."

I decided to return to our room, resigned to the belief that either these people didn't like me or I didn't like them, when Adams invited, or rather confirmed the belief, that I would join him and a few fellows for a sociable smoke, away from the masses.

My initial reaction was annoyance at his assumption that I smoked marijuana. It seemed he could have at least expressed enough interest in me to ask about my preferences, but then I remembered I was out of weed and I recognized that there were plenty of people around who would have been happy to indulge in an attitude adjustment with him.

Actually, the fact that I partake has always seemed a bit out of character for me; I mean, it is illegal, and my Dad sure as heck wouldn't like it if he knew. But he didn't, and I guess I kind of figured it probably helps to have one clear thing to repent, because it makes Confession easier. Maybe for me, marijuana was that thing.

Well, that and, of course, masturbation.

Anyway, ignorant as we were of the hall director's standing on the subject, the four or five of us retreated to our room.

"Come on in, fellas. We haven't had time to pretty up the place, just having arrived and all."

He consulted me. "Dude. We gotta get some tunes. You haven't got a stereo, huh? I had one at home, but it was pretty cheap, so I gave it to my little sister. Figured I'd bunk up with someone with major tunes." He smiled. "Tunes are like toilet paper, man. You don't miss 'em 'til you don't have' em."

I started to say I was considering buying a stereo in the spring, but once I caught myself in the position of explaining my purchasing plans, he had lost interest and was rummaging around in his duffel bag, searching for his stash.

***

Most ganja makes me introverted, much more so than usual. Some makes me paranoid, and I hate that. Consumed with the feeling that everyone knows I'm high, and that they disapprove of me because of it. Like when you have that dream where you're playing naked Twister with the mom from next door and your Catechism teacher comes in the door. I think these are fairly common reactions to smoking marijuana. However, there are some few people who seem to gain control, gain perspective, seemingly gain verbal wisdom. Other people are drawn to them – to their strength, their ideas, their awareness. They lose ego and gain understanding. Calm, collected, centered.

Like how it would be if Jesus smoked marijuana.

Some pot makes me giggle, and the stuff Adams pulled from his duffel bag was giggle dope. I laughed uncharacteristically when he suggested I roll another joint.

"No way Cib, my fingers are numb," I laughed.

He feigned seriousness. "Hey, Dude, listen. I was a sophomore in high school, behind the county football stadium with Rachael Sommers, and I swore a blood oath to the gods I'd never roll another joint for as long as I lived."

He chuckled at the memory. He shook his head, dejection struggling against grins.

"You got to do it for me, Buddy. I gotta have another toke and I can't compromise my principles.

"C'mon," he said. "Roll us one, man. You can do it."

I laughed, took the cracked yellow Frisbee full of clean brown weed and squinted my eyes accusingly. "Okay," I said, "but don't complain if it falls apart, and don't wait for me to ask you about Rachael Sommers and the football stadium."

He shook his head. "Deep, dark secret, Buddy."

I couldn't tell whether he was oblivious to the rapt attention of the other fellows in the room or whether he was milking that attention for the finale to the story.

"Terrible, terrible episode in my life. I'll tell you about it one day only after you've told me you once peeked in on your granny or farted in confession."

The other fellows were awed by our jocular familiarity, and I loved the illusion. They probably figured Adams and I went way back together. Maybe all the way back to kindergarten.

***

I was in Kindergarten. I think about kindergarten a lot.

I remember it well, refer to it often. I was happy there. Miss Carlotti was my teacher. She was young, and tall and pretty with long black hair. She was even prettier than Miss Jeannie from Romper Room. She wore dresses, sometimes with spring flowers, and sometimes colors like peach and red and green. She had an easy smile and brilliant white teeth, ringed in soft, rose colored lips.

At least I think she did.

I don't know about the rest of the boys in my Kindergarten, but I was in love with Miss Carlotti.

I remember Buella Walker from Kindergarten. A lot bigger than all the other kids, she wore cotton dresses, red checks or blue checks, sewn from picnic table cloths; dresses assembled like feed sacks with cutouts for the arms and her big head, which was covered with stringy, usually greasy looking brown hair. Her hair hung down like dirty straw, cut straight on her forehead and stopping just above her eyebrows. It climbed up over her ears, and then dropped to her neck. She wore white tennis shoes and black socks.

I wonder now what in God's name her parents were thinking when they named her Buella and dressed her that way.

I remember all through the year her upper arms were covered with a red, bumpy rash.

Buella Walker was mean. She was bossy to everybody. She used to threaten me on the way home from school, push me and stuff. Once when she was standing way on the other side of the field between the school and my house, I yelled out at her; I called her Boo-Boo Bueller. She was awfully far away, and I was close to home.

Buella Walker chased me down and beat me up.

It was Kindergarten when kids started calling me Gopher. It's not a great name, and I always hated it. But sometimes it's just easier than Johnny Gophe, because no one ever gets the pronunciation correct and you get tired of saying "no, it rhymes with "off," not "oaf.""

It didn't matter to Buella Walker because she never called me Gopher anyway. She called me Freddy Frog, Crawdad Turd. I don't know why.

Buella Walker could touch the white part of her eye with her fingertip. She could roll her eye all the way back in her head and then turn the upper eyelid inside out. Then she'd grin like a skeleton, blood-red half moons hanging down over dead white eyeballs.

I wonder where she is now. I look over my shoulder when I think of Buella Walker.

I never knew what happened to her. She never showed up in first grade. She didn't flunk Kindergarten, because she just wasn't around anywhere anymore.

I never heard of anyone flunking Kindergarten except David Valiuso.

David Valiuso was a goofy guy. Goofy is a funny word, and David Valiuso was a funny guy. And he was goofy.

He had a long, drawn olive skinned buck-toothed face. Terribly buck-toothed and his ears stuck out from the side of his head. Really.

David Valiuso was a class clown, but he was one of those sad clowns that nobody ever laughed at. Most of the kids ignored him. Miss Carlotti always talked to him very seriously, like she was telling him his dad had just died.

One day, at recess on the gravel playground with swings and Monkey Bars, David Valiuso snuck up behind Buella Walker and started scratching his armpits and making "Oooh Oooh Oooh" monkey sounds. He tried to run when she turned around, but she grabbed him and banged his head with a foursquare ball.

David Valiuso and I were friends for a couple of weeks once. He wasn't in any kind of demand as a friend, and I don't know how much I really liked him. I secretly thought he was funny, but I could never shake the knowledge that no one else liked him, and no one else ever would. I guess that's why I stopped being his friend.

The truth is I did like David Valiuso. He was my friend. I did think he was funny.

I know that seems strange. It does to me.

Anyway, the next year everyone else was in first grade, and David Valiuso wasn't around. I never noticed until a few years later, when he was part of the third grade, the class behind me. I didn't talk to him.

In Kindergarten, we built castles out of huge, different-colored cardboard boxes. We ate snacks. We played on the playground, and we took naps on rugs under tables. When we woke up, Miss Carlotti was there.

Kindergarten was great. I wish I was there now.

You know how in Kindergarten, they tell you, "Yeah, this is good, but just wait until first grade"? And then they tell you the same thing in sixth grade, "Yeah, but just wait until junior high." And then high school is even less then junior high, and college, even though they swore that would be the ultimate, is the least of it all.

And then, real life. The tops. Way cool.

I matriculated into real life. I am there still.

And now I believe an enormous mistake has probably been made, a convoluted bureaucratic bumble, and I reported for the wrong duty, received incorrect, or at least inadequate, orders.

And, like the real world, I have proven to be much less than was promised in the Kindergarten catalogue.

Many bad things have happened. A lot of things, to many people. To the O'Neills, Lance and Daniel. To Becky Dreiling, for God's sake. To Adams and Nattie Sinclair.

I hope good things came to Miss Carlotti.

"You always sit up and take notice
Whenever the eyes of your friend
Reflect the depth of your pain"

- John Gophe

Chapter 6

More than anything else, my old man believed in his principles. Man alive, did he ever. I learned that lesson well because of a fight he once had with my mom.

She won the battle, like they say, but boy did she get annihilated in the war.

I don't think my dad left us simply because he lost that one fight with my mom, but I recognize now that the larger principle involved was big enough to eventually drive him out of the house.

On the surface of it, they fought about Knights of Columbus picnics, basement remodeling, and college-level red cardboard-bound dictionaries. And, of course, about the Teazas. I understand now that the real conflict was over his principles governing behavior and her desires for herself and her family. Hard to argue with either one of them.

But couples rarely fight honestly about stuff like that, come to think of it. They waltz around the edge of the issues, getting just close enough to the center that the other person's foot is bound to stick out somewhere and trip them up. Then they get angry and yell about clumsy feet instead of what's really going on down there in the vortex of the middle. As if they poke each other with knife-sharpened sticks but wrap rags around the points, either because some modicum of love or need requires they ultimately protect the other person or, even worse, their cumulating and mutual disdain drives them to hurt the other just enough to cause pain and blood, but not enough to deliver the mortal blow. This way fresh wounds can be inflicted tomorrow.

When I was little they fought the first way. By the time I was ten or eleven, it seemed like an awful lot of fresh wounds were being inflicted around my house. After Christmas in sixth grade, my dad moved out. They never divorced, partly because of me but mostly because of the Sacrament of Holy Matrimony. But everything sure changed. One day we just weren't a family anymore. We didn't do any family things, we no longer hung out with other families. My dad kept his men friends from church, and my mom saw the same women. But we never saw any of them as families anymore. When the love was gone between them, the family disappeared as well. I saw them both a lot, because my dad bought a duplex next to the field over by my elementary school. My mom and I stayed in our house. She had to get a job at J.C. Penny's. She worked behind a counter at the catalogue-ordering department. She works there still.

When I got to high school, my dad moved to Albuquerque, and I spent summers with him. I didn't much care for Albuquerque, and I don't think he was that thrilled to have me around, but, you know.

Anyway, the fight they had was toward the middle of the summer after fifth grade. The whole thing actually started earlier, in the late spring before school got out.

It was an after school evening. The doorbell rang and my mom opened the front door onto the droning wide-street suburbia and found this little door-to-door dictionary salesman nervously buffing his brown shoes against the gray pant leg of his cheap suit there on the huge concrete slab of our front porch. Nervous and pathetic, like most door-to-door salesmen, he was working himself into a sweat trying to keep his best foot out of his mouth and forward.

I was sprawled out on the bumpy olive-green Berber of our living room carpet reading the evening-paper comics; my dad lounged nearby with the news section tucked into the worn arm of his recliner. I sat in it only when he wasn't around. We both glanced and listened toward the entryway (we never called it a foyer; maybe ours wasn't fancy enough, or maybe we just didn't know the word).

My mom wasn't great with door-to-door salesmen. Actually, she wasn't too great with strangers of any occupation. Not shy, just sort of reserved in a scared kind of way. Typical suburban housewife, I guess. She spent half of her life living in her father's house, and then she moved into her husband's house, where she did the best she could to raise me, make casseroles and do the laundry and stuff.

Usually my dad would listen to her stammer at the salesmen for a bit, and then casually join her, either to gently move the scarier ones along, or chew the fat, sometimes even buy something, from the others. He bought a lot of things he didn't need that way, but I never saw him give anyone a handout, if you know what I mean.

There were two parts to this deal – one part was a brown dictionary for kids in elementary and junior high called the Junior Scholastic; it had pictures of flags and lists of presidents' birthdays and whatnot. The other part was a red dictionary that would give your children a leg up in high school and serve them well on through their entire college years. An investment, really, in their complete education. It was called the Collegiate, and I still lug the son-of-a-gun around with me. Partly because it serves occasionally to amaze me, since it often doesn't contain a word when you go to look one up, which is bizarre. I mean, how worthless is a dictionary that's filled with thousands of words you never need to look up, but sometimes doesn't contain one that you do? It's almost scary when you don't know a word, and then you discover the dictionary doesn't know it, either.

Mostly, though, I still have the worthless red Collegiate dictionary because my old man bought it that night from Fred Teaza.

***

I remember when the school principal brought Catherine Teaza into our classroom that year, nearly at the end of school in the fifth grade. We all had to say hello like when a new kid comes, and then she sat down at an empty desk the row over from me and one up. I could hardly look at her, she was so pretty. She was quiet, and mostly I remember her eyes. Bright green, with black circles around the green. The evil eye, or the eye of God; I couldn't remember which, but she was sure pretty. You could hardly help staring at her eyes, but it was scary for me to go in there.

It wasn't long after this that Mr. Teaza showed up at our door with his pathetic little sales pitch and useless dictionaries. My dad not only bought two sets of the books, but also invited the guy in for a beer and ultimately had him signed up with the Knights of Columbus.

After he was inside, I recognized him as the father of that family that had just started coming to our parish.

And I've got to point out, the Teaza family could sure draw attention away from the Mass. They were like some big blotchy mole on an old lady's cheek − pretty disgusting, so you were compelled to stare, especially, maybe, at that black hair growing out of the middle. But no one talked about it as if it was, embarrassingly, not there.

The first time they showed up at 10:15 Mass, a lot of heads turned as the Teazas entered the vestibule, and a number of heads followed them the whole time as they made their tortured way up to an empty pew at the head of the church.

And I say heads over and over because I can't help it, and I'm sure everyone in church that morning was thinking heads, too.

The dad came in first, and the girl Catherine, who like I say turned out to be my age and in my class, brought up the rear. His pathetic little gray salesman suit drooped from his body, and Catherine wore a pretty dress with a little white straw hat, like girls had to wear in church back then. Their clothes weren't real new, you could tell, but clean and neat, like my mom said later. I swear to God I don't remember a thing about the dad or the girl Catherine Teaza that morning, because like everyone else, my eyes were riveted to the freaky human carnage walking in between. I think the order was dad, mom, youngest son, oldest son, and then Catherine the girl.

By far the first thing you noticed was the oldest son, because he had that big head disease, and his was enormous. Really big. Remarkably, he held it straight up and smiled.

This head wasn't shaped like a giant melon, but rather like some gigantic overgrown heart, narrow and almost normal down at the chin, but then rising and spreading and flattening into a purplish mass at the top, sort of flat up there but really big.

He was I guess 15, and he not only had the biggest head in the church, but certainly the biggest head in the world. Really big. Otherwise he looked pretty normal, and he was very attentive to his younger brother in front of him. This kid, maybe seven or eight, was a little pinhead brother. He was obviously severely retarded, and he had a tiny, deformed head. Big nose and crooked bucked teeth jutting out from this tiny little head. And he had one of those hands with only three fingers hanging on the end of an atrophied arm. I guess it sounds pretty funny to think about, but the two of them together, with their remarkable heads, were scary like a human grotesque that makes your stomach boil and your nostrils burn. As they walked up to the front of the church that Sunday, the big head brother sometimes put his hands on his younger brother's shoulders, softly guiding him or whispering to him; and sometimes the little pinhead lurched along on his own, wobbly and jerky so his thick glasses bobbled about on his nose. It was terrifying to look at, but after they sat down, and your stomach and nose got a chance to settle, you sort of got used to these two freaky and dichotomous-head brothers.

But you never got used to looking at the mom.

You know how in scary movies, you never get truly frightened by the monsters, because they're so obviously not real? How the really frightening things were more like Night Gallery and always involved some kind of dysfunctional grotesque but familiar humanity? That was Mrs. Teaza, not only that morning in church, but for that entire summer that I knew her. She was a little woman. Not petite or tiny, only little. She had one of those short, salt-and-pepper, dowdy, nondescript, downtrodden, mousey wife haircuts, and her thick wire-rimmed glasses frequently slipped down her nose, like those of her retarded pinhead son. She didn't look old; she looked like shriveled skin aching with a blue pallor. I think if you saw her alone, wandering the streets or even cackling atop a bell tower, you'd probably feel sorry for her, pity an unfortunate. But because she was always surrounded by her deformed family she exuded an emotional and psychological stench, like a macabre parody of motherhood. When you looked at her, all you could see was that claw of a hand clutching at her withered breast, or that enormous head pushing its way out of her crotch. Those things, those two boys, grew inside of her, and that fact drenched her body in an aura of oozing failure.

Once they all sat down and finally got settled into a pew, you could tell all the moms were glaring at all the kids, warning us not to stare. But the Teazas wouldn't go away.

During the priest's homily, and even the reading of the Gospel, for that Sunday and every other all summer, God and the Mass took a back seat to the Teazas. To their entrances and exits, to their chaotic shuffle toward communion and the pace-slowing return to their pew, to the fact of them in our presence.

The little retarded pinhead had this thing where he made these sounds, these awful noises. Kind of like grunting and moaning and wailing. Deformed human sounds. I guess it's likely that if someone had inexplicably brought some kind of animal into church that morning, and those sounds were coming from the animal, well then maybe they wouldn't have been so bad – you'd feel sorry for a trapped or scared or hurt animal. But as the priest continued droning on and on about keeping Jesus in your life throughout the week, the retarded pinhead brother kept making these horrible grunting, groaning sounds, and they echoed and banged around inside the otherwise peaceful church. Those retarded noises wiped out the priest's and everyone else's increasing efforts to ignore them.

There's something unsettling anyway about being inside of a church, kind of like you're supposed to feel pleasant and loving and peaceful, but there's always this overwhelming sense of heavy. Like quiet and somber with sick-sweet incense and candles and prayers, a hum of people trying or pretending to be better than maybe they really are, while a hidden and overwhelming omnipotence watches and takes notes.

Those retarded, deformed sounds that morning were nauseating; they made putrid curdles in your stomach, like when you eat really soggy corn flakes disintegrating in too-sweet warm milk.

Deformity. In God's house. I mean I know church is where you're supposed to be loving and accepting and all, but maybe because you're in God's house, because the Holy Ghost is actually in there with you, maybe human deformity reeks particularly. The Sacred Blood of Jesus dripping an infectious plague.

Soon after their startling entrance at our church, followed by the trailing quiet whispers afterwards downstairs in the church basement during coffee and donuts, my dad started inviting the Teazas over to our house on Sunday afternoons for barbecues and stuff.

It was embarrassing.

I just felt sorry for the pinhead brother and sort of liked the big head one because he was protective and gentle with the little guy, but I could never stop being terrified by the mom. When they sat around the picnic table on our back patio, or on those folding lawn chairs with the green webbing for seats, I could tell that the girl Catherine was embarrassed only by her mother, who embarrassed herself and all of us just by being so dadgummed happy to be invited over.

It was pathetic.

I was embarrassed that summer during the annual Knights of Columbus picnic, too. Even though my old man hadn't said so, it was pretty obvious that late July morning when we were all getting ready for church that his intention that our family adopt the Teazas was about to extend beyond coffee and donuts and our backyard. He was planning to have us hang out at the picnic with them. The stomach buzz hit with a roar. Since I was 11 years old, I settled into sullen and acted mad.

The church picnics were always a little weird, anyway. Because we lived at the boundaries of our Parish, I didn't go to school with very many of the kids from church. So you only saw them at church or at Wednesday night Catechism. Or at the annual Knights of Columbus picnic. Church friends.

When I was really little it was better, because we went to Saint Christopher's, which was a cool old church downtown with enormous stained glass stations of the cross, marble statues, and a tall stone bell tower. But then the town turned into a sprawling suburb and the parish got too big so all of us living west of Franklin Street were sliced off and we got a new church, Saint Jude's. We went to church in the high school auditorium for a year and a half until our new church was built. Our church was so big and ugly when it was finished that the high school auditorium was better. On the outside our church looked like a big round circus tent with a metal cross on the top. It wasn't even a steeple, just a cross sticking out of the middle of the roof. Inside it was like a miniature arena it was so darn big, with about five different entrances, so you could easily celebrate the Sacrament of the Eucharist with someone and never see their face. Industrial shepherding, factory sheep. The ceilings all around the curved edges of the church were pretty low. At least the church rose high in the middle. The altar was set into a dormer-like sanctuary built out from the big round room. That was supposed to be the front.

All along the continuous round outer wall were these cheapo dyed-burlap Stations of the Cross. That colored felt on dyed burlap motif became popular in a lot of churches about the same time they started having guitar masses and loosening up about Latin and ladies' hats.

Everybody talked about how nice to be more simply honoring the mostly simple life of Jesus, and how the church was becoming more human. Less on Saints and stained glass, more on Jesus and loving hearts. Like Protestants, I guess. Here's what's strange about that. How come these people, mostly conservative and placidly suburban, suddenly thought it was cool to start thinking about Jesus as this simple, wise soul who went around saying, "Peace Be With You," but at the same time bitched about hippies on the television news – basically people seeking wisdom and a simple life – who went around saying, "Peace, Man"? And they even put it in as an official part of the Mass. You know where the priest says, "May the Peace of the Lord be with you," and the congregation thunders back to him, "and also with you"? Well, they added this new part, where the priest says, "Let us offer each other a sign of Peace" and you had to turn around and shake hands with whoever was standing next to you and sort of murmur, "Peace be with you."

I hated that part, almost as much as I hated going to confession. They both created this uncomfortable buzz in my stomach, that nervous feeling that just builds and builds until you do the thing, and then the nauseous buzz disappears as if floating right out of a piercing in your side. I used to try to be prepared for where in the Liturgy that part came up, so I could be bending over tying my shoe or picking up a dropped missal or something, but I was too chicken to even try that, so I would just shake hands, and look into strangers' eyes and say, "Peace Be With You." If I had been really brave, I guess I would have parted my fingers and flashed a peace sign.

It seems at least probable that hippies might still be with us if they'd have gone around saying, "Peace Be With You" instead of, "Peace, Man." I guess they would have co-opted a lot of Catholics, anyway.

And maybe the cheapo burlap Stations of the Cross instead of stained glass were just a heck of a good way to save a ton of money. That's probably why they built the church so big, so they'd never have to build another one in that part of the state ever again.

Actually, I liked going to church in the high school auditorium a lot more than going to Saint Jude's. Velmont High School was just down the street from us, so we walked, every Sunday morning. No other Catholics lived on our street, so we were the only family that paraded by every Sunday all dressed up.

The high school auditorium was right inside the front doors of the school, so every Sunday morning the school lobby was a Catholic vestibule; dressed up people standing around visiting on their way into or out of Mass. It was funny, because right in the middle of the lobby floor was the high school seal – The Velmont High School Viking. A mean looking guy with one of those horned hats glaring up at you from a mosaic of tile on the floor. When I finally got to high school, I learned you weren't supposed to walk on the seal – seniors made sophomores who nervously wandered onto it kneel down and polish tiles. That only happened to me twice. Nobody from church bothered to stay off the seal on Sunday mornings. What if high school kids came into Saint Jude's after it was built and blew their noses on our burlap Stations of the Cross? That would seem awfully sacrilegious, but how would they feel if they knew we were tromping all over their Viking every Sunday morning? Plus, the Viking seal was a whole lot nicer than our burlap Stations of the Cross.

Inside, the auditorium looked like any high school auditorium. Rows and rows of fixed wooden chairs whose seats flipped up when you got out of them and a concrete floor sloping down to the stage, which became an altar once a week on Sunday mornings.

At first everyone kind of laughed each time the congregation stood up during the Mass, because the racket raised when all the chair seats flipped up drowned out the priests. It didn't take long before not catching your seat with your hand became really against the rules, and it got you dirty looks, especially from your mom, but it was still funny to do it. You had to stand up, sit down, and stand up so often that kids had lots of chances to raise a little ruckus in church.

Right from the first day, the priests said people didn't have to kneel, since of course there were no kneelers and the concrete floor was so hard. But you sure looked around to notice who sat down during the kneeling times and who toughed it out and knelt. It always looked wimpy to me when men knelt on both knees. My dad always knelt on one knee, like a football player or a discus thrower or something. I tried kneeling like that one Sunday and it felt really cool, like you were lots stronger than everyone else, and also like you weren't really begging anyone for anything. While we were walking home, my Dad told me he didn't think it looked very respectful for a boy to kneel that way, so I never did it again.

My mom didn't like it when I walked back from Communion clasping my hands together in front of me.

"It looks like you're trying to cover up your private parts."

"What am I supposed to do with them? I don't think I should put them in my pockets."

"Certainly not. Just let them hang at your sides, naturally."

I tried it once, but it felt uncomfortable, and a lot of other people must have looked like they were covering up their private parts, so I did too. She got over it.

We always went to 10:15. Nine o'clock was the guitar Mass, but we never got to go because my dad was the captain of the 10:15 ushers. It seemed like a great job, because ushers never had to sit with their families. They pointed people to empty seats and got people to slide over when the place filled up and opened the doors at the end. But the coolest was they walked up and down the aisles using a long pole to thrust a wicker basket in front of each and every man in the congregation, when it was time to collect the money. Kids could put money in, too, like a quarter or thirty-five cents, but the ushers wouldn't stop the basket in front of you. They just sort of let the basket slide in front of you, so you had to be quick to get it in.

Every kid in Catechism got a box of little colored envelopes to put the money in. Different colors for different church holidays, I guess, and pale green money-colored ones for regular Sundays.

It was a big deal.

Our church got a lot of money every week, maybe saving for stained glass or a Saint Jude mosaic seal. I know some of it was used to help families in the parish. I know that, because I know the church bought the Teazas a bunch of school clothes and some kind of deal down at Bob's Best Beef store. They were new clothes, too. I never told anyone I knew that.

I heard my dad talking to the Catechism secretary one Sunday morning after Mass in the church basement during coffee and donuts. They were talking pretty quietly, but I was pretending somebody needed a coffee cup filled with water out of the slow fountain by the bathrooms so I could stand there and listen. She said she didn't know if she should give the Teaza children boxes of envelopes. "You know," she said speaking even more softly, "given their circumstances."

"Hell yes, give 'em their boxes," my dad said, "Kids love those colored envelopes. Besides," he said, and he winked at her, "the more boxes of envelopes you give out, the more we can suffer God's children to pitch them into the collection baskets on Sunday."

I didn't figure it out for a long time, but that was the first Sunday my dad invited the Teazas over for a barbecue.

It was okay, because no one else was around, and, after awhile, I just played with them like they were regular kids.

We had one of those really normal square backyards: flowers and tomatoes and strawberries and stuff along the back fence, one of those huge high blobs of concrete patio stuck onto the back of the house, and a big patch of square grass in between. It was a really normal backyard. It was a pretty good one.

The first time the Teazas came, my dad decided to pay all us kids to pick bugs out of his vegetable garden. A quarter for every grasshopper, two quarters for every tomato worm. Those big gross squishy green worms with the little red horns on their heads. I thought paying us all that money to pick bugs was crazy, because it was already part of my weekly chores, and I only got five dollars allowance for a whole month. But when I started to say something, my dad gave me that raised eyebrow look – that "keep it to yourself" look. For some reason I also took the look to mean "and you damn well better make sure that the Teazas find most of the bugs."

I did, they did, and he shelled out quite a few quarters that day. He did the same thing every time the Teazas came for a barbecue, which they did, as I've said, a lot more frequently than I would've liked. I lost the bug picking job that summer, and my old man deducted a dollar twenty-five from my monthly allowance because of the fall-off in the workload.

That first time we picked bugs they put a plastic bucket in the little retarded pinhead's deformed claw, and he sort of lurched around, making those noises and following me and the other two Teazas. Of course he couldn't find any bugs, so his older brother, whose name I think was Bernard but they all called him Sonny, found a fat green tomato worm and dropped it in his little brother's bucket. The retarded kid didn't even notice it at first, but then he took it and stuck it in his mouth. Just the green head with the little red horn on top stuck out between his chapped and cracked lips. When he bit down, the slimy green tomato worm juice spritzed out between his crooked teeth. The girl Catherine just stared at him for a moment as the tomato worm juice dripped down his chin. Then she started sobbing and ran to the front yard and sat in their old beat up car. Mr. Teaza came out into the yard and stuck his finger in the kid's mouth, took out the chewed-up worm and wiped the pinhead's mouth and chin. Sonny hurried through the gate and got into the car and talked with his sister.

By the time the two of them came back around, my dad had already counted out quarters for bugs in every bucket. The girl Catherine wasn't crying anymore, but sniffling like you do when you can't stop, and she held on to Mr. Teaza's elbow, as my dad gave her her quarters and told her some dumb story he said he just remembered about how he went to work one day with a split in the seat of his pants and didn't even know about it until he came home that night. The story made the girl Catherine laugh but I'd never heard it before.

***

Two or three weeks after the Teazas first invaded our back patio on Sunday afternoons, my dad decided we were ready to finish off part of our basement for a family room. He hired Mr. Teaza to do the work, because he supposedly had experience on account of once having worked as a carpenter's helper or something.

It was strange having someone who came to your house as a kind of friend show up as a worker. He'd usually arrive in the morning, a half hour or so before my dad left for work. The two of them would take coffee downstairs and discuss the project – what had to be done next and how to do it. Except on the mornings when I had swimming lessons, I usually stood around with them. Mr. Teaza was a nice man, but you always felt a little sorry for him, just because. It didn't seem to me Mr. Teaza was that good of a carpenter; my dad had to tell him a lot of stuff to do. It took him a long time, more than two weeks, but he finally got the concrete walls framed out and the paneling put up. He installed a checkerboard of brown and red glue-down carpet tiles.

It was funny watching him pull up to our house in his little beat up car – sometimes with a stack of two-by-fours roped to the top, sometimes sheets of paneling. By the way my mom watched him out the kitchen window, you could tell she didn't see anything funny about it. In fact, I could tell my mom didn't like having him in the house at all. She spent most of those weeks out shopping, or taking me places, or meeting for coffee and playing bridge.

"Of course I like him," she insisted to me. "Why wouldn't I like him?"

But she sure spent a lot of time with my dad complaining about the quality of his work, and the day he started on the trim work, she asked him to stop at two o'clock because she had a headache. Then she waited for my dad to get home.

"Where's Fred?" he asked when he came through the door. "Don't see his car out there."

"I asked him to leave early. I think you should go look at the basement."

My mom and I followed my dad downstairs, and I thought she might shoot through the newly installed and poorly patched ceiling when he turned around and asked her "What's the problem?"

"You've got to be kidding. What's the problem? Look at this trim work."

He looked around. "No one ever said the man's a master carpenter," my dad said. "What the hell difference does it make? It's a basement."

"It's our basement," my mom said, sounding sad and mad at the same time. "It's our home. That's what difference it makes."

"The man's doing the best he can."

"The best he can isn't good enough. Why should our home look like it was schlepped together so Fred Teaza can feel good about doing the best he can? He doesn't have the skills to do this job."

"Oh come on. His skills are fine. I'm not paying him to make this look like a showroom, I'm paying him to finish a basement."

"Don't be ridiculous," she said. "Look at all the joints, they don't even meet. The walls aren't straight; there are gaps between the sheets of paneling. We can't have this kind of work in our home. I can't live with this. This is embarrassing."

"What the hell do you want me to do? Fire him? You know damn well he needs the work."

She was quiet for a moment. It's not like she was a mean or selfish person.

"Maybe you could just tell him...something. Something else." She glanced at me. "This is our home," she said, very softly.

"This is our basement," my dad emphasized, but also sounding nicer. "I hired Fred Teaza to refinish it, and I'll be damned if I'll do anything except pay him when he completes the job. Period."

There was a short silence where they locked stares that I watched turn back into glares. Then my mom said it was time for me to wash up for dinner.

The silence between them lingered around the house for the rest of the evening until I went to bed. I never heard the end of the fight but, when Mr. Teaza arrived the next morning, my mom was already gone, and my dad told me he didn't want me coming down to the basement with them for coffee. I went riding my bike and, when I got back, both my dad and Mr. Teaza were gone. They still came over the next Sunday, and even though my mom acted a little nervous and Mr. Teaza was especially nice to her, thanking her for everything, nobody said anything about the basement.

It never got finished, and my mom and dad were never the same afterwards. It snowballed, like I said before.

A few weeks later was the annual Knights of Columbus picnic, and shortly after that summer came to a close.

The morning of the picnic, things were pretty tense around our house; my folks barely speaking, only being polite. I spent the whole day fighting that stomach buzz thing because I was petrified people would draw what was to me the obvious conclusion that somehow the Teazas belonged to us. I think my mom felt the same way, but she cut me off when we stopped in the foothills along the side of the road so my dad could go back and make sure Mr. Teaza understood the map inserted that morning in the church bulletin.

"That's not a very Christian attitude, Johnny."

"I just don't see why they have to come with us. Why couldn't they just come up by themselves?"

"Your father thought they'd be more comfortable coming with us."

"Well, what about how comfortable I am? It's like they're suddenly his new family. What about us, his old family?" I felt brave, saying these things to her. Of course, it was just the two of us, inside the car. If you want to know, I wouldn't have been so brave, if my old man could have heard me.

"Sometimes when you want to do the right thing, or the good thing, you have to be willing to make sacrifices. Besides," she said, turning away from me and looking ahead through the windshield, "it won't be that bad. I'm sure no one will stare."

She said it, but she didn't believe it.

So he gets a better place in heaven because he's willing to humiliate his family by doing a good thing? What was the big sacrifice for him? I mean, he was doing the good thing, but we were making the sacrifice. And we were probably adding thousands of days in Purgatory because we didn't want the good thing to be happening in the first place. So it was kind of like a double sacrifice for us. When you think about it that way, you kind of get the feeling God has a strange way of keeping score. You can't pretend to want to do the good thing, because He'd know you were just pretending, and you'd be in trouble with Him for not being honest. On the other hand, you get in trouble if you're honest about not wanting to do the good thing in the first place. It seemed like a gyp. The only way you didn't get extra days in Purgatory was if you already wanted to do the right thing to begin with.

And then I thought how strange that I would debate with God His Divine method of record keeping but would never do so with my old man. I mean I feared God like you're supposed to, but He didn't scare me. Too far away. His punishment, or wrath, or whatever, just too colossal, too remote. Plus, you could always get prayed out of Purgatory, and with Confession you always start again at zero. (Except, though, if God forgives you through Confession, why does He send you to Purgatory at all? To punish you? Shouldn't forgiveness mean that He loves you again? Shouldn't love mean that He doesn't want you to suffer? If Purgatory is to teach you a lesson, what's the point of that? When you get out of Purgatory you go straight to heaven, so what good are lessons for earth when you're in heaven?) Whatever. The point, really, is I never would let my father know I questioned his method of measuring me up.

He wouldn't have been mad but, Jesus, would he have been disappointed.

My dad hopped back into our car and ground the Chevy station wagon back into gear.

"They seem awfully crowded together in that little car," my mom said.

Filled up with heads, I thought.

"Maybe we should have invited the little girl to ride with us. She's awfully sweet," my mom said, "but kind of quiet."

What's she supposed to talk about? Headlines? Head Cheese? Headquarters?

"Was she quiet last spring in school?" I could see my dad's eyes in the rear view mirror.

Uh oh. This was it. He was setting this trap for me, wanting to know how she was treated in school; wanting to know mostly how I treated her in school.

"Kind of."

"Kids talk to her? Play with her?"

"Yeah."

"Any kids mean to her?"

Here it came. "Yeah, sometimes, but she was only there for a few weeks, and then school ended," I finally said.

He just drove for a while. The car was a real family-mobile, so it didn't do that well in the mountains. It groaned some as the transmission lugged down while the car struggled up the hills. The engine strained just like my stomach, waiting for him to shift gears or punch it home.

"You ever mean to her?"

"No."

I knew he wouldn't shift down, there was no relief coming from the hot friction against weary metal. It didn't matter to him that I didn't pick on her at school; it didn't matter that I did the right thing. His only concern was that I had the right thoughts. That I did the right thing for the right reasons. Anything less was disappointing. Suddenly, it was all so unfair. First I was mad because I had to go to the picnic with the Teazas, and now he was mad because he had questions about whether my soul brimmed with adequate purity and goodness. And now I felt like a bum because the reason I didn't make fun of the girl Catherine Teaza at school was I knew my dad would have been disappointed in me if I had.

Well, that, and because I liked her. I didn't want her riding in our car because I was shy around girls even then, but I liked her. She seemed like the half of a Siamese twin who got separated and who left all the scars on her deformed sibling. She was quiet, but not shy quiet, just protective quiet, like she was always watching, waiting. Like I said before, she was never embarrassed about her brothers, only about her mom. And except for that eating the green tomato worm thing, she acted like her brothers were just fine, as normal as anyone.

They sure didn't look normal when they all piled out of their little beat up car, when we finally got to the parking lot of the Chief Rockpoint picnic grounds.

Like usual, we were early, and this time it was good, because our freak show didn't have much of an audience sitting under the huge roofed area where all the picnic tables were set up. The few families who were already there worked hard to not watch us carry all our stuff from the cars. Sonny and I each grabbed a handle and lugged our enormous green metal Coleman camping cooler. My mom and the girl Catherine carried some paper grocery bags stuffed with hot dog and hamburger buns; Mrs. Teaza brought some stupid wilted flower arrangement, and Mr. Teaza sort of shepherded the retarded little pinhead. My old man led the way, slapping backs and shaking the hands of all his Knights of Columbus buddies.

These Knights of Columbus picnics brimmed with lots of Sunday afternoon energy. You know how Catholics are well behaved and sedate on Sunday mornings and then let loose the rest of the week? Well, they especially let loose at the annual Knights of Columbus picnic on a Sunday afternoon. It was a blast. Wide-open spaces where there was nothing kids could do to get in trouble. We had to use our manners around the moms, sure, but the rules were riddled with winks.

Like how, the year before, Mark Halper stole a raw egg from the egg toss basket and climbed up the rock and tree outcropping rising above and beyond the horseshoe pits. He did it after lunch, so everybody was starting to gather around and get ready for the games. The egg toss was always last, the finale, so getting to the egg basket was a piece of cake. He stood up there with his egg, and of course he lobs the raw egg into the crowd, and here's the weird part. Out of a crowd of people big enough to fill a swimming pool, he hits his own sister, right in the forehead. Didn't hurt her, just scared her, and dripped slimy egg down her face. That's the kind of thing he or any of us would have gotten our butts whacked for, normally. But it was, after all, the annual Knights of Columbus picnic, most of the mothers were probably thinking, as they sort of clucked their heads and passed along comfort to Mary Margaret, who was Halper's sister and a teenager. I imagine most of the dads were thinking, and all of us kids were openly celebrating, what a great shot it was.

The men encouraged us to run wild at the annual Knights of Columbus picnic. They burnt meat on the barbecue, told jokes that embarrassed their wives, and stayed focused on draining the beer kegs. The moms sat around, running a loose hollering day care for the little kids and gossiping about who knows what. They drank soda pop in bottles, or Rose' wine in plastic cups. One of the moms hung out with the men. Mrs. Strickland, the only woman I ever knew, when I was a kid, who drank beer. At least she did every year at the annual Knights of Columbus picnic. She was a great looking mom, too, even though technically she wasn't, because she and Mr. Strickland didn't have any kids. He was a big shot at the bank, and she wore short shorts and had tanned legs, and I always blushed whenever Mrs. Strickland talked to me.

***

We had boring priests at our Parish. They were old, like our dads, and were called Father Jones or Father Smith or whatever. Their last names, like Mister Somebody's Dad. Secular priests. They wore black pants, black shoes, black shirts, black jackets and those little white priest collars. I had cousins in another state, and their priests were Franciscans, and they wore brown sandals and hooded robes, and you called them Father Bob or Father Matthew or whatever and, even though some of them were old, too, you could talk to them like you really knew them, I guess because they had real names, not Dad names.

What was neat about this year's picnic was Brother Mike, a young guy not yet a priest. He had to wear black clothes but without the collar. He sure didn't act like Father Rainier, our Pastor, or Father Cummings, our Assistant Pastor. Brother Mike was the one who was in charge of guitar Mass. He was in charge of the CYO for teenagers, too. When I had to serve 6 a.m. Mass before school, the old priests usually let Brother Mike do most of the work. They woke up just soon enough to actually celebrate the sacrament. Brother Mike once told me to mix in a lot of water when I was pouring with the little crystal cruets, because he said he couldn't drink very much wine that early in the morning.

The only thing Father Rainier ever said to me in all the years I served Mass was that quick little blessing at the end, back in his chambers. You know, where, after you walk out in the procession and you're still wearing your choirboy cassock and surplus and you go into his little room and you kneel, he mumbles some blessing and touches your head? And once Father Killian, the visiting priest, did the regular blessing and touching your head, and then he did the secret sacred touching back in his little room, but as an altar boy you're not allowed to talk about that or tell anyone, so I can't.

The priests didn't really talk to the kids at the Knights of Columbus picnic, either. They circulated around some with the moms and whatnot, but pretty soon they were hanging out with the men and with Mrs. Strickland, burning meat, telling jokes, and draining beer kegs.

Brother Mike organized the games that year.

It was funny to watch how the high school girls acted around Brother Mike. I guess he was kind of like a hippie for Catholic Suburbanites; his hair was down over his collar, sometimes his ideas were a little bizarre, he played the guitar, and he was fun. He was a man, but not like a dad or a priest. Most of the moms and almost all of the kids, especially the high school girls, really liked Brother Mike.

***

The kids' games were the usual kind of picnic games – ring tosses and passing balls from spoon to spoon and relay runs and gunny sack and three-legged races. Usually the Catechism nuns ran the games. It was okay, but sort of like old ladies yelling a bunch of rules and pretending to have a good time. But the year Brother Mike was in charge, he joined in the games with us, so it made them seem a lot more real. He also had different ways of picking partners. Everybody pulled a colored ribbon out of a bag, and the ribbons had different numbers of knots tied in them, so your partner would be whoever else had red with three knots or purple with four knots or whatever. You picked different partners for each event, so it kept everyone mixed up together.

For the last two years, Scott Gilchirst and I were three-legged race partners, and we figured out this secret way to win. We won really big the year before, but we agreed not to tell anyone else what the secret way of running the race was, so I can't. For the three-legged race this year, Gilchirst got partnered up with some high school girl. She wasn't really pretty or anything, but she did, you know, have tits, so I was afraid he would tell her the secret.

I might have, if I got a high school girl with tits.

For the three-legged race, I picked a green with four knots. I would never have told anyone, but I was secretly wishing the girl Catherine Teaza would get green with four knots, too. I don't really know why. It's not like I even had the guts to talk to her very much, but she was wearing shorts and a flowery kind of shirt and, if you really want to know, I liked looking at her. She picked a while after me and got red with one knot; Mark Halper stepped up and picked the other red with one, and I suddenly felt like he'd better be nice to her. He was usually kind of a bully, sort of a mean kid who laughed loudly all the time. But when I sat on a rock and watched the rest pick their three-legged race ribbons, it looked like the two of them were having fun, sort of messing around as they tied the rubber thing around their ankles. Oh well, at least I could watch her laugh and have fun.

I waited awhile, and then sure enough, Sonny also picked green with four knots, and when Brother Mike hollered out for who had the other one, I thought for a moment I might just pretend I hadn't picked yet and throw my green with four knots behind the rock. It's not like it would have been a big sin or anything. And even though he'd probably feel badly, he wouldn't be mad at me because he wouldn't know I had it. Anyway, it seemed like it was someone else's turn to be his friend. Like I said, he was a nice guy, but jeez.

I held up my ribbon and said, "I've got it."

Sonny sort of smiled, but he looked disappointed too, and I swear to God I think it was because he felt badly for me having to tie up with him. See, how can you not like a guy like that? He walked over to where I was sitting.

"Guess we're partners."

"Sure," I said.

"I'm not really very good at running. Do you like three-legged races?"

"Nah, I'm not any good at them either." It felt fine to say that.

He sat down, and just when I was thinking of suggesting maybe we shouldn't run the race at all, we saw his mom walk over from the picnic tables and get in line to pick a ribbon.

Usually the moms just watched the games, but when Brother Mike picked yellow with no knot, and no one held up the other one when he called out for his partner, a lot of moms put down their glasses of rose' wine or their bottles of 7-Up and came over to pick a ribbon.

Mrs. Teaza stood there in line and sort of giggled and spilled some of her wine out of the little plastic cup that she held with both hands. Other moms and kids spread out a little, sort of like giving her some room, and I thought again how pathetic she looked standing there, hoping to run the three-legged race just like anyone else. She was acting goofy, hollering over and over that she'd get the yellow ribbon with no knots. Sonny didn't say anything, he just watched her, acting like he was ready to jump up and do something, but I couldn't imagine what.

And then suddenly, Mr. Teaza appeared next to her, with the little retarded pinhead clutching the tail of his Dad's red flannel shirt.

Mr. Teaza had spent the whole picnic roaming around with the pinhead, not stopping anywhere too long, like if he kept him moving no one would have to suffer those weird laughing grunting noises too much. The pinhead held onto him and sort of lurched along, as Mr. Teaza just shuffled from one group to another. I remember seeing them take a long walk along the creek. Earlier, I had watched my dad bring him into the man's circle around the fire pit where the pig was roasting, but even my old man didn't try very hard to keep him there, once the retarded little pinhead started up with those grunting noises. Truth be told, my dad was probably looking nervously around for tomato worms. I mean, come on.

Mrs. Teaza was standing in line behind Mrs. Strickland, the banker's wife who drank beer and wore hot pants. Looking at both women, I couldn't imagine any two things more dissimilar, except maybe that deal with those two heads. Mr. Teaza very gently tried to take the plastic cup of wine from his wife, but she yanked it back and tried to gulp it down.

"You can't keep the yellow ribbon away from me," she bellowed.

The little retarded pinhead let out a wail and pulled against the dad's shirt. Mrs. Strickland moved to get out of the way of the commotion, and some of the wine from Mrs. Teaza's cup sloshed onto Mrs. Strickland's tight-fitting white blouse.

"Damn," Mrs. Strickland said.

"Keep away from that yellow ribbon," Mrs. Teaza mumbled.

"In your dreams, Honey," said Mrs. Strickland.

"Sorry," Mr. Teaza said to Mrs. Strickland, who was fumbling around with a napkin, daubing at the wine staining the white fabric stretched tightly across her boobs. Mr. Teaza started to hand her the red handkerchief he carried around to wipe the snotty nose of the retarded little pinhead, but he took it back when she glared at him and his wife swatted his arm.

"Keep your hands off that bitch," Mrs. Teaza said. "Just get me that yellow ribbon."

"Let's go get some coffee," Mr. Teaza said, softly pulling his wife with one hand and leading the retarded little pinhead with the other.

"Shit," Sonny said, very quietly. He got up from the rock and went to help his father, taking the arm of his little brother. First he started coming back over to the rock where I was sitting, and then he turned and led the kid, wailing and making grunting noises, down to the creek.

Brother Mike watched the whole thing with his face resting in his pressed-together hands, like he was praying, or maybe hiding. He had long fingers, almost like a woman, and for a moment he looked like pain captured in stone. Finally, he passed the sack holding the ribbons to Mrs. Strickland and watched Mr. Teaza guide his wife to an empty picnic table at the far end of the covered area. They sat down there and you could see Mrs. Teaza was still carrying on, but she was losing steam and winding down; her husband sat across from her at the picnic table and held her one hand between both of his, and it was strange, because his hands were also pressed together like praying in stone.

I looked for the girl Catherine, figuring she had probably gone off somewhere and was crying again. I thought maybe this time I would go sit in the car with her. But she wasn't crying. She was sitting next to Halper on a huge ponderosa pine log down by the creek. They were still tied together at the ankles, waiting for the three-legged race to begin. Certainly she had to have seen what happened with her mom; everyone at the picnic saw it. But she just carried on with Halper like nothing. They were throwing pinecones at a boulder out in the creek. Just sitting there pitching cones, laughing and fooling around.

That stomach buzz thing started up again, and it grew stronger and more uncomfortable each time I looked from the girl Catherine Teaza to her parents at the other side of the park. First, for his sake, I wished Mr. Teaza's wife would just fall over and die, then I sort of wished Halper would, and then it overwhelmingly donned on me that I wanted to stay as far away from the girl Catherine as I could.

I mean, who could blame her for ignoring her mom that way, but I couldn't imagine being able to actually do it like she was doing. It didn't seem sad; it was scary. A tumbling run of surviving; not the gnashing of teeth kind but the holed up in a cave type. Back to the wall, yellow eyes glowing, measured breathing masking a wild heart ready to strike with weapons of pretty charm and pine cone laughter.

***

When the annual Knights of Columbus picnic ended that year early in the evening, we didn't drive back with the Teazas. The whole picnic kind of quieted down after the Mrs. Teaza thing. Mr. Teaza sat with her for a while, and then he rounded up his family and packed up his car. When he came back to the picnic table to get his wife, she was hunched down, shivering. Mr. Teaza took off his red flannel shirt and wrapped it around his wife's shoulders. She weakly pushed him away when he tried to help her to the car, and she staggered to it by herself.

Mr. Teaza sat at the picnic table in a sleeveless undershirt and watched her for a bit, then he just sort of sat at the picnic table and watched nothing. Finally, he got up to go and made his way toward my dad over at the beer kegs and the barbecue pit.

I could see goose bumps on his bare arms as he shook my dad's hand.

"Thanks, Jack. I think we'll be pushing off."

"Find your way down the mountain all right?"

"Sure," he said.

"We'll see you next week," my dad said. "Take 'er slow getting down."

"Sure will," Mr. Teaza said. "Thanks again."

But we didn't see them the next week. My dad was real sick, so my mom and I got to go to the nine o'clock guitar mass. It was the first time all summer the Teazas didn't come to our house for a barbecue. The following week, they weren't even in church, and then they weren't anywhere anymore.

In the fall, I started sixth grade and the girl Catherine never showed up at school. And that was that. They just disappeared, as if they all piled into their little beat up car after the annual Knights of Columbus picnic, drove down the mountain at sunset, and then just kept on driving forever into midnight.

Kyrie Eleison

It oozed again last night, and the nuns came quickly, dragging as always their haggard virginity and fulsome longing for my flesh.

They poke around in my room, and I lie very still. I feign sleep, quiet and still as if lifeless in a tomb. But the sisters are not put off by my simplistic subterfuge, and their rosary chant fills the air above my bed with incense, heavy and sweet and choking my soul. Just like the begging moan of the droning damned. I don't invite them in, and I don't demand they leave. They'll do their work in the night, in my room, and move on. They feed on the crevices and orifices of my body, poking and prodding and peering. Often they rip the flesh around my nipples and drink the blood there. The nuns love the ooze and need it and feed on it.

This is not the first time, and I'm of a mind each time they come to lodge a complaint with the landlord; I don't believe it responsible for him to so injudiciously rent out rooms.

The nuns all live in the largest apartment at the end of the hall. I do not begrudge them their special status, their spacious accommodations. Obviously I, too, respect the cloth and the men and women who are called to it. But I think I'm well within my rights as a fellow tenant to expect reciprocal rights of privacy. Their apartment is nicer, that's fine and as it should be, I being alone and there being so many of them. But the nuns also control the main room, a not lavish open area the landlord allows for community use. It's good of him, certainly, for without trouble he could rent it separately for storage or meetings or weddings or such. But he does not; he allows us, my neighbors and me who share residence in this building to use that space. My room is very small; others are small also, so he's put a television in the community room, chairs and a few tables. Nothing fancy, to be sure, nothing pretentious or ostentatious but comfortable all the same, and he doesn't have to provide this; he does so on his own and, therefore, I try to get along with the nuns at the end of the hallway who monopolize the community area and steal into my room looking to satiate themselves with my blood and with my body. I have not lodged a complaint with the landlord and, perhaps, after all, I will not.

But all the same, their late-night flesh-driven scavenger hunts can be annoying. I am compelled, when I am of a mind to consider their actions, to draw the obvious comparison with little girls on a sleepover, running about merrily collecting a diverse listing of outcast humanity. It changes nothing when they bring the priests along; as if in so doing they believe they are manipulating the divine hierarchy and creating another sacrament or two.

And after all, for those little girls rollicking about amid the innocent joy of their scavenger hunt, the prize is simply in the seeking. In the hunt. The nuns are driven by an obsession with stealth and acquisition. Into my room and into my body and after my blood.

***

My room, as I've said, is comfortable enough, suits me quite well. The rounded metal tubes constructing the bed frame are black, and I take some pride in the contrast this suggests with my white linens, which are kept clean and tucked neatly beneath the mattress. The small desk and chair I have situated pleasantly beneath the window. I can look out across a courtyard teeming with tulips in the springtime and grasses thereafter. This flowering courtyard is another recommendation of the landlord. The grounds are clean and well kept, so that even though my apartment is somewhat small, I enjoy the sense of the beyond, the outdoors, the growing smells and cycles of the garden. That the window itself sticks and will not open is a minor inconvenience only; I know the fresh smells are there; I can imagine, and therefore frequently do, the busy insects among the marigolds and the overall striving for sun and health.

My body, as one might imagine, carries that subtle stench of an over-worked kitchen garden. Too much compost, too much manure not well turned nor dried properly in the sun. A country gentleman's garden, overwrought and overrun by the untimely arrival of spoiled city grandchildren. Used up, bled dry, and mostly fallow.

Over my bed in my room hangs a Sacred Heart picture. I accept that the nuns take this as a standing invitation. My mother brought the picture on one of her Sunday visits and insisted on helping me hang it that very day. It hung in my bedroom when I was a boy, and she said it should continue to bring me comfort, so I thanked her and told her I missed the picture and was happy to have it back.

In the picture Jesus looks unsure. Not happy nor sad, not weak nor strong. Unsure. Long robes with lots of folds and layered colors – lavender and rose, purple and ivory. His hand is weakly flashing some version of a peace sign. His hair hangs down straight and brown, well past His shoulders, and His half-smile is sickly and sweet and a bit sorry. Unsure.

Jesus' heart is the undeniable focal point. It has been somehow moved. It is beating outside of His chest. It is outside even of His robes, and it is dripping blood. To the nuns, this is like chum meat in shark waters. It draws them, calls them, oozes and excites them. I would remove the picture and bury it beneath the sweaters in the bottom of my chest of drawers, save for the fact that my mother is comforted in the supposition that the picture brings me comfort. In any event, I have no strong feelings regarding interior decoration and, like Jesus himself who called to His Mother while breathing His last, I am happy to give her this solace.

I wonder, though, and have done so often, if the Man with the well-combed dark hair parted in the middle and with flowing purple robes and with the sickly smile and the heart dripping blood outside of His chest is a depiction of Jesus after His death or before. It is no remarkable feat to rise from the dead if you are also in possession of such bodily control that you can, at will, place your heart outside of your chest, so I generally conclude He is looking at me after His death, though his effeminate countenance and condescending smile offer me little in the way of eternal confidence.

Certainly I would not buy a used car from this man.

When I was a youngster my mother used faith and her own wanting powers of reason to answer such questions. For example, if Jesus knew all along that He'd die for my sake through betrayal, and thus I'd be saved, then how in the scheme of things could I fairly hold Judas Iscariot responsible? A pawn, and nothing more. Judas defended himself as such, yet Jesus disdained and condemned him nonetheless.

Free will, my mother said. God knew ahead of time the decision Judas would make of his own free will. Thus the entire stage was set.

My concern exactly.

Later, once I began putting together more reasonably thought-out dilemmas and she had aged a bit, she merely patted down her growing bosom, strutting and clucking as a pigeon whose young had tumbled from the nest.

And of course she prayed for the salvation of my eternal soul.

She was angry, and then hurt, and finally afraid when I surmised that Jesus was either a liar or a hypocrite for claiming He was born of a Virgin. The dilemma, really, is quite compelling: We Catholics, we Marians, are prohibited from questioning Mary's place in our ancient Palestinian opera: Pure. Innocent. Long-suffering. Willing always to intercede on our behalf with Her Son and His vengeful and hostile Father.

But here's the rub. What kind of a narcissist opens His arms and welcomes us as brothers and sisters, tells us He is just like us, demands that we be just like Him in goodness and love, and then says, "Oh, by the way, I was born of a Virgin, and you weren't."

Well, hold on a moment here.

I don't mean any disrespect, I really don't, but how can I be expected to emulate Jesus and follow in His footsteps and be just like Him and reserve my eternal room in my Father's house and all, when I don't have the same head start? After all, I came about because two sweating and grunting and slightly flabby human beings got naked and disgusting, and possibly a little drunk, and then poked and licked and fondled nasty parts of one another's bodies.

I mean if Jesus is supposed to be my Big Brother, dying for me and recommending me to our Father for my eternal place in the Big House, it hardly seems fair that I be compared to a Man whose beginnings included a pure bolt of light, made of love and life, entering a Virgin Girl and then animals breathing softly on Him to keep Him warm in a manger.

Is that fair?

And actually, it's no knock on Jesus, finding Himself as He did in the role of Big Brother. By birthright, big brothers simply make out better. As the younger sibling, I accept without complaint my position – buried in the back of the hand-me-down closet. I strap pillows with rope while I wait for Jesus to grow out of his brand new shoulder pads; He gets new shoes, His old are re-soled for me; He is first in line to the throne; I will distinguish myself in business or the military and then cynically live out my time chasing women and scooping up the horseshit behind his coronation parade.

I do not blame Jesus for this commanding head start of His; it is not His fault. Neither do I carry the vengeance of the bastard second son; my lot in life suits me fine. But God forgive me, I do blame our Father.

I know that considering these things is another provocation for the nuns to bleed fluids from my body, poke and prod as they do. They sense the impurities pulsing through my veins: the questions, the logics, the confusion. A dialectic of blasphemy.

I too rebel against these thoughts, my random yet persistent questioning of eternal truths. However, I am unable to completely suppress them, which I imagine is another reason for allowing the nocturnal scavenges of the Good Sisters. I will, ultimately, suffer the indignity of their purulent interests for the slim hope that they will ultimately succeed in bleeding the impurities from my soul.

I wish them luck. I pray for them.

"Regardless if it's your local machine shop or
The goddamn president of the United States;
If you let someone else put the engine back together,
You never know maybe the assholes filed down the teeth
On your fucking flywheel."

- Lance O'Neill

Chapter 7

He jammed the toe of his black work boot against the floorboard
of the Valiant and listened in resigned agony as the starter clicked
and clicked but refused to engage. Daniel O'Neill was all packed
and anxious to get going before the sunrise. He had hoped to get
out early and allow the goodbyes of last night to suffice. He
listened again to the aggravating, empty click of the starter motor.
No dice.

No luck, the young man thought.

"No shit," he said aloud.

Daniel O'Neill leaned back against the freshly vacuumed seat
cover with a self-deprecating smile.

"Of course not this morning," he said to himself. "Of course it
won't start this morning."

Daniel couldn't wait to get away – away to college, away from
the sticks, away. Mostly, right now, Daniel couldn't wait to get far
enough from Lance so he could buy a new starter and bolt it in.
Even though Lance had never really been much of a prick about
being right about replacing the starter, Daniel would be damned if
he'd admit it while he and his uncle were anywhere near the same
county.

Besides, in the two years since they'd finished the overhaul and
repair, he had become an expert at parking the car so that it was
always aimed for an easy rolling start. Except, of course, right now,

parked on his own circular driveway, as flat as the sea of grass surrounding him.

Daniel O'Neill, on the morning of what he often swore would be his final one at the farm, got out of the 1965 Plymouth Valiant and began pushing it around the gravel drive toward the hill in the dirt road running in front of the farm. Once everything got rolling he'd hop in, pop the clutch and be gone.

***

The car had belonged to his dad. His mom and his uncle, they all spent time in it together, but it had belonged to his father. He had waited all his life for it. More than fishing, more than Pete, more than his bike, Daniel loved the 1965 Plymouth Valiant. He remembered how it sat out behind the barn when he was a little kid. They used it as a fort, as a base, as a clubhouse, and as a hideout. He remembered when, only a week or so after his grandfather died, Uncle Lance hitched the car to a rope tied around the chest of a cow and guided it into the barn.

"Guess it's yours now," the man told the boy. "You need to fix it up."

Daniel O'Neill wasn't near old enough to drive, and he didn't know anything about cars. So he didn't know what his Uncle was talking about, but he liked the idea nonetheless.

And so for years the 1965 Plymouth Valiant sat undisturbed beneath the hayloft in the corner of the barn. The car belonged in the barn; the old man was just plain mean in keeping it outside. After it sat in the barn awhile, he helped his uncle jack it up and place bricks beneath both front and rear axels. They removed the sun-beaten tires and left the wheels leaning against the wall.

When hot summer winds blew across the prairie, they swirled hay dust through light shafts in the barn and animated the floor; sometimes it looked like the 1965 Plymouth Valiant roared to life on the barn floor, speeding without direction toward no place whatsoever.

Uncle Lance knew a lot about cars, or at least he knew a lot about his old Chevy truck he tinkered with all the time. Daniel

O'Neill could always tell when his uncle was planning to leave the farm on one of his mystery trips, because he'd spend several nights out in the barn dinking around down beneath the faded green hood of the old truck. It was one of those moldy green old-fashioned bubble-fendered old man kind of trucks – like a thing that had been around forever.

"Simple," Uncle Lance often said. "Like gravity or love. No new fangled crap getting in the way and mucking up smooth operation. No surprises. Straight-forward machinery; smooth mechanical operation."

It was funny how his mom never acted mad whenever Uncle Lance left the farm. She'd spend the days and, oftentimes, weeks while he was gone going about everyday business like nothing was different, like nothing was changed. The first time he left, which was only a few months after he first came, Daniel O'Neill thought Uncle Lance was gone for good.

"Just a spell, I imagine," his mom had said. "Don't get too used to the quiet. He'll be back."

"You want him to come back?"

"Doesn't probably matter, Sweetie. He'll be back when he gets a mind to, whether I want it or not."

It seemed so strange. Daniel O'Neill knew his mom liked having Uncle Lance around the farm. He did more and more work since the old man died, and she laughed when he was around. Daniel O'Neill could tell they were good friends, and he could tell his mom needed to have a good friend around, what with his dad being killed and the old man dying and all.

So did Uncle Lance have important things he had to do when he left the farm, or did he have other friends somewhere else, or what?

He was always the same when he came back, and he never said where he'd been, and his mom never asked, but for several days afterward Daniel O'Neill felt like the house near choked with some kind of enormous tangle. Everyone talked carefully and politely, but it was all messed up. Nobody was straight and nothing was smooth, like a bird's nest in a fishing pole. His mom always seemed to warm up and get over it after a few days, and then it was back to normal and almost like Uncle Lance had never left in the first place, but Daniel O'Neill couldn't help feeling that a bit of drag built up each time, like a fishing pole building little knots; first a couple, then a few more catching on the first, and then more, then more again, each time. You could keep casting, but less distance, and it got harder and harder to hit the soft holes beneath the shaded overhang of willows, or drift a worm without jerking it when you slowly reeled it in.

Why couldn't they just stay friends, all the time and always? Why couldn't his mom understand Uncle Lance had important things to do somewhere else, or someone else needed him? Why couldn't Uncle Lance take his mom along, or take them both, or just stay put and send someone else? Then things would be so much smoother, like a sleek and synchronized open-faced spinning reel. During those times when Uncle Lance disappeared, Daniel O'Neill wished everything wasn't so much like his friend Pete's stupid tangled Zebco closed-faced fishing reel. His whole life was like someone else's rusted Zebco with fat 12-pound line, hundreds of knots, tangles, and a missing handle so that you had to wedge a stick into the crank to turn the thing.

He changed the line in his own Zebco every spring, taking particular pain to ensure that the new line remained smooth, as he meticulously worked the double-handled crank, spinning the line off the spool nailed to a strut in the wall of the barn. For years he had dreamed of owning the black Garcia-Mitchell open-face with retractable bail that sat in the window of Henderson's Hardware store. It was the kind of reel they used in trout streams in the Rocky Mountains. Kids, hicks, and hayseeds lived in Kansas and cast with Zebcos; real fisherman angled with open-faced reels.

But Daniel O'Neill caught more than his share of bass and catfish, and actually, he was proud of the care he gave his Zebco reel; it wasn't top-of-the-line, but it always worked, and he kept the reel clean and oiled and the line fresh and free of knots. Nothing was ever perfect, anyway, but you could always make things work.

His friend Pete, for one, never got it. Pete spent no effort maintaining his equipment. He just wouldn't learn.

Even at fifteen years of age, when any other idiot would know better, Pete still used the same line that was on the reel when both boys hopped on their stingray bikes years ago and pedaled to town and bought the matching reels out of the cheap case down at Henderson's. Daniel O'Neill had spent years watching his friend screw around with knots and tangles and frustration so that the reel wouldn't cast for shit – brittle line spitting in spurts out of the little hole in the face and creating nothing but a succession of ten-minute bird's nests.

Daniel O'Neill wasn't competitive about fishing – he would much rather have spent the years watching his only fishing buddy reel in trophies. But during all the time they spent dragging stink bait across the bottom, searching for bullheads or popping lures out of the grass trying to trick largemouths, Pete's only catch of any significance was a half-pound bluegill that the son-of-a-bitch still talked about, and if truth be known, it was probably a blind fish that most likely just accidentally impaled itself on Pete's hook.

But Daniel O'Neill didn't offer advice. A man ought to be able to catch his own fish, not because it makes him more of a man, but because it simply wasn't another guy's place. Who knew what the technique of the day might be? Who was to say this bait was superior? Giving fishing advice entailed, for Daniel O'Neill, an unacceptable level of hubris. This didn't prevent him, especially as they got older, from occasionally venting a bit of frustration with his incompetent friend, who fished always with form and without substance.

"The bass ain't wait'n on your nonsense, cut the sucker and re-rig."

"I don't have enough line left, I can't cut it." Pete worked furiously on the mangled knot sticking out of the hole in his reel.

"I've got to get this untangled or I'll lose half my line."

"Cut it, clip a bobber on, and fish for bluegill in the shallows. You've already lost the battle with the tangle, Buddy. Don't make it worse by losing the day as well."

Invariably Pete spent the best part of an otherwise perfect bass fishing afternoon fooling with a hopelessly lost tangle of worn-out fishing line.

Daniel O'Neill figured, all told, Pete'd spent weeks and used up the best part of their youth, screwing around with a tangled mess while countless tadpole hatches meandered away.

"Just cut the fucking line and re-rig, Man. We're here to catch fish, not reinvent a ridiculous mess. Cut and re-rig the friggin' pole."

"It's a rod, not a pole, and we're here to exhibit some modicum of technical prowess in the face of natural, reactive response. I'm going to untangle this and catch fish without cutting my line."

"Horseshit," Daniel O'Neill said. "We're here to catch fish."

And he knew, either right then or later, that that's the day their friendship finally died. Oh sure, it carried on for several years more. It included the final bonding of high school, the parties out at the lake, and the late-night crazy tractor drives tearing up somebody else's dad's pasture, but Daniel O'Neill knew at that moment when he lazed with Pete atop the west bank of the cattle pond, fishing in the hot still summer of their 15th year, that there was no future in their friendship. He knew it would slowly run its course, play out like a well hooked but tired bass, and then finally float belly-up and be done.

Different paths, different needs, different lives.

Of course he was sad the moment this revelation first hit him, but it wasn't sadness that moved him that day at the pond. It wasn't the loss of old times that focused his attention on Pete, fiddling with meaningless endeavor. Rather, as Daniel O'Neill painfully watched his friend slide away, he silently celebrated the glorious march of the inevitable.

"Fish is fish, Pal," Daniel O'Neill finally said. "I reckon' huntin' 'em is at least as important as catchin' 'em."

Saying that was like cutting Pete loose and watching him flip-tail towards the cool depths of the pond, swirls and memories fading into gradual ripples of complacent water.

Most astonishing to Daniel O'Neill was the ease with which his friendship with Pete slipped away; how easy it was for him to move on. The two boys had been inseparable since fourth grade, and suddenly, a wedge appeared between them during one fishing trip, and over the course of that summer it split them clean. The flaw in the grain clearly didn't appear on a single fishing trip; it had developed deep between them over the years while on the outside the bark of their friendship matured, gained strength, enveloped and covered them over. A good, healthy-looking friendship, growing straight and strong. They shared sophomoric metaphysical revelations, teacher-baiting strategies, stories of wet dreams and assorted fantasies. During the school year, they trudged together in the mornings to the bus stop, taking comfort in their mutual academic confinement and making plans for recess, or gym class, or for freedom in the afternoons.

But the center wood lacked strength.

The sapling of young boys fielded its share of bark nicks and broken branches – the kind of petty jealousies, name-calling, and easily hurt feelings natural to boys busy honing their peculiar and unique slicing edges, which would cut the way clear through their lives ahead. Daniel had always been physically stronger, Pete more willing to take risks. Pete figured problems, Daniel O'Neill felt them. Early adolescence found their friendship like a gnarled hackberry clinging to the side of a windswept hill. Resilient. Entwined. Inhospitable to outsiders. Over the years the stout wood had withstood much pruning and winter freezing, like when Pete's rich Grandpa surprised his grandson with a mini-bike that 13-year-old boys wouldn't be caught dead riding together, leaving one best friend home alone chucking baseballs against worn barn timbers while the other best friend sped across dry packed pastures, chasing rabbits and wind burn.

Daniel O'Neill took pride in his stoic insistence that Pete enjoy the new mini-bike and not worry about leaving him out, but he zinged the baseball with a pained fury each time the little Briggs & Stratton crested a hill and laughed at him with barely muffled strokes of compression and exhaust.

Their friendship survived the mini-bike, growing around that knot and building strength. But the boy knew, even then, that within the tree, deep and hidden near the center wood, an imperfection loomed which would ultimately rot an otherwise lifelong friendship and fell the tree, casting splinters and dust for years to follow.

Daniel O'Neill was unable to salve the scar of his missing father. Pete knew his deepest secrets save this one – no one with a father was forgiven. The boy had allowed, indeed encouraged the hole to grow and gnaw inside himself.

On the one hand he knew he wasn't the only person never to have known his father, but on the other hand, he knew no one else without one.

It wasn't Pete's fault and the boy understood this, but Pete couldn't fix it, either. It wasn't his mother's fault, but she also had no caulking for the empty space, which cracked jaggedly between the boy and the rest of the world. Uncle Lance was just mean – a painful reminder and an unacceptable replacement. The boy initially spent a few weeks helping his Uncle work around the place and then he lied to his mom, saying he'd rather ride bikes and go fishing. His mom said okay, but Daniel O'Neill still remembered the huge fight it caused.

"It can't work this way, Becky. We need some space; you can't hover. Besides, he's a strong kid, it'd do him good to break a sweat."

"He's just a boy, Lance. He's only 11 years old. He's got his entire life to work and sweat and worry. He's just a boy."

"That's not the point, Beck."

"You can't just take it, Lance. That won't ever be any good. He's got to give it to you."

"That's still not the point."

Becky Dreiling fixed her gaze on her hands resting on the kitchen oak table. She marveled at how similar the grains of her hands were to the veins in the dull and faded wood. Wind-burned and often wiped up, she imagined. She still took pride in her long soft hair, but she believed in the six months since Lance's sudden arrival her face had hardened, or changed, or didn't sparkle, or something. Not less attractive, she allowed to herself, just different. She thought long about Lance hunting for the treasure of Daniel's affection. With some curious distaste souring her tongue, she thought about his cavalier willingness to breeze in and pick up the pieces, or worse, to break some of his own. He had said so often, "I'm the only father he's going to get, so I'm the best father he's ever going to have." She felt her face twitch as it fought back tears while she tried again to see it as clearly as he did. If she agreed, would that really fix it for her son and for their lives?

"You have to be patient, Lance. It's all so new to him. It's going to take time."

There was a long silence and the boy, crouched still and quiet at his secret listening post, imagined Uncle Lance was pulling a cigarette from his shirt pocket or pouring coffee again from the ceramic pot at the stove.

"Just give it some time," his mother said again.

"Time I've got," Uncle Lance finally said.

In the months after Uncle Lance's arrival, Daniel O'Neill had finally discovered a decent place to listen from his bedroom to the almost nightly conversations in the kitchen below. Pressing the side of his head to the ornate, black, cast iron, heating wall grate in his bedroom didn't provide nearly the clarity of the banister in the downstairs hallway, but Uncle Lance had already caught him on the stairway twice. His new place offered security, because once he was sent to his room for bed, they never checked on him until hours later.

There wasn't nearly as much crying anymore, and often the tones were muffled when the voices hushed, so that the sounds wafting up through the shafts of the old gravity forced coal furnace sounded more like a droning vibration than conversation. It gave the boy a feeling from a very long time ago, a time well beyond his recall when he sat with his head nodding against his mother's chest and she spoke softly to him, her voice coming from deep inside her ribs and her breasts. He didn't hear her voice, but rather felt the sounds. The vibration moved through her and into him and lifted him and took him back inside of her, so once again they shared the same rhythm of breath. He must have been little more than a baby, and the deep misted memory of those long ago primal lullabies often whirled with the hum coming from the heat vent, so that he would awaken hours later when Uncle Lance carried him to bed, where his mother sat waiting to tuck him in. The tears in her eyes sometimes dropped to her hand, and she rubbed the side of his cheek where curious indentations from the cast iron grate froze a grotesque mechanical smile into the side of his head.

Other times, when the voices rose a bit in anger or frustration, the boy listened hard, trying desperately not to hear, like in that song of darkness my old friend. He wanted the words, but not the meaning. The boy knew there were issues in the house, great unresolved movements of emotion, and he fed voraciously on the ripples and undercurrents while studiously avoiding the waves, as if he believed he could ride the tides forever while denying the greater pull of the moon.

***

Lance said little during the first few weeks of Daniel O'Neill's sophomore year in high school, but the boy's mother grew increasingly concerned about Daniel's solitude. He walked home alone from the bus stop; Pete rarely came around anymore; except for football in the fall, he hung around the house, or more frequently the barn, alone.

"He'll be fine, Beck. Just needs some space," Lance said one afternoon as the two stood before the kitchen sink and watched the boy turn in from the road, kick stones across the leaf-strewn dirt driveway, and then saunter into the barn.

"I know, but it's hard to watch. And he's more than alone, he's almost morose. Sometimes I can't stand to watch him; it breaks my heart. It seems more than some adolescent angst. Like this enormous weight, and I can't help but think I dropped it on him, that I'm at fault, and that Danny's dying, and you, and the whole goddamn mess I've made are all somehow running around in his brain. I know I screwed up, and I know it's too late to go back, too late for him, and I know it's hurt you, and it's too late for that. I watched the separateness eat at you for years, and it hurt to see it, but I thought it was best for my child, so I bore it. But now I can't help but believe the separateness is eating him, and it's likely to kill me.

"I was wrong. It wasn't the best for him, or for you."

Becky Dreiling stood behind him at the sink and rested her head against the strong pull of his shoulders and back.

Lance O'Neill was unbelievably lost and tortured. But she knew he was also decent and honest and dignified. He cared for her a great deal, and he showed it in ways she could respect. Nothing flamboyant, nothing loud. Lance O'Neill, for all his physical strength and inner turmoil, was a gentle man. As she stood next to him, watching the barn door that had only just taken her son from the afternoon light, she realized that, even including Daniel, Lance O'Neill was the best thing that had ever come into her life.

"It was wrong for what it's done to us," she whispered.

"No shit," was all Lance said.

Lance O'Neill was, above all else, a patient man. He had to be. He worked constantly to suppress the rage lurking just behind his eyes. This was a pissant way for her to break his resolve of restraint. She knew it and used that horseshit, innocent, feminine, manipulating crap to scrape fingernails across the inside of his skull until his teeth ground and his jaw ached from the goddamn restraint; and as the blood dripped behind his eyes and burnt his tongue he simply said again, more quietly, "No shit."

He nearly exploded with the urge to rip something, maybe the fading kitchen wallpaper with its stupid, fucking, repeating pattern of little yellow roses and obnoxious fucking lace, or maybe her face, smiling sadly as if she alone carried weight and pain, or maybe the head of goddamn Roy, barking incessantly out in the yard and running around like a happy goddamn idiot, greeting the boy at the road and barking and running circles around him and following him into the barn. Goddamn tail-wagging dog looked like a goddamn fool.

On the other hand he could stand quietly in the kitchen and listen to her in silence. With great difficulty he chose this course, forcing to the fore whatever remnant of rational thought he could muster at the moment. He didn't want to kill; he wanted to rip and shred, but he honestly couldn't guarantee himself that he could stem the red rush of his rage, so he was patient and restrained and held it all back.

Becky Dreiling knew she was poking a hornets nest, but her hand held fast to the stick, because once again she needed to reassure herself that the usually dormant insects could still be aroused. Or, more to the point, that she could still do the arousing. She didn't really expect any resolution to this old argument. She argued both sides of the issue, and she knew that using him as an unwilling foil was cheap and unfair. She brought it up again mostly because she could, and because it shone light into that dark and rotting room where she blamed herself for her son's aimlessness and for her lover's soul-forsaken lack of life.

She could handle the guilt of possibly lying to her son; she could accept stealing or muddling or confusing his lineage and his heritage. She was okay with having assigned Lance to years of living with them on the farm in limbo, but she couldn't forgive herself for the fact that she needed to perpetuate their pain, because she needed the guilt to punish herself.

She reached her arms up over the roll of his shoulders and clasped her hands at the front of his neck.

"Sometimes I just wish somebody else, or something else, or somewhere else would begin making the decisions for me."

Lance said nothing and did not move. He allowed her face to rest against his back while he took slow, deep breaths.

***

Daniel O'Neill didn't have an enormous reservoir of friends, but neither was he a natural loner, so, slowly, during his fifteenth year, after the falling out with Pete and based on repairing the 1965 Plymouth Valiant, he and Uncle Lance began grooming a curious friendship.

"I can get a learner's permit in July," Daniel blurted out one Sunday morning.

"God help all pedestrians," said his mom, poking a piece of cantaloupe with a toothpick.

They lounged around the big oak dining room table with springtime sunlight streaming through the bay windows and the newspaper sections spread all over hell and back. Increasingly, Daniel O'Neill enjoyed the Sunday ritual of black coffee till noon, fruit cut and arranged on hand-painted heirloom plates, cigarettes, conversation, comics, and taking it easy. By the time he got into high school he began devouring the sports first and then moved through the columns in the editorial section. He even read his mom's section – arts and women's crap. Lance never let go of the front section until he had commented on every last ridiculous news story. His mom mostly skipped around, a lifestyle feature here, new music review there, fetching fresh coffee from the kitchen, emptying the ashtray. Musing and drifting with the placid pace of Sunday.

Several months ago she'd quit hassling him about smoking, and Lance said he didn't give a shit as long as the boy bought his own with his own money. "I hate goddamn cigarette whores," Lance said at the time. "Talk about your filthy habits." So the boy relaxed on Sundays and joined in and felt like a real part of the family. He was astonished at the power of cigarettes. One day he's some kid sneaking butts out of Lance's work coat inside the barn on a Christmas morning, the next he's a part of his own family, dragging like a pro and watching the smoke make soft gauze in the sunlight near the valances of the windows.

Lance caught him out in the barn last Christmas, and the boy's disdain for the expected cigarette lecture turned to caution when Lance nonchalantly pulled his fixings from his own breast pocket, rolled quickly, and lit up himself.

"Suckers'r old," Lance said, nodding his head toward the old dirty fleece and cracked brown leather coat hanging on a nail. "Must taste like rolled ragweed by now."

Daniel O'Neill sat in the front seat of the Valiant with his legs sticking out the opened driver's side door and watched the man lean against the rear bumper of the old car.

"You gonna tell my mom?"

"Tell her what? Tell her you're being bad? Tell her you've lit up the long slow suicide? Tell her she's dropping the ball and losing her angel? Tell her you're growing up?"

"I dunno."

"Can't stop time. But she's the boss, and unless you want to spend the rest of your life packaging yourself in frilly paper and cute ribbons, you ought to suck it up and tell her yourself."

"Okay," the boy said. Some hesitation, and then he said, "You know, thanks."

"Yep," was all Lance said.

And all things considered, his mom was pretty cool about it. She did give him the health lecture, and the age lecture, and the don't start young lecture, but Daniel O'Neill knew he had an ally, so mostly he laughed and playfully accused her of feeling like an old lady because she had a son who smoked, and the whole thing came off easily, with surprisingly little in the way of sparks or excitement.

"One of you has to be with me, but I can drive on the roads and into town. It's so kid's can learn. Whaddya guys think? I'm ready." He giggled, "I been good."

"What's wrong with driving the truck out in the pastures? You've done that for years," his mom said as she cast a sideward glance at Lance, letting him know she knew. "It's safe, and you're not nearly as likely to run over puppy dogs or little children."

"Yeah, but you have to learn the rules. Any idiot can drive circles in pastures. I need other cars, stop signs, speed limits."

"Can't go into town for a burger out in the pastures," said Lance.

"Right. Exactly. Pastures are for kids. I'm ready for the big time, Mom. Racing down Main Street. Flooring it, trying to beat a train past a crossing. Crashing through hardware stores."

"Uh huh." Becky Dreiling had no intention of relenting easily, but she knew relenting was inevitable, and she smiled to herself as she recognized again the subtle power of the alliance against her.

She could squint her mind a bit and see two men sitting at the table with her, sharing and laughing. Strong and angular men, given more to grunts and expressions then long-winded explanations. Soft men in the macho kind of way she loved. Macho. She cringed at the word. But even so. Macho crawled across a wet cedar roof during a goddamn midnight rainstorm, nailing and patching and keeping the kitchen dry; macho stuck its greased hand and arm inside a bellowing cow, speaking gently and patting the hind quarter, while slowly turning a breech calf; macho said nothing and sipped beer while she rambled on and on.

The boy could do worse. Becky loved the model. Increasingly, she loved that her son fit the mold.

She could squint again and see a couple of boys, ornery and conniving and lovable. Boys kept secrets. They giggled with conspiracy. Boys blossomed like strawberries – lots of runners and wild growth shooting off in all directions, anxious to set down their own tiny roots. Runners with twig-thin umbilical cords needing a quick and painful pinching – a gentle but definite separation from the mother plant if you ever expect to get any fruit. Boys willingly crashed tricycles into walls, testing and teasing physical laws. Boys cuddled only when exhausted, smiled only when a step ahead, took it all in and gave more of it back.

Lance actually laughed when he was with the Daniel. He seemed slightly lighter, playful, content.

The dynamic between the three of them pleased her, and though she often stretched like a short hypotenuse to bring the two other points of her family together, she was enormously comfortable with the triangle growing in her household. Growing, she realized with a twinge of painful memory, like a repeating DNA pattern in her life. Biology.

Biology and geometry. She wondered. Where did that flash of high school science come from? Becky Dreiling had hated algebra; she struggled to recognize any reasonable application of such obtuse formulas. But geometry was different. Geometry exploded with design, with invention, with architecture. Biology was glorious, dynamic, and alive. She smiled to herself again on that comfortable Sunday morning when she saw clearly that her life had finally crested whatever certain hill it was that determined biology was her destiny and she was extremely unlikely to ever really utilize geometry.

"Middle age, maybe," she said aloud. "Now there's a hell of a hill."

"Don't worry, Mom. Just because I drive doesn't mean you're middle aged. You're not an old lady. You're well seasoned. Marinated. But still fresh and tasty as a springtime daisy."

"Crummy metaphor," his mom said. "Crummier sentiment."

Lance popped the top of his Zippo lighter.

"Can't cruise the front porches of cheerleaders out in the pastures."

"Don't even start. That's nothing but the first brick in the decrepit cobblestone trail of grandma-hood."

"Ah, Mom. Everyone loves a Grandma. Don't worry. I'll still love you when you're a roly-poly little grandma. I'll visit on Sundays, just like this, and we'll talk about the sales down at the Ben Franklin, and your blue hair will shimmer in the light, and Lance, well, you know, Lance will have moved on to a young woman by then, but, you won't mind cuz you probably won't remember him anyway."

"Young woman wouldn't put up with him." She flicked a toothpick in Lance's direction. "Sullen." Another toothpick. "Sensitive." Flick. " Stubborn and opinionated." Flick, flick. "Testosterone overload." No toothpick; she willingly gave him an opening. No response. "Young woman, my butt," she said.

"That's the idea behind marriage, Ma. Can't go running off with a young filly if he's tethered to the barn. You know? Tie the knot"

His mom laughed. "As if you'd know anything about it."

Lance smiled, and began relating the wisdom of not buying the cow as long as you could get the milk, but he didn't finish, because

Becky Dreiling had picked up the Old Wharf Bar & Grill shot glass filled with toothpicks and wamped him squarely in the chest.

"Nice shot," Lance said.

"Crummy sentiment," Becky said, stabbing methodically at a piece of cantaloupe.

***

"This beast's sat up on blocks so long it'll probably take us 'til you're sixteen to get her going."

Lance and Daniel had decided to begin work on the old car that very afternoon, and as Lance walked around the jacked-up car, blowing his nose into his red hip pocket bandanna, Daniel O'Neill remarked on how the thing had changed somehow, now that he would soon be driving it. Freedom. Fun. Wheels.

"Gas money. Insurance. Sobriety," Lance said. "And don't forget, right now it's a bucket of loose bolts. It won't really be yours 'till you've banged and bloodied your knuckles twisting a wrench, hit your head on the open hood, lost little parts down through the wheel wells, and cussed the timing half a dozen times. Don't kid yourself, we got some work ahead of us."

"Sure, but you said you'd help. How hard can it be? It used to run for the old man, we'll get 'er goin'."

"Making it run's only a small part of the deal. You got to get to where you feel the son-of-a-bitch. To where you know its smells, its stutters, its little invariable pain-in-the-ass idiosyncrasies and bitchy little problems. This is internal combustion, Cowboy, and it's as different from bicycles and bass fishing as knee lengths are from menopause."

"I swear to God, Lance, you've lived with us here for more'n five years, and, as often as not, I never know what the hell you're talking about."

"No wonder and not your fault," the man said. Lance pulled a canvas tarp off of his upright toolbox over next to the workbench and wheeled the seven-drawer monstrosity toward the car.

"Cool," said the young man. "The good tools."

Lance rested his arms atop the toolbox and gazed about, first at the car, then at the boy and finally up toward the light stream in the hayloft.

"Anyway, little girl knee-length socks isn't really right. More like faded blue jeans and sun-drenched blond hair. Lot's of love and laughter. Fair amount of commotion"

"Like in the picture of you guys on the mantle."

"See there, you know more than you think you do."

"Yeah, but what's the menopause?"

"Don't really know, or can't say, but that's not really right, either. Maybe just real life, I guess. Shit," the man said. "Never mind. Get yourself a socket wrench and a short 5/8's socket, and let's get this hood off."

***

Daniel thought pulling the engine was incredible, and he thought Lance's deliberate pace admirable. It happened on a Saturday morning in the late spring. Lance dug an ancient pulley winch out of a wooden box under the tool bench, and he set about untangling the chain and greasing up the pulleys. Daniel climbed on to a metal milk crate perched on top of the Valiant and chained the pulley around one of the massive roof trusses spanning the length of the barn. After they pulled the engine hood and leaned it near the ladder leading to the hayloft, Lance used a long pitchfork to slide the pulley into place eight feet above and directly over the engine. One chain dangling from the pulley looped down several feet and returned into the top pulley. Two loose ends dangled from a second chain, and Lance bolted the last link from each of these into the holes which had secured the engine to the motor mounts.

Daniel O'Neill couldn't quite figure out the mechanics involved, but when Lance pulled on the looped chain, the slow clacking and clatter of the pulley lifted the sonofabithching engine up and out of the front of the car.

"Jesus," Daniel said at the time. "Look at that."

Lance left the engine swinging off the barn rafter, and they took the car off its blocks and pushed it out of the way. The Valiant looked like a skeleton after the engine came out. Most of the car stuff was still there – axels, doors, scratched and dusty windows, tan body paint, and upholstery spilling from ripped seat covers. But now, without the engine and virtually weightless, the front end jutted grotesquely up into the air.

The car looked ridiculous parked against the far wall, impotent and crippled. Its engine hung for days six feet off the ground while Lance fired up the old arc welder and built a sturdy metal bench beneath the swaying engine. Finally, on a Tuesday night, Lance satisfied himself with the stoutness of the bench, and they slowly lowered the engine on to it. They spent several nights pulling components and carefully setting each on a wooden workbench. Lance sent the teenager hunting around for enough metal pans so that each component sat in its own little container. Some, like the oil pump, the carburetor, and the valve and lifter assembly were taken apart and luxuriated in reservoirs of gasoline, screws mixing with loosening sludge in the bottom of the pans.

Others, like the starter and the alternator, sat dry; dirty nuts and bolts from each thrown in. Daniel O'Neill taped the connecting bolts of the six entwined cast iron arms of the exhaust manifold to the flanges and set the hunk of metal off to the side. He couldn't decide whether the manifold was more like an esophagus or the lower intestines, exhaling waste or pushing it out. In any event, the corner of the barn began looking like a mechanical morgue; parts lying about like discarded organs – some to be replaced, some repaired. Oil soaked into the wooden bench or into the dirt floor leaving dark stains of petroleum blood.

They pulled the head and extracted the pistons there in the barn. Lance knew a guy in town with a machine shop who agreed to hone the cylinders for a couple cases of beer. Lance pro-rated $159 out of Daniel O'Neill's piddling $15/week allowance and bought a set of oversized pistons and new rings.

"This engine's a Slant Six," Lance had told him many times. "One of the most simple, efficient, and beautiful engines ever created. She's deserves the best of everything – from you and from your intentions."

Lance methodically explained every part and every function to the boy, so that slowly he began to understand how a series of perfectly timed sparks jumped from the distributor rotor and traveled along the plug wires, where the spark jumped again across the gap at the end of the spark plug and ignited tiny little gasoline explosions inside the cylinders; how these explosions erupted against the top of each piston and forced the rapid up and down motion of the pistons; how the ends of the pistons were connected to pushrods and how these were connected to the crankshaft and how they pushed down on one side and pulled up on the other, turning the crankshaft in a circular motion; how the shaft attached to the big metal fly wheel at the back of the engine; how the pressure plate in the clutch pressed against the fly wheel; how the spline in the transmission turned when the throw-out bearing in the clutch released; how the transmission took the turning motion, geared it up or down and sent it along the driveshaft to the axels; how everything was hooked together so that ultimately the wheels turned and the car ran.

They worked together at nights in the barn for weeks, well into the summer. Daniel O'Neill's initial impatience with the pace of the repairs and his uncle's meticulous insistence on attention to detail ultimately gave way to a mesmerizing fascination, not so much with the principles of internal combustion, but with Lance's quirky obsession with those principles.

"This is going to scare the shit out of you, once you fully understand it," the man said early on.

"Ignorance is scary. I've never been scared of anything I could learn. It's just a machine. I can figure it out."

"Not talking about the machine. Talking about the principles."

"Of a car?"

"Of internal combustion. It's an incredible force, and it's screwed up everything. Changed all the rules. Nothing anymore is real."

Lance flicked his glowing cigarette butt into the dirt floor of the barn. "Unreal bullshit," he said.

Lance wasn't usually nor often given to filling the air with words, and over the years Daniel O'Neill had grown comfortable with a certain consistency of his uncle's verbal reticence. But tinkering with the Valiant's classic slant-six engine drew a constant drip of opinions from the man, like a curious and then nagging leak of crankcase oil. As Daniel O'Neill listened and asked questions, the pool of opinions increased; it spread and covered him like cranking down overhard on a pan bolt might force a gasket crack and create oil puddles all over the floor.

Mostly, Lance just rambled.

"Three primal elements, fuel, fire and air – well, fuel's not really primal but never mind – combine with a natural force, geared and leveraged motion, to create an astonishing array of harvestable power. We don't know what in the hell to do with the power except increase it, and we've not only shit in our nest but also dug an enormous trench surrounding it which we'll ultimately tumble into and die.

"Damnedest thing, internal combustion" Uncle Lance winked at him. "It'll scare the shit out of you."

Lance maintained the steam engine helped man become better and internal combustion turned him into a monster.

They were installing the newly re-built carburetor atop the intake manifold one evening, and Lance picked up the lecture almost where he'd left off the night before.

"Innocents harvested these forces. First we made the Industrial Revolution with all its dehumanizing filth. Now we race around with our heads up our ass and our hearts in the stars to see if our evolution can keep pace with our technology. It took us 100,000 years to adapt to walking upright, another 100,000 to get comfortable with simple tools. What in God's name makes us think we're equipped to keep pace with this bullshit," he asked, kicking the fender of the car and reaching into the back of the toolbox's third tray for an adjustable wrench.

"I think cars are cool, as long as someone doesn't drive off the road and land in a ditch. If we wanted to get to Montana, we could drive it in a few days," the boy said. "Before cars, it would have taken us months."

"Sure, but that's just a result of the fact that since we can get there in a few days, we think we must. Not necessarily a good thing, just an inevitable one."

That's how the conversations usually went, and as the summer evenings lengthened and the work progressed, the conversations became increasingly dialectic, and Daniel O'Neill learned about life from a substitute father with a philosophical burr up his ass and a passionate yearning for simpler times when things made sense.

His mom gave him a good healthy dose of natural order and innate wisdom, but he shared Lance's cynicism and distrust of convention, so that he often marveled at the molding powers of upbringing over genes.

The simplicity of internal combustion interested him; his ability to fully understand it awed him; the fact that he could create a temperament for this particular machine fascinated him. But they had worked on the thing for almost six weeks and had yet to even turn it over and see if the fool machine would run. In the beginning, everything was exciting. Now it was repetitive to the point of moronic, and Daniel O'Neill figured a little well thought-out debate might be a good way to spur Lance on to greater speed.

"Yeah, okay, but take a look at this carburetor," he said. "It's just a bunch of well honed metal pieces, stuck together in a way to mix up gas and air. I mean basically, that's what it does, right? It seems either radical or paranoid to see some kind of evil in that."

"Twist those bolts slow at first, help them find their threads before you start cramming them home. Wiggle the carb so the bolts can settle." Lance reached around the boy's outstretched arms and realigned the gasket, which looked to Daniel O'Neill like a piece of bread with all the bread cut away, leaving only the crust laying flat and squished, sealing the two metal surfaces.

"Nothing at all inherently evil. In fact," Lance said, handing Daniel a ½-inch socket, "something of a marvel of well-machined efficiency. But think how corruptible it is, how open to human manipulation." Lance attached one end of a bent, stout piece of wire to the throttle spring and snapped the other end onto the butterfly control of the carburetor.

Daniel looked at the throttle linkage and traced the throttle cable over the octopus arms of the exhaust manifold, down around the block and in through the firewall, where he knew it attached to the accelerator pedal inside. He imagined romping on the pedal, pulling the linkage and opening the butterfly valve. Gas poured into the chamber and the engine screamed out in throaty rpms. The sound rumbling through the muffler in his head sounded like freedom, like furious dust clouds obliterating small towns through rear windows, like wheels spinning away from this barn and toward anywhere else.

"An old lady driving through quiet Sunday morning streets on her way to church will gently, maybe even tentatively, work the throttle," Lance said. "She'll be a bit surprised every time the thing goes a little faster when she steps a little harder. She's fully in control because she's frightened. She's working the machine with respect because she doesn't understand it. A hot rod kid might romp on the same throttle and piss and moan cuz it's not fast enough. Maybe he understands every aspect of putting all those elements together – fuel, fire and air. Maybe he understands the extra little spurt of gas makes the pistons race faster up and down inside the cylinder walls. So he's got no respect, cuz he's got no fear. Now the machine's working him."

"That sounds like bullshit."

Daniel O'Neill thought now might be a good time to allay the knock on hot rod kids, so he spun the ratchet wrench quickly to tighten the four carb bolts. He'd watched Lance manipulate a ratchet wrench often, and he felt confident in his ability to get the extra turns on the bolt by twisting the extension forward with the fingers on his left hand on every clicking backstroke of the wrench – a real pro kept the bolt turning on both forward and back strokes. Hot rod kid, my ass, he thought.

"Not bullshit," Lance said. "The kid's lot's more likely to wrap the machine around the concrete pillar of a bridge; little old lady won't. It's an illusion of power, of control, and it's fed by greater knowledge."

Daniel O'Neill knew he still needed Lance's help, mostly because they still had to work through the electrical shit – plugs, plug wires, and, as Lance kept mentioning, some solenoid problem in the starter, whatever the hell that meant, but enough already. The guy's stupid little philosophies about a bunch of moving fucking metal – well oiled or not – etched a buzzing flatline of insufferable indifference across the boy's attention chart. Let's just get the thing up and running already.

They'd been collecting dirt and grease beneath their fingernails for almost two months, dicking around in this dark fucking barn, and the son-of-a-bitch refused to move along and fire the thing up. Daniel O'Neill started believing his Uncle was procrastinating so as to extend his soapbox for philosophizing on bullshit. He realized the increasingly mind-numbing soliloquies might actually go on for fucking ever and he'd never get to see the car actually run. Shut up already. This was the problem with grown ups; they reveled in taking a minor and mostly obvious point – like machines are a pain in the ass – and driving the sonofabitching obvious point right into the ground. Who gives a shit? Let's just get the thing running.

"Jesus, Man," Daniel O'Neill thought to himself, "shut up already."

And ultimately, the man did. Lance knew the boy was boiling with anticipation. He had prolonged the process to ensure a quality job, to make sure the boy understood how the thing worked, so that he would be capable of fixing it and avoiding small town rip-off mechanics when something inevitably went wrong.

It was, as Lance loved to say, one hell of a well oiled machine. As the summer drew to a close Lance constantly drilled the boy on the finer points of troubleshooting. Analyze the big picture. An engine needs only two things to start and run – fuel and fire. If it won't run, it's not getting one or the other or both. Pull on the throttle linkage and peer into the chamber. You can see the gas shoot in through the jets. If not, no fuel. Pull a spark plug wire, stick a nail in the end and hold it near anything metal. Crank the engine and watch a spark jump off the end of the nail. If not, no fire. After determining the status of those two primal ingredients, the chase becomes a mystery: clogged fuel line, shot fuel pump, too much or too little air, sparks flying at the wrong times, the sort of simple stuff that was like gravity – non-negotiable physical laws.

The job was finished and Lance knew it. The boy understood everything he needed to know about the car. Except his stubbornness about the starter. The thing was shot, but the kid insisted he would live with it and save the twenty-three dollars. It made Lance laugh, this youthful rebellion. He didn't worry too much – the kid already understood how to push-start the car, and Lance was sure he'd change the thing out as soon as he got out of sight of the farm.

Otherwise, the block gleamed with its new coat of black paint. Lance had no doubts all the new gaskets were snug and sealed; the high performance plug wires jutted off the distributor cap and snaked smoothly down to the six spark plugs; they had rebuilt the carburetor with care and precision; the alternator had new brushes and, save for the starter solenoid, the thing was done and Lance knew it.

He hadn't really believed two months working on an old car could replace years of distance and distrust, but the time together created a pleasant sort of complacency. Lance long ago allowed that the distance between him and the boy was as inevitable as the mood swings of a woman dealing with sexual guilt and maternal muddling. In the beginning his love for Becky prevented him from pushing her to give both him and the boy their due. During the last few years he decided he just didn't give a shit anymore. But these last few weeks with the boy gave him a different perspective altogether. Certainly he couldn't make up for years of lost time, but the Valiant represented another option, a neutral meeting ground.

And then, so typically, he screwed it up. When he saw the chance to breathe in, refreshing and cool, and breathe out and breathe in again, he screwed it up. Rather than sit back into nourishment and calm, he stuck his face into a flaming inferno. He seared and cauterized possibility. And he hurt the boy badly.

What in the hell did it really matter who owned the Valiant, who drove it and why? Was he really such a fucked-up mess that he couldn't even remember what it was like to believe in something? To need to believe? Was it stupidity or meanness and evil that made him slice hard into the heart and twist like a bayonet with blood grooves?

"Or just pathetic," he mumbled.

Afterward, when Lance sat by himself in the barn, he pulled out the whiskey, so he wouldn't feel the boy's pain. After a couple deep swallows it was easy to convince himself that truth was most important. The little shit needed to grow up and needed to grow tough.

"I didn't make the goddamn rules," he hissed in the empty barn.

He drank most of the bottle that night and he and Daniel never spoke of the Valiant again.

***

More than two years later and bound for college in Colorado, Daniel O'Neill sat in the 1965 Plymouth Valiant. Duffle bags filled the back seat, scholarship papers stuffed in his backpack, trunk crammed with his stereo, fishing gear, and albums. His intention had been to fill a coffee thermos in the dark kitchen, slip out quietly, and slip away. Now, he would push the car out of the driveway and roll quietly down the dirt road hill that led from their farm to the Interstate. Daniel O'Neill always got a kick out of coasting down the hill with the clutch pedal pressed to the floor. He'd turn the key on without starting the engine, gently shift into third gear and then, at 20 miles per hour and with a certain exhilaration, he'd pop the clutch. Instantly, all hell would break loose. Third gear was perfectly synchronized with the roll of the back tires, so gravity and the road put motion into the transmission and the gears began turning effortlessly, while furiously turning the crankshaft. The fuel pump had a lever resting on the crankshaft; as it spun, the lever pumped gas from the tank through the carburetor and into the cylinders, where the pistons, now racing up and down, compressed the gas and air mixture into a highly combustible state.

Sparks were already flying into the cylinder heads because the key opened a circuit from the battery. Powerful explosions erupted in the cylinders and the Valiant roared to life. Now, these explosions began forcing the pistons up and down; those natural forces of gravity and mass and motion and the hell with all that.

Daniel O'Neill, getting out in the Valiant.

Finally, after years of anticipation, the Valiant belonged to him – fully, completely, totally. He rolled down his window and screamed unfettered joy into the cool morning. He was one with the Valiant, and it was delivering him from broken pieces of yesterday into a wild and complete tomorrow.

"Life," he screamed again. "Get ready for another O'Neill and the 1965 Plymouth Valiant!"

He sat back then and relaxed, the Slant Six engine running smooth and well oiled, effortlessly taking him away. Daniel O'Neill and the Valiant, two old friends visiting together calmly on a lazy front porch, or on a sunrise Kansas ride.

*"Life is like toilet paper, man.
You don't miss it until you don't have it."*
                                    - Cib Carkus Adams

Chapter 8

Hooting, laughing, and hollering, we were out prowling on a Friday night in a college town: in our college town, in our new hometown. Our new home away from home, tacked onto the Western Slope of the Rocky Mountains.

We cut across a cemetery on our way to the weekend's fraternity parties. Rowdy, raunchy, and filled with ourselves, half a dozen college guys masked in merriment and engaged in innocent autumn alley-catting.

The graveyard was on the far side of the city's park. Gravestones pockmarked the side of a hill that once defined the south edge of the town. Rail workers, no-name drifters, and anonymous fortune seekers were buried near the bottom of the hillside sloping towards a creek. Nineteenth Century townsfolk rested respectably near the hillcrest behind a wrought iron fence encircling the First Presbyterian Church on Main Street.

The small creek bordered by cottonwoods and willows meandered around the base of the hill. The water separated the hill from a tree-filled meadow. Stone levies had been built on the meadow side of the creek. As the town was cultivated over the years, the cemetery also grew, at first wild and overgrown spreading down the hill and then finally overtaking the meadow. The water now cut the cemetery down the middle. Frequently placed footbridges connected the respectable dead meadow dwellers with the less fortunate dwellers marked by their tiny stones holding onto the side of the hill. The town re-named the place Overlook Point back in the 1950s, but most of the locals still called it Paupers' Hill.

The footbridges themselves were old. Rough cut red flagstone bricks curved up and out of the ground on the poor side. The grass jutted up at the edges of the bricks and reached the second level of gray mortar. The bricks gently arched over the small stream and then effortlessly rested back into the earth, secure again in respectable soil.

On this side the lush lawn was cropped close and manicured. It grew square and evenly around the headstones.

The tombstones on the hill were small and unassuming. Small markers for people moving through a small town, who undoubtedly led inconsequential lives and rested forever in unremarkable graves. Good for them, they're probably better off now than when they trudged along six feet up. The view's not so good, but few concerns, and the stress of waiting for the end is over. Their problems were as far behind them as ours were ahead of us. Arthritis. Poverty. And for the meadow folk on the other side, ungrateful kids marrying badly. The sapping realization that most dreams are crap, and the rest won't manifest. Constipation.

The cottonwoods along the creek, the cedars and firs and other pines in the meadow had escaped 100 years of city planning and design, so some of them were very old, and the cemetery carried this great age like a haggard woman hunched over her kettle of experience and sorrow. Down in the meadow stood a scattering of enormous family mausoleums like sentinels to death with dignity – dead, perhaps, but certainly not buried on the hill.

Careful concern for eternal placement.

Our concerns were immediate and basic. Getting to the weekend fraternity parties. Getting a bit more drunk before we got there. Meeting girls. Wisecracking about dead people. Bellowing out The Who's chorus – "Hope I Die Before I Get Old." Shaving the wild hairs and sowing the same oats. Meeting girls.

We were half a dozen college freshmen out of an October evening, obnoxiously celebrating the blood in our veins and the thrill in our feet.

Adams had a pint of Scotch tucked into the top of his left boot. A guy named Stu carried a plastic gallon milk jug filled with rum and coke. I lugged a canvas laundry bag filled with 24 cans of 16-oz Schlitz beer.

"I think these old farts are happy they've finally got some young blood dancing on their graves," Stu's roommate said. "I mean, they're dead, and they were old when they died, and they were probably old all their lives."

He took a swig from the rum jug and handed it back to Stu. "We're here, Old Farts," he yelled, "and we're never gonna die, and we ain't gettin' old!"

He jumped atop a cube-shaped block of granite death.

"Gopher!" he called down. "Toss me up a beer."

He caught the can and popped the top, spraying foam on himself and on the tombstone. "Forever young!" he screamed.

"Nothing better, Johnny G, than watching a boy who can hold his liquor," Adams said. "Suck it down, Cowboy."

"You got Cowboy right," Stu's roommate said as he pitched his empty can into the creek. "Once we hit that party and the girls see me, this cowboy's gonna mount up and ride."

"In your dreams, Fool," Adams said. "Leastways, it doesn't count if she's already passed out."

"One look at him, and all the girls will pass out anyway," somebody said.

"Or he'll scare 'em away, and they'll all pass out the door," someone else said

Adams grunted and Stu's roommate jumped down off the headstone. "Girls don't stand a chance once I get there," he said.

"Moron," Adams said.

I sat down on a small stone and opened a beer, suddenly overcome with an overwhelming sense of contentment. Everything fit. Everything belonged. These other guys were suddenly good friends. We were happy. We belonged here, and we belonged together. The beer wasn't so cold anymore, but it sure tasted good.

"I could stay here all night," I said. "The heck with the Frat party, let's make our own party right here."

"Eat shit," Stu's roommate said. "We're going to that party. Nobody's chickening out now."

"I'm not chicken, I'm drinking beer on a gravestone. You can go to a party anytime you want. When do you ever get the chance to party with the dead?"

"These dead could drink you under the table," Stu's roommate said. "They've already beat you under the ground. Shoot that beer, Gopher. Burrow down there with them. Show 'em what you've got. Shoot it. Anybody got an opener?"

"I've never done it," I said. "I don't know if I can."

"No opener," someone said. "Use my Swiss Army, and just cut a hole in the bottom."

"Bullshit," Stu said. "These are 16-ouncers. You can't shoot a sixteen ounce can of beer."

"Dead-Boy can do it," Stu's roommate said. "Burrow, Gopher, burrow. Shoot the beer."

"Leave him alone," Stu said. "You can't shoot a 16-ouncer."

"I can shoot a 16-ouncer," I said. "How do you do it?"

"It's easy, Gopher, nothing to it," someone said.

Stu's roommate took over. "I'll cut a hole in the bottom of the can. You get your lips around the hole and then grab the edges with your teeth, like you're about to chew through one of those trees down there. Tilt the can up, pop the top and shoot the thing down."

"Nothing to it," I said.

"The whole thing, Gopher," Stu's roommate said. "Just relax. Keep your head back and keep your throat open. Breathe slowly through your nose. Don't think, don't swallow. Just keep your throat open and let the beer run down. You gotta do it in 12 seconds or less, Gopher, or you're a Mole."

Stu's roommate giggled and grabbed the red pocketknife. He clicked open the larger of the two blades. "Gimme a beer."

"Bullshit," Stu said. "12 seconds for a 12-ouncer. These are 16-ouncers. You can't shoot a 16-ouncer."

"I can shoot one," I said. "Gimme a beer."

"Grab one out of your bag," Stu's roommate said. "Grab a nice cold gonad out of your little furry bag and shoot that sucker."

"Leave him alone," Stu said. "He's gonna be pitching gonads if he tries to shoot a 16-ouncer."

I dug in the laundry bag for a can of beer and handed it to Stu's roommate.

"Shoot it," someone started chanting. "Shoot it. Shoot it."

Stu's roommate turned the can upside down and drove the knife blade into the rounded aluminum bottom. He twisted the blade to enlarge the hole.

"Hey! Watch the blade," someone said. "Don't screw up my Swiss Army cutting cans."

"Shoot it, shoot it, shoot it." More joined in the chant, eerie and quiet and somehow cheery there in the graveyard. "Shoot it, shoot it, shoot it."

I sealed the opening with my lips and turned the can upright. A bit of beer wet my tongue, but nothing came out.

"Don't suck on it," Stu's roommate said. "Wait until you pop the top. It'll come all right then, just be ready."

"Shoot it, shoot it," several fellows chanted.

I closed my eyes and forced the back of my tongue to the bottom of my throat.

"Do it," Stu's roommate said. "Just remember, relax and breathe slowly through your nose. Don't hold the beer in your mouth, just let it run down your throat."

I took a long, slow breath through my nose and popped the top.

All heck broke loose in my stomach. The beer rushed down my throat like it came out of a garden hose on full blast. I concentrated on my nose, breathing slowly.

"Don't swallow," Stu's roommate yelled. "Shoot it."

The blackness behind my closed eyes filled with little pictures of beer shooting out of a fire hydrant.

"Stick with it, Gopher," someone said. "Shoot it."

I opened my eyes. My throat closed in the back and I took a strong quick breath through my nose. The fire hydrant exploded and beer sprayed out my nose; beer ran down my chin, beer soaked my shirt.

"Critical pressure," someone said. "Awesome."

"Jesus, what a mess," someone said.

"What a puss," Stu's roommate said.

"Shit," Adams said.

"You can't shoot a 16-ouncer," Stu said.

"Nice try, Gopher," Stu's roommate said, giggling. "I've never seen anyone shoot a 16-ouncer."

"Asshole," Stu said to him. "You can't shoot a 16-ouncer."

I felt wonderful, and I opened another beer. On the other side of the cemetery dogs started barking.

"I had a dream like this," I said, "except the dogs were howling and chasing us, and we were running through the cemetery and tripping on gravestones."

"I had a dream too," Stu's roommate said.

"What was yours?"

"That only sissies dream and sit in cemeteries. Let's go, Gopher. Grow up and let's move. Just because you look like a baby doesn't mean you have to act like one."

"I know what you mean, Johnny G. There's something cool about a cemetery," Adams said, handing me his bottle of Scotch. "Except us, right now, everyone who comes into a cemetery is here to think about someone they once knew, probably loved. Nothing but positive, peaceful thoughts. No hate, no anger. Everything else is just dust and bones. There's really no death here. I mean, if I was dead, the last place I'd hang out is a graveyard. The dead folks are all off somewhere else. Probably standing in line waiting to get back into the game. Cemeteries are like junkyards for old busted-down cars. No owners, just broken, used up machines. It's cool. Of course," he said, taking the bottle back from me and slipping it beneath his pant leg, "this cemetery's been here for over 100 years. It's not going anywhere. If we don't hit the party, the Babes will be left with nothing but Frat Heads and morons like Stu's roommate. Doesn't seem quite fair to the Babes."

Gosh, Adams was a good guy. And even though Stu's roommate was an asshole, he was a swell guy too.

"Just because I don't want to spend the night in a cemetery playing with myself doesn't make me a moron," Stu's roommate said.

Swell, I thought. "Let's go on to the party."

I stood up, emptied my can, and flung the laundry beer over my shoulder.

"This beer sure is good," I said, opening another.

"Stick it in your teeth and can it, Gopher," Stu's roommate said, laughing. "Get it? Teeth? Can it? Gopher? Too bad your name isn't Beaver; then you'd at least have a chance with the girls. You know? It'd be better to go for her, Beaver, than to Gopher her beaver." He cackled and reached into the laundry bag. "Burrow me a beer, Mole."

"Leave him alone," Stu said. "Let's go."

"Listen to those dogs," Adams said. "They may be fuzzy Fidos normally, but tonight they're running in a pack and there's a bunch of 'em and they're coming our way. I say let's definitely get the hell out of here."

"Scared?" Stu's roommate asked. "Chicken of a few dogs?"

"Stay if you want," Adams said. "I'm not screwing around with a pack of dogs."

"I agree," somebody else said. "Let's get out."

"I agree," I said. "I'm not chicken of a few dogs. Let's get out."

We started moving again, hopping over headstones, laughing and following the creek toward the city park. The barking got louder, and some of the fellows echoed with barks and howls of their own.

"Shit," Adams said again. "They've caught the scent of assholes. Let's move."

We fanned out into an efficient military retreat formation.

"All we have to do is kick them in the stomach when they lunge for our throats," someone said. "Right in the soft part, below the rib cage."

"I have a cousin who joined the marines," someone else said. "They train you how to fight dogs in the marines. What you do is, you slam your fist right down a dog's throat. You'll get your hand cut up a little, but the dog can't do any real damage when it's got a fist stuck down its throat."

"No," someone else said. "Fight them on their own terms. Don't run. Never run, because they're faster. When they come at you and jump up, grab their throats and hang on. Kick 'em, break their leg, whatever, but hang on to their throats."

"You guys are idiots," Adams said. "Dogs in a pack will attack. Even pets, when they're out at night and running in a pack, will attack. They're faster than us, their teeth are sharper. They'll go for the smallest one, or the slowest, and they'll chew you up. They're like coiled springs of muscle and knives. Anybody who wants to fight a dog is an idiot.

Look," he said. "There they are."

And there they were, a dozen or more, coming out from a stand of maple trees 20 yards upstream. Out front leading the rest was one of those big police dogs. A big black and tan German Shepherd. Behind this one were six or seven other big dogs – black and yellow labs, a Collie-looking thing, some scruffy mutts. Behind these were a bunch of little hangers-on. The shepherd stopped and growled with genuine menace at us. We all froze. The dog hunched down slightly on his front paws and rose up a bit on his hind legs. You could see the hair standing up on his shoulders. He snapped at one of the black labs, sending it back into the ranks. The dog yipped and squealed, then circled around behind the shepherd.

"This is not cool," Adams said. "This is not cool at all."

"Oooh," Stu's roommate said. "The big, tough, high school football quarterback hero, stud is scared. Run away, Stud. Run away."

"Idiot," Adams said.

Why fight them at all," Stu's roommate said. "Let's just tap into the football stud's peaceful, positive, graveyard energy and make them our bosom buddies. Let's just link our peaceful spirits with their peaceful spirits."

Stu's roommate leaped onto Silas Bowman's big black marble headstone – "1904-1967, Good Father, Community Man."

"Ohmmmm," Stu's roommate began chanting. "Ohmmmm. Ohmmmm. Find peace, little doggies. Ohmmmm. Ohmmmm."

Some of the other fellows took up the meditative chant. "Ohmmm. Ohmmm. Ohmmm."

147

The sound wafted out into the cemetery. It found its own rhythm and got louder, sounding like monks, or Druids calling up the dead. " Ohmmmm. Ohmmmm. Ohmmmm."

The shepherd sat down, cocked its head and listened. A little Beagle-mix gamely tried a howl.

"It's working," someone said. "Keep it up."

A pulse-pounding hum, the sound lingered and floated through the cemetery. It rolled across the marble and granite stones, meandered across the water, and settled like incense into the trees.

"Gosh," I said. "It is working. They're just sitting there." I joined in, lent my voice to the pagan hum.

"Ohmmmm. Ohmmmm. Ohmmmm."

"Wow" Stu said. "Unbelievable."

"Bullshit," Adams said. "They're probably just getting ready to take a communal dump so they'll be lighter on their feet when they attack. Let's go."

We started walking again, slowly, backwards, and humming and Ohmmmming as we went. A few of the dogs stood up, but they didn't move. The Beagle-mix and a Dalmatian howled low and mournful. The German Shepherd sat as still as a dignified general overseeing an orderly and negotiated armistice.

We reached the wrought iron fence sealing the cemetery and we hopped over, one by one, into the park. Stu's roommate guarded our flank, Ohmmming with the passion of a bugler heralding the last man out of the back door of the fort. My laundry bag caught on one of the pointed iron spikes adorning the top of the fence. Stu grabbed the bottom of the canvas bag and flung it over. The bag flew over my shoulder and the momentum flung me to the ground on the other side.

"Ohmmmm," I hummed. "Foamy Oamy beer."

Someone laughed at that, Stu's roommate jumped over and we were out.

"Later, Canine Brothers," Stu's roommate said. "May the peace of the Ohmmmm be with you."

"Nice work," Stu said.

"What bullshit," Adams said.

***

Greek Row roared its party voice on the other side of the park, away from the creek that filled the duck pond. Seven enormous Frat houses backed up to the park. Music and laughter and light poured out of each one. We were looking for Sigma Phi Something, but music blasted out of all of them, and people milled about up and down the street. The whole block felt like a rowdy all-night street carnival. The backyards were separated from the park, and from each other, by tall wooden fences. Beer kegs covered with ice and blankets sat in plastic garbage bags.

Lots of laughing, talking, loud music, hooting and hollering everywhere.

Girls were everywhere too. Tiny petite girls wearing short skirts or cut-offs. Beautiful girls in bare feet wearing overalls. Athletic girls. Smart girls. Suntanned girls. Girls were everywhere, and they were gorgeous.

"Jesus, look at all these girls," someone said.

"Yippee ki yay," Stu's roommate said.

It reminded me of a Dr. Seuss book.

"Big girls. Little girls. Girls everywhere you look.
Skinny girls, busty girls. Girls from a glamour book.
Suntanned legs and bouncy boobs, Girls for me and girls
for you.

Nice girls. Friendly girls. Girls who want some sex.
Smiling girls. Laughing girls. Girls who'll take a check.
Girls are girls, they squat to pee. Girls for you and girls
for me."

"C'mon, you guys, spread out," Adams said, shattering my ridiculous rhyming reverie. "We look like a busload of gawking Boy Scouts on a field trip. Johnny G., let's go inside."

"See you later, fellows," I said.

"Good luck, Gopher," Stu's roommate snickered.

"Asshole," Adams said over his shoulder.

The biggest frat house was a gray brick three-story Gothic looking building with lots of windows out front. People crowded onto a stone porch that ran the length of the entire front and along one side. The grass in the yard was already starting to go dormant, which seemed good because it was taking quite a beating with all the trampling under so many feet.

I had left the laundry bag in a ravine in the park, and as we squeezed through the crowd on the porch, I didn't know what to do with my hands. Stuffing them in my pockets made my elbows stick out, which made it hard to get past the partying crowd. Letting my arms hang at my sides left my hands down out of control, and I was mortified when my left hand rubbed against a girl's butt. She turned, and instead of punching me in the stomach or slapping my face, she smiled and winked at me.

"Adams," I called. "Hold up."

But he was already several feet in front of me, pushing through the crowd and heading for the front door. I watched him disappear, swallowed whole and then gone. The porch was packed, but suddenly it was just me and the girl with the cute wink and the great butt stuffed inside tight cut-off jeans and her auburn hair flowing down onto an oversized white sweatshirt. Her short legs were muscular, and I had to force my eyes away from the back pockets on the cut-offs.

She was beautiful. Curvy and full and clean shiny hair down her back, like in those Playboys my dad used to keep hidden on the bottom shelf of the upstairs linen closet. Her skin was smooth, and she had these incredible green eyes, and they were looking right into mine. I was slightly intoxicated, so I couldn't be sure my own eyes were making contact, but she was sparkling and radiant and wholesome like Mary Ann, and she was still smiling, and I knew I had to say something.

I felt like Gilligan.

"Sorry," I said. "It's pretty crowded, kind of tight. I'm just coming in."

150

She laughed and her eyes sparkled, and she did that great thing women do when they put their hand over their mouth when they laugh, because they don't want to hurt your feelings. I started to say something dumb like how's the party so far, but suddenly she and everyone standing around us turned and watched this old beat up car hobble up over the curb and park right on the front lawn.

A guy got out and slammed the door.

He leaned comfortably against the car, smiling a bit as he surveyed the crowd. Except for the beat up old car and his flannel shirt, the guy looked almost dangerous, like a mechanic-biker type – red bandana wrapping his head, blue jeans, work boots. Except for his easy smile, he looked scruffy and almost mean, like one of those Iranians on TV who had just taken our hostages.

The girl with the wink and the butt looked up at me and winked again.

"Daniel O'Neill and the Valiant," she said. "This party just got a whole lot better."

He saw her then, and just by the way he came walking right over to her, I could tell immediately I had absolutely nothing interesting to say to her.

She glanced at me quickly and laughed again.

"Hard to get back inside," she said to him, after he had pushed his way through the crowd to where we were.

"Looks like," he said, throwing me a look. "I figure once it's hard, leave it inside. Come on," he said, taking her arm, "It all depends on how you approach it. We can go in the back way. Not quite as tight back there."

She laughed, and off they went.

He led her back down the porch stairs. I watched them go around the back of the house.

"Easy come, easy go," some guy said to me.

"I guess," I said. "She was great. Did she know him?"

"Everybody knows him," the guy said. "But don't sweat it, Buddy. It's a full house in there. Like spearing fish in a barrel. Keep your head up, Man. Work on the rest as circumstances demand."

One-liners. I wished I had one.

I stood on my tiptoes but couldn't see Adams. He must've gotten through the front door. I wedged myself a little closer to the front door and thought of the girl with the wink and the butt. I didn't need Adams. Grow up, Gophe. I was a college man now. She winked at me. She wanted me. I couldn't get her thighs out of my mind, nor the feel of her butt, nor her sparkling eyes, nor that wink. She winked at *me*. The heck with that Valiant guy, he just had a good one liner.

"You're on your own, Adams," I said out loud to no one in particular.

I backed out, weaseled my way to the stone steps and spilled out into the yard. I took stock.

Around the side was a painted cinder block garage. It wasn't as old as the house but was in worse shape. Boards covered the windows of the garage door. Two little concrete wheel paths ran up from the street and disappeared beneath the garage door. It seemed like a sign – "Come this way, come here."

Maybe the wink meant around the corner. Maybe her two legs meant those two concrete wheel paths. Maybe she was waiting behind the garage, just passing time with the Valiant guy until I found her. Maybe I should bring her a beer.

I peered through the wooden slats of the fence encircling the backyard. She wasn't part of the crowd pressing around the beer keg. If I could just get over the fence and into the backyard, move to the front of the line and fill a couple of cups, I could saunter behind the garage and find her, offer her a beer and think up a one-liner – "Pretty cozy here behind the garage," or "Good party but the garage is better," or "I like garages too."

Well, anyway, something would occur to me.

I slithered along to the back of the fence, glanced once at the empty park behind me, pulled myself up, and vaulted over. As kids, my next-door neighbor best friend and I perfected an effortless and soundless method of getting over tall wooden fences. You grabbed the top with both hands, put your butt low, and climbed your feet up sideways until they reached the top. You perched there for just a moment and then vaulted over, hitting the ground on the other side like a cat on all fours. It was easy, it was fast, and it didn't make any noise. I landed in the backyard of the frat house without a sound. Nobody even looked my way, and, as per the plan, I kind of sauntered over to the keg.

"I lost my cup," I said to a very big guy with huge curly red hair who was carrying a stack of plastic beer cups. "Know where I can get a fresh one?"

This guy was a giant, kind of stupid looking but also mean looking. His eyes were bloodshot and his face was pockmarked and covered with dirty looking red whiskers, and he just stared at me. He weaved a bit, and then he grabbed the side of the house for support.

"You get one when you come in the front door and give 'em your five dollars. Hold on to your cup, 'cuz that's how we know you've paid."

He looked at me some more. "Where's your cup?"

Oh man, I was about to get the bejesus kicked out of me by a gigantic drunken Scotsman with a strong sense of party ethics.

"I gave mine to a girl," I blurted out. "She accidentally stepped on hers. I was just trying to help her out, and now I don't have one." I quickly searched the faces of the people near us, looking for a drunk-looking girl I could point to in case he demanded tangible substantiation.

The red headed Scottish Gigantor narrowed his eyes and looked at me some more.

"Stupid move," he said. "Chick's not worth a beer cup."

"Not even," I said. "Moment of weakness. She was cute and thirsty. Dumb thing to do."

"No shit," he said. "But nice move. Name's Big Bill."

He thrust out a huge hand, attached to a massive arm covered in freckles and red hair.

"John Gophe."

"They ever call you Gopher?"

I wasn't sure what the right answer was. "Sometimes."

"Fuck 'em. Don't ever let 'em call you Gopher, and don't ever let 'em steal your beer cup. Ever."

"Okay, Big Bill. I won't. You've got that right. You're right about that." I felt like I was fooling around with a rattlesnake.

"Here," he said, and he pulled a plastic cup off the bottom of the stack of cups nestled like a sleeping cat in his huge forearm. "Don't give this one to no chick."

"Heck no," I said, wondering if it was insane to ask him for a second cup for the girl with the wink and the butt.

"Chick's not worth a beer cup."

"Damn straight," said Big Bill.

I moved into the circle around the keg and watched as a little guy stood holding the flexible beer tap, dutifully pouring beer into cup after cup thrust at him. A few people said thanks, but most just regarded him as an extension of the beer keg, sort of a freshman automatic refiller. You see the same thing at church. Somebody holds open the door for the person behind him, and then everyone starts passing through, nobody reaching out for the door until the person holding it can't let go without catching some old lady's cane, so he ends up holding the door for everyone as the entire congregation files out. I could tell this little guy holding the beer spout was looking for some sucker to pass the responsibility to. Having held my share of church doors, I was determined not to get stuck. Besides, the girl with the wink and the butt was waiting, somewhere.

I got to the front of the line and held my cup out, but the little guy wouldn't fill it. He kept avoiding my cup, filling those attached to pretty hands, or big hands, or Frat hands. He worked well and I marveled at his technique, moving the tap from cup to cup, even setting his own beer inside the round aluminum lip of the keg when it needed to be pumped.

"Not too much," a dark-haired fellow holding a big German stein warned him. "You'll get foam. Pump it just a few times, and pump it more often."

"Okay," the little guy said.

"It's a little tricky filling a stein," the Frat fellow said. "You've got to pour it down the side more." He held out his stein.

"Okay," the little guy said.

I held my cup right next to the stein. The plastic rim of my cup touched up to the big gold lion coat of arms emblazoned on the outside of the stein. I watched the foamy head slowly rise in the stein and I raised my cup higher. The stein filled up, and the little guy moved the tap across the top of my cup and began filling a girl's cup. He never took his thumb off the lever, so a little trickle of beer dribbled into my cup. The guy was good.

The beer flow slowed. The keg needed pumping.

"Let me hold your beer for you while you pump it," I offered.

He handed me his cup and worked the piston sticking out the top of the keg a few times. Perfect, I thought. I'll make him fill mine before I give him his back. I briefly considered getting my cup filled and then making off with his to give to the girl with the wink and the butt, but then I realized I didn't want her to get any germs from this geeky little guy.

The beer from the black plastic hose poured faster each time the little guy rammed the pump down, and the girl's cup filled quickly. He held the hose tap with both hands, ready to move it again.

"Move it my way, little fellow," I said to myself.

"Thanks for holding my cup," he said to me. "Let's fill yours," and we exchanged possessions.

Suddenly I was the guy holding the tap.

My cup filled quickly, and as I prepared to move the nozzle and pass the hose, another empty cup appeared, gulping the flowing beer. Then another. And more.

"Don't pump it yet," the Frat fellow said to me. "It's pouring perfectly right now."

"I wasn't going to," I said.

"Good, but you'll need to soon."

So there I was, hosting the keg, head down, eyes on empty cups or on the ground, dutifully pouring beer for other people I didn't know. I hoped the girl with the wink and the butt wouldn't see me like this. Nothing but hands and empty cups everywhere, floating around the beer barrel amid a sea of feet.

"Not too much foam," someone said.

"Pump it," the Frat guy said. "It's slowing down." But he wasn't a Frat guy now; he was just a pair of tennis shoes, a hand, and a German beer stein.

"Thanks," a girl said. But she wasn't a girl now; she was a pair of lavender sandals, a silver charm bracelet, and an empty plastic beer cup.

"Thanks, Pardner," a pair of work boots and dirt under the fingernails said. "How'd you get this job? The other guy had it for the last three refills. That boy had a hankering for it. I was gettin' to like him."

I looked up, and it was the Valiant guy, Daniel O'Neill. I noticed he had a ponytail sticking out from the red bandana tied like a skullcap on his head. Up close, his eyes were a musty gray and creased quite a bit in the corners. Actually, if you looked closely enough, his eyes weren't really gray at all, more like platinum, or silver. He looked nice when his eyes smiled, even though his mouth didn't. He clearly did not remember me from the front porch, even though he had sort of stolen my woman.

"Just next in line, I guess," I said. "Want to take over?"

He laughed and downed his full cup of beer.

"You look as though you've got it under control. I'd think it was fine if you'd pour this one full." He held out his cup.

More people were spilling into the backyard. The music, blasting from speakers set in second story windows, got louder.

I started to introduce myself, seeing as how we were sort of sharing the same woman for the evening, but he cut me off, all excited when a new song blasted into the backyard.

"Hot Good God damn, "he said. " Fogerty. Damned if these slickers've got some musical taste, after all. Maybe even Jerry Jeff next. You one of these fraternity fella's?" he asked me.

"Just came to the party," I said. "I thought about pledging in September, but I didn't. Seems like a pretty nice group of fellows."

"Nice for sheep and sleeping close," he said. "Nice enough."

Some guy standing in line started bitching about having only one keg at the party.

"For five bucks, you'd think they'd have more than one," he said to no one in particular. "This waiting in line, while some little dweeb pours beer, sucks."

I looked up, feeling foolish for taking offense. He had long greasy hair, dirty bell-bottom jeans, and tire-tread sandals. An embroidered white cotton shirt hung from his shoulders; the embroidery was peace signs and birds and things that made people like my dad mutter "hippie."

Some of the girls standing around the hippie took a few steps away and made some air.

"Beer ain't goin' nowhere," Daniel O'Neill said. "It's a party, Man, relax."

Big Bill, the big redheaded Scotsman, appeared and bumped shoulders with the hippie. "Problem?"

"Screw you," the hippie said.

Big Bill didn't even flinch. He reached out, grabbed the hippie's empty beer cup and smashed it in his hand.

"You don't got no cup," Big Bill said. "No cup means you didn't pay at the door. Didn't pay at the door means get the hell out."

"My ass," the hippie said.

"Careful, Son," said Daniel O'Neill. "This here bull's a big one, and he looks mean."

"My ass," the hippie said.

Big Bill's cheek kind of twitched and quivered. I kept pouring beer, though the demand had died as everyone watched and waited. Creedence Clearwater Revival screamed about being down on the corner.

"Don't know whether to pick up this keg and bust you one over the head or just pitch you over the goddamned fence," Big Bill said.

"My ass," the hippie said.

"Wrong answer," said Daniel O'Neill.

Big Bill handed his stack of cups to some Frat guy standing silently by. He grabbed the back of the hippie's embroidered shirt with his left hand and clutched the belt holding up his jeans with his right hand. He lifted the hippie chest high, took a few steps and flung him clean over the six-foot fence. One of the hippie's sandals fell off. The backyard erupted into cheers.

"Fuck an A, that was incredible," Adams said, appearing out of nowhere and slapping Big Bill on the back. "Nice work, Big Bill. Nice piece of fucking work.

"Johnny G!" he called. "Major dude, Johnny G! What the fuck you doing, pouring beer? Got a union card for this crappy job? What's the deal, G?"

Adams grabbed the beer tap from me, shot me a "what the hell's wrong with you" glance, and poured himself full.

"Big Bill, need a fill-up? Gimme two of those for the big guy," Adams said to the Frat fellow holding the stack of plastic cups.

He drew two cups full and handed them to Big Bill, poured me one, and then dropped the hose on top of the keg.

"Did you see that big son of a bitch?" Adams said. "In-fucking-credible."

"Kind of a fella you always want for you, rather than against you," the Valiant guy, Daniel O'Neill, said.

"No shit," Adams said, slapping him on the back as well. "First pick in any draft." Adams grabbed the beer hose from the Frat guy and poured Daniel O'Neill full up.

"Here's to Big Bill," he said, raising his cup and dropping the tap hose again. "Big son of a bitch, Big Bill."

"I'll wet one with you on that," said Daniel O'Neill, gulping his beer down.

***

We stood around the keg and partied for quite awhile longer. Adams just picked up the tap hose and filled us up whenever he felt like it. Adams and Daniel O'Neill warmed up to each other right away. The more beer I drank, the more they seemed like two halves of the same loaf; Adams boisterous and confident and carefree, Daniel O'Neill mellow and confidant and content. They fooled around with Big Bill, they one-upped each other with stories of high school football heroics, they talked and joked around with a lot of people who came to the keg, many of whom seemed to know Daniel O'Neill.

I was part of the circle, but I didn't say much. The beer just kept ironing out the edges in my mind and everything felt fine. I didn't really have anything to say, and, besides, the beer also made me aware that my lips couldn't be trusted to do their job well. Plus, I wasn't good at talking like these two were. They had an easy time of just going back and forth; you could tell other people liked standing around them, listening but not really part of the circle like I was. It felt like when two dads used to hang around a front yard visiting of a summer's evening. Kids from all over the neighborhood would get drawn in and just hang around also, not really part of the conversation, but part of the scene. It always felt better if one of them was your dad, because then you were a more important part of the circle, even if you didn't have anything to say.

Suddenly, I felt a burp burning at the top of my stomach, and then, because I realized I might be about to throw up, I handed Big Bill my cup and staggered over and sat down next to the fence.

"What the hell I'm supposed to do with this?" I heard Big Bill ask.

"He's fine," I heard Adams say. "Just needs some air."

"Looks kind of rode hard to me," someone sounding like Daniel O'Neill said.

My head was spinning and the back of my neck was tingly hot. My eyes might have been closed.

"He's fine," it seemed like Adams said. "He's a goer. Just give him a sec."

I liked knowing Adams was there, believing I was all right. It made me feel like I probably was. I could just close my eyes again, and get a little air.

***

"Johnny G! Let's go. Get up, Man. We're outta here." This sure sounded like Adams. I opened my eyes; he and Daniel O'Neill were reaching down to pull me up to my feet. My mouth was a

159

little dry, and as I licked my lips, I could see the backyard was almost empty.

"On your feet," Daniel O'Neill said, plopping me there. "Tomorrow you'll tell the story around town how you walked out of a party and had to step over the unconscious heap that once was Big Bill."

I looked around and saw the Scottish Gigantor slumped against the back porch, snoring like a lion and still cradling the stack of plastic cups against his chest.

"You outlasted them all, Johnny G," Adams said. "And the killer news is, this night is about to get one hell of a whole lot better. Remember that little 'dry' problem we've been having lately?" Adams nodded toward Daniel. "Well, Bunky, our green and gold sticky-weed ship just came in."

"Green, gold, yellow, and red," Daniel said. "Only the best."

"Excellent," Adams said. "I'm ready. I'm dying." He nodded to me. "We walked."

"I've got wheels," Daniel said. "Out front."

Adams put his arm around my shoulder like friends would do, and I knew if I walked along with him I'd get around to the front of the house just fine.

There was hardly anyone left in the front yard, either, but Daniel's old car was still parked in the grass next to the porch.

"There she sits," Daniel said.

"Right on," Adams said. "I don't guess anyone at this party's likely to give you shit about where you park your car."

"Reckon not," Daniel said. "If they party, they know this car."

"What is it," Adams asked. "An Impala? A Falcon?"

"Fool!" Daniel said. "That's the car God made when he took the day off just to build his own car. 1965 Plymouth Valiant. Slant Six. God's engine. A perfection of simplicity, history, and reliability. A piece of art cleverly disguised as a piece of shit."

"Works for me," Adams said. "Can't wait to hear the history part, one day. Sounds juicy. Whaddya say, Johnny G?"

"It's a really nice car," I said.

Adams laughed and shook his head. He gave me that "you're pathetic" look and called out "Shotgun!"

He opened the passenger side door and slipped in, his elbow sticking comfortably out the open window even before the door completely closed.

"Okay," I said, and I climbed in the back.

Talk about feeling like part of the circle.

Daniel drove across the grass, down off the curb, and out onto the street. We cruised all over town that night and into the early morning. Daniel stopped every now and then to go inside a house. Adams sat up front in the shotgun seat like he'd sat there all his life. The back was fine with me, space to spread out. I probably nodded off some, too. It seems like we met up with some girls and rode around in their red convertible for a time, maybe even getting home that way. But what I really remember is riding around in the Valiant, that night and so many nights after. It certainly wasn't a fancy car or any kind of hot rod, so that made the ride even finer. Lots of people knew the car because they knew Daniel, and they always seemed pleased when he stopped in. Because Adams and I rode with him, they seemed pleased to see us, too. It didn't take me long to figure out that the reason people knew Daniel and the Valiant was because Daniel O'Neill always had, and often sold, the best weed in town. Whenever we'd show up at a party, you could see it in people's faces, like we were the ice-cream truck rolling down the neighborhood streets of their childhoods.

But that was just the Valiant from the outside. The Valiant other people saw. The Valiant no one really knew. On the inside the Valiant made our world. It contained us and defined us. It made us whole. There was a great stereo system with speakers front and back; it had both a radio and a cassette, and we kept it cranked loud. We usually had cold beer in a cooler that shared the back seat with me. In the beginning we were like cowboys, or knights, or army comrades, we three, riding together and getting around.

"Here comes the Valiant," I often imagined people said, or "Seen the Valiant tonight?"

It was fabulous. It was completion. It was belonging and it was whole. Daniel was the Valiant the night Adams and I met him; after that, I imagined that we too had become the Valiant. I truly felt like I owned the world, back in those days when we'd cruise around, all of us together, taking a Valiant ride.

I never got the shotgun seat; Adams was always faster at calling it. But that was fine, the back seat became my space, and as the weeks rolled on through that winter and into the spring, a lot of exciting things happened back there as well. Not that it became my domain or anything like that. Everyone, including me, recognized that the 1965 Plymouth Valiant was Daniel O'Neill. Then, like I say, it somehow became all of us. Daniel driving, Adams riding shotgun with his right elbow stuck out the window no matter the weather. Whatever happened with me in the back seat could in no way compare with the energy those two created up front. And if you want to know, nothing much happened with me in the back seat. The action was all up front.

Sometimes early on Nattie Sinclair rode with us, and, when she did, she sat up front, in the middle. Later that spring, after we all moved in to Nattie's old Victorian and lived together, the four of us like a family, well then we all rode together all the time. It was wonderful, like riding around in the Pope mobile. I loved it, and I'm pretty sure we all loved it, all in our own different ways.

Adams loved calling for the shotgun seat, even though, after a short time, it was clear to anyone that seat was his. Adams just liked the game, the competition of calling for that seat. He liked the challenge of winning it, even though neither Nattie nor I ever really tried to get it from him. Nattie loved it because I think she loved the energy of being with us. Well, maybe not me, but you know. She liked men a lot and she talked about liking men a lot. It seemed funny and even a little silly in the beginning when she insisted on calling all of us, even me, men. I guess because I'd never thought of myself as a man, but always a boy. A man was a grownup, like Mr. Somebody's Dad. But here's the really funny part. After a while, because Nattie thought of me that way, I almost did too.

Anyway, Nattie seemed to come even more alive when we were all together in the Valiant. Adams and Daniel like bookends in the front, hooting and hollering and carrying on with Nattie between them, teasing them, laughing with them, winking back at me and loving every minute. Me with the back seat all to myself, pleased as punch to be part of the ride.

I guess I could talk a long time about what Daniel loved about all of us and the Valiant, but then I'd have to go a long way to talking about what he loved about just the Valiant.

And then also of course what he hated about the Valiant.

That's a story I don't know if I can tell, or if I should tell, or if I want to tell. I mean I'm not trying to keep secrets or anything like that, but I came to realize that Daniel and the Valiant was something special. A rare thing. Maybe even unique. I didn't fully understand it then, and I probably still don't now, but I know enough, and I knew enough to understand that Daniel O'Neill and the 1965 Plymouth Valiant were connected in the same way you'd imagine a palm tree is wed to a hurricane, or a harp seal is hooked to a polar bear. Something in a way you didn't want to get too close to, but something you couldn't take your eyes off of. So why Daniel was in the deal, why he was in the Valiant, was more complicated than it was for the rest of us. And not just because it was his Valiant. For Daniel, hanging out in the Valiant was more than grins and good times, like Adams used to say. It was something about his dad, and something about his uncle, and a lot of somethings he didn't want to talk about, so clearly it was something about family, which I believed made the whole thing a little more intense, a little even sacred. And I also believed, secretly I guess, that if it was about family for Daniel, then it made it about family for us. Like I would have done anything for those three and the Valiant, and they would have done anything for me.

"Of course God is a woman.
If God were a man, swallowing semen
Would dissolve cellulite."

- Cib Carkus Adams

Chapter 9

My head got drenched the night before, and then the next morning it got dried, all in alcohol. It bellowed beneath the terrible pressure squeezed out by hundreds of tightly wrapped rubber bands. I woke up inside of my head while my eyes were closed. All of me woke up inside my head while my eyes were closed.

There was quite a commotion going on inside my head; chaotic activity with a lot of racket and disorganization, like when somebody's dad agrees to pay all the neighborhood kids a quarter to clean out his garage on a Saturday afternoon. One of those slow summer Saturdays, where everybody's kind of lazily riding their bikes in big circles up and down the street; maybe someone's dad is hand watering a big green hedge over there, maybe someone else's dad is trimming roses or washing the car on down a ways.

And then someone's dad starts the arduous job of cleaning out the garage. After the first couple of trips he takes hauling garage stuff down to the end of the driveway; he has created a kid magnet, and the bicycle circles begin their slow collapse in front of the house. Pretty soon someone stops, straddles the front bar on his bike, and asks if he can help. In no time at all bikes lie scattered all over the front yard and half a dozen or so kids are gleefully hauling everything in the garage out. The dad is kind of directing things, helping the older kids take over, saying where everything should be put down and basically working his way out of the job.

Pretty soon the garage is totally empty, except for now it's filthy and everyone is sent home to get their own broom.

Bikes scatter again, and by the time everyone gets back with their broom the dad's got a cooler and he's icing down a case of Coors beer. Then some of the other dads start wandering down, some of them carrying lawn chairs and some of them deciding to spread out and relax on the grass.

Being inside my head felt like being a part of that garage clean-up: kids going nuts, hollering and dragging stuff out of the garage, dropping things all over the front yard. Dust flies, an old barbecue grill looses a rusted wheel, busted fishing poles get even more tangled, everything clanging away and crumpled in the corners.

And then the sweeping part. Now the garage is just a shell – concrete floor, framed stud timber walls, dirt and dust. You got to pick a corner or a section of wall and you got to sweep it up. You'd start with little, precise broom strokes to clean out between the two-by-four wall studs, brushing all the dirt and cobwebs and junk off the lip of the wood and down onto the gray concrete. The surface of the concrete is super smooth, not like the rough stuff out on the driveway, so the dirt slides along beautifully in front of your broom. Clean behind you, from all directions along your corner area, all into a little pile. When it's done well, there are neat little piles swept all over the garage, and now the concrete feels cool and so clean and everything is quiet in there.

So there inside my head I slowly swept the clanging quiet, starting in the back of my head, sweeping circles into piles as I worked my way forward to the garage doors of my eyes.

But it was clumsy sweeping up half-ideas and dusty memory. Each time I got close to my eyes, the pounding and clanging grew again in intensity. It seemed smart to keep my eyes closed for a while.

And finally I considered just staying put, collapsing back into the coolest and cleanest corner, far away from the commotion at the doors and in the driveway beyond. My thought then, as I say, and increasingly my determination, was to stay inside my head and keep my eyes closed, maybe for a few more minutes and maybe for the rest of the day. The belief persisted, as enduring as the pounding in my brain, that certainly with my patience, more sleep, and God's master plan, I would either die or Monday would eventually arrive.

My second thought involved the realization that perhaps my eyes wouldn't open, sealed shut, not in spite of hours of sleep, but because of them. Sealed, not with mucous-dried crust in the corners, but by eyelid muscles fully atrophied by debauchery.

Man alive, I wished I were dead.

Last night somebody, probably one or all of those former high school volleyball players from New Jersey, apparently snuck back into the dorm room, dragged me out of my bed and clumsily poured me into the corner on the floor.

Half my body was crammed beneath the foolish little dorm desk, which on a good and upright day crushed against my knees. On this morning, the wood-grain Formica desk clutched my head and neck and crookedly wedged the rest of me between the closet door and the wastebasket.

I couldn't move, my eyeballs stuck against the blackness, and my mouth was dry, as if someone had stuffed a dried-out sour dough roll into it.

I reflected, scrunched there on the floor while my head continued building critical mass. Pounding-Boom. Pounding-Boom. Pounding, pounding, pounding-boom.

Memories of the night before grudgingly crept back into this mental maelstrom. There were these cheerleaders, or no, actually they were former high school volleyball players from New Jersey, but they were cute and bubbly and bouncy like cheerleaders, and they could probably do the splits and they were in our room at some point in the evening.

Memory wobbled out, looked around a bit and collapsed again, like the sheepish dad who had an afternoon beer buzz and a twilight mess in his front yard. It seemed increasingly plausible that these girls, cute and bubbly and giggling from a night of throwing back multiple sex-on-the-beach shooters, that these same girls were impishly capable of finding moronic New Jersey humor in actually stuffing my mouth with a dried out sour dough roll.

There was sure something in there that didn't belong.

And it was big, and it was dried out. I tried to dislodge the roll with my tongue, but it wouldn't budge, so I remained still and began mapping a strategy to reach up and grab the thing with my hand.

My left arm was twisted up and behind my head. I couldn't feel the arm, but I knew where it was because the thumbnail was embedded behind my ear.

I dragged my right hand, connected I'm sure to my right arm, up across my chest. My fingers crawled over my chin, and the dried out sour dough roll flinched like a turtle's head.

Apparently it wasn't a dried out hunk of bread sucking moisture from my mouth.

Those giggling, bubbling, cute little bouncy former volleyball players from New Jersey had cut off my tongue, left it out in the hot sun for a week, stomped on it a few times for good measure and then put it back in my mouth, all in the course of one night I now wished I could obliterate and swore I would never repeat.

Maybe I was dead.

I really needed some water, but I needed to move first.

I had no idea how long I'd been crashed with my feet sticking in the closet and my head wedged against the wastebasket beneath the little dorm desk, but my entire body felt very much like I'd been cast with plaster into this position. "Study in Papier Mache: Pathetic Freshman Demise."

I disentangled my left arm and clutched both legs beneath the knees, guiding them out of the closet. I swung them out toward the room and waited for the rest of me to follow, hoping the final impact would jolt my eyes open.

My neck felt like the venetian blinds must have felt last night after I crashed into them – tangled and broken metal sinews fully incapable of folding smoothly. My eyes finally opened, and they were immediately seared shut by the weak sun limping through those tangled blinds, shining distortedly and casting broken shadows across Adams' bed.

One of his black cowboy boots sat straight up on the unused pillow still tucked beneath the gold spread.

I remembered something about that cowboy boot.

Something about a contest of flipping beer bottle caps into it, something about Adams finding three cute and bubbly girls in the main hall, something about them somehow getting the impression that I was the champion beer bottle cap flipper from some dinky town in Minnesota, something about what a great coincidence that I drank the same drink they drank, something about all of us piling into their convertible Camaro and driving all over town looking for a liquor store where Adams or I hadn't already bounced a check, something about buying beer and whatever ingredients we needed to make our giggly cute and mutually favorite drink – something called sex-on-the-beach-shooters – something about ending up in our room, flipping beer bottle caps into a cowboy boot.

Like my lips, the memories were cracked and dusty, but they continued clearing into some kind of cohesion as I rolled over onto my hands and knees and finally stood up.

Pounding-BOOM.

Man alive! My mom was hoping I'd have a full and broadening social life at college. Did she want it for me so badly she would have approved of Adams and me, shamelessly lying to three former high school volleyball players from New Jersey who were cute and bouncy, all the while slamming ridiculously named drinks and competing for the beer bottle flipping championship of the universe?

I don't know, but I can't see her cheering last night.

"Look Ma, no brains."

That was me last night, the star of stupidity. Bottle cap flipping champ. I remembered perching on my left foot and leaning back while extending my right foot in the direction of the black cowboy boot on the bed. I draped my left arm around one of the cute and capable-of-doing-the-splits in New Jersey former high school volleyball players, squinted professionally, and took aim.

And then, in some surreal slow motion montage, the laws of physics reversed, and I recoiled from the preparatory energy of flipping the beer bottle cap. The cap dribbled off my thumb and forefinger and I shot myself backwards, crashing into the venetian blinds covering the only window in our dorm room.

I sort of doubt that's what my mom had in mind, but the splitting New Jersey giggling high school Hollywood bouncers loved it, and things get a bit foggy for me after that.

I think sex-on-the-beach-shooters contained vodka and fruit juice and other stuff, and I know Adams was spiking every batch with his reserve of Johnnie Walker Red, and I can't imagine a rational reason to attempt beer bottle cap flipping or bar recipe tinkering, ever again.

I sat back down on the side of my little bed, unused but not unmade. If I wasn't dead, I should be and wished I were.

A sedate death, coming quickly and making no mess, presented a radically improved alternative to living in a 12-foot by 12-foot experiment chamber with Cib Adams.

A clean death was a good prescription to the malaise caused by the last few months of close proximity to this guy – to the constant hemorrhage of my finances, to the anemia of my school work, and to this imminent explosion of my brain, pounding away inside of my head. Pounding, as I've said, Boom!

Adams was incredible, and he was killing me.

Class schedules, dorm curfews, and passed-out chums only spurred him to increasingly creative methods of "getting down."

"Dude, let's give it a rest. Your butt's going to mold to that hard little chair," he said to me early on during our first semester, while both of us were supposed to be reading up for our first test in Western Philosophy 101.

"Let's bag this studying crap and get the hell out of here for awhile. I've gotta get some blood flowing back up into my brain, what about you? Let's blow this gig."

"Adams, I can't just breeze through this stuff. I don't like the idea of flunking the first test I ever take in college. I don't even know what these guys are talking about."

"Philosophy, man. They're just talking philosophy. It's a no-brainer, buddy."

"No-brainer? Baloney no brainer. These guys are like the biggest philosophers in Western history, and I don't even know what they're talking about. Whitehead. What's Whitehead all about? William James. Descartes, for crud's sake. What's all this duality stuff? I mean it, Adams, I don't know what they're talking about. Determinism, for crud's sake. And this is an essay test. I sit here and I read these guys without understanding a word they're saying, and I've got to write intelligently about it at ten o'clock tomorrow morning, and I don't have a clue. I'm serious. You go if you're finished. I can't."

"Horseshit, Buddy. These guys've got you rattled cuz you see pictures of them wearing stupid little white British collars, because they're dead, and because they're using a lot of bullshit words to state some pretty obvious stuff."

"What are you talking about? Scholars have been studying these 'guys' for decades. You think all these scholars are idiots, spending years studying simplicity?"

"Hey, Johnny G, rule number one on scholars. They're not studying the concepts, they're studying all the bullshit around the concepts. It's job security. They stroke each other and stroke themselves and shoot wads all over the material and think they're writing brilliant papers, analyzing a cum stream. It has nothing to do with the concepts. Everybody knows the concepts. You know this stuff. It's natural knowledge. Kids know it. This class, these scholars, it's just bullshit trying to get us to confuse and hide the knowledge in the pursuit of it."

Adams stood behind me and lightly slapped the sides of my head. "Lose the fear, Buddy, throw out all the bullshit ladders leading to the attic and get to the good stuff stored up there.

"The Dualism of Descartes, what a crock of shit. All he's talking about is the physical is on one side, the mental is on the other, and they're constantly fluxing and balancing with each other defining the human condition – you know, a synthesis toward the spiritual. Which, by the way, is just a jerk-off way of saying who we are. It's just mind/body dualism, Buddy. The one can't cross to the other, and each is necessary for both. So you write your essay, and you

170

come up with your own idea, or you disagree or whatever, and when he reads your stuff, the Prof's nipples get hard cuz he's been reading essay after essay of freshman crap, and you write something intelligent and different, and you ace the test."

"You're out of your mind," I said. "There's no way it's that simple. And besides, I don't think we're supposed to be disagreeing with these philosophers, I think we're supposed to be learning them and understanding them."

"Dude, get a clue. Just because these guys are dead and in a college textbook doesn't mean they have a corner on the reality market. You're not learning shit if you don't interpret them. And you're wasting a lot of time and enduring a lot of brain damage by sitting here, scared to death of a bunch of blustery old farts. Slap 'em, man. Challenge 'em. Poke 'em in the eye with a wink of your own. Everybody, including Descartes and Whitehead, is sitting in the same reality. You've got just as much right to interpret it as they do." He slapped my head again. "Let's go get a pitcher and a pie, and interpret that reality for awhile."

"Adams, I've got three more chapters to read, and I don't even understand the notes I've taken. I can't go get a pizza. I think you're out of your mind. I'd like to pass my classes this semester."

"Suit yourself, Buddy. I've got to get out of here."

Adams sat on the edge of his bed, pulled on his boots and stuffed a pack of Kent's into the flap pocket of his jean jacket.

"Seen my Zippo? Shit, Man, every time I... Hold on, never mind. Got it."

He put on his jacket and grabbed his hat.

"I'll be back for you in an hour," he said. "And Buddy, for your own good, I'll drag your ass out of here.

"And listen here, Johnny G, don't sweat it. I don't know what the hell Whitehead is talking about either. If I have to write an essay on him, I'll just say he's some tight-ass anal aristocrat who used his brain to think himself into crossing conflicts, categorizing character as antithesis of human reach and endeavor. You know? I mean, the hell with Whitehead. Anybody that fucking obtuse probably sat around as a kid and read the dictionary all day long. Who the hell cares what a moron like that thinks? You know? Fuck Whitehead."

And Adams was serious. And he aced the test. I got a C-minus, complete with a written lecture from the prof, who obviously enjoyed no physical manifestations of pleasure in reading my essays:

"Mr. Gophe. Although your essays are well written, they demonstrate little understanding of the basic concepts involved. Consider re-reading the material and an overall increase in the rigors of your study. **C-***"*

***

And now Adams was killing me with partying.

My feet were still flat on the floor, but the rest of me sprawled motionless on the bed when Adams pushed open the door and came into the room.

"Softly," I hoped, whispering inside my head still. "Close the door softly."

"Dude! Champion Dude! Johnny G, the bottle cap Dude!" He threw his jean jacket on his bed. "You awake, man? Jesus, Bud, you look like shit."

I tried not to move. I hoped he'd go away.

"Wake up Buddy, we're walking to clover. Double score last night. TD and two-point conversion. You're gonna love this. Wake, up, man."

I could hear him pacing about the room, like some huge bull, snorting and stomping, busting with energy, the smell of fertile cows flaring his nostrils.

What was the deal here? I had watched the guy drink last night. I saw him throw down the shooters. I laughed along with the girls when he pulled out and repeatedly filled his trademark scrotum-shaped Scotch shot glass. I know he emptied most of the beer bottles, supplying contestants with twist-off bottle caps. What was the story on this guy? I hadn't moved from my bed all morning, and here he was, tearing into a box of Dolly Madison powdered sugar donuts, strutting around like he'd just spent a week at a health spa.

"Dammit, G. Get your butt up. Those three lovelies are gonna turn out to be our limousine trip out of this dump of a dorm. It'd be a lot better if both of us were conscious. C'mon, man, get up!

"Jesus! This room smells like a hog took a shit in a brewery. You really look like hell, Buddy. Get your ass up!"

I rolled over, resigned.

"What's wrong with you, Adams?" I sort of focused in his direction. "Shut up and get out of here. Where've you been this morning?"

"This morning, Buddy? Try last night. Left late. You've been cuttin' all by your little lonesome, all night long. Tried to get you to go with, so did the girls. Son, those were some beauties. You missed out and missed big. Thought about staying here with you, I really did. You know, sending three drunk and horny lovelies on their way and tucking you in and making sure you had your blankie up around your neck all night long."

"Go away, Adams." An admittedly weak defense, but my gloves were down and the guy had me backed against the ropes. A decision would be nice, but I knew the knockout was imminent.

"Wanted to stay with you, Buddy, I really did. But the Babes needed someone, you know, and they were so sweet about asking. Janice, Babe number two, was determined to bring you along. I gotta tell you, I've never seen a guy more determined to crash and miss out with such beautiful tight-bodied Babes. Hot damn, Buddy. What Babes. But really, I'm concerned about you. Did you have a good night's sleep? Stay warm? All cuddly, just you and your little winkie?

"Whooee," he screamed, "Buddy, did you miss out!"

Up until that moment, the most dangerous thing I'd ever done in my life was continue to masturbate, even though I wore glasses. But for just a moment I felt a slight surge, and it seemed possible I would get up and strangle this idiot.

"Adams, I mean it. Shut up! You're driving me crazy, and my head's about to explode. Get out of here, will you?"

"Can't do it, Buddy. No time. We've got to get moving, and we've got to get you looking a bit more presentable. Let's go! Up with the day, Son. This is our ticket.

"What's wrong with you?" I sat up and cranked my neck several times from side to side." What are you talking about?"

"Babes, Buddy. No, wait, better than that. Women. Real ones. Classy. Cool. I'm serious, man, the Chicks last night introduced me to this gorgeous, incredible woman. I mean, unbelievable. I'm in love, you will be too. Let's go. She invited us to brunch."

Adams opened the top drawer of my chest and grabbed a pair of my underwear. He stretched the waistband like a slingshot and flopped the underwear in my face.

"Jeans are cool, but grab a clean shirt. One of those button down ones, so you don't look like such a kid." He gathered his cowboy boots. "C'mon, I'll tell you about it while you're in the shower."

So there I was, severely hung over, thinking I would sleep all day and now being led by a maniac down the hall to the showers. I felt like a penitent sinner following a perverted priest.

Usually the showers were pretty empty on Sunday mornings. Guys were mostly hung over, sleeping late, or a few of the good ones had already eaten breakfast and were hitting the books to get ahead for Monday.

Sunday nights were shower crunch time, everybody getting it out of the way so they could sleep late Monday morning before rushing off to class.

So on Sunday nights, the place felt like a cattle processing plant – naked guys mindlessly herding themselves in and out, soaping up, rinsing off, toweling down.

If there had been keg parties during the Sunday football games, the guys were subdued, hung over from Saturday and then drinking again on Sunday. Blank stares, lackluster movement, inevitable procedure. Going through the motions.

The stalls were empty when we walked in. Adams plopped his boots on the floor and set his box of powdered sugar donuts on a shelf below the long row of mirrors. He walked out and returned with a chair from the lounge. One of those orange, molded plastic chairs with metal legs like on Sesame Street. He propped it against one of the sinks, pulled his boots on over his bare feet, leaned back in his chair, stretched his legs, and clunked his boots on the rim of the next sink. He settled back and stuffed half a powdered-sugar donut into his mouth.

I looked at him propped there – sort of rugged American Individualism Does Toilets, and I realized there was absolutely nothing incongruous about seeing him in the bathroom like that. The guy always belonged.

I remember from art history class, Michelangelo said he didn't actually carve his sculptures in the stone. Rather, he used a hammer and chisel to chip away the unnecessary pieces so the figures already in the stone could get out. That was Adams. No matter the environment, no matter the pieces around him, he just took over, chipping away all the pieces that didn't fit until Adams emerged.

He always looked the same. He always dressed the same. Black cowboy boots. Blue jeans. Jean jacket. T-shirt. Sometimes the T-shirt was brown or rust, sometimes black or white or blue, but it was always the same T-shirt. He carried a gold pocket watch inside the right flap pocket of his jean jacket. The gold chain looped out and down in front of the pocket like those little monocle chains old guys used to wear. I watched him as I stood in front of another mirror, brushing my teeth.

A lean, large, and loud guy, propped in a bathroom, fully content, munching away on powdered-sugar donuts.

A fellow came in and stepped up to the long white communal urinal. He looked at me and looked at Adams. Then he quietly retreated into one of the private stalls. Adams didn't seem to notice him, but suddenly, out of nowhere Adams said, "I hate it when somebody's watching and you can't pee, don't you Johnny G?"

He chuckled and grabbed another donut. I headed for the shower.

The college dorm showers always reminded me of junior-high gym class. One big, open stall covered with little brown tiles. Tiles everywhere – floor, ceiling, walls. Ugly tiles that were undoubtedly clean but looked like mold or something worse was growing on them.

One big drain in the middle of the floor sucked in the communal wastewater. A couple dozen stainless steel nozzles stuck out of the back and two side walls. Little nubs of nozzles that looked like penises and either sprayed hard enough to sting your skin or dribbled in giant drops.

Maybe the showers were different for girls in junior high gym class. I heard they had individual, private stalls. I don't know. But if they were individual, why were they individual? I mean, what was it that girls had that they weren't showing to each other? Maybe they had individual stalls for privacy from each other so as to increase the mystery of privacy from us.

But then that would require an extraordinarily well thought-out conspiracy on the part of somebody – designing private girls' showers to make boys curious and crazy – a conspiracy to rival the one thought up by whoever decided to give junior high school kids raging hormones, awakening sexuality and acne, all at the same time.

I don't know anything about junior high gym class for girls.

They had their own separate little gym upstairs above the music room. You never saw them in gym class. They would file into their locker room at the top of the stairs and then file out an hour later. Their hair was never wet. You never saw them carrying gym clothes around. You didn't see them having outside gym class during the warm months; you never heard the sound of balls, or jumping jacks, or running, or anything up there in their little gym.

What did girls do in junior high gym class? Did they perspire? What did their gym smell like? What did their showers smell like? What did they smell like when they perspired, or when they showered?

The boys' gym smelled like sweat mixed with the emerging body odor of adolescence. The locker room smelled like sweat mixed with Borax soap and urine. Plus mildewy towels and the pungent terror of boys self consciously gauging the relative sprouting of their pubic hair.

For the majority of kids who shared a similar stage of genital development, junior high gym class was shocking and uncomfortable. But there were always those few poor fellows weighing in at either end of the spectrum: guys hanging little pencil thin worms less than an inch long, surrounded by nothing but barren baby's-butt skin, or, on the other end, guys with hairy legs, sporting a dense-growth forest between them. Either way, they didn't fit in, and not fitting in was the one leprosy of junior-high.

All in all, junior-high gym class smelled like a spitting fire of confusion, which I guess pretty much describes junior-high.

Like I say, I can't imagine for a moment what God could possibly have been thinking when He came up with the idea of combining hormones, adolescence, and junior-high.

Apparently He decided to make it a little easier on the girls by giving them private shower stalls.

He threw the boys all together in a communal shower stall, and then he inflicted us with an uncontrollable urge to check out other penises. You'd try hard to be discreet – stealing a quick glance or aiming your eyes about a foot off the ground, as you toweled off your hair and tilted your head so it looked like you weren't really looking at anything at all. But you couldn't stop yourself from looking; and you knew the guy knew you were looking, because you knew every time another guy was looking at yours.

Maybe it was a dominance thing, maybe just curiosity. But, as it turns out, it wasn't just a junior high thing. It still happens. All the time. At health clubs, public swimming pools, while looking in the mirror. Even in the college dorm communal shower.

I didn't think too much about it while I showered and Adams ate powdered sugar donuts because he was on about women. He liked them a lot.

"Know what I mean, Buddy? You hardly ever meet a woman. Chicks and babes are everywhere, you know? And they're great, and you need 'em – a real purpose in life. But Jesus H., a woman, a real woman, is rare."

Adams gave out one of those construction guy-whistles – kind of sexy and between his teeth. He grinned at me and gave me the Adams wink.

"Good Lord," He giggled, "There sure as hell is something pretty knock-down different about a woman.

"I'm not talking frilly or prissy or anything like that. You see a chick throwing a Frisbee, and it's cool, and you make all the remarks, the whistles, the catcalls. Boorish, really, but a hell of a lot of fun. And no one's hurt, cuz the chick's out there in her tight-ass little cut-off jeans.

"You know, and the sun's hitting her blond hair; she's barefoot with one of those little bell bracelets on her ankle – cute as shit, even if she's rough around the edges, and she knows she's sexy.

"She knows she's got gorgeous sun-tanned legs, and she loves it when you watch her bend over to pick up the Frisbee, and who gives a shit? You know? She wants macho and you want a piece of ass. The rules are simple and the game's a slam dunk."

And Adams just kind of rambled on and on about chicks and women. I caught some of it, but he did tend to get carried away with the sounds of his own storytelling. The entertaining thing about him was that you could listen or not. Tune in and skate along with his analogies and metaphors, or just drift on about your own business. It's not like he talked just to hear himself, but he usually pushed a pretty broad broom toward a very abstract pile. Even if you didn't catch every bit of debris being shuffled along, it was easy to follow the general collapse of the circle. Just like cleaning a garage, where you sweep hard around the edges of the walls and underneath the workbench. Then you move the broom around the smooth concrete, pushing the dirt and dry leaves toward the garbage can in the middle. You generally had a pretty good idea where the pile would end up, so it wasn't critical to follow the precise movement of every broom stroke.

When I was first getting to know Adams, I'd frequently apologize for lapses in attention.

"Sorry Bud," I'd say, interrupting his rambling. "What was that?"

"I don't know," he'd say, laughing. "Weren't you listening either?"

Standing naked in the shower listening to him ramble on about women contorted my own thoughts about girls into some pathetic effort of drilling peepholes in bathroom walls. I had no idea where this current sweeping of debris was headed, but naked and unprotected as I was, and increasingly graphic and erotic as his descriptions became, I moved one hand a bit nearer the cold water faucet, just in case.

"Chicks are great but a woman is incredible. Everything about a woman is different. I don't know what," Adams said, "but it's all different.

"Same tight, sexy ass. Same legs. You know, but different. You watch a chick play Frisbee, and you imagine being on top of her in bed, just pounding away. But with a woman, it's different. A woman is like color and light in Monet or Cezanne. A woman is where the eye enters the art of life.

"You imagine her standing on one of those arched stone bridges crossing a stream. The bridge is filled with sun, and you're down in the water. You're down below, maybe ten, maybe fifteen feet. Maybe you're fly fishing, just kind of lazily moving the fly through the air, drifting it around the water, just kind of letting it go. There's pine trees everywhere, and wind high up in them.

"You can feel the cold pressure of the water against your hip boots, and you can see everything in the crystal water – rocks, gravel, floating sticks and feeding trout. You start working the fall-off in front of a rock, casting your line back and forth across the stream.

The line arcs through the air like some gigantically gentle green spider's web. Now it catches the sun, now it dips into shade.

"Back and forth in great arcs, you've got 20, or maybe 25 feet of line flowing into the air from your fly rod. The rod bends and whips the line, and the line moves and floats with this subtle, majestic energy because of controlled, tight motions of your wrist and forearm.

"You finally get the line where you want it and you place the fly at the start of the current, well above the rock. You get this incredible rush because you didn't disturb the water at all. The fly lands perfectly. The line trails off and settles in a picture perfect loop above your fly. You watch the fly and the leader float with the soft current as you slowly strip in the line. You can hear the water kind of gurgling over rocks, and you can smell it running swift and deep in the channels. Everything's gentle, everything's soft until the fly hits the rush of water around the rock.

"Your arm tightens, you loosen your grip on the rod and wait for the fish to hit. You have to be alert, because the fish are wary, they're always a little on guard.

"The water bubbles into a froth below the rock, and you can't see the fly, but you watch the line for the hit, and she's up there with the sun at her back. She's not really looking at you, but she's looking your way, kind of past you, kind of into the stream, into the water, but past the water. Looking and seeing different kinds of things.

"Her dress, thin, gauzy cotton, is backlit with the sun. The light comes through, so you can see into the dress. Like the fly line, inside the dress is this quiet explosion of flowing lines and fluid movement.

"The energy starts down low at the ankles and calves. It moves slowly down there – a soft swirl – but you can feel the tension, feel the growing momentum. The thighs are a little bowed, they go out at the knees and there's a flowing arc moving back and forth between them. Her thigh muscles are relaxed but they bend taut like your fly rod. Then everything picks up speed, racing up the inside of her thighs, and the lines crash back together and collide into her hot fury of hair.

"The lines and the energy swirl again and move gently back out into her hips, and then in again flat and strong at the stomach. It starts to feel like white-water rafting, and you begin to confuse the calm stream. You get dizzy with the motion and disoriented with all the fluid lines and flowing motion. The toe of your hip boot is suddenly above your knee, then it's below the gravel, then it's out of the water all together. The current suddenly starts flowing in all directions at once. The sun somehow finds your back and your fishing vest soaks in sweat. Your eyes sting from the sweat coming off your forehead. The gently swirling eddies around rocks and small currents at the shore start speeding up and the swirls become whirlpools and the rocks become boulders. Everything moves faster and faster. The drag on your fly is intense, tugging and tiring your arm.

"You can feel her stomach muscles struggling to hold all the lines together, and then Wham!, the motion erupts out again and circles into breasts. Her round nipples never completely relax, they're always on guard, always on watch. It's those little erect nipples, showing nonchalantly under her clothes, that keep you coming back.

"Dag," I said, suddenly and acutely aware of that familiar groin pulse. I thrashed about, searching frantically for thoughts of fishing while reaching for the cold water faucet.

"And you know," I said, desperately grinding the gears in my mind, jolting my groin out of four wheel high, "it doesn't matter how well you false cast, how well you drift the fly, how much like a real insect it looks. For all its art and grace, fly-fishing isn't an exercise in imitating bugs. You could go all day without a single strike, and as long as you believe the next drift might bring a fish, you can enjoy the dickens out of a day of fly fishing."

"Exactly," Adams said. "Fly fishing's good just by itself. I could watch a guy reeling 'em in all day long with worms, but I'd never switch off flies, even with no strike, no fish, no nothing."

"But that's because you believe you *might* get a strike the very next drift," I said, relieved that my own little fly rod had finally relaxed. "If you knew there wasn't a trout for a mile upstream or down, you'd lose interest. No matter how much you enjoy the act itself, no matter how peaceful and serene the river, no matter how perfect your casts, no matter how much you don't care whether or not you catch a fish, you've got to know you *might*."

"Absolutely. Good point!" Adams said, enthused nearly off his chair. "Good fucking point."

At that moment, I could have had a boner from here to junior high and not been embarrassed. "Good point" was the highest compliment Adams ever paid. I didn't even know for sure what point I'd just made, exactly, but Adams liked it and I loved it. Later, I would hate myself for taking such pleasure in his acknowledgement, for repeating my role as his prized duck. He never encouraged me to seek his approval; he took no obvious pleasure when I did, but I hated wearing the obsequious feathers of a sycophant.

"And that's why extraordinary women are the same way," Adams said. "Just like fly fishing. Chicks are like drowning worms, any idiot can catch one. Fly fishing's like a gorgeous woman."

He sat back and popped another donut into his mouth and then sat there like a little kid munching contentedly. "And you know," he finally said, "it's not about sex and you never catch the fish, and the burn in your gut never goes away."

***

I realize now I could have stopped the whole thing there and then. Adams was a fly line finagler; the truth is he was a lousy fly fisherman, and I didn't have the guts to tell him. He was enamored with manipulating the line, with false casting, with creating all this fluid motion nonsense and ridiculous flowing line. From that moment on, he believed Nattie Sinclair stood above him on the bridge all gorgeous and see-through. She wasn't, and I see that now and could have made him see that then.

But he said "good point," and I lacked the courage to push on and make him understand that his flowing lines and false casts were silly affectations that would get him hurt, or at least explain why he never caught fish.

From the moment he met her the night before, through all our college craziness and into the hell of Becky Dreiling's farm, she spit the hook back into his willing, smiling mouth and then she set it hard. She darted and flashed about him like an enormous and blood-red cutthroat trout; wiley when he crouched low for his stealth approach, fast as a shark when she hit his line, and strong as a whale when she pulled him in. Fishing for Nattie Sinclair was dangerous. Adams never had a chance and he never saw it coming. In the end he'd lose more than his line.

He tied lazy knots in his leader. He picked fly patterns poorly. Like all idiot playboys or mediocre fishermen, he concentrated exclusively on delivering a good line. Nattie Sinclair, like an experienced German Brown or a woman out for herself, saw beyond the line and watched for the fisherman.

Adams played people and situations better than anyone. He was the champ. But there wasn't a malevolent hook in his creel. He inhaled life as a series of "yucks" and "hoots." There wasn't even a lure of self-preservation in his tackle. Before Nattie Sinclair, it didn't matter. He easily dominated, so he had no need to watch out for himself. His exuberance, quick smile, wit, and intelligence protected him well enough.

But with Nattie Sinclair he spilled his tackle into a jangle of entangled hooks – he became a trout farm water-beater who stupidly hiked too far up the canyon chasing a gold medal stream.

"Like Ken Kesey might say, any kind of hot sauce will do,
As long as it comes from Avery Island."

- Cib Carkus Adams

Chapter 10

I stopped going to Sunday Mass the day Adams and I first attended Nattie Sinclair's Sunday morning soiree.

I had never missed Sunday Mass in my life; even as a kid on camping trips or vacation, my dad would search out a church and we'd go to Sunday Mass. It was sacrosanct. Sunday Mass represented the tradition, it represented my father's religion, it represented where I was supposed to be.

But Adams absolutely insisted we were going to attend this Sunday morning soiree. I missed Mass that morning. The next weekend I officially became the kind of Catholic my father despised – a Saturday-nighter. Mass at five o'clock on Saturday night. It didn't feel the same; it was too easy, so not much of a sacrifice, not like waking early and getting all dressed up and going on a Sunday morning. Because of Nattie Sinclair, my Sunday sacrament now came from what increasingly felt like paganism – celebrations of intellect, celebrations of food and song, celebrations of joy and style. Sunday soirees.

***

"Death to form. Die for content."

That's how Nattie Sinclair began every Sunday morning soiree.

"Ladies and gentlemen, welcome to my home, and to this soiree. Help yourselves to the food, to the ideas, and to the enthusiasms spread out before you. Let's enjoy ourselves and challenge ourselves and most of all, let's celebrate the death of form, and let's kill and die for content."

Everyone always took it seriously, so I did too. After a while, it struck me as ritualistic and almost sacred. It came to sound like a blessing. At first, I was pretty sure a soiree had to happen in the evening, and so I figured Nattie was just trying to be rebellious or contrary. But after awhile, and to this day, the actual meaning of the word changed for me. Nattie Sinclair had that affect on people. At least she did on me.

The morning Adams and I first entered Nattie Sinclair's Bohemian world, we stood on her front porch. I was feeling guilty about missing Mass and Adams was excited about getting to know this incredible woman he had met the night before, who turned out, of course, to be Nattie Sinclair. That's the same night I tried to commit suicide by alcohol and fraternity nonsense. I may have already talked about that night, I don't remember. If I did my continued existence may be something of a surprise.

We stood there on this big wooden porch, and Adams rapped on Nattie Sinclair's front door with a brass doorknocker that was two split, bare, female legs. All the way up. You grabbed the ankles and pounded them onto bedposts.

"Ah, last evening's poet warrior," Nattie said when she opened the door.

"Doing battle only with internal demons and the beauty of a new day," Adams said, sounding like he talked that way all the time.

He was right about her. She was not a girl, she was a woman. She was our age, but she was drop-dead gorgeous in a real mom kind of way. I don't mean she looked like my mom, or anyone else's mom I'd ever seen, but she exuded this alluring combination of familiarity, sexiness, and nurturing. She was a woman.

Remarkable emerald eyes, ringed in black circles, twinkled with trickster delight. Her blue jeans didn't go up into her waist like most girls wore them but stopped at the top of her hips, so the tucked in white T-shirt suggested her waist rather than accentuated it.

She wasn't wearing a bra, but she wasn't big and floppy and large. It's a silly word but I thought "perky"; her breasts drew this incredible line on the outside of her torso. Maybe that's what I mean about mom gorgeous; cleavage is somebody's girlfriend – mysterious and compelling and off limits. This soft, outside the body tear-drop line of breasts I was staring at, while standing next to Adams on Nattie Sinclair's front porch, was safe and inviting and felt like being home. I shifted my feet and scraped the wooden slats of the porch to draw attention away from my boner as I stared at her breasts.

"Who's the sidekick with pectoral envy?" She smiled at me.

"Just hung over and far from home," Adams said. "Johnny G, say hello to Nattie Sinclair, our hostess and brand new best friend."

I sort of gulped like a little kid and shook her hand. "John Gophe," I said. I wished my hair wasn't still wet from my shower.

"If you're a friend of Cib Adams you're a friend to this house. Welcome," she said. Come in."

It felt like we were walking into some kind of cinema satire of a beatnik coffeehouse. Guys with berets and goatees, girls in long straw skirts and white puffy blouses, bare feet and black coffee. I had seen some of these people hanging around the art building, and others looked like they were too old for college.

This was a real house, with real furniture and real people milling about. It was as far away from our regimented dorm life as my button-down suburban finger sandwiches were from Adams' voracious appetite for the entire feast of existence. Adams and I looked like we were costumed for a Halloween party: me in khaki's, topsiders and a white oxford shirt; he in his denim and cowboy boots. Adams mixed and mingled with his usual ease, but without the bravado I'd seen and admired so often. Suddenly, in this urbane living room, he was graceful and gracious, and if I didn't know better I would say he was modest, or even soft and sweet. I kept waiting for him to emerge from this chrysalis of understatement and beat his gregarious wings. He was calmed by walking into this world of magic; he too had fallen beneath the spell of this seductress of fantastical truth.

Nattie Sinclair slipped her arm through mine. "Come," she said, "let me introduce you around."

I almost couldn't stand to look at her, and I sure couldn't stand to look away. I'd never been this close to any woman this beautiful in my life, certainly not one who was touching me. It reminded me how I used to feel about that girl, Catherine Teaza, when I was a kid. They were both exquisite, especially the eyes. Vibrant emerald green with thin black circles ringing the edges of the irises. Nattie used them to look right into your soul while, curiously, not seeing you at all. I wasn't remembering the names of any of the people I was being introduced to. Having her on my arm was fabulous, the same way wearing a nice suit to a funeral or a wedding makes you feel important, only a thousand times more. Everything about her said gorgeous, caring and warm, class and beautiful style. She kept telling people I was a promising young man with a writer's eye and a child's heart.

"Our salvation," she told a brown-haired woman with huge boobs and tons of necklaces, "from this empty decade devoid of soul."

"Thanks," I said. "But I doubt it. How do you know anything about me, anyway? Whatever Adams told you is probably not true."

"Mr. Adams is raw material. Promising," she said, turning and catching his eye from across the room, "but raw. No, Mr. Gophe, your reputation precedes you this morning. Our resident wizard beguiles us with impressive tales of your literary accomplishments. He sees great things from you. We're delighted to have you in our circle."

For some reason I thought of the hags, those Weird Sisters, in Macbeth. It was bizarre having a stranger describe me. She might be crazy, but the many curious books on the shelves, smoking incense, and other exotic stuff all over the house suggested she might really know a wizard, so I kept my mouth shut and just smiled. I finally sat down on a couch next to the brown-haired woman with the huge boobs and gypsy dress. The tops of her big boobs kind of bubbled and bounced around at the top of her blouse, like she had two water balloons stashed in there. Her skin was really smooth and dark golden, almost olive, and it was hard not to stare at these fake jewels and seashells she wore, riding up and down on these enormous swells, in and out of her cleavage.

She asked me about my favorite authors, who I liked and why. The buzz in my stomach felt like when the clock is ticking and you haven't finished the essays for a test.

"Don't you agree that contemporary American fiction died on the tracks with Kerouac?" She shifted a little closer on the sofa. I did everything I could think of to keep from looking at those boobs trying with vigor and enthusiasm to jump out of her blouse.

"Died on the tracks with Kerouac?" I said, stalling for time. I thought it was Neal Cassady, and, in any event, it seemed to me the issue was more complicated than that.

"I think Pynchon and Gaddis are interesting, and John Barth may be brilliant," I said, feeling pretty safe because that was the basis of a lecture I remember from Contemporary Lit, and the Prof was the chair of the department.

"Horseshit," said a voice behind us. The gypsy woman and I turned and saw a guy who looked awfully familiar from the night before at the keg party.

"Daniel O'Neill," he said, extending his hand. "We met for the second time at the Frat boys' shindig last night, and you didn't remember me then, either. Shit, son, last night you looked rode hard and put away wet. You clean up fine. You write well, too. Remember Janeway's creative writing class? I sat in the back, in the corner."

"You're the wizard," I said, suddenly remembering his curt comments and astute criticisms.

"Ah, so you've met Nattie. Be mindful of her. That one's a witch who sees wizards when she doesn't understand whiskers. So naturally she makes me a wizard. Simpler, really. Just a failed Irish farmer from Kansas."

"A farmer with the blood of kings running in his veins and dripping from the severed hand of honor claimed for the common man," Nattie said as she slipped up behind him and lightly kissed his cheek. "An Irish farmer who belongs for a hundred years in the service of the queen."

I watched their eyes lock, an explosion of emerald and platinum, and then he turned back to me.

"They won't be reading John Barth in a hundred years, and Pynchon won't be teaching anyone how to read anything once the fad of the ridiculously obtuse is gone. Barth is a brilliant technician, but it's masturbation, not creation, when your subject's the craft and the process; Barth does it again and again.

"They'll read some Hemingway in a hundred years, and all of Faulkner, and a lot of Steinbeck, and that single pop-fart of art Fitzgerald put out amongst all his other self serving drivel and diarrhea."

"Hemingway was a horse's ass," Nattie said. "If he was here this morning, you'd be more inclined to send your boot through his pompous crotch than take seriously his macho ranting."

"For shame, Nattie Sinclair. Making the mistake of confusing the art with the artist. Gertrude Stein was a bitch, Sylvia Plath a manic-depressive married to an egomaniac. Their art, because it's real, stands by itself. Imagine what a prick Little Bobby Zimmerman might be if he sauntered into the room right now."

"True enough," she allowed. "But you do tend to overstate the value of simplicity for its own sake."

"Not simplicity, raw-edged endeavor. Not a goddamn thing simple about Dostoyevsky, or Camus, certainly not Shakespeare or Uncle Leo."

"Yes, but don't you think *Anna Karenina* is really just an overblown and overstated miniature glimpse into a relatively common slice of life?" The gypsy woman with the enormous boobs didn't seem too sure of herself, and she looked at Nattie for support. "That story line seems kind of simple to me, although I like the book," she said apologetically.

"Course you like the book," said the Wizard. "Exploring the day to day intrigues of an unhappy woman searching for greater meaning seems simple enough, but along the way you just happen upon ageless questions concerning what we want, and what we get due to what we expect. Not a hell of a lot simple about that."

I felt like it would be a really good idea if I said something, preferably something intelligent. I was floundering in a whirlpool of a warped reality. This is what college was all about, this is what all the class discussions were preparing me for, this was my chance to put my dad's tuition money to good use. I had finally arrived at a place beyond practice, beyond preparation. Trouble was, all likely candidates for intelligent response were hiding out, shy or suddenly stupid, refusing to emerge from the crevices inside my brain. I had absolutely nothing to say. There was not a coherent thought to be found. So I blurted.

"I guess it seems stupid, but isn't art, at least in literature, less something created brand new and more like an energy that just floats around until somebody happens upon a strand of it and rides along with it somehow and gives it form?"

"Value based exclusively on individual interpretation?" Nattie sounded either intrigued or incredulous.

"I guess so. I mean, if I sit down to write or paint, and I think it's brilliant, and it flows and it's real, but it does absolutely nothing for anyone else, gives not one other soul a vision of anything beyond, I don't think that's art. If it is, than every 12-year-old girl who writes in a diary is an artist. I think that's craft, or therapy, or something, you know? Maybe sweet or true, but probably not art. I don't know," I said quietly.

Adams walked over holding a plate piled high with quiche and purple grapes. A rush of relief swelled over me. He might be full of baloney, but I welcomed and anticipated his off-handed slam against the mental gymnastics we were engaging in, relief mostly because I believed that the longer this went on, the more likely I was to miss one of the parallel bars and smash my face into the balance beam below.

"I agree, Johnny G.," he said nonchalantly. "Kind of like searching for Tabasco to put on a slice of quiche." He motioned over his shoulder, toward the kitchen. "Fellow in there insisted I was insulting the chef by rummaging around for New Iberia's finest. Couldn't seem to convince him it was possible to improve on perfection. One man's Tabasco is another's cream cheese. This quiche is perfect with a dash of the sauce. Same quiche is perfect, to another fellow, without."

My God. Here he was, doing it again. He was going to convince these people about something to do with artistic merit by discussing Tabasco sauce.

"But all that means is either everything is perfect, or nothing is. Relativism," Nattie said with a slow smile, "is rather passé, don't you think?"

"Relativism is the only real thing there is. Everything that matters, everything we do or don't do has meaning only to the extent that somebody, somewhere, gives a shit."

"Birds don't read the classics and winners of wars write the history," Daniel O'Neill offered.

"Exactly. Good point. Imagine how different our values, our morality, our sense of truth would be if the Indians had kicked ass on the invading Europeans, or if alley cats had started walking around on two feet before monkeys did. Anything that's real is totally dependent on whoever's around to care and take notes."

Most of the 20 or so people in the house had gathered around the sofa like a casting call for a "College Life" movie. It was one of those pure moments in life, albeit filled with post-adolescent self-importance and a good smattering of intellectual nonsense, but I remember it often when I sit these days alone at night trying to look up at the stars. The skies now are so foggy and hazy and cluttered with the disappointments of growing up and being alive. That fresh and exhausting enthusiasm with a world brand new has long ago calcified. That's the source of the world's insanity – everyone mourns the closing of their college chapter, even if they didn't go to college. But everyone got close to the edge, got to the experience of cutting loose and adventuring as a first time explorer, and then retreated and compromised and gave up and gave in. I know it's the source of mine.

Well, that and Becky Dreiling's farm.

You can read poetry all your life but you can only read it the first time one time. I don't so much want to go back to those days as I want to bring them with me.

Everything is pathetic now and everything was fresh then, and what makes me crazier still is that I know that's not even true, but rather a self-defeating outlook symptomatic of my condition.

"There's only one thing with its own reality, needing no interpretation or communion with humanity," Adams went on. "The first thing, the impetus for us, and for anything of meaning."

"I could have guessed your Hollywood cowboy image was really a facade for typical Midwestern meat and potatoes values. Home-cooked meals with the family around the table and God safe in his church on Sundays. God died in the 60's, friend," a beatnik beret guy said, "and he's been castrated and cremated since."

Nattie Sinclair's eyes glowed and she leveled a glare at the beatnik. I learned later she set no limits on topics or disagreements, but she had no tolerance for personal attacks, prejudice or banality.

"God's certainly an important part of our need for a collective myth," Adams said with no hint of hostility or defensiveness. "But I think you would agree, 'friend,' that man created God out of his need, not the other way around. But well before there was God there was the creation of man, and that act is the one thing that makes any of this relevant."

I watched Nattie almost sigh with relief, and with the pleasure of being able to sit back and observe with no need to police the situation. There in Nattie's living room I was seeing, for the first time, the schematic of their relationship, the wiring diagram that kept the thing sparked and alive. They fed off each other while they fed each other. They often had entire conversations without ever saying a word to each other. I don't mean that unspoken, soul connection nonsense of Romance novels. But in a room full of people, one or the other or both could engage in conversation with others and, at the same time, actually be talking back and forth with each other, generally without anyone else catching on that they were just props in a much larger production; props who not only were unaware of their unimportance but who didn't even realize there was another show going on.

"That's a reality worth a second look," Daniel O'Neill said. "We started as dust and will end as dust. We're just like dogs and largemouth bass, only carrying around a bigger computer in our briefcases."

"But certainly there are qualitative differences between us and other animals," Nattie said. "Even if we don't usually live up to the billing, we are the headliners, the stars of the show. We are aware, conscious, capable of loving and despising, aspiring and inspiring. There's something different, something very special and unique about us."

"We eat quiche," somebody joked.

"Of course there's something different," Adams said. "Everything about us is different."

"Brain chemicals and complicated circuitry," said the beatnik beret guy.

"Nah, those are the tools we've developed over the centuries to keep up with our humanity."

"Then if not God, who or what created us?"

"Poetry," Adams said.

The big-boobed gypsy enthusiastically agreed. "There are so many times a good poem speaks directly to the essence of humanity, lifting us above the mundanc. Poctry is divine."

"The Muse," a serious, blond-haired woman named Barbara said, "is directly from the gods. The Muse is a terrible lover and a comforting enemy. The Muse is the ultimate, and the Muse brings poetry."

"What I mean," Adams continued, "is that poetry actually created man. Not defined or improved, but created man. And so consequently, poetry created God."

"I don't get it," somebody said. "You mean, like, poetry is a supernatural force?"

"I mean that poetry is ultimately primal symbol. Of course it's a manipulation of language, but at its core, it's pure symbol."

"So's language," somebody said.

"Yeah, but language requires thought. It came much later. It was born of poetry."

"So how's that make poetry the great heavenly father?"

The beatnik beret guy said this, and though he didn't seem ready to throw in the towel of devil's advocate, he sounded less accusing, more interested.

"Okay," Adams said. "Imagine a group of apes standing around a rock or something, grunting and screaming at each other. Suddenly, a little ape screams at a big ape who just stepped on his foot. But he doesn't holler and gnash his teeth and bare his claws, he screams sounds in a rhythm. The rudiments of poetry. Then he repeats it. Now he's not just verbally reacting to pain or fear, he's threatening to get even, or planning to run away, or maybe calling his buddies. He's aware. At that instant, symbol in his sounds created consciousness in his brain. The grunting and screaming are direct audio responses to emotions. But now, the little monkey is not directly expressing his anger, he's repeating something that *represents* how pissed off he is. Symbol. Poetry. Embryos of language and thought. Ancestors of consciousness."

"Monkeys and apes are different animals," the beatnik guy said lamely.

"Yeah, well, whatever," Adams said to him. "That's not the point. The point is, that first rhythmic grunting was the first poem, and it created thought and consciousness and self-awareness, which for all practical purposes created reality. Then it created God, and things got pretty interesting after that."

"This is the first time since I used to sit as a kid and contemplate cow pies that I've had reason to question my own philosophy," Daniel O'Neill said. "Interesting."

"Interesting indeed," Nattie said, casting a glance at the beatnik. "But how's that different than monkeys of today, who make repetitive, rhythmic and identifiable sounds to express fear or anger or belonging? They haven't evolved into humans."

"Uh oh," Daniel O'Neill said. "Another philosophy shit-canned by rationality."

"Probably no different," Adams said. "But if I explore that track, then ultimately I probably have to give up my nice little theory about poetry being sacred and creating reality. Who was it said man must ultimately make a leap of faith, and it's that ability to make the leap that gives us the glimpse of the divine?"

"Jesus," somebody said.

"No, Samuel Coleridge."

"John Lennon."

"Some wimpy apologist for Jell-O logic," the beatnik said with incredible satisfaction.

"Whoever. Since it's probably true we can't ever really know, I think we all have the right to create our own comforting myths. That's mine."

Nattie listened to Adams with a smile. She looked at him as if she were standing over a puppy that just got run over but was still clutching the rear tire of the beer truck in its little teeth.

"Mr. Adams, that was either the biggest crock of manipulated bullshit I've ever heard, or the most graceful retreat this living room's ever seen. Do you like the quiche?"

"Delicious," Adams said, returning her smile. "Did you make it?"

"I did. Try it with Tabasco sauce."

"It's perfect with Tabasco sauce. I love it with Tabasco sauce. I think I'll have some more with Tabasco sauce."

"Help yourself. I never use Tabasco sauce myself, but I made this one perfect for Tabasco sauce. I'm glad you like it."

"I love it."

***

Daniel O'Neill moved in to Nattie Sinclair's house at the same time Adams and I did, after I returned from the summer in the fall of our sophomore year. The four of us were already spending an awful lot of time together what with cruising around in the 1965 Plymouth Valiant coupled with the intense, immediate attraction between Nattie and Adams. It was like we almost all lived together already, even when Adams and I were still in the dorm. It made sense to share a house and the expenses. I got money sent from home; I think Nattie Sinclair had a rich great aunt, or was maybe a trust fund baby. Adams roofed houses on Tuesdays, Thursdays, and

Saturdays to make money. I pretended to have no idea how Daniel O'Neill paid his share of the expenses.

My room was in the partial basement, a cot on a concrete floor surrounded by a soft brick foundation. An old black and red braided rug covered most of the floor. There were some cobwebs and a little dust, but Adams and I threw up some sheetrock on the ceiling rafters, and Nattie hung some fabric stuff to cover some of the rusty orange brick walls, and it suited me fine. Daniel O'Neill had a pullout couch in a sunroom off the kitchen; he and I shared a bathroom back there. Since he was always up at dawn and out till forever, it often seemed like he didn't live there at all.

Adams and Nattie took over the entire second story of the house. They had a bathroom, a bedroom, and a sitting room where Nattie kept her easel; and Adams lifted weights and watched her paint.

Adams gave me his dorm collection of drinking mugs to decorate my room, but I never unpacked them from the cardboard box. We all shared the main floor's dinky living room and huge kitchen. Adams liked to spend time figuring out where and how somebody had remodeled the kitchen some time ago. They had cut into the living room and used a small main floor bedroom, so the kitchen wrapped around half of the main story. A wood-burning stove sat inside a hearth of old bricks, and if you built the fire right it never smoked and would heat the entire house. The floor was all old brick too, so in the winters it heated up nicely. We spent all our time together there. We used to spend hours sitting around that fire playing pinochle, a game we all learned from Daniel. You never really figure on how much time you spend in a kitchen until you share a house with other people, like gathering around the communal fire pit.

My favorite time around the fire pit was pretty early one Saturday morning when it was just Nattie Sinclair and me. I couldn't really sleep; preparing for the homecoming football game coming up in the afternoon made sleeping seem almost sinful, but in a positive, motivating way. I knew I'd have to hustle after the game in order to make it to five o'clock Saturday Mass, and then hustle out of there to catch up at the parties, so relaxing in the morning seemed like a good idea.

From up in the kitchen, soft nesting noises filtered down into my room. I threw on my robe and slippers and shuffled up the stairs and into the kitchen.

Nattie usually didn't fool with making a fire; she'd just crank the gas furnace up and call it good. But this morning she had a hot blaze going in the wood stove. Her flannel robe was already slung over a chair, so she was only wearing a long white T-shirt that hit her just a bit above her knees.

She turned casually when I walked in.

"Morning, Johnny." She smiled and I just stood there looking at her, like I was watching the unfolding of history.

"Good morning," I finally said.

Nattie Sinclair smiled at me again before turning back toward the sink. She tilted her head back over her shoulder.

"Coffee's pretty good. I think I'm figuring out the great mystery of percolation. Want a bagel?"

"Sure, okay," I said. "Or I can get it."

"Don't bother. Grab some coffee and sit down, Johnny. I'd love to get it for you. I'll even make you some eggs. I've got some kind of euphoric domestic buzz going on here this morning. I feel like I could work in this kitchen forever."

And she looked like she could. A kitchen goddess, nurturer in a nightgown. The sunrise streaming through the window above the sink hit right onto Nattie; it illuminated her. Since it was a T-shirt you couldn't see into it, and I was kind of glad. But the sun and the shirt made wonderful shadows: the fabric was just a little snug around the front and sides of her breasts, and again just a little down at her hips and rear end. Everything else was free-form cotton that you just knew smelled great. I sat down at that kitchen table, and I could have sat there forever, just taking it all in. I don't remember if we won the football game or not that day, but whenever I think of homecoming, I think of Nattie Sinclair. At some point that morning, I remember she smiled warm at me and said, "This is so nice, Johnny. This feels like being home."

Usually Daniel was the first one up. Always before the sun he'd build a fire, make coffee and then do stretching and meditation. He did this Chinese thing. I watched him do it once when he didn't realize intestinal disorders had awakened me early.

He repeated a routine in the dark kitchen where he moved slowly around the hot wood stove. He formed his body into shapes of different animals – a perched crane, or an attacking bear, or a coiled snake. He'd hold each position for a long time, a minute or so, and then carefully contort into the next. He did maybe a dozen of them, several times over for almost an hour, dancing ever so slowly around the wood fire. And he was stark naked the whole time.

It was bizarre to watch: tiny cross-hatches of light coming from the grate slits on the cast iron wood stove getting all distorted by this shadowy human animal as it gyrated around the fire.

And that's how it felt living together that year, the four of us. A primal dance around the edges of reality. Fire pits. Witches and cave drawings. Nattie Sinclair held things with her eyes, and things got lost there. Deep things, dangerous things, nonsense. She oozed familiarity, not so much like someone you knew but like someone who knew you. At first I thought I actually did know her from before but then I realized I was just sucked into her realm of familiarity, like what people call Déjà Vu. It's not a memory of something you've seen or done before; it's more like a signpost telling you you're on the right path. Being around Nattie Sinclair was like that. It was important to her that we feel and act like a family. Important to all of us, sure, because it was important to her.

She was the energy, the lubrication in the house. She didn't feign excitement like a Cub Scout mom, but she was the center of our little world. I didn't know anything, really, about her life outside of our house, almost like she had no other life, came from nowhere, going nowhere. She never talked about plans for her future, never talked about where she grew up or what her family was like, not even the occasional Christmas memory or Fourth of July picnic anecdote.

Everything was immediate for Nattie Sinclair.

Over the course of the year our house became like this underground culture center of the campus. We kept up with the fancy Sunday brunches that Nattie called soirees. She was very particular about who got invited and about who didn't get invited back. We had poetry readings on Tuesday nights.

Adams never made the poetry. He'd hit the bars on Tuesdays with his roofing buddies, shooting pool or throwing darts. Nattie said it was just as well. She said poetry was for the sensitive and civilized. Adams would belch or pinch her butt, and she'd smack him in the face with a closed fist, and then they'd kiss like crazy, knocking over chairs and making a commotion, while stumbling and tumbling upstairs to their bedroom. They didn't seem to mind making it pretty clear they were having one heck of a lot of sex. You know, which I wasn't, but even that was fine. You kind of felt like you were having sex when you lived with Nattie Sinclair. I don't mean actual sex, of course. I don't think Nattie Sinclair would anymore have sex with me than she would with Sancho Panza. But she was an incredibly sexual creature. She was real sexy, sure, but I mean sexual as well, like in some way everything was sexual to her – men, road trips, the universe, watching football games on TV, whatever. With Adams, I think she got a jolt of physical sex, but she liked it all ways – philosophical sex, spiritual sex, dangerous sex, I guess even the sex of the mundane. Sometimes I tried to figure out what kind of sex she got from Daniel O'Neill. I think now maybe it was the sex of mystery, or of anticipation. Maybe unrequited sex.

Adams of course loved "getting laid," but if you looked closely you could see little changes in him. Cib Adams was no cretin, even though he was pretty tough. He didn't act cool, but he was macho like John Wayne in a John Ford movie. He was just as smart as she was, and I know he liked poetry and literature because we used to discuss it all the time when we lived in the dorm.

He always had ideas when I first met him: always talking, scheming, laughing and joking around. He carried himself like a walking Western movie poster – frozen in a pose bigger than life but sort of paper-thin. It was like Nattie took scissors to the poster and carefully cut him out, discarding leading ladies and scar-faced villains. She shredded the supporting cast of Hollywood starlets and removed the background train wrecks and cattle stampedes. She rounded and softened the edges to eliminate paper cuts and then began filling the form with some of her own content. His biceps no longer flinched impulsively like a tiger but pulsated rhythmically when he stroked her hair.

Adams and Daniel O'Neill hit it off almost as well as Adams and Nattie. Of course I don't mean the furniture crashing sex thing, but they took to each other strong and fast. They loved debating. Even when they mostly agreed on something they'd find ways not to agree. They both talked a lot about not growing up with brothers, and wishing they had, and feeling like now they did. They didn't really include me, and even though I didn't grow up with any brothers either, I didn't take it wrong. They both had been football players in high school, and they loved to throw the ball around. I joined them often but the truth is I'm not the most athletic guy. That's another way they were the same. They were both good to me. Lots of guys would have made fun, maybe, that I wasn't good at catching or throwing. They never did. It's not like they treated me like a baby or took care of me or anything like that.

But they always pronounced my name correctly, if you know what I mean.

"Like whiskey, life is poison.
Both kill innocence and breed reality."
- Nattie Sinclair

Chapter 11

The midnight adventure in the 1965 Plymouth Valiant started normally enough. The four of us were in Dante's Bar, marking the end of Spring Semester. I had no way of knowing it would be the last normal day of my life.

The place was packed, even though it was only eleven-thirty in the morning. End of semester celebration is like a carnival in a college town: boisterous, light-hearted, and filled with summer potential. Our table was crammed tight, right in the middle of the fray. Nattie was telling me about the lease on her house; we were talking about whether we all four should get on it for the summer and fall, or let it go and find something else. Something that maybe suited us better. I had already told my folks I wasn't going to go home for the summer. Back and forth between them, all the hassle. My Dad of course was fine with it; my mom cried, but I told her I'd visit for a couple of weeks. It was strange, because these three people sitting with me in a bar on a Tuesday morning seemed more like family than, you know.

Anyway, we had to decide what we were going to do on Nattie's lease pretty soon.

Adams and Daniel O'Neill were arguing over which was more valuable, the 1965 Plymouth Valiant or Adams' Zippo lighter. It was a pretty cool Zippo. It sported a sterling silver "1935 Varga Girl" on the cover.

The Varga Girl spilt at the waist when you popped the cover of the Zippo. Her hair and dress blew back toward the flame, which shot up from her behind each time she bent over for a light. Not surprisingly, I guess, she held a tiny Zippo to light her own cigarette. Adams said the Zippo was a graduation present from his dad. Adams didn't like his father very much, but he always made a big deal out of the Zippo.

"I agree, the Zippo's a classic," Daniel said. "A classic like the Valiant."

"To Valiants, Zippos, and our friendship." Adams raised his glass of beer and looked each of us in the eye. "Classics all around."

"That's a perfect toast," Nattie said after we'd all taken a sip. "Both the Valiant and the Zippo symbolize us as not just good friends, but as a true family. Both are heirlooms you guys have and value, and both are from people you're estranged from." She looked at Daniel. "Even death is an estrangement, you know? By bringing them together, you've brought together a family. Do you notice how none of us has plans to go home for the summer? Like why leave home to go search for a home?"

"Well said, Darling."

Adams sat back, just eyeing us all, a smile creeping larger. "Wanna trade?" he finally said. "Trade your heirloom for my heirloom? Seal it for real?"

"It's like blood brothers, sharing blood," I said.

"But more, and bigger," Nattie said. "It's sharing families and histories and issues and connection." I watched her look first at one, then at the other. Solemnly, like a high priestess.

"It's sharing it all," she said.

Then nobody said anything, especially not Daniel.

"Wow," I finally said. "That sure is interesting."

"Wow," Nattie said. "That sure is."

Daniel O'Neill just smiled.

"Tell you what," Adams said. "That's not fair. Even though the Valiant's not worth much in dollars, it was your Dad's. He drove it. Sat in it. My old man got the Zippo as partial payment from some client who dealt in antiques. You know? Typical shit from my old man. Just because it's worth lots in dollars, he figures it's worth lots to me."

"The strength and focus of my childhood was knowing the 1965 Plymouth Valiant belonged to my father," Daniel O'Neill said, sounding a bit more Irish than Kansas. "I wouldn't have traded it then for all the jewels in the crown. But later, when my uncle helped me rebuild it, he tried to steal it from me. He tried to tell me the Valiant had really been his, not my dad's at all."

Daniel and Adams locked eyes, and when I looked between them I almost cried for the love I saw inside of their stare.

"So I'll trade you my uncle's half, and I'll keep the half that holds my father.

The Zippo for half ownership of the Valiant," Daniel said. "I get the Zippo, filled full with 'Dad' shit, and we both get the Valiant, also filled with our fathers."

They both fell silent, considering.

Then Adams got caught up in the excitement of the idea. He couldn't stop himself.

"I'll trade the Zippo, plus extra flints, for half ownership."

Finally, Daniel said "I get full ownership of the steering wheel horn cap with the Valiant emblem. Plus full ownership of the Zippo. Plus half ownership of the Valiant. Plus the extra flints."

"What about when the flints run out?" I asked

"Good point," Adams said. "The flints can never run out. Not ever. You need a flint, even fifty years from now, you've got a flint."

"Flints are sacrosanct," Daniel said.

"Done," Adams said.

"Plus," Daniel continued, "We christen the Valiant with a road trip. Today. You all have to come with me back to my mom's farm. Couple of weeks."

Adams and Daniel looked at Nattie and me.

"I'll go," I said.

"I'm in," Nattie said. "Guess that makes up our minds about the lease. We can get something bigger when we get back. She got that conspiratorial look. "Or maybe we won't even come back," she said.

I knew she was joking, but we all just looked at each other.

***

Several hours later, we had all packed a bag of clothes and the cooler of beer. Nattie called some of the soiree gang to come over and take food and the plants. She put a few things in several boxes and asked one of the women to hold it for her. She pulled her brass doorknocker off the front door, and by three-thirty we were on the road heading east over the Rocky Mountains.

We drove into a beautiful late-spring Colorado afternoon. Blue skies dramatized by wandering clusters of clouds. For the first time ever, Daniel road shotgun. As usual Nattie sat between them, and for a long time I just enjoyed watching her. Her hair looked like New England autumn as it flapped around in the wind and fluttered into the backseat like tendrils of wind-blown contentment. Nattie Sinclair looked really happy leaning against Daniel with her feet stretched out across Adams' lap, and I could have sat there and looked at her forever. She was pretty and smart and funny but she belonged to Adams, who popped beers, flipped butts out the window, and drove the Valiant through the mountains like a madman.

***

We had been driving for quite some time, hours at least, because it was starting to get dark. All of a sudden the road turned sharply ahead of us. The mountains opened up and the entire basin of the Great Plains lay before us. The lights of Denver spread out on a giant square grid; we descended like bats upon millions of fireflies.

"The Queen City," Adams said. "There she sits, there she lounges."

"My mom always used to say the rosary on road trips," I said, not sure how this would be accepted. "I can lead it, if anyone wants to say one. You know," I said, "just for safety."

"How about instead you pull out your prayer book, and we each pick out a prayer," Nattie said. "I've been dying to get my hands on it. I used to have the same book when I was little."

"I didn't know you were Catholic," Adams said.

"Yeah, well, whatever," she said. "How about it, Johnny?"

"Well sure," I said, hoping there wasn't anything sacrilegious in letting a pretend-Catholic read my prayer book. I reached into my backpack and passed it up to her. I got it when I was little, at First Communion. It's black leather and it's called The Prayer Book and it's filled with all different kinds of prayers – for the days of the week, for the months, for different saints, to protect the Pope, everything. Each prayer tells how many days of indulgences you get by saying it, which is I think how many days out of Purgatory you get, or maybe you're praying someone else out of Purgatory and hoping someone prays for you; I'm not really sure how that works.

"How about a goddess prayer?" Nattie asked, looking through the table of contents. "We need a goddess prayer." She reached up and turned on the dome light of the 1965 Plymouth Valiant. "Here's a whole section of Blessed Virgin Mary prayers," she said. "That's close enough."

She flipped to that section and started thumbing through different prayers. Just as I was beginning to buzz uncomfortably with her not seeming very respectful of the book, Nattie Sinclair let out a squeal.

"Ooh, here it is. A perfect goddess prayer. This is it. This is my prayer, my favorite prayer for all time. I'm always going to say this prayer. Listen to this," she said, "it's a prayer to our Lady of Help:

> *Say not, merciful virgin, that you cannot help me, for your beloved son has given you all power in heaven and on earth. Say not that you ought not assist me, for you are the Mother of all poor children of Adam, and mine in particular. Since, then, merciful virgin, you are my mother, and you are all powerful, what excuse can you offer if you do not lend assistance? See, my Mother, see, you are obliged to grant me what I ask, and to yield to my entreaties.*

Hot Damn!" said Nattie. "Now that's my idea of a prayer. Forget this groveling, I-am-not-worthy nonsense, just give me what I want and shut up about it."

I didn't think it was funny at all that she was making up such a blasphemous prayer and then laughing about it. I took the book back from her but was stunned to see that it was an actual prayer, credited to Saint Francis of Sales.

Who, other than Nattie Sinclair, would say a prayer like that? Surely our Blessed Mother would not want anyone talking to her that way, and yet there it was, in my Prayer Book, an official Catholic prayer coming right after the prayer to Our Lady of Perpetual Help and right before the one to Our Lady of La Salette.

I felt sick to my stomach to even think about it, but for the first time in my life I wondered whether God really was a Catholic; I just couldn't imagine him letting them talk to His mother that way.

***

Daniel O'Neill slipped the Zippo out of the watch pocket of his Levis and flipped the metal wheel. The spark hopped and darted inside the darkness of the backseat and then popped into blue flame.

"You're about to throw a rod, Brother. Pull this sucker over and cool her down. Told you 20 miles ago, told you 20 miles before that. She won't make it another 20. Won't be able to tell you again. Pull the son-of-a-bitch over."

We'd been driving forever; It was dark as pitch; no moon, tons of stars.

"Hey, Man. The deal was whoever's driving is the owner. I'm driving. Your half ownership doesn't start until you're driving."

Adams' tone was smiling, so you knew they were back to batting things back and forth, mostly for fun. But this wouldn't be the first time I'd watched Adams push something just to see how far he could.

"Fair enough, though brilliantly stupid," Daniel said. "Deal's a deal. My new Zippo here, of which, I'd like to point out, I'm now full owner, will keep firing regardless. Hate like hell to seize this Slant Six out here in the middle of nowhere, though."

"Out here in the middle of the night, no less," Nattie chimed in. "This adventure will turn into something uncomfortably symbolic if we get stranded in the middle of the night, in the middle of nowhere." She reached for the bottle stuffed tight between Adams' legs. "Seems like the middle of the country, as well."

"Coming up on it, about three and a half hours away," Daniel said. "Hays, Kansas. Forty miles from the geographic center of the United States."

"How do you know that," I asked him.

"Read it somewhere when I was a kid. Maybe National Geographic"

"So really, as far as you know, it could be 400 miles from the geographic center of the United States," Adams said.

"And once we get there," Daniel said, "we're about there."

"Black Prairie Darkness, Shattered In Stars, Swallows Youth Of America Returning Home In Search Of Roots. Or no," Nattie said, "that's not it. Not searching for roots, really."

"Hoots," Adams exclaimed. "Yucks and hoots and the pure hell of the adventure. That's our goal. Screaming across the wasteland at midnight in the Valiant. Which," he said, taking the bottle of Jack Daniel's whiskey from Nattie and passing it over to Daniel O'Neill, "will purr like a lion after a zebra, steady and strong from here to anywhere."

"She'll pop a gut in no time unless you let her cool off. Or actually, Cowboy, you're right, but your metaphor's off. A Wolf or coyote pack would run down a zebra; but this contraption really is just like a lion, or a tough bastard of an old man. It goes like hell in fits and starts, but never steady and strong. It pounces, sleeps, and stalks."

"Whatever. This one's a goer. I can feel it. I'll bet you a case of beer this baby'll be running strong long after your Zippo's sucking fumes and striking dry wick. By the way," Adams said, taking the bottle back, "have I told you lately how much I appreciate the opportunity to buy in? One half ownership in the 1965 Plymouth

Valiant with a goddamn working stereo for the Zipster? I fired up a lot of Kents with the old Zippo, burned a lot of bongs, but I gotta say, never got laid in the thing. Never drove the son-of-a-bitch to Kansas in the middle of the night, either."

"Plymouth Valiant steering wheel horn cap, plus Zippo, plus extra flints. It's the extra flints made the deal."

"Don't forget to tuck those flints underneath that little cotton thing in the bottom," Adams said. "You'll lose them for sure if you don't, like I told you. That way you'll never be out of one when you need one. You know? Just like toilet paper."

"Got 'em. Thanks. Butt out. I'll take over on the Zippo now. It is mine, after all. All mine, not just half."

Nattie giggled. "Good point," she said, laughing out loud. "You guys traded property, not wisdom. If you'd done that, you'd pull this sweet little car over and let it cool while Daniel lights your smoke with his brand new Zippo lighter, which," she laughed, "doesn't have to cool down every 200 miles."

"Besides," Daniel said. "Case of beer's a pussy bet – no offense, Darling. You want to bet on the durability of this demon, bet a snort."

"Hell, I can't wait that long between shots. I've owned a Zippo, I'm learning Valiants, but one thing I know for certain is this here prime time machine gets awfully rusty if it doesn't get a shot of Jack a hell of a lot more frequently than every 200 miles.

"By the way," Adams went on, "Have I told you lately how much I appreciate you turning me on to this wicked nectar? Beats the shit out of scotch. I'll never put that musty, peat-moss crap to my lips again. I'm a Jack Daniel's boy now, and I'm proud to say Daniel O'Neill, descendant of the first and great Kings of Ireland, heir to the honor and bravery of royalty, Daniel O'Neill made me now and forever a Jack Daniel's boy. Best goddamn drink invented by God or Devil, and I'll swear to that."

"Wet yourself with beer," Daniel allowed, "but drink only the best when you've got it and drink milk when you don't."

"The sacred O'Neill mantra," I said. "I think I'll steal it."

"You've got be able to drink it first," Daniel O'Neill said.

"Don't you dare, Johnny," Nattie looked back at me. She winked at me and the little buzz in my belly grew into an awfully pleasant urge to pee my pants.

"These two want to ruin and corrupt you only because they fear purity. You stay just the way you are. Don't give these two macho shitheads your soul. Whiskey's poison, Babe. It kills innocence and breeds reality."

She smiled again at me and took the bottle from between Adams' legs. She unscrewed the bottle from the cap, and then she gave me the O.K. sign with the cap curled in her fingers' circle. She took a long drink.

"Just look at us."

"I'd like to drink it," I said. "It just makes me kind of sick. I'm not trying to be pure, though."

"That's the magic, Baby. Nobody's pure who tries. The gods either bestow a piece of themselves or they don't. And they don't," she said, ramming the bottle hard back into Adams' crotch, "bestow it very often, or to just anyone."

"Screw you." Adams laughed the way he always did when he agreed with a criticism of himself.

"Pull over, lover."

"Don't pay her any mind, Suburban Stud," Daniel said to me. "Woman's only trying to emasculate you because she's over the edge herself. Besides, you'll get enough of a buzz when your former roomy here loses the bet and snorts one. Likely it'll blow his damn socks off."

"Never been a shot invented could do that," Adams said.

"I'm not talking shot, Cowboy. I'm talking a snort."

"What do you mean, a snort?"

"I mean a goddamn snort. Whole capful, right up the nostril. Snort it."

"Bullshit," Adams said.

"Don't blame you. Few can do it. Fewer try."

"Oh Johnny! It's happening! Can you feel it? All that pungent grade-A testosterone filling the air? Rattling horns? Pawing hooves? I just love it! Hair rising on the back of the neck.

Pheromones. Ooh," said Nattie, "guy stuff. I need a shot to calm my drip."

"Bullshit," Adams said again. "Nobody snorts a capful of Jack Daniels whiskey."

"That's the bet," said Daniel O'Neill.

I got a real kick out of watching the show: Daniel laughing while holding the temporary upper hand, Nattie squirming with delight while the wheels in Adams' brain spun like crazy, figuring out his next move.

He was silent for a long time; for several miles, just staring straight ahead and driving the Valiant in the darkness.

"It's bullshit," Adams finally said. "But I'll do it if you do it."

"Okay," Daniel said. "It's a deal. But I've already done it. Did it once, won't ever do it again. But to the day I die, I can say I did it."

"Bullshit."

"Big red-headed buck backs off, reconsiders, lowers his rack," Nattie said.

"You saw him do it?"

"Never had the pleasure. Love to watch. But if he says he did, that's good enough for me. He's now my new hero, my new wonder boy. Come here, Lover," she said to Daniel. "I've got a need to snuggle with my new man."

"Horseshit," Adams said.

The entire inside of the Valiant erupted with the trilling love laugh of Nattie Sinclair. She stretched her body full out across the front seat, half on Adams lap, half on Daniel's. Her hair and arms flapped out the window behind her, fluttering across Daniel's chest; one foot nestled with the bottle jammed in Adams' crotch, the other rested on the dashboard above the oversized steering wheel.

"God," she screamed, "I love my men."

She leaned up enough to wink at me. She stretched back out and I watched a serpentine writhe of her face, and then her breasts, and then her belly, and then gone.

"All right," Adams finally said, taking his foot off the accelerator and guiding the car towards the gravel lined shoulder of the black highway. "Here's the deal. I'm gonna do it. If you're full of shit and you've never done it, and you probably are and probably haven't, then I'll be in an exclusive club and only you will know you don't have the credentials to get in. If you really have done it, then we'll both be in and we can put our feet up together and watch everyone else try to get in. But either way, at least the four of us here will know for certain that I'm in, because you'll see me do it. No one here knows that you have."

"But remember," Daniel said, "you'll do it once and the very first thing you'll do next is swear to God you'll never do it again."

He took the bottle as the Valiant rolled to a stop. "So the only true credential is a man's word."

"That's true for you, not for me. I'll have witnesses."

"Wet and ready," Nattie said.

"Maybe I'll do it too," I said.

***

I rubbed my legs and back, using the wide tan trunk of the Valiant like it was a stretching bar attached to an invisible wall in an abandoned dance studio. The distant clunk of work boots pounding along a midnight blacktop highway vibrated in my mind's eye. Daniel O'Neill had this outrageous kind of otherworld energy, and I marveled again at his staying power. Stuffed into the backseat with the cooler and some suitcases and fishing gear and boxes and all the rest of the stuff that wouldn't fit in the trunk, I felt like I'd been trapped in a coffee can for the last four hours, crunched forward with the foil-lined lid compressing my back and forcing my face into my knees, yet there he was jogging along an empty stretch of blacktop highway on a cold spring midnight in the middle of the Great Plains prairie. The hood on his sweatshirt was up and for a moment I felt like I was watching a monk burdened with lost faith pounding down the road to hell, getting smaller and smaller on his way to a curious death.

"How in the world can he go off running like that? Where does a reservoir of energy like that come from?"

"In work boots, to boot," Adams said. "He looks like a damn convict out there, plodding along. Plodding and plotting."

"A wizard," Nattie said. "I keep telling you guys, and you keep blowing it off. There are people who don't fit in, and he's one of them. They're here for a short period of time, just sort of passing through. Right now, he's a wizard with wings. Five minutes ago, a wizard with wheels. Can't you feel it? There really is something very different about him. It scares me sometimes. And it attracts me always."

I knew exactly what she meant, even though what she said was silly and made no sense. Daniel O'Neill was an awfully nice fellow and I liked him a lot. But he was kind of different.

We had spent hours together at the house, just he and I.

He had this enormously wide-angle view on things. Beyond detached; more like removed. Like a ghost, or I guess like Nattie said, a wizard. He went to most of the parties with us and attended his classes like a regular student, but he carried this detachment with him all the time. He was a real personable kind of fellow, just distant, like someone standing alone on the bank of a river being fed by sunlight, watching everyone else thrash about in the currents trying to catch fish for food.

I remember once in our Russian Lit class we were discussing some novel, I think it was Turgenev's *Fathers and Sons*, and he was arguing against the whole class. The prof in this class never really took part, she just sat back and listened, occasionally throwing out beacons or mileposts. Gradually Daniel started making more and more converts to his position, and pretty soon people were sitting back saying, "cool, never thought of it that way." I talked to him about it later when we were sitting out in his sun porch bedroom, and he told me he hadn't even read the book. He was just picking up the trail from things people were saying and piecing together the direction from clues being dropped. It was one of those things where you say "I can't believe it," but you believe right away.

We were pretty close, he and I. Well, we weren't really very close, because with me there's not an awful lot to get close to, so he wasn't all that interested in me, but we spent a lot of time together when Nattie and Adams were out doing their thing – Daniel called it the romantic death dance.

"They'll kill each other sure, those two."

"Heart attacks, probably," I answered with a laugh.

I always tried to be clever around Daniel O'Neill. I don't know if he just wasn't interested in clever or whether I wasn't ever clever enough. I kind of stammered, "You've got to be in pretty good shape to have that much sex." As soon as I said it, I knew that's not what he meant.

"Shit, son, that's nothing but youth and hormones. Excitable experiments exploding in copulation. Bunny rabbits with brains. Though actually," he said, "you're right in one way. It's like the herd bull going after the queen bee. Seeming nothing but sex on their minds, but it's power disguised as humping. Him tired of the always willing and docile cows, and her sick of the boring buzzing of fawning drones. It's a hot dance and fun to watch, but they don't mix, see? Can't breed the two. She'll sting like hell over and over; he'll butt and snort and stomp, and finally they'll be used up and die. Or worse yet, just dissolve. But never really connect, never create anything."

But see, here's the thing. He could have been jealous of her, or of him, or of them both. I thought then he was looking for problems in their relationship because he wasn't part of it. Maybe he loved her. Maybe he was one of those fellows who liked other fellows and he loved Adams. I sure never saw him with girls, so I think he was stuck on something, why else was he hanging around? My mom always said homosexuals lived in big cities, but I was beginning to think she was mistaken; I think they can live anywhere. And though I still believe they're breaking God's laws, what if Daniel O'Neill was one? He was, like I've said, a good guy, and it seems rather cavalier of God to be throwing away perfectly good souls simply because of who they sleep with.

See, that was the crazy part of going away to college. You're supposed to be getting an education and broadening your mind, but it can get really weird when you start meeting other people who come from different towns, different backgrounds, different childhoods. Growing up where I did, everyone pretty much got a handle on life with the same tools. Like one family might use a big push broom, and another might give all their kids whisk brooms and those little dime-store metal dustpans, but everybody in my childhood basically spent their time working to collect the same kind of debris; you know, clean up similar messes.

I just thought everyone everywhere did the same.

I mean I'm not stupid, I'm talking about when I was a little kid. I know better now, but it's all still shocking sometimes. I guess what I'm saying is that ever since I got to college I began having ideas I'd probably just as soon no one told my mom about, if you know what I mean.

Anyway, the reason I say that about Daniel maybe being homosexual is this: once he said to me it doesn't have to be soft and round and sweet, it can be just as good if it's coarse and hard and acrid. See? Like I say, I liked him a lot because he wasn't afraid to stretch stuff, to look beyond, to see more. Sometimes we'd sit there outside his little porch bedroom in the backyard, not saying anything, just looking up at the night sky, and I'd feel like I wanted to be like him, and I wanted him to like me. I don't think Catholics can even be homosexual, so I don't mean I liked him in that way, but I always felt good when he was around. That's why I listened closely to Adams and Nattie while we three lay in the middle of the midnight highway, stretched out head to head forming a trinity along the faded white lines, talking about Daniel O'Neill.

"He's like Satan," Nattie was saying, "and I don't mean evil, but like the omnipotent and powerful Satan, like what Satan would be like if he finally threw in the towel and joined back up."

As I listened to them, out in the middle of the silent nowhere, I imagined I could still hear the faint clunk of Daniel's plodding boots on the blacktop. I felt this slow hovering combination of mundane forces building to a critical energy pinnacle, balancing me on the point, poised to burst and shoot me away. The further away he got, the louder the pounding rhythm of his boots became, sounding increasingly like the rhythm of his heart, pounding away in my head so like he was there, listening somehow through me.

"Bullshit." Adams was saying. "He's just a misplaced Irish lad from Kansas."

"No, there's one hell of a lot more than that going on. That's like saying Satan's just a regular angel who fucked up, and he's not. He's not, he's God's equal opposite. It's like Daniel's back on God's payroll, but with a separate agenda. Doing good and being nice, but with a strong and silent undercurrent of mean and sad and pain."

"Bullshit. He's no more mixed up nor mysterious than any of us. He's a farm boy. There's nothing more normal than that."

"Yeah, okay, but what's the deal with that? I mean, have you really thought about that? Why's it suddenly so important for him to go back there? Out of the blue this morning he says he's leaving. Something really heavy's happening down there. And I'll tell you something else. I wouldn't be surprised if he doesn't come back to school with us in the fall."

I guess I always thought she knew everything about him, as if that secret of hers was somehow tied up with him. With Adams she was playful, with me kind of protective, but with Daniel she was insightful, like he fed her mystic neurons or something. They meshed well, so I figured they knew each other well, not like brother and sister so much as a husband and wife who unfortunately married other people, or like partners who had to dissolve the business, or like secret sharers.

Or something. But the thing is, Nattie and Daniel somehow just went together. I didn't know a lot about his childhood, except he grew up on a farm and his dad was killed in Vietnam. I couldn't imagine what kind of person Daniel O'Neill would be without Nattie Sinclair; it seemed to me like they had always been together. Usually when you know someone, and then you find out who they used to be and where they came from, well then they change somehow, they're different. Maybe less mystery, or things get explained, or something simple like they have the same hair as their dad or smile as their mom, but it's like you see more of the canvas and brush strokes behind the image. Nattie and Daniel just were, like they'd only been born in college. No families, no past, nothing else defining them or pulling them or putting them together. I liked

Cib Adams a lot, I mean he was my roommate, and you always feel special about your first college roommate. Every time I looked at him and Nattie together, I got this little quiver of bad things happening. I wouldn't tell this to just anyone, but I was happy it was Adams with her and not Daniel O'Neill. I guess because I thought Adams could handle her better, or survive her more, or at least hold onto himself. I liked Nattie Sinclair a lot. I don't say I thought she was a good person, I mean I don't think she was bad, but maybe like good wasn't her defining characteristic. She was fascinating, like Daniel; she was an awful lot of fun, like Adams; and she was beautiful, like, something, like someone I never knew, or maybe like someone I dreamed about never knowing, so it makes them kind of real. Maybe it was the contrast. She was sort of mysterious, sort of metaphysical, sort of like a Temple Priestess, like a stone shadow flower who chooses when to open. Or like the wind with an emerald center. She ate the world slowly and completely. Feared and fearless. And then, on the other hand, she was this gorgeous girl next door. Sweet, sweet smile. Long, blond, brunette, strawberry sort of full palette hair, always clean and shining. Drop dead body. Actually, she looked a lot like Cib Adams. Great breeding stock, those two. Poster People for the Future.

Anyway, they kept each other in check, while propelling themselves forward. I remember sitting in our house one night during the winter, playing pinochle on the floor of the living room in front of the fireplace. Daniel taught us the game. Nattie and I were always partners, and Adams always had scrap cedar from roofing jobs for the fire, and Daniel and Cib and Nattie drank Jack Daniel's in glasses with ice. I remember thinking, and giggling to myself at the thought that the two of them were like a slinky going down a flight of stairs. Every time the slinky hits a stair below, it pulls itself together, gathers energy and coils up and then jumps out again, like a mechanical yin and yang. Over and over, always teetering on the edge of destruction.

I used to spend a lot of time searching for the perfect defining image of Cib Adams and Nattie Sinclair. Like I've said, their

216

relationship was compelling, something you wanted to be a part of. I was convinced there was a perfect image of it somewhere. The slinky didn't last long. I came up with and ultimately discarded others. I didn't know it at the time, but the ideal image of them was right out there on the prairie with us. A huge cottonwood growing down by a creek bed. Enormous and perfectly shaped. But when you looked at it you realized the trunk split low to the ground, so it looked like two trees growing from the same spot of ground. Each of these trunks was also big and straight and strong, but the tree was slowly growing itself apart. It was right out there with us in the middle of nowhere on our midnight Valiant ride.

They were sure something to be around.

Nattie Sinclair loved to listen to Adams talk, and as I've said, he could go on forever, often just droning on and on describing rather mundane details of scenery. He used to talk almost nonstop last fall when we'd gather in the enclosed back porch and watch football games on television. Just on and on about really obvious stuff – the length of a player's hair or the yard line where a receiver made his cut or how many big fat bodies were tangled up in the pile. Nattie always sat close to him: sometimes he'd be on the floor resting against her knees so she could drape her arms around his neck and rest her chin on his head; sometimes she'd lay across the back of the couch and he'd lean back into her breasts, talking and describing the game the whole while. She'd just listen.

Nattie Sinclair liked to be close, and now I looked at her differently and wondered why. She touched people a lot, stayed near people. Sometimes flirtatious and almost fawning, sometimes business like or even aggressive, but she stayed in other people's space. She had this way of making you feel like you were a part of her, a way of making you feel good or special or at least pleased, because she was gorgeous and she smelled gorgeous. It never made me uncomfortable; it made me feel I was part of her world. You could always tell immediately if Nattie liked someone or not by how close she got to them. After living with her for awhile I just kind of took to letting her blaze the path for strangers – either welcome or get the hell out. Like a watchdog, or those birds that used to keel over in mine shafts, alerting the miners to danger, Nattie became like a first line of defense into our little world. If she took to someone you'd know it because she'd get close to them, take their arm, comment on their fragrance. It always seemed kind of sexual but it wasn't sex, she didn't seem to care if it were a man or a woman – if she liked you she was in your space, if she didn't like you, she kept away. If I was Adams I might have gotten jealous, but he never seemed to. They had some shared understanding, and he never seemed to notice or mind when she got real close to other people. Like I say, Adams really was a good guy. You can't live with someone for a long time without seeing faults and things that bother you about them, but all in all Adams was a good guy. Sometimes his loud prancing wore kind of thin, and sometimes you simply didn't have the energy to keep up with him, but you couldn't help liking him. And often it was kind of sweet to just sit back and listen to him describe the way things looked. I know that was part of his and Nattie's deal: she loved smells and sounds, he loved to talk about colors and sizes and their relationship to function.

Anyway, Adams and Nattie could talk forever, like they were doing now lying in the middle of the highway, sometimes he soft and listening, guiding and improving her thoughts, sometimes the other way around. I think conversation to them was like fertilizer, strengthening an ever growing intertwining of roots and limb.

"I told you I talked to his mom on the phone the other day," she said. "But what I didn't tell you was how strange it was. Daniel seems like somebody who dropped from the stars or crashed out of the side of a mountain. He doesn't seem like someone who has a mom. She was nice at first, but I don't think he'd told her much about all of us living together."

"Probably thinks he's shacked up with a bunch of city slickers in a hippie commune. I know that's what my old man thinks."

Nattie giggled. "The opportunities for developing future business connections and relationships are of unparallel value in a fraternity, C.C. That's where you belong. Sow your wild oats, C.C., but do it within the circle of similarly like-minded young men.

Remember, some of today's fraternity pledges will be many of tomorrow's business successes. Be smart, C.C. Don't throw away these extraordinary opportunities by over-frolicking with the bizarre or downtrodden. Stay with your own kind."

Adams scoffed. "You got it, all right. That's definitely him and his bullshit lawyer babble. What a fucking stiff."

"Maybe," she said, "but still your dad, nonetheless. Stiff blood maybe, but still your blood."

I laughed out loud, hearing Nattie sound like Adams' dad.

Nattie was really good at sounding just like other people. Not so much her voice changing, more like impersonating. She could nail those sounds in people's voices that dripped attitude.

Adams got really angry just thinking about his dad.

"Stiff's right on. What a geek. The son-of-a-bitch still gets together with some of his college fraternity brothers. A bunch of middle-aged Greek geeks, with their geeky little kids and their geeky little wives and their geeky little plans for their geeky little lives."

"Nothing particularly geeky about corporate law, mansions and Mercedes," Nattie said. "The only geeky thing in this scenario is adolescent rebellion against affluence." That was all Nattie. Then it was Nattie and Adam's father both together. "Time's coming when you'll have to grow up and take your place in the patriarchy, C.C."

"Call me C.C. again and I'll spit in your face and break your heart, just like I did to him." Adams pulled a smoke from the pack of Kents tucked in the flap pocket of his jean jacket.

"'Cept with him, I broke his fingers and left home. But a heart will hurt just as badly and take longer to heal."

"Broken fingers," Nattie said. "No damn wonder he never calls. Can't dial. That doesn't excuse," she said with true disgust edging her voice, "you ignoring or not returning your mom's calls. If you don't call her when we get to O'Neill's farm I'll call you C.C. for the entire summer, and you can spit until your tongue dries up and falls out. You're an asshole to ignore and avoid your own mother."

"I don't really ignore her, but shit, man, her entire life living with him is this outrageous grind, like a mouse who got plucked up and dropped by the tail into the goddamn garbage disposal. He flips the switch and grinds her up whenever he gets it into his goddamn mind to do it, because he's an asshole, and she just spins around and spurts blood. I'm tired of plucking little tufts of hair off my face and picking little mousey feet out of my teeth. I can't help her and she won't change. I can't be around the stench of rotting rodent anymore. It's her life. I didn't choose him, she did."

"That's crap, disguising jealousy of your father with pity and noble disdain for your mom. That's horseshit."

"Jealousy my ass. He's the one who wants me to be some hotshot lawyer, not me."

There was a bit of a silence, a silence between them that used to make me uneasy. I didn't grow up around people who talked this way to each other – real straight and to the point. I used to think they were mad at each other, but they never were. They would just think for a bit and then carry on wherever they left off.

"Well anyway," Nattie finally said, "I was talking about Daniel's mom, not yours. The other day on the phone, she wasn't a hick or a hayseed at all, nor some prissy Southern Belle. In fact, she didn't even have an accent. So if she doesn't talk that way, why in the world does he? And she asked a lot of questions about me, and when I said something like I'll bet he's anxious to come home for a visit, she just kind of sighs, and says something like, yes, I guess he probably is. Not like she didn't want him or miss him, but like she knew he might never come back anyway. And another thing. She kept asking about me and my studies and my plans, like she was really my mom and Daniel was some college friend she had heard me talk about, and I had to explain why I was bringing him home for Christmas or something."

"Maybe she wants to be your mom instead," Adams said.

"Don't laugh, that's what it seemed like. And the funny thing is, and remember, this phone conversation went on for something like 45 minutes or an hour or more, for a time that's what I wanted, too. I almost felt like she *was* my mom, but my real mom, not this bogus biological excuse of a mess I got instead."

"I thought you told me your mom died."

"Yeah, well, whatever, that's not the point. The point is, for the first time ever in my life, I felt like I belonged to someone. I fit in somewhere. My life somehow made sense. It felt," she said, "as if my dictionary finally held every single word I ever needed to look up."

Something in my scalp tingled like crazy when she said that. The blacktop beneath me became fluid and wavy and watery. I got sucked into the melting eager asphalt. I crawled across the blackness and clawed my way up to the trunk of the Valiant. I shuddered as a grotesque wave of nausea gripped me, and the stars began whirling up in the sky. I closed my eyes and held on.

Suddenly I knew why Nattie Sinclair liked me so much. I understood why she treated me like her favorite little brother, or like a precious stuffed bear from her childhood.

Except Nattie Sinclair didn't have a childhood. Her parents didn't die in a car crash. She wasn't raised by a rich great aunt. She wasn't an only child, and she wasn't alone in the world.

I suddenly and violently realized that Nattie Sinclair was her own creation. She changed her past, changed her name, changed her memories, and maybe changed her hair and her face as well. She had to invent a new person because she couldn't stand to part the curtains of her childhood and look into the wreck of her putrid home. She couldn't stomach peering through the dirty gauze because she couldn't stand to stare into the troubled little face of Catherine Teaza.

***

We were back in the Valiant, screaming along in the midnight, and I needed to not think for a while. It took no time at all for the conversation to start back up, so it was easy for me to just be quiet.

"Let's hear about it, Daniel," Nattie said. "Tell us about this farm. Are we in search of roots? Tell us what we're searching for."

"Yeah," Adams said, grabbing the bottle of whiskey from her and throwing one back. "Tell it again, George. Tell how I get to tend the rabbits."

"Well," Daniel said, taking the bottle Adams passed over. "There's this farm, see, out in the middle of nowhere, kind of like the country around here, except it's different because at this farm the wind doesn't really blow, it kind of settles in, and it doesn't bring coolness nor hope, it just moves dry.

"An old man's farm, one that smells like an old man and looks kind of like an old man, with wrinkles and sunburns and whiskers. Cattle there are sick. Tree branches breaking all over the place, vegetables in the kitchen garden rotten on the vine. Like ancient and plague-eaten Medieval lands, everything is slowly decaying and drying and dying.

"There's women there, but they're just there, no real joy, old and haggard; kids are about, but no laughter.

"One day a warrior knight sends a magic seed, a seed to flourish in the wasteland and return bounty and plenty. The seed was a son, but the warrior knight lost his life in a far away battle, so he could not return to sow the seed. Others spread it too casually, buried it too shallow, irrigated it poorly. The seed sprouted, but was crossbred foolishly and spliced and grafted recklessly. It withered. It wouldn't grow right.

"We're going back not looking for roots, but to till the soil, hoe the weeds, and plant again. The roots there now are poison; if we're searching for them at all, we're searching only for ways to ferret them out, pinch them off, and watch them die."

"Jesus," Nattie said half seriously, "and I thought this was going to be fun."

"Nobody really possesses this farm," Daniel O'Neill went on, "though a daughter who's a mom lives it, an Uncle who's a dad works it, a son who's a ghost leaves it, and a father who's dead curses it. All of them existing in the shadow of the patriarch, who got a disease in the brain. A disease that made his spirit sick and then killed him. Farmer Ben the Fisher King. Ben Dreiling, a keeper of the Trinity, a keeper of all that's secret and all that's sacred." Daniel paused a moment, and then he said, "And when he dies it's all destroyed."

222

Daniel takes a breath, and you can feel its sucking, encompassing violence squeeze the air out of the Valiant.

"Almost," he says softly.

"In the corner of the Dreiling barn is a relic – a symbol of simple times, of times when everything runs smooth and well oiled, when people work diligently, animals grow healthy, and machines operate well. The relic follows simple and natural rules, harnessing the great powers of the universe. It is the freedom chariot of the lost warrior, and then it is not."

"Jesus," Nattie says again, very quietly this time.

"Sounds like Willy Loman eats Soylent Green," Adams cut in. "Why we going? How do we fit in? The energy of youth or the pathetic naiveté of our own enthusiasms? What do we do?"

"Don't know yet. Just watch, I guess. Maybe stoke or piss on the dead coals trying to heat the old fires. Maybe just for the going."

It was now that darkest part of the night, pitch quiet outside and black. An extraordinary prairie Milky Way danced an excited exuberance all around us. A blanket of incredible stars, galaxies. The universe. God's backyard. We'd driven again without stopping for a couple of hours, and my butt had long since given up and gone numb. The quiet storytelling quality of the conversation squeezed the extraordinary revelation I had had of Nattie Sinclair out to the corners of my brain, so finally I could close my eyes and stop staring at her.

I dozed off for a while and when the smell of Jack Daniel's woke me it took me awhile to be amazed that the three of them were still at it, drinking like demons and driving the Valiant in the darkness. They're all crazy, and I'm here with them, so I'm crazy too, I thought during that groggy time when you're trying to stay awake and everything becomes surreal: darkness outside seeps in through the car's rusting scars along with the hum of the engine; the buzz of the wheels spinning along the blacktop pulls you in and out of dreaming so that sounds begin to smell and colors sing. Nattie wasn't sleeping but she was quiet, listening to Adams and Daniel O'Neill going back and forth, talking mostly nonsense in that way they had of assigning a great deal of importance to frivolous or silly discourse.

I tried hard not to listen, not to think, not to wonder. A deformed piece of time and space had just spilled out across the prairie, escaping from a dark little midnight crevice. It swallowed us up and nothing was the same.

Something skewed; something else twisted. A macabre tilt in the darkness out in the middle of our midnight nowhere.

I float in the Valiant like a madman.

Book Two

"It is possible to hold on so tightly
That you miss the reality of falling off."

From *Ride the Wild Bison*
- by John Gophe

Mysterium Fidei

Adams is a very busy man, but we visit together, sometimes, he and I. He's become quite important and very busy, so I hold no malice that his visits are less frequent and not at all regular anymore. At one point, and pleasantly so, he stopped by always on Wednesdays after work, before his softball games. And then after awhile he said he'd have to start coming Sundays when he could make it, on account he was too often late getting to softball. Certainly the physical camaraderie provided by weekly softball games and beer with the fellows is commendable and important.

The real reason, though, for the scheduling change: Adams does not care to be with me at supper.

I don't blame him for this.

Because I chose one of the more modest units without a kitchenette, I elect to share my evening meal in the community room at the end of the apartment building. The food is fine and I've perfected ways of unobtrusively not listening, so the conversation is good. But the last supper Adams had with me did not go well, so he no longer shares this with me.

Most of the residents save their loud socializing for the privacy of their locked doors. Actually, I hate my neighbors and am embarrassed about them each time Adams comes. Except for the nuns, the rest are loud and obnoxious, lots of late night parties with people screaming and yelling and banging on walls. I don't bang back because who knows when I might have need to cut loose myself someday, or maybe even have some fellows over to drink beer and play pinochle. Might as well build some credit while I can and put up with the cretins in my building. I'll have my time, it will come.

On those rare occasions when someone decides that some compelling reason exists to enter my space – not a tenement house, this, much better, really, not on the best side of town, perhaps, and not overly well lit, but a strong history from the heyday of this town, and the utilities are not unreasonable – and that compelling reason brings their knuckles rapping, or in the case of that one unfortunate incident involving a bingo wager in the community room, brings their fist crashing against my door – Number 37B – on those rare but compelling occasions, I do not answer.

At least not any more.

I am certainly no recluse, nor eccentric, nor do I relish confinement. I could go out, for a meal from time to time. Fresh air. I am no social mole nor unbalanced half-wit. I spend none of my time cackling from the rooftop nor fondling myself in the bell tower. Certainly I could go out; I could pass myself off outside as easily as anyone. I mean to say I neither attract stares nor draw pathetic comments.

I choose not to, so I do not go out.

I liked it better when Adams came regularly, when I knew when he'd come. I could clean up a bit and sweep and be ready for him. He doesn't know that I know his Wednesday visits ceased not because of softball but because of that last supper. I don't blame him so why confront him?

Except Sunday visits don't always work for him, the time isn't consistent, so I'm edgy when he does come, having waited so long, and then sometimes, more so lately, he doesn't even come at all.

I miss the old Adams. He's now working hard to be grown up. He sits and crosses his legs, and we visit about my mother or his practice or what's going to be for supper. He doesn't like talking about the old days, so we usually don't. So much so that I worry sometimes he doesn't remember them at all. And then I start to worry even more that if Adams doesn't remember, than those old days exist only because I remember. Not that Adams is my only connection back to those times, but he is, he is. The rest are silent.

Even though Adams struggles to be calm when he visits, I watch him cross and uncross his legs, and I know he's uncomfortable. He can't wait until it's time for him to leave. Maybe he's got to meet someone, or maybe he has a different appointment or something else important, but when Adams visits me he waits until he can leave.

Sometimes he'll pace around my place, straightening pictures hanging on the wall or pulling off and then replacing books from my shelves. Once he even opened the drawers of my dresser and checked on my supply of underwear.

I mean, come on.

But it's better that he comes than he doesn't; it's much better.

Adams is a very busy man. Many important people depend on him, many important things he needs to attend to; he has just so much time to go around. He's doing extremely well and I couldn't be happier for him.

Usually by 3 p.m. or 4 p.m. on a Sunday I can rest easy and figure he won't make it this week. Any number of things might have come up, important things and important people needing his attention.

I made a joke to him once about attorneys and armadillos. It was about hard shells and living wills; I guess it's kind of an inside joke; you have to know a lot about them to get it.

Often when Adams comes he suggests going for a walk or maybe even taking a drive. But there are many reasons not to do so. Things out there that he can't see. Best to stay in my apartment when Adams comes to visit. It's not that I think Cib Adams brings these things with him, or they follow him to me like he's a conduit, but I believe much better not to risk it. There are other times, and other reasons, for going out. Quite some time ago Adams thought it would be a swell idea for me to come to his house for a barbecue. Just a few people, he said, neighbors and some folks from his office. A few beers, he said, some burnt cow and horseshoes in his back yard. Mellow, he said, no big deal.

Well now, there was quite a thought. I lie in bed and wonder about many things, like who Cib Adams pretends to be when he's not visiting me. He has a house, apparently, with a backyard, in a neighborhood where co-workers from his office come for barbecues. How does he blend in? Why do his neighbors believe Cib Adams fits in with them, that he belongs among them? I imagine he must need to borrow clothes from somebody to pull off the ruse. Perhaps from his father, as that's become his look, but I can't imagine the number and complexity of problems that arrangement might cause.

Adams pretends many things these days; for one thing, he pretends to work with his father, sharing and building a practice with his father. Building a facade, I say, but not to Adams. A facade, a colorful nylon business tent sporting tethers of bright wire and polished steel. A blinking neon façade falsely anchored to a dry-land prairie aching for teepees and fire. Not his element, if you know what I mean. And I say this because I know what he wants, I know who he is.

I watch them through the clean spaces in the glass of my window, his father and Adams. I watch fascinated while they stalk wild bison.

It's not right how they do it; the searching's not true, because they hunt the herds from helicopters. The whirling scream of the blades raises dust and covers up the tracks in hard packed dirt, yellow and beaten by hooves. Now angry scared, now pounding a fury of dust and afraid. Nowhere do they stop, his father and Adams. Never do they thrust their nostrils into the dry air and wait for the rancid smell of the buffalo. Never do they wait for the calm and the quiet to pick young bulls from the herd, or old cows to clean and cull the herd. Rather, they are always rushing and whirling and afraid.

I've seen them do it, shooting long and gleaming rifles from helicopters. Their kill rots on the ground, the earth cries rivers and spring rains, but they don't care. Their kill rots on the ground beneath their whirling and screaming arrogance, and they don't care.

Adams does this to pretend. It's not how he is. It's not what he would do.

Adams is very busy, very important, so he pretends he no longer needs to plunge his arm deep into the steaming cavity of hot blood and last breath, clutch the final beat of a purple-red heart, and pull with his fingers the massive muscle of running gasp and afraid.

I feel for him, his predicament with his dad. I imagine sometimes that I scream for him at night. "Pull over," I shriek, "slow down. Please," I plead, "slow down. Pull over."

I can say without embarrassment that Adams' life is more complicated than mine, I understand this difference between us. He visits me maybe as a reminder, as a link to hunts that are real and no more and mean something.

I have the time to be there for him. I have the time so I am. He would do it for me, I'm sure, if I needed him that way. I imagine a philosopher may once have said the measure of any true relationship is if something's unimportant to you but you do it anyway because it's important to him. The content of what you do is irrelevant, all that matters is the form of why you do it.

That's true in this grounding thing I do for Adams. It's important to him, so if you see what I mean, that makes it important to me.

And I really don't know if this should be part of the philosophy or not but it's also important to me.

It is important to me.

I run with Adams in the darkness, not late on cold nights but later and darker yet in the early mornings right as or just before the birds wake to squawk and chatter and sing. I can lead him because I've jumped in it before; into this not-yet-morning sweet darkness of dew. Dropping almost from leaves on trees quiet and slow with the autumn late night morning we run together, Adams and I.

I slip out easily, and he waits patiently when he comes for me. I know always where he'll be. He flings off his clothes, naked sometimes when I arrive; he remains modest other times, but when we run together it does not matter.

Across darkness, it's always morning darkness and it doesn't matter when he comes because we run together when he does.

Full with ragged breath and long arm-pumping strides, Adams sucks in deep long gulps of air, and then I do. The day pounds out toward dawn, our footfalls leading the darkness across the prairie, pounding along dry creek beds where cottonwoods lean away from the wind and suck after water deep down running sweet long ago.

When Adams comes, we run together leading the darkness toward morning and then toward nothing but the darkness before sunrise. The horizon impossibly distant and far, miniscule sometimes, a thin nothing line stretching without separating black morning sky from black morning empty. I know we can't reach it and Adams runs with me toward it, and we run together when the darkness of morning kicks in.

It moves away from us, but I push him, and we pursue and persevere, panting for air, for breathing clean air and sweet pounding of our feet running together in the darkness. We will never reach it, I know, but when we do I want to get there with him, at the same time falling prone and exhausted upon the earth. Sweating and spent, sprawling on the earth, needing only air sweet and wet in the darkness of morning, we collapse from the running, sure, but also from the running having done this together.

That's when I pray Adams will reach deep inside me, split my chest with his panting and exhausted need, clutch out my heart and eat it raw.

He's a very busy man, but we run together, sometimes, Adams and I.

"You can never go home again,
Unless you've never been there to begin with."
- Nattie Sinclair

Chapter 12

Standing in the middle of his own barn, Lance O'Neill smiled through the smoke of his hand-rolled cigarette. He watched the enthusiasm spill out before him around the enormous wood cook stove. He allowed it to move up and out, from his belly up and then out through the widening grin of what he knew Becky would call a too infrequent smile. "My too infrequent man," she thought it was cute and clever to say. "My too infrequent man."

For Lance, this smile began growing hours earlier; it began in the middle of the night, actually well after midnight. It began the moment after he was jolted from sleep by the bleating horn of the 1965 Plymouth Valiant. During those crazy few thoughts between sleepfulness and awake, Lance's head as usual filled with images: portraits of Danny and Valiants, pictures of painful and then gone. But as he felt Becky shift in the sheets and then sigh, Lance O'Neill woke fully and realized Daniel and all of that back there had finally come home.

Lance stayed put in the small four-poster, completely still. He sucked in Becky's sleeping presence as she lay with her back to him, and he listened to the commotion going on outside. Daniel and, it sounded like, an entire regiment was spilling out of the Valiant and onto the circular gravel driveway. The voices and sounds were excited, youthful, and worn out. The end of a road trip. Christ, it took him back. A road trip ending here, well past midnight in the middle of nowhere. Lance heard the clean metallic clack when the Valiant's doors slammed, the trunk closing, the crunching of young boots on crushed rock.

"Becky," he whispered as the crunching voices moved toward the front door. "Beck, wake up." He ran his hand along her back, then down into her waist and up the curve of her hip. He rested it there, patted softly. "Becky," he whispered again. "Guess what?"

***

And now it turns out not a regiment at all, just Daniel and a couple of buddies and one gorgeous co-ed. Lance opened the door and joined them on the porch while Becky was still upstairs, making ready to come down and see her son after so much time. Lance watched the guys fiddling and fooling with each other on the front porch, stretching and jabbing and loosening up. The co-ed stayed back a bit, leaning on the railing and inhaling the night air, deeply and over again. Watching her, catching her scent, made Lance think of Becky, those many years ago, those many lifetimes before. God, the similarities. Arriving on this same front porch, in the same '65 Valiant, in the same middle of the night, wondering where in hell they were. But now he was the old man and these on the porch had their lives out ahead of them, mistakes and joy and so much pain.

The introductions went quickly and then quickly again with more laughter and hugging and commotion when Becky joined them a moment later.

Daniel looked good. Quiet, like always, but good. Strong. More confident. Maybe even happy. The buddies framed quite a pair. The big one was clearly tough and smart. Strong as hell. The other one a sweet kid and a little lost. Daniel's whiskers still hadn't grown into much of his face but the face itself was good, had grown. A strong jaw line. A good jaw line. An O'Neill. Becky's smile, sure, and certainly her gentleness, but Daniel carried the look of an O'Neill: the double-edged eyes holding both the fierce pride claimed by all princes of Ireland and the constant hauntedness of all lace curtain Irish. His eyes shone; Lance had always loved looking at them. A bizarre combination of his own and Danny's green hazel mixed with Becky's blue. Lance was not alone in finding fascination in Daniel's platinum eyes.

The co-ed, talking animatedly now with Becky as if they went way back, had extraordinary eyes as well. Emerald green and encircled with defined black rings. The eye of evil, or the eye of power, or the eye of madness, Lance couldn't exactly remember which. He looked at the two of them closely. One blond, one brunette. The one beautiful and familiar and taking first steps into the second part of life; the other young and beautiful and probably just beginning to get a taste.

God, he loved women.

She'd only just arrived and he could already imagine driving off with her in the pick-up, a road trip. Bar hopping from dinky town to dinky town, shooting pool, heading toward Denver or Kansas City – a downtown hotel, a bottle of champagne, a long hot bath. Nice restaurants, crisp clothes.

Last autumn Lance swore to give up wandering, and he had. With Becky's help he was beginning to understand what it was all about. But he also realized what Becky didn't know – some amount of wandering was a good excuse for philandering.

"This is no time to reconsider a sworn oath," Lance thought. "Watch yourself, fool."

***

"Who's hungry?" Becky asked. "Who's tired, who's thirsty?" She smiled at the co-ed. "Who needs to wash up?"

"Thank you," said Nattie Sinclair. "I absolutely love these guys, but I've been stuck in a car with them for the last part of what seems like forever."

"Twelve and a half hours," Daniel said.

"I think we smell great," Adams, the big one, said. "G.," he said to the little guy, "check your pits."

"I'd love a tour of your house," Nattie told Becky. "I'd love a tour of your bathroom."

"There's a plan," said Becky. "Lance, why don't you take the posse out to the barn and show them around, show off your facilities. If you all aren't too tired, I'll throw a few things together and we can eat a little before you sleep.

"And you," she said to her son, shaking her finger at him while her eyes moistened a little, "welcome home, and why don't you ever tell a person anything?"

"Don't know enough, I guess." He smiled back at her.

And just like that, the farm and the barn filled up.

***

"Holy shit," Daniel said when he slid open the door and Lance hit the light switch. "This place's sure changed. What the hell..."

"Glad you like it," Lance said. "Imagine it does look a bit different."

"No shit," Daniel said.

"This is killer," Adams said. "This is unbelievable. It looks like some giant tree fort, or hidden boys' club. That a bedroom up there?"

"Hay loft," Lance said, "just some furniture, bed and dresser and chairs and whatnot. No more'n a bunkhouse, really."

"Hey, if this barn had looked like this when I was here it'd been a lot easier to get me out here, sanding wood and cleaning up. Look at this place. A real woodshop. Organized and efficient."

"A tribute to the old man, mostly," Lance told him. "Turns out the old bastard had a fondness for woodworking. Poor son of a bitch worked so hard as a farmer he must have never had time. Figured it was right to keep the place cleaned up and working. Not so much like the old days. Not a bad woodshop, you think?"

"Not bad at all," Daniel said.

"Talk you grunts into a cold beer? Sort of an end-of-the-road-trip nightcap?"

"Hell yes," Adams said.

"Man alive," the young kid, John Gophe, said while running his fingers along the top of the wood stove. "This is beautiful. I wish it was cold enough to have a fire. It almost is," he said hopefully. Becky and the co-ed – both looking refreshed – sauntered in through the big sliding door.

"Always cold enough for a fire," Lance said. He smiled at Becky and winked at the kid. "Sometimes you just have to move the cold around." Lance motioned to Adams. "Hop up there and open the loft up to the night sky. We'll move some air through and allow this young stud to heat us back up."

Adams sprang into action. "You got it," and he bounded up the heavy timber ladder. Almost immediately pounding and cussing and banging spilled down below. "I'm on it," Adams hollered down. "Don't worry, I've got it."

"Hold on to something," Nattie called up to him. "Get a grip, Man, get some traction."

Everybody laughed, and then Daniel said, "Just crack the door. Undo the latch and slide the door open a bit. Quit fooling with that window. It'll never open."

"Don't never say never to Cib Carkus Adams," Nattie said. "You tell him he can't do something, and that's all he'll try to do. Dogged," she hollered out so Adams could hear, "like a fever that won't let go."

"More like fourth and two and won't be denied," Adams yelled down.

Lance wondered if Becky also recognized the interplay between these two, the teasing banter and undertones that again took him back to another lifetime – when he and Becky and Danny laughed together always and drove the Valiant forever. Something very strange about these kids showing up tonight, something both calming and alarming. Not really déjà vu, more like a remake with new actors.

Lance laughed to himself when he thought that the new movie twist for the younger audience was the little guy – John Gophe. Lance couldn't quite figure him out, and he sure as hell couldn't place him anywhere in the memory banks. Shy and sweet and very bright but as turned inside out as anyone Lance had ever met. Lance had no idea why, but when he looked at John Gophe he thought of pineapple upside down cake. Perhaps getting out of bed and drinking Pabst Blue Ribbon at four o'clock in the morning had something to do with it.

Lance explained to the boy how the wood stove worked and how best to start the fire and where the different woods were. John Gophe listened intently.

"It's pretty damn simple," Lance said. "Just have fun with it."

After awhile Becky gathered a few empty platters and nodded toward Nattie.

"We're heading inside, let you carry on with boys-will-be-boys. There's all kinds of places to sleep. Maybe you all want to lay claim now?" She mostly said this to Nattie Sinclair.

After a brief silence, Lance said, "I don't think Becky or I care who any of you all sleep with. Everybody's welcome to bed down wherever and with whomever. There's a spare bedroom in the front of the house, and the sofa in the den pulls out into a bed. There's also a couch in the living room. The loft out here in the barn's got a bed, some floor mattresses and a couple of couches. It stays more'n warm enough with the wood-burning stove, and there's plenty of wood around. It's got a bathroom and a shower with cold running water."

"What about hot water?" Nattie asked.

"All you want," Lance said, "But you've got to make it on the stove." And then he sounded almost apologetic. "All kinds of light and electricity, though."

"Yeah," Becky laughed, "for all the hair dryers and blenders you'll want to be using."

Lance laughed also. "It really is kind of primitive."

"Sounds like the place for me," Daniel said. "I'll take the bed up in the loft."

"Me too," Gophe said. And then he stammered, "I don't mean I'm going to sleep in the bed too, just up in the barn loft."

"Good," Lance said, winking at Becky. "I'm likely to spend a bit of time out here myself."

There was a brief silence that lingered. Everybody waited for Adams and Nattie to claim a spot. Adams didn't let the silence linger long. Lance recognized a familiar edge when Adams finally said, "Well, sounds like boy's camp has been set up. I'm here too."

"Great!" said Nattie. "I'll take the clean warm spare bedroom in the house with women and hot water."

She said it with so much exuberance and humor that even Adams smiled. Lance suddenly realized he was practicing his old bar tricks – making assumptions about who did or didn't want to sleep with whom. "Yep," he said again, to nobody in particular. "I believe I'll spend a fair amount of time out here as well."

"May I look aghast at the loft before I retreat to feminized civilization?" Nattie asked.

"Sure Doll," Adams said. "May very well be your last invite."

When Nattie reached the top of the ladder she squealed. "This is so cool."

"It has all the makings," Lance agreed. "Sure as hell."

"What's with all the ropes and pulleys hanging all over the place?" Adams asked. "Looks like a gymnasium in here."

"Monkey pulleys," Lance told him. "Makes it a bit easier to get around, mostly to get up and down. Watch this."

Lance clomped over to the nearest rope and stepped his boot into a hanging loop. He reached over his head and pulled at a hanging knot, holding the end in his hand. A loud clanging came from the side wall where a series of heavy metal scrap was connected in intricate array. Lance floated up to the loft.

"It's all about pulleys and counter weights," he said. "I can pretty much get to any part of the barn, high or low, from pretty much anywhere. Just like a one-legged Tarzan, the Monkey Man."

"They're not monkey pulleys, and not a one of you is allowed to call them that," Becky said. "They're angel pulleys." She looked at Lance, and he could feel Daniel watching closely. "Angel pulleys," she said again.

The women went inside, and then things began winding down. Sofas, overstuffed chairs, John Gophe at his perch on a wooden stool in front of the stove.

And now Lance looking around, and breathing in, his life slowly settling into an aroma of oil soaked sawdust here in his own private haven, drinking beer before sunrise in his own barn filled with young bucks just arrived and on God knows what kind of adventure or folly. Lance freely admitted to himself a contentment that had been welling and building for some months.

"I love this barn," Adams said. "I'm never leaving."

Lance raised his own beer bottle and clinked it against Adams'.

"I'll wet one with you on that. Gather around, gentlemen," he called out, "this space and this road trip scream out for a christening, and now's the time."

"Hold on," Adams said. He sprinted out of the barn and then rushed back in clutching a nearly quarter-full bottle of Jack Daniel's from the Valiant. "Damn nearly finished this thing on the way in," he said. "Seems appropriate to kill it here, now that we've arrived." He twisted the cap off and put the bottle to his lips.

"Hang on, Cowboy," Lance said, scoffing at Adams' exuberance. "Drinking from the bottle's for drinking alone or drinking in sorrow. John, grab some of those baby food jars filled with those little wooden dowel plugs; we can dump the plugs here in this bucket; I'll sort them out later. Poison's all the same, boys, pick your needle."

"What have we got?" Adams asked. "Strained peas? I'll take the carrots. O'Neill," he said to Daniel, slapping him on the back, "thanks for the ride, Man." He grabbed a couple of empty baby food jars from John Gophe and held them out. "Pick yourself a good one."

"Vegetable beef," Daniel said. "I'll clean out my own, with my own bandanna."

"Fair enough."

"I'll take lima beans," John Gophe said. "I used to throw up on them, just like I probably will Jack Daniel's."

"Not today, Johnny G. We've arrived. We have indeed arrived," Adams said. "This is a morning starts everything new, including," he giggled, "your little problem with tolerance concerning the ways of men. A thing of the past, Buddy."

"I'll take the squash," Lance said.

Adams poured the mostly clean jars full all around, passing the neck back and forth across the tops of the baby food jars, making them even, and then forcing the capacity to empty the bottle.

Lance held his jar at arms length. "To the midnight arrival of youth and adventure; to all of you, plus the lovely young lady inside the house, being welcome here in this little wind sweep we call home. Slainte."

"I only took a sip because I wanted to save some for a toast of my own," Gophe said.

"That's the stuff," Daniel said. "Pace yourself. We're all doing the same."

"Okay," John Gophe said. "Here goes. I've got one. Daniel, thanks for bringing us. Now I know why you wanted to come back here. It's a wonderful place to be, a great place to come from. This barn is really special. I feel like I've been here all my life. I feel like I could do anything, or be anything, here in this place. I could stay forever. Mr. O'Neill, thank you for having us."

"Jesus," Adams cut in, "This could take a while. Mind if I take an interim nip? Just to tide me over?"

Lance swung Adams a fast look. "John, you're doing fine. Carry on. And by the way, my father's not here, so just call me O'Neill."

"Okay. Thanks, um, O'Neill. Anyway, I just want to say that it was pretty weird coming here, what with the midnight and all, but now I can really, you know, see why we came, and I'm just real happy to be here. So, uh, cheers. And thanks again. To everybody. For everything."

"Well said," Adams smiled, draining his baby food jar. He finally laughed in spite of all effort at maintaining a respectfully somber tone. "A good toast, Johnny G., deserves another."

"Hang on, Adams. I need some air, or a beer, or something. I think I need a little break."

John Gophe made his way to the barn door and staggered out into the awakening hints of sunrise.

"He okay?"

"He's fine. Just takes him awhile to get his legs about him."

"Not true," Daniel said. "We may have lost him for the duration. Something like a crippled mare. Awful sweet, and real happy to hang around licking sugar."

Almost immediately after stumbling out, John Gophe returned, supported on either side by Becky Dreiling and Nattie Sinclair.

"Look what we found wandering in the yard. What's wrong with you shitheads, throwing babes outside in this condition?"

"I'm all right," Gophe said. "Thanks. I'm good." He reached out for the wall and sat down on a plastic five-gallon bucket.

"Ladies!" Lance said. "Perfect entrance. Just in time for welcome toasts and salutations."

"Better idea," Becky said, "is to get these kids to bed before the sun comes up and we start losing all of them."

She shot Lance a look and he could see immediately that he agreed with her. It was time to call it a night, or a morning, or whatever.

***

It wasn't the snoring that kept me awake that first night sleeping up in the hayloft at Becky Dreiling's farm. You have to get used to sleeping amid noise and clatter when you sleep in a dorm. It wasn't the excitement of arriving from a road trip, either. We had gotten in so late, almost four in the morning, that the road trip party just kind of turned into a barn party – all of us, Daniel's mom and everybody, standing around in this enormous barn drinking beer, telling stories, laughing and acting comfortable like we were a big family who'd just come home for Christmas or the Fourth of July.

Daniel's uncle Lance had a metal 7-Up cooler filled with iced beer. There was also a pretty nice stereo set-up, and Daniel's mom had brought out all kinds of platters of cheeses and bread and sausages and crackers and dip, and we just stayed in the barn like it was some elegant parlor.

Actually there was much more than a stereo; the barn was like a cross between a Gentlemen's' Lounge and Geppetto's woodshop. All kinds of saws and power tools and workbenches and woodbins and cabinets filled with oils and stains and rags set up on the far side of the barn, beneath the hayloft. A big wood-burning cookstove surrounded by overstuffed chairs and couches filled the open side, near the huge sliding door. You couldn't help but feel at home. The minute you walked in you were comfortable. Even though I had ridden like a madman in the Valiant all night and drank like a wild man until dawn – by rights I should have been passed out or dead – I was wide awake up in the hayloft bedroom.

The sun pounded loud outside beyond the barn door, but that's not what kept me awake either. The sky had already gotten light by the time we went to bed, and all the snoring certainly showed everybody else was sleeping fine. It wasn't the sunlight that kept me awake. The day was out there, too, but that also wasn't calling me.

I felt both excitement and unsettled. Everything in this barn and at this farm sparkled new and exuberant – the feeling of little kids wild and joyful at an extended family picnic. Everything was possible and anything might happen. Out of space and out of time.

And yet, like a stomach buzz refusing to subside, I couldn't shake my midnight revelation that Nattie was the girl Catherine Teaza. That's what kept me awake.

Familiar. Strangling. Nurturing. My own childhood chased me down and followed me here. It had jumped out and, like a shadow along a blacktop highway, clutched me hard and hitched a ride. It made me dizzy and it made me nauseous. Like a horrible hangover where the whiskey is everything you thought you'd left behind.

Nattie clearly didn't recognize me, or, if she did, she too didn't want that old stuff anywhere near the new. Anywhere near the now. Was she outside the barn calling me, waking me, needing me. Wanting me?

Dag! There was the rub. Nattie Sinclair had never wanted me, and the girl Catherine barely noticed me. That's what needed to change. I was smacked hard with the clear realization that that needed to change. I needed to change it. That's why Nattie Sinclair was the girl Catherine. That's why I was wide awake. That's why something was calling me out, calling me up, calling me into the now. That's why I was called down from the hayloft and out of the barn. The old me would have creeped down the ladder, making no noise, knowing I wouldn't be noticed. The new me, the now me, grabbed the top of the ladder and swung my legs over and plunged down.

The dirt floor of the barn felt smooth and cool and very deep below my bare feet – deep enough so my stomach sank effortlessly down into it, down and connected deep, and it was calm. I realized I should crawl back up and fetch my sneakers; I wasn't allowed to go barefoot. I started back up the ladder, and then I was hit again square by a gigantic wave of something fresh like new school clothes, hit by something brand new like no footprints in a February snowstorm.

I realized with absolute and sudden clarity that I could go barefoot if I wanted. I needn't sever the connection between my feet and the cool earth floor. I stood still and wondered. My feet were so clean, so white, and so soft and tender. When I was little, my father got so angry when he saw people not wearing shoes. Sister Mary Pat, my third grade teacher, warned ominously that the ground teemed with all manner of germs and bacteria. Shoes protected us from a base malevolence and spiritual sloth.

I wiggled my toes like a toddler. My feet slid across the cool dirt toward the huge sliding barn door.

I could feel the day and the sunlight against the cracks in the door, either voraciously gnawing to claw its way inside or beckoning with sweetness like a siren song – calling and singing and gently inviting me to step out.

I opened the barn door.

She didn't see me at first, and then she didn't see me at all. I stood frozen and stared, watching Becky Dreiling move gently through the kitchen garden in the morning sunlight. I didn't move a muscle, like a squirrel who's seen a cat. Becky Dreiling, thinking for sure we were all asleep, in the morning sunlight in the kitchen garden. Becky Dreiling, relaxed and smooth and totally alone except for me and the sunshine and a tiny pair of panties.

She was bending over, facing away from me, and as I looked closely, I could see she was releasing something from a clear glass jar – a spider trapped gently inside the house and gracefully let to wander again in the kitchen garden.

And then she started to turn my way, her back toward me now, but her breasts and her face and her flat stomach turning now my way and I was about to see them. Her breasts. Not pictures in a magazine but real flesh in the sunshine, turning my way. I only had to hold my ground and stay still and keep watching her turning while she doesn't know I'm there, standing and staring and frozen and still.

Her blond hair wafts like flowing invitation, she's turning toward me. For just a moment she's not a mom and she's not a woman, but a gently turning planet, like the earth turning toward me. This is it, this is what you wait for, this is how it happens. This is the time to stand and hold my ground, because she's turning my way and she doesn't know that I'm watching; and when she turns all the way and sees me, I'll hold my ground and I'll have had a split-second look that I'll remember forever. I'm there watching and frozen and staring and, just as she completes her turn and her breasts are about to be there in the sunshine, I move and I flinch and I bend down and I look for a job so that she doesn't think I was standing there staring.

I look to be busy doing anything other than be frozen and staring and watching her turn.

A piece of wood is in my hand. My hand is in the firewood box, and I'm looking for kindling and building a fire. I suddenly know with a certainty that a fire in the wood cook stove demands the utmost care and complete attention. I cannot waver, I cannot look away from the seriousness of fire, and when Becky Dreiling turns finally and sees me, I will be busy and focused, engaged with the clearly important business of tending the fire. It will be as if I don't even know she's there, so intent am I on tending the fire.

Who can say anything about tending the fire except it's an extremely important job that must always be done, especially early in the morning for coffee and heralding the sun? When Becky Dreiling looks at me, I won't be standing and staring and frozen. She will see that I am busy and focused, tending the fire.

I have become the keeper of the hearth.

"Life roughs you up.
And then it sands you smooth."

- Becky Dreiling

Chapter 13

Lance came busting into the kitchen and Nattie could immediately tell what kind of morning was ahead for him and Becky. First he flashed a gorgeous good morning wink at Nattie and then he slipped his arm around Becky's waist.

"Top of the good goddamn morning, ladies. You both look like golden slivers of prairie sunrise."

Becky turned towards him, and then she planted a cute quicklickity little bite on the bottom of his ear.

"What's so up with you this morning?"

When they both laughed into one another's eyes, Nattie felt transported. She loved the mornings following one of Lance and Becky's infrequent nights together.

The kitchen filled rapidly with a soft sexual breeze; it would linger until late afternoon, and Becky and Nattie would luxuriate throughout the day in its wake, breathing in a subtle and ongoing orgasm.

Nattie loved the sexual separation taking place at the farm. Girls inside, playing house; boys outside, playing who knows what in the barn. Even though they sometimes ate together, the separation was strong, because none of the intimate time was being spent together. The sleeping time, the bathroom time. The morning time, before anyone has a chance to put their day face on, before anyone changes, while everyone is simply who they are. Nattie welcomed the exhilaration, and she loved the tension building like a great wall of dammed-up water (actually, like a great wall of pent-up semen), threatening to crash through and wreck havoc, or create life, or destroy them all. She loved it.

Sitting and watching Lance and Becky play and cavort around the kitchen – he was going on and on about some rocks or something he found – Nattie realized again how little she was missing sex herself. Hell, she thought, as good as it is with Adams, I think I could forsake it forever if I knew I could live out my remaining days in this kitchen. A pulsating narcotic aphrodisiac; a low level constant cum. Spending time with Becky offered access to a mythical feminine energy: like thrusting your head through a hedge of zinnias to breathe in the fragrance of the air between women.

"No, I mean it. Listen to this," Lance was saying. "This is a coup, the steal of the century."

"Plus," Becky laughed, "Sounds like it's just sitting there, nobody using it."

And then they both laughed together when he said "and I've got a ready battalion of pumped young men corralled out in our barn, just busting to do some heavy lifting."

"Nattie," Becky said, "feel like bailing the boys out of the pokey at four in the morning tomorrow?"

Nattie looked up from her gentle daydream of flow with Becky.

"He wants to sneak the boys into town and steal city property tonight."

"No, not quite." Lance bustled about, throwing crackers and cans of sardines and Vienna sausages into a sack.

"Assisting the town in the process of reclamation and recycling of refuse." He laughed again, and gave Becky this affirmative eyebrow wiggle. "Unsightly refuse," he told her.

"Unsightly," she said, "and likely to be retrieved by a higher authority sometime very soon."

Then they both laughed like hell. "Yeah," he said. "That too. That's why we've got to hurry. But right now, it's just lying there, waiting for someone to pick it up."

For Nattie, part of the fun in watching these two was the mystery in so much of their discourse. It made no difference what they were talking about; Nattie enjoyed floating along with it and suckling at their connection. She marveled at the energy between them and saw it often in a picture on their mantle. She could see the fibers in their clothes drawing together; the skin between them was quivering and there was a tension in their hair. The picture is of them with another man who Becky said was her husband.

Behind them in the photograph is a mountain lake with a spread of camping beach. It seemed a familiar beach and a familiar lake, an important setting, Nattie thought, in our collective childhoods. Shared myths and fantasies.

Nattie believed that her looking at the photograph gave Becky great pleasure.

Lance flew out of the kitchen as chaotically as he entered.

"Men," Becky said to Nattie. "You gotta love 'em."

"That I do. Every one of them."

***

Nattie realized early on that living with Becky was its own kind of incredible. Life changing, she thought. Magnificent. Nattie swallowed whole all there was to learn from Becky. She was intuitive, and more importantly, Becky was a woman who trusted her intuition. She was more interested in the feel of things than the facts of them. She listened exquisitely well and heard everything. She was centered and safe and strong. Nattie was fascinated with how Becky regulated her life to the lunar cycle.

She owned and often consulted a Wiccan almanac. It contained healing spells and described not only what phase the moon was in but in what constellation of the Zodiac. It was filled with all kinds of other information, and Nattie looked through it frequently. Becky had candles and trinkets and incense on an altar in the front room. She spoke of the goddess and of balanced energy. She began every month with a new moon ritual that included cleaning and oiling a beautiful, enormous, three-legged cast iron pot. It sat outside on the ground near the front porch, amid flower gardens and a patch of cool grass. Becky had insisted Nattie join her last week in the ritual, and Nattie was breathless to do it again at next month's new moon. Becky tended her garden vegetables out back on the last quarter; she made and froze food of all kinds at first quarter moon. Last week, at full moon, they listened to Melanie loud on the stereo and drank red wine. They set up easels in the big kitchen and painted with acrylics on canvas. They sang and laughed and remembered while Melanie sprawled all around them, as big as the land with the velvet hills in the small of her back and her hands playing in the sand. They celebrated with her, loud and raucous and joyful, swimming in all of the water, knowing that all the rivers are givers to the ocean, according to plan.

Making and arranging their lives around the earth's natural rhythms and the cycles of the moon gave Nattie a sense of calm and clarity unparalleled. It gave them a connection to each other and to something much larger. Nattie couldn't help but notice that focusing so keenly on the moon dulled all separation from boys and men out in the barn. The something much larger didn't exclude men, necessarily, but it didn't seem to require much of them, either.

The closeness and ease made Nattie believe they could talk about anything.

One day, Nattie asked, "What do you know about Daniel that explains why he's still a virgin?"

Becky was not dumbfounded at all, but Nattie watched her quickly identify and eliminate, in her own mind, the various uncomfortable aspects of that question.

"That's interesting news to me," Becky finally said. "I'd want to think about it awhile. Why? Are you sweetly trying to slip me some inside information?"

"No, no, not at all. And it's not like I've gone to any great efforts myself. I love him a lot just the way he is. He's an extremely important friend. I guess I just always figured he came from a pretty uptight upbringing. I figured that's why he seemed so asexual. But this," Nattie said, nodding around the kitchen and smiling at Becky, "this is hardly uptight."

"No," Becky agreed. "No it's not."

Becky oozed through small chores in the kitchen, her form nearly as fluid as a flowing stream. The room was bright, now, full morning on its way.

After a bit of time, Becky said, "How well do you know Daniel?"

"He's detached from everything, in a way, and at the same time he's tightly centered around some astonishing inner strength," Nattie said. "It's extremely attracting."

Nattie looked right at Becky and her eyes squinted a tiny bit in the corners. "He's never told me himself, perhaps he doesn't even know, but I know what's different about him."

She watched Becky Dreiling wonder what secrets there might be about her son, and Nattie watched her wonder if she wanted to know what those secrets were.

"Daniel doesn't believe that you're born, you live, you die, and then go to heaven or hell. He believes in reincarnation, where individual souls keep coming back, adopting new personalities and new lives each time. He believes souls float around the universe in packs, in huge groups of maybe several thousand souls. When the souls are together, and not down here on earth living their respective lives, they exist as a single entity, like hydrogen and oxygen molecules have identity, but when you put a bunch of them together, you get a drop of water.

"So his idea is that these souls choose what kinds of lives to jump into based on what they have yet to learn – maybe they need to learn something from being poor, or being crippled, or being murdered, or being ruthless."

"Never sweet or helpful? No nice lives for souls to fall into?"

"Oh sure, every kind of life and personality you can think of. We've all been, or will be, everything."

"Just goes to show you," Becky said, cutting in so she could catch up, "if you don't tell your kids what to believe, they're liable to believe anything."

But she smiled to herself, and Nattie could see this glorious moment of recognition, or self-recognition, flash through Becky's eyes.

"Comfortingly similar to a lot of the things we believed when we were his age. Very Tao. Very Buddhist. Very Berkeley."

"I guess," Nattie said. "Not much chance of us coming up with anything really new, I guess."

"You'd be surprised," Becky said slowly. "So what does Daniel believe? That he was a rapist in his last life? Or is he beating himself up believing he was a child molester, and he's paying now for those sins."

"I don't know what he believes, or what's up with the sex thing. I just know what I believe."

She waited, and then Nattie said, "I think this is his last time around, his last incarnation, his final trip on this physical reality. After this life, he won't be back."

"Ah," Becky said, almost betraying a satisfied smile. "An old soul."

"Exactly. Very old."

"Well," Becky laughed, "a woman could do worse than a wise old soul for a son."

"I don't know about wise. I just know old. Very old."

"So suddenly this doesn't sound good. Like senile old?"

"More. I think like bored old. Like understand it, accept it, even love it old, but definitely seen it all before old. Ready to move on old. Spent the last several lifetimes packing, waiting for the silver spaceship old."

"And his eyes growing weary from the yellow haze of the sun."

"Right. Exactly. Great song. And that's it. Ready to move on."

"So if he's already done it all, what keeps him interested? What's fun about life?"

"I think that's exactly the issue for old souls like Daniel. Souls on their last leg. Very little interests them. So easy for old souls to be hobos, to be bums. Brilliant bums, or unbelievably compassionate bums, or drunk bums. Can't seem to find a foothold anywhere bums."

"That sounds so sad," Daniel O'Neill's mother said. "What do you suppose keeps them interested in life? What keeps them going?"

Nattie smiled warmly at her, sharing the concern and the burden.

"I think that's the key, finding out what delights a man like that."

Becky finally just shook her head. "I've spoken with him so little since he went off to college," she said. "And I've not seen him at all. Having him back here suddenly, with all of you, is so strange – almost like I'm watching Salvador Dali mow lawns in the suburbs – the prodigal son meets up with Lazarus.

"I do love, though," she said to Nattie, "hearing your perspective on him."

Becky was quiet for a bit, and Nattie waited for the revelation she knew was coming. Nattie reveled in this bridge she and Becky constructed, this story-telling and soul-massaging connection.

"I think it's also very possible," Becky said, beginning slowly, "mostly because of mistakes I've made, that Daniel carries around some significant sexual confusions. He may not be an old soul at all, just a very confused one. Not necessarily confusion about his own sexuality, more like confusion just about sexuality in general.

"God help him, he was conceived by people caught in a raging vortex of irresponsible exploration. We truly believed we were charting new territory in the human condition. My," she said, while her head moved back and forth from wonder to disgust, "we thought we were all so smart. Everything was okay with us. Big-time rebels. Look at me, changing the universe by refusing to change my maiden name. Keeping my maiden name. Big deal. Oh so brave, so enlightened. Anything that stretched limits or pushed boundaries, we embraced. If your theory of souls turns out to be wrong, then I think Daniel is a great example of how someone as meaningless as me can indulge herself and release a curse. We created a plague; not so much because we went too far with anything, though God knows many of us did, but because of the Pandora's Box we opened. Every generation breaks some rules; we were so damn smart we simply decided rules didn't exist. Rules were pitiful, mere subjective baubles of bourgeois reality.

"My," she said again, and again shook her head, "we were all so smart.

"When anything goes, anything can happen. We believed anything would naturally be positive and good, simply because we conceived of it. Not one of us stopped to think maybe anything could be bad."

"If everything's in color, then nothing's in color," Nattie offered.

"Exactly. If everything's true, then nothing's true. And Daniel was a result of that kind of thinking. We were so in tune with the universe. We were all so goddamned evolved."

"There's a fabulous story lurking here," Nattie said. "I can smell it. Have you told it in a while?"

"Not in a long while, and never completely." Becky looked at the younger woman with a sly sister smile. "It's a pretty good one. Pretty revealing, though, and maybe dangerous, too. And you know, I've thought about it a lot since you guys arrived. I get this burn of uncomfortable déjà vu when I look at the extended little family you and these three guys have developed.

"The closeness and care you all have is obvious and beautiful to watch, but it scares me."

"Scares you why? Scares you how?"

"I'm sure I'm just imagining my past onto your future. But I get that same sense from you all that you've somehow placed yourselves out of space and out of time, like all the rules are off. That's a thrilling and exhilarating ride, but it's one that scares me, for you."

***

Becky and Nattie changed into cutoffs and T-shirts before heading outside to work in the strawberry patch – to clean it and prepare it for the summer.

Becky said the new young plants were called "runners," and the older, established plants she called "mothers." Both women held a dandelion digger, a long metal spike which resembled more than anything a hardened serpent's tongue. They used them to loosen the earth and to dig out the first sprouting of wild violet and choke vine; and mostly they used the tools to separate the young plants, the runners, from the older mother plants.

Strawberry tending, Nattie suddenly realized, is matricide.

The mother plants nurture the new plants through an umbilical cord while the new plants put down tentative, and slowly strengthening, roots.

After several years of bearing both fruit and young, the mothers need to be plucked out to make space for the children. And because so much growth energy has gone into putting out runners, the older, larger plants slowly lose their ability to bear fruit.

"Eventually, they'll die out naturally. But if we pull some of the older ones, and cut the cords from the established babies, it makes the entire patch healthier," Becky said. She began telling her story as they worked, though mostly Nattie just watched, kneeling in the dirt and pulling nothing more than an occasional dead leaf.

Becky worked quickly, wasting no time deciding between the mother plants she pulled out and the ones to which she granted another cycle of bearing fruit and nurturing young. Runners with well-developed roots she snipped from the mother and gingerly aerated with her dandelion knife. She pat fresh dirt around the tiny plant, and Nattie followed along, letting trickle fertilized water from a metal watering can.

Strawberries, Nattie thought, are not particularly pretty plants – they look matronly rather than fertile, and Nattie wondered what degree of pleasure Becky derived from the finality of her decisions in her effort to shape her patch.

But soon Nattie forgot about fruit and got carried down into the roots of Becky's story. She began slowly, building with simple details.

***

"I married a good friend of mine when I was very young."

Becky looked at Nattie hard for a minute. "That's not an excuse, I was just young. I was a wife. He was Lance's brother, actually, and I married him in college, because I believed it would keep him out of Vietnam.

"I don't know what you know about that, what you've heard, but Vietnam was a horrible obscenity, an appalling filth of ego and lies. It made so many of us do so many things. Anyway, Lance knew why I married Danny, but it hurt him like hell nevertheless. And in the end it didn't matter, because both the sons of bitches went off and joined up anyway."

Becky stopped abruptly. She sat motionless on her haunches, staring at a mother strawberry plant clutched in her gloved hand. Nattie could tell she'd just heard the succinct summation of the entire story, and she let it sink in.

"Danny O'Neill died in Vietnam because we played around and paid no attention to what in the hell we were doing.

"Danny had a shitty low number, and he had stupidly dropped out of college. Lance's number was a lot better, and the bastards were still mostly honoring college deferments, even though they were starting to play games with that, too. Danny planned to wait for his number to come up and then take a big, in your face, political stand.

"Lance said the hell with it; he wanted us all to move to Canada. Danny was contemptuous, said that was cowardice. God, they used to fight about it, screaming back and forth. Lance was a year older, and the brother thing between them was always intense.

"So I thought I could solve it by making Danny fall in love with me and then marrying him and bringing him here to run this farm. Danny was so proud; I knew there was no way he'd go along with the ruse. I had to be pretty damn convincing. Lance knew what I was doing and didn't like it, but he agreed because he could see how set Danny was either getting himself killed or thrown in jail over a principle. I had some vague plan of setting it all straight after the draft problem had passed us by. But in the meantime, Lance and I agreed to stop sleeping together."

Becky looked at Nattie again hard. "We agreed to stop making love."

After Becky said this, she was quiet for a long time. She sat back on her heels and twisted a strawberry blossom in her fingers. The yellow center of the tiny white flower stained her hands and crushed easily. Her pain slowly rose to her surface as more details of the memory bubbled up. The serpent tongue in Nattie's hand was motionless, transfixed.

"Danny fell pretty hard. He told me he loved me within three days. He asked me to marry him within three weeks. Within three and a half weeks, we did. It changed him completely. I couldn't believe it. No longer intense and angry and proud, he was becoming all these pieces of lighthearted, optimistic, and happy.

"He took his life savings, cashed out an insurance policy he had, and went and bought an almost brand new car. That same car," Becky said, nodding her head toward the front of the house and smiling wistfully, "that you kids arrived here in. *Not fancy*, he used to say proudly, *but reliable as you could like.*

"We called it the 1965 Plymouth Valiant because that's what it was. No marketing glitz, no Fifth Avenue charm. A solid, workmanlike automobile. It became our home as the three of us left college and left California. We gaily assured the draft board we'd stay in touch, and we took off to live on the road.

"Danny fell in love with this farm when we stopped to see my dad on our way to our honeymoon. The two of them, my father and my husband, hit it off like they had grown up together; they stayed up talking both nights we were here, laughing and making plans. He really liked my dad, and Danny got excited about moving here and helping run the place. It was my dad's dream; pass the farm on to a son. For me, it was like some perverse mating ritual; marrying me stripped him of his intense attachment to the great issues of the day: economic justice, social equality, intellectual freedom, individual morality. Suddenly, he decides all he needs is a nice life on a beautiful farm with his new wife whom, it turns out, he loved a great deal.

"I had created a mess; that was clear to me by the time we arrived at this beautiful lake in the mountains of Colorado. Pactolus Lake."

"Pactolus. Isn't that the mythic river flowing with gold?" Nattie wasn't sure how or why she knew this, but she did.

"Maybe," Becky said. "I think so. I think it's the river where King Midas washed off his ability to turn things into gold. Which,"

Becky said after a wistful pause," is actually very appropriate. Anyway," she continued, "we were going to camp for a week, all three of us. Danny was so excited. We'd fish, throw Frisbees, cook over an open fire on the beach. He had such a sweet vision, he was so happy: his own car, his only brother, his new wife.

"Lance got angrier and angrier as the days went on, and it was all directed at me. More and more, he wanted to spend what little time we had alone together talking about how we would end the charade, or fighting about how much I was enjoying myself.

"It was scary. He was getting crazy with jealousy. *I don't know what to do*, I told him. *I don't know what to do.*

Did you fall in love with him, too?

I love him a lot, and I don't know how I could hurt him.

Are you in love with him? Lance was furious.

I can't hurt him, I said.

"I still hear those conversations, over and over in my head."

Becky's voice burned with pain when she told this next part.

"Lance asked me again if I was still in love with him. I just cried, and he held me, and while my husband walked around the shore of a beautiful Colorado mountain lake I made love to Lance O'Neill inside of my honeymoon tent for the first time in two months.

"That same night, because I was confused and scared and felt guilty, I also had sex with my new husband, Danny O'Neill. It was like he became blinded to reality. He couldn't tell there was a thing wrong. He was peaceful and happy. I was frightened to death when he went out of the tent afterwards and sat by the fire with Lance. I just lay there and listened to the two of them talk.

Lance, Danny told his brother, *tonight I'm a truly happy man. I'm glad you're here with me. Although,* and I cringed when Danny said this, *I really feel for you, knowing you had a shot at that woman, and you let her get away.*

"He laughed loudly, and I could hear him clasp Lance across the back. I lay in that tent listening to the tick of a testosterone time bomb.

"I didn't have to wait long. Lance just came out with it, sat there and in two minutes told Danny everything. Of course Danny didn't believe him, and it was refreshing for a moment to hear some of the old fire come back into his voice.

"Both of them knew I was listening from inside the tent.

Do it, Becky, Lance called out in the dark mountain air. *Tell him it's all a lie. Or tell him I'm full of shit. Tell us both you're not in love with me.*

"I just cried and couldn't say anything and Danny finally got up and took another very long walk along the lake. I don't know where he slept that night. I don't know where Lance slept, either. I slept in my honeymoon tent by myself. The next morning, Danny threw some clothes in his backpack, walked to the highway and hitched into town. Lance and I packed everything into the Valiant and went looking for him. We found him two days later in a bar. I was utterly exhausted so Lance dropped me back at our shitty little motel room and went back to join his brother. The two of them sat talking in the bar until it closed, then walked around the streets of this dirty little mountain town.

When they came to get me the next morning, they both looked as crummy as I felt. They told me they were both off to enlist in the goddamned army, and just like that, they jumped on a bus and they did. I cried and laid around in the motel room for a few days, unable to get out of bed. Then I packed up the Valiant and came back here.

"Within a couple of weeks my exhaustion turned into what I thought was a stomach flu." Becky shook her head, fighting off tears. "Of course, it turned out not to be stomach flu at all, and from that day to this I've never had any idea which of my honeymoon lovers is the father of my son.

"I fooled around with things I shouldn't have gotten involved with; I played with emotions I had no right to manipulate. I believed God was dead, so I believed the old rules no longer applied to me. I've lived forever since with two stakes of pain and sorrow ripping into me. Pain I caused, sorrow I created. A horrid, unspeakable affliction cast onto the two men I love. Their lives lost and ruined like two points of destruction and despair driven violently into my flesh."

Becky didn't cry but her sadness soaked Nattie through. After a short while she almost smiled.

"Sometimes," she said, "I blame them. And that's my sin. I blame their lack of vision, lack of expansion. I blame their lack of ability to open up, like a full moon, and embrace the trinity that might have been."

***

"The smells in this kitchen are wonderful," Nattie told Becky later in the week as she lounged over morning coffee while Becky worked at the sink, slicing and chopping and whatever. "Storybook smells, smells of myth and belonging."

"Childhood," Becky agreed. "This kitchen always smells to me like childhood. Wonderful, nurturing. I'm so mellow and grateful in this kitchen," she said. "Not a religious contentment, but a spiritual one certainly. Like being back in your childhood, where you spend your mornings waking up in the lap of an angel."

Nattie hesitated for a moment, uncertain.

"Not my childhood," she said softly.

Becky turned and smiled almost sadly at Nattie without comment. Nattie looked for some sign in her eyes that she understood, or was willing to understand, or that everything was okay now, or that none of it mattered now. A sign of recognition only, perhaps.

Becky is extraordinary, Nattie thought. Beautiful, soft and strong. Accepting and gracious. A wise woman of the tribe.

Finally, Nattie decided to tell Becky some of it.

"My childhood was ... different," she began. "A comical grotesque, filled with all kinds of things that left little room for me. My mom, she didn't cook in the kitchen. She really didn't do very many mom things. Her kitchen never smelled like this. Her kitchen usually smelled like those little plastic fake lime juice things. You know? The kind little pathetic moms used believing they were covering up the smell of Vodka? She, um, she had a sort of bad hand dealt her, I guess, but she was pathetic anyway."

Becky stopped slicing into the pile of meat and veggies for the stew or whatever it was Johnny planned to cook today out in the barn. She dumped the pile into a clean bowl and whisked it into the fridge. She wiped her hands on a tea towel slung over her shoulder and then sat at the table across from Nattie.

"You can tell me anything you like, Nattie," she said. "You can tell me whatever feels right."

"I'll just tell you this," Nattie said, "and if you don't want to hear it, that's fine, just let me know and I'll shut up."

Becky nodded and smiled. Nattie felt an enormous embrace — she climbed into a softness and breathed it all in, and then she breathed it all away.

"So here goes. The smell I really remember from my childhood is this attic we had when I was really little. The attic was up these stairs at the end of a long, dark hallway. You went down to the end of the hallway and there was a door, smaller than the other doors that went to the bedrooms and bathrooms. Behind the little end door was one of those lights with a string hanging down that you have to pull, and then long and narrow steps going up to the attic. It was like the mirror reverse of your attic. Farmhouse attic off the sunny kitchen, childhood attic at the end of a long dark hallway. I'm sure yours is much nicer inside."

"Lance keeps it locked."

"I noticed."

Nattie didn't say anything for a moment, and neither did Becky.

"Well, anyway, at the top of the stairs in my childhood hallway was this dusty, filthy, poorly lit attic. A lot of junk up there, some of which was probably there when we moved into the house, not even our junk. You know? We lived in a house filled with landlord junk. Anyway, my mom used to spend a lot of time up in that attic filled with crummy light and dried-out spider webs. She sat kind of hunched over in this dinky little rocking chair, just rocking and staring out a filthy window and sort of mumbling to herself. It was grotesque, and now, as a grown-up, I sometimes wonder if she actually was crazy, which would be a nice dramatic addition to my genetic trash pile. I don't know if she was or not. But I know she was grotesque. Or macabre. Or something.

"She used to make me come up there and sit on her lap sometimes, when I got home from school, and she'd clutch me and rock me and mumble and tell me a terrible story, the same story, over and over.

"She always smelled. Not smelled badly, really, just smelled, sort of like sweet decay. That's the smell I remember from my childhood."

***

Becky wept. First for Nattie and her memories, and then for Nattie despite them. She wept just for childhoods lost or ruined or gone. For some time neither woman spoke. The moist warm air already filling the kitchen opened wide like a chasm, waiting for them to tumble in.

"Bless your heart," Becky said, without meaning to and surprising herself. "I'm sorry."

Becky watched Nattie's eyes glisten and then dry. She searched the younger woman's face, wondering how many different wounds conspired to make Nattie who she was, conspired to bring Nattie here to sit at her kitchen table. Becky was astonished that such a vibrant, happy, and wonderfully infectious spirit could carry this depth of inner pain. She felt overwhelmed with the desire to reach out and stroke this beautiful head of auburn-strung sorrows.

"The other day, when you told me about your marriage, you confessed a deep sin," Nattie finally said. "Do you think the sin has defined you, has become your fate, or are you forgiven?"

"Which sin do you mean?" Becky smiled. "I've committed my share."

"The one about believing both your lovers were somehow at fault – they were two damaged points of an otherwise perfect trilogy. Or maybe it was a tripod."

"A triptych. A trinity that refused to come together," Becky said. "I did see it that way, and it does feel like a sin. A sin of hubris, I guess. A sin against the continuum of history. My sin against the Brothers O'Neill. I don't know, but surely a sin."

"But are you forgiven?" Nattie repeated, "Or will it forever describe who you are?"

"I can't imagine God forgiving me, even if I believed in him, and even if I went to confession, which I haven't done," she said ruefully, "in an awfully long time.

"Lance and I can't even talk about it, or we don't, or we won't. I don't really know which. But certainly he can't forgive me." Becky swallowed hard before saying, "I sure as hell doubt Danny forgives me."

"What about forgiving yourself?"

"Greeting card nonsense," Becky said. " Doesn't mean anything. Doesn't matter. Doesn't help."

"That's for sure," Nattie said.

"You're awfully young to be feeling the weight of such deep remorse." Becky reached over and stroked the back of Nattie's hand. "You're the one who's been hurt. It's not your fault. You've committed no sin."

"I betrayed my father," Nattie blurted out.

"Wow," Becky said. "Are you sure?"

"What do you mean?"

"I mean that often, especially when we're young, we believe our actions are bigger, worse, than they actually are. 'Betray'," Becky said, "is a big word."

"Take it from me," Nattie said. "It's probably not big enough."

"Do you want to tell me about it?"

"Yes," Nattie said. "Yes I do."

She picked her words carefully, feeling each step before taking the next.

"There's a fair amount of, uh, problems in my family, in my bloodline," Nattie said. "When I was 12 years old and met Gregor Mendel in school, I discovered that the problems were not only in my bloodline, but in my blood as well. It was in me. I came home from school one day – we were living in yet a different house by this time – but I still came home in the afternoons and watched my

262

mother rock and cackle. Different room, different house, but the same grotesque. This was well beyond the time when she made me sit in her lap, but I used to watch her just the same. I don't even think half the time she knew I was there. I was watching her, feeling disgusted, also thinking about the other, um, the different genetic warnings in my family, and I suddenly had the horrible realization that I would never be able to look at my own children for fear of seeing the deformities I might pass down to them."

Like breathing a soft epiphany, Becky asked quietly, "What was the story your mom told you?"

"What do you mean? Which story?"

"The horrible one she told you over and over when you were a little girl and she rocked you?"

"My mother used to sit and tell me how my father brought evil into our family. She said that's why things were the way they were in my family. She said he drank with the devil and agreed to let the evil in. I loved my father a lot – I still do. He is by far the most decent man I'll ever know. So I was confused when I was little, because he seemed so wonderful to me. But when you're six or seven, you can't really know what a fucked up abortion your own mother is, so you believe whatever she tells you. At least I did.

"The evil was in my father, she said, and in my brothers, and if she wasn't careful, it would get into her, too. But she insisted that I was different. And as I think about it now, I realize that's probably part of why I believed her, because her twisted little story made me the secret princess.

"She said my dad wasn't really my father. My real father was a warrior hero who carried gold across midnight beaches, who found her, who loved her passionately for one night and who vanished before morning. He left a seed within her, and he blessed the seed with her tears. That seed became me. She said my true father was pure and good and strong, and no evil was part of me. I was different. I was special.

"My sin was wanting her story to be true, even though I knew that meant abandoning the father I loved."

"God could have made us nicer to each other.
It wouldn't have killed him."

- Daniel O'Neill

Chapter 14

My stomach buzzed queasy at the creepy part of saying those two words – peg leg. Archaic. Disrespectful. Almost funny and very sad. Nothing, however, compared to the strangeness of the leg itself. Man alive, talk about creepy. Everyone else acted like it was no big deal, like they didn't even notice at all. It was everything I could do to try and act the same. But I stole as many looks as I dared when I could be sure he wasn't looking anywhere near me.

You could hear it plainly when he was up in the loft. It clomped around up there scary and unsettling sounding maybe like the creaking mast on a quiet night aboard a sailing ship with wooden decks. But when he was down with us on the hard-packed dirt of the barn floor, everything was quieter, almost soothing. The peg leg sunk into the dirt ever so slightly with each step he took, as if every repeated depression, every silver-dollar size divot speckling the barn floor was actually some exercise in personal grounding. Either way – clomping and crazy and freaky or quiet and soft, Daniel's Uncle Lance seemed to go out of his way to bring attention to the thing. First just having it, and then having so many of them. It would have been almost funny if he had a different one for every day of the week, but he had an entire rack of them, hanging like sports or hunting trophies along the wall behind where the wood cook stove was. Some very simple, cut and finished and polished, some extremely elaborate in their decoration – pieces of bone, or beads, leather and metal. All kinds, like Indian totems or warrior clubs. Every day Lance strapped on a different one, and though he did it without drama or fanfare, it felt like a solemnizing ceremony, exotic and even a bit primal. It made the whole boys' club thing more serious, like the peg leg became the emblem or the crest of the boys' club, just as the bloody hand defined the O'Neills. Everything about the boys' club was strange and exotic, and the peg leg made it all the more bizarre and intense. As if living in a barn painting our faces in the harsh hues of heathens and savages was as regular as you could get.

Daniel's Uncle Lance loomed over all of us, even taller than Adams. A decent bit over six foot so that perching half balanced on a peg of polished wood made him seem taller but at the same time more fragile – like powerful and towering but teetering all at the same time. Like dangerous but without meaning to be, or able not to be, or even wanting to be. And I know what you're thinking, and I couldn't help but think it too, especially since he did look like a stern ship's captain – straight black hair longer than I'd ever seen on an uncle or a dad, down to his shoulders. Some silver jewelry, even an earring. Strong nose, angular face, probing, sometimes frightening eyes. Lots like Daniel in the mouth and nose and hair and cheekbones, even in the laugh and dry humor, but nothing like him in the eyes.

Eyes dark, like I say, but not mean. Maybe tough, maybe tired. Almost dangerous, maybe, and so calm. Maybe even treacherous but not mean. Lance's eyes could catch you; his eyes could grab you, clutch at you and hold you but like something from the inside eating its way out and not the other way around. And then he would wink and it would, all of it, let you go and be gone. Everything was fine again, or even sometimes better than fine.

Better than fine. On that very first night, or, actually, early morning when we arrived at Becky Dreiling's farm it happened that we named the boys' club "Better Than Fine." It became our toast, our anthem, our motto. As Adams liked to say, "If it's good then it's good, but if it's even the least bit good it's *better than fine.*"

I don't want this to sound bad, and I don't want to brag, but if you really want to know I'm the one who came up with the name for the boys' club. I was the one who named our boys' club "Better Than Fine."

It was kind of accidental, of course, as I was merely saying something about how it felt *better than fine* to be standing around in a Kansas farm barn in the wee hours drinking iced-down cold road trip beer. Adams clicked the neck of his beer bottle against mine and said with just a hint of his trademark defiance and an enormous amount of exuberance, "I'll wet one with you on that."

We all joined in and before you knew it we had an official toast and we all started calling the barn "Better Than fine."

And you know what? It was. The boys' club felt a lot like being in that land of Donkeys where Pinocchio goes when he's bad. There was lots of arguing and laughing and making up the game as we went along. Like one time Adams and Daniel disagreed over having consideration about playing the stereo if someone was trying to sleep. They argued for a while; I listened; and then we all voted on it. It became part of the ever-expanding ten-rule charter. I think the ten-rule charter ended up with 27 rules, but the one about the stereo said if you couldn't sleep through the music then you either weren't tired enough and you should get your butt up and party some more, or you weren't drunk enough and you should get your butt up and party some more. Most of the rules in the charter were like that.

A good part of our time was spent just goofing around, talking about whatever, listening to albums cranked loud on the stereo, drinking black coffee or cold beer, and finding whatever to do. Nattie and Becky Dreiling usually stopped in a couple times a day to see what we were up to, but they left us mostly alone.

I'm not trying to sound macho or anything, but we immediately began to feel very strong and complete in our boys' club. Me cooking all our own meals atop the wood stove that Daniel kept constantly stoked with scraps of oak or mahogany or pine from his woodworking projects. Adams and Daniel's Uncle Lance throwing darts. The three of them laughing and arguing and imagining up new barn projects. Goofing off. We lived together out in the barn like we were living out of place and out of time, doing whatever we wanted whenever we wanted and not ever having to explain to anyone why. You could just do whatever you wanted, and you could spend a whole day doing it, if that's what suited you.

We had so many great toys to play with, and everybody sort of had their own projects going on. Daniel made most use of the woodworking tools. It was real obvious he knew a lot about power tools and had used them before. It was great to watch him work, because he did every project the same way. I learned a lot just paying attention to him.

He'd pick through a basket full of pieces out of the scrap pile and then sit at one of the workbenches and smoke a cigarette and look at the pieces of wood. And then he'd just start. He wore a small leather tool pouch and carried a tape measure, a pencil, and several kinds of squares and carpenter's angles. Then he'd just go from one work station to the next, doing whatever needed to be done to each piece of wood – ripping straight edges on the table saw, then cutting to length, usually on compound angles, with the miter saw. Next he'd run stuff through the jointer so that all the edges came out clean and straight, or he'd run curvy cuts through the band saw. He spent a lot of time at the lathe, turning angles into round.

Then he would start to sand.

Man alive, Daniel O'Neill could sand wood. There was a nice belt sander, a palm sander and something called a spindle sander, and after running each piece through each one, Daniel sanded everything by hand. Everything, every piece. Each time he finished a piece, each time he sanded it finally, lovingly with 440 grit, he invented kind of a ceremony and he made me a part of it.

"Gophe!" he'd holler out, sounding for all the world like he was rhyming with 'soft.' "Stroke it real and breathe it alive!"

Then he'd throw the piece to me, no matter where I was in the barn – at the wood–burning cook stove, up in the loft, or at the stereo. I'd feel it and run my fingers over it awhile and then throw it back and holler, "From dust to dust. Life sands you smooth!"

They were exquisite, these little pieces of all different wood. It seems like I would say they felt as smooth as glass, but that wouldn't tell you anything about how they felt. Smooth as skin, maybe. I remember, back in our dorm days, Adams describing to me how smooth the skin was on a woman's inner thigh, high up on her leg, high up inside next to... you know. Muscular and just a bit quivering, these pieces of Daniel O'Neill wood felt like that place I'd never touched on a woman. Soft like something that makes you hurt in your stomach, like when you ache for your grandma to hold and rock you; soft like the fine powdery dust, invisible as it rises from the barn floor; soft like a real smile from your best friend.

The pieces themselves were curiously compelling – each one very different or sometimes exactly the same. Each one from a different kind of wood, so the grains were different – different tones and colors and hues. But all starting rough and splintery, and then being sanded from 60 grit, which was almost like a rough rasp, all the way down to 440, which was like polishing. You almost couldn't let go of them, they were so smooth and soft and spoke to your soul.

They really didn't look very much like anything, but somehow looked a lot like pieces of something, something larger and eerily human – almost, and I hated to say this, so of course I never would have, but almost like a bunch of little peg legs or peg arms or peg heads or peg torsos. Peg people, and I'm sorry for thinking that. If I thought about that part of it too much it got kind of creepy, so I tried not to.

Daniel sanded every piece carefully by hand, and then he'd toss it to me for the baptismal sacrament. "From dust to dust," I'd say. "Life sands you smooth." I'd toss it back, and he'd place it on the workbench in front of him while he lit a Winston with his Zippo. He sat and smoked in silence while he stared at a fresh scrap of wood. The next thing you knew, if you were watching closely, not spying but just paying attention, the next thing you knew, the finished piece was gone, disappeared, and he began the process all over again with a nice virgin piece of wood.

The only piece we saw him finish was a gift he made for Adams. After only a few hours of working – cutting, carving and sanding – Daniel O'Neill gave Adams a perfect replica of the original horn cap emblem he had removed from the 1965 Plymouth

Valiant. The wooden horn cap emblem had rich grain that shone and danced through the polish of the varnish. It looked so alive, it looked for all the world like a mechanical body part; it looked like a heart. The heart of the Valiant. Adams immediately took it out to the front drive and snapped it into the center of the steering wheel. We all toasted, celebrated, and took the rest of the day off.

Other than that one item, we never saw what the finished pieces looked like, they just disappeared. We never saw what he was making.

Daniel didn't speak all that much when he did woodworking. I don't mean like he was a stoic, he'd join in some of the debates or throw out one liners in the Mickey Mouse stuff, but mostly he was quiet and made very strange little things out of wood.

The two men – well actually that's not right because Adams was the same age as me, but he and Daniel's uncle sure got along together like a couple of old Knights of Columbus buddies – basically they just carried on. Playing jokes on each other or on us; shooting pool on the old beat-up bar room pool table that was set up beneath the loft; throwing darts at the board that was behind my station at the wood cook stove. After a few days Adams and Lance started looking around for projects they could do, improvements on the boys' club, they said. The first one was a disaster – they tried to rig a system where you could pee from up in the loft and it went down to the toilet. It didn't work at all and we quickly made a rule that, if you were upstairs, you had to get off your butt and climb down the big ladder if you needed to take a leak.

Daniel often joined in when they got into really steamed debates on ridiculously complex topics that seemed to have no meaning. A lot, actually, like a college dorm, except not co-ed, so the drinking, arguing, laughing and carrying on didn't have that added tension of trying to get the attention of girls. Just the straightforward nonsense of boys and men being boys.

It felt like a big out-of-town summer family wedding when you were a kid. Dads and uncles fooling around for the whole weekend – laughing, telling stories about work, arguing about sports or politics. All the moms staying inside making Jell-O salad. But nobody really buttoning the collar button until the actual ceremony of celebrating the Sacrament of Matrimony, where some more than a few sat in the pews, a bit flushed and a little red-eyed. I guess I always thought the dads were more relaxed and more fun when the moms were inside on account of they wouldn't get yelled at, but once I got to college, and especially living in the *boys' club barn*, I realized it wasn't a fear of women so much as it was freedom from needing to impress them, or from needing to bask in their approval.

Don't get me wrong, I really liked Daniel's mom a lot, and you pretty much already know how I felt about Nattie Sinclair. But it was fine with me that they mostly stayed out of the barn and out of our business. All was smoother when it was just the boys. That, plus whenever they came into our world the air among us got a little tense and testy – competition for attention, like I say. Anyway, we were all pretty happy, fooling around out in the *better than fine boys, club barn*.

I designated myself as camp caretaker, and since no one objected or seemed to want the job, it suited me fine. I swept a lot of sawdust, kept the tools in their rightful places, played harmonica when the stereo wasn't on, kept the fire going, and pretty much constantly cooked atop the stove. Even though the fellows made fun of me, I always wore a white apron I had found in the mudroom in back of the kitchen. It was great to wipe my hands on and all, but mostly it just made the job feel so much more like mine. Camp Caretaker.

I spent entire days sharpening knives and then finely dicing onions or cutting sliver-thin slices of tomatoes or sawing through fresh bread or slicing cheese for snacks. I chopped all manner of vegetables to throw into the stockpot that I kept moving around the top of the wood stove, increasing or decreasing the heat instantly by moving the pot to follow the path of the burning wood inside the glowing firebox. The hottest spot – scalding water – was left rear, over the back of the firebox. The coolest was right front, over the oven and away from the flu.

I don't want to be the one to say it, but I got really good at knowing what kind of fire I needed depending on what I wanted to accomplish – a sucking hot and angry fire to start coffee or make dishwater, a mellow and consistent one to simmer soups and chili and stews, hot again but only fast hot to brown pork or fry steaks.

I almost always kept a pot of coffee going on the stove, perked over the hot areas and then moved off near the side to stay warm. Also, I always kept a big pot of soapy water slightly warm, for your hands and whatever. Every day, somewhere about midmorning, I'd start a pot of some kind of stew or soup or whatever I felt like making, filled with lots of beans and meats and vegetables. Early on I figured out that I could use the old metal 7-Up beer cooler as an alarm clock: Once it cracked open for the first time of the day it was time for me to start out on that days' "pot of eats," as Daniel took to calling it. Becky Dreiling was already starting to get a few summer things out of her garden, and she brought me whatever else from town, so I had a great supply of peppers and onions and garlic and peas and just about whatever else I could think up. She bought me all different kinds of meat, and we had a great *boys' club* refrigerator.

I kept my own dried beans, and soaked them overnight as the need arose. I also had a bag of brown rice, and a box of kosher salt. By the way, don't ever cook any meat if you don't have kosher salt. I only used a little salt when I sautéed my meat. All the rest of the flavor came from whatever fresh I put in the pot. More than once, Becky Dreiling offered for me to take any spices I wanted out of the kitchen to add to my little boys' club larder, but I enjoyed the challenge of flavoring with fresh. Also, I don't think spices are sissy, necessarily, but neither do I think those old guys had anything other than salt in the chuck wagon on cattle drives long ago, if you know what I mean. Plus, it's not like I was cooking up any recipes or anything; I didn't even know how to cook. I just looked at whatever ingredients I had on any day and figured out some new way to put them all together. I guess we could easily have survived on bread and cheese and tomatoes and Tabasco and beer, but I took to the cooking job and wouldn't have traded it for anything.

Daniel's mom complimented me often about the flavor and always about how healthy I was cooking. She said she was amazed at what I was coming up with, but of course she was just trying to be nice to me, because, as I've said, I was just using whatever was available; I didn't really know what I was doing.

She and Nattie would usually wander in and out during the day and sometimes even taste whatever I had going atop the wood-burning cook stove. They'd chat a bit or joke around, and then Nattie would say something teasing like "Smells great, Johnny. I see you're cooking with beans again today." Then they'd giggle together. Sometimes Nattie would even make these ridiculous farting sounds, and then they'd laugh like crazy and leave the barn.

I guess we all knew we were sort of being made fun of, but like I said, the dynamics between everybody were so different than usual that none of us took offense. Mostly the dynamics between all of us guys, and between Nattie and Becky Dreiling. It was a little bit like what I imagine summer camp must be like, or life in the medieval church. The girls and boys mix and spend some time together, but a lot of segregation, too. You could really watch this strong connection between Nattie and Becky. They took a lot of long walks together, and did a lot of kitchen things – like for instance they made us a lot of homemade bread. Also a lot of sewing and baking and crafting; a lot of farmwife household stuff. It was like Nattie stumbled into nesting Disneyland; she was thriving on this crafty homey down-to-earth rhythm.

You could tell that Mrs. O'Neill didn't usually spend all of her time that way, and every few days, when she had to go into town, she'd get all dressed up and brush her blond hair down, and when she walked across the driveway I'd stand in the sunshine of the barn door and watch her like I was about to cry. Not like I was a baby but like something very deep inside me tugging and holding and being caressed.

A captivating flow of hair and light and colorful fabric and tiny silver and all about smile. She looked like a hippie from the old days but not angry and protesting and mad. More like she wasn't just Daniel's mother but she was everybody's mother. I don't just mean all of us at the farm, I mean everyone's mother. The mother of everything. Kind of like the Blessed Virgin Mary, although that's not right, because even she was only Jesus' mother. I know we're supposed to think of Mary as our mother too, but the truth is that's a little scary, because of God. Like when you'd knock on some kid's door to see if he could come out to play and the mom answered. She was always nice to you and asked you easy questions but it was still scary because you knew the Dad was inside the house somewhere.

Anyway with Becky Dreiling it wasn't that way at all. I don't mean to say better than the Blessed Virgin, of course, but Becky Dreiling was easy to talk to and you felt like a kitten sitting in her lap. Or you felt like earth in her hands – rich and black as she cultivated you, full of possibility as she gently worked roots into you, settled and content as she raked you smooth.

I wouldn't say this to very many people, if you know what I mean, but Daniel's mom sure was pretty. Like Nattie a little, pretty in the eyes that you couldn't really ever get the courage to look all the way into. But not like how Nattie had that glamorous magazine-cover look. Becky Dreiling was more like the best sister on Petticoat Junction.

Anyway, Nattie was having a blast. In all the time I lived with her I'd never seen Nattie Sinclair cook more than a one-course meal and always from a can. I had seen her throw away shirts when they lost only one button, so it was fun to watch her hang out with a mom and take so much joy in learning all these really basic Grandma things. Nattie took particular delight in telling us all about learning to sew.

Me, I was having fun just fitting into the barn, watching and learning, cooking, fire tending, and sweeping up. Then one day I was amazed, astounded really, when Lance O'Neill asked me if I wanted to use all the woodworking tools and make him a leg.

"Be honored to clomp around in one that had your mark on it," he told me. "If it appeals to you to do so."

"I don't know anything about it," I said. "I wouldn't know how to begin."

He laughed when I told him I really didn't see how it worked and I wondered if he could give me plans or diagrams or drawings or something.

"I'll take care of the connection and the user's manual," he said. "All you've got to do is form it up: either do it on the lathe or fiddle around on the table saw and then finish it however you see fit. Whole bin over behind the band saw filled with good sticks of hardwoods. Pick one you like and off you go."

"Don't even start," Daniel said to me. "Next thing you know he'll have you sanding every piece of wood in this barn. You'll never escape, you'll never finish, and you'll never be done. Don't even start."

"Old hang-ups of a young man," Lance said to the both of us. "Things have mellowed a bit around here," he said to Daniel. "It's all fun here now, kind of like summer camp."

"Ooh, how about I get a pony ride? Maybe," Daniel said, not sounding mean but not sounding nice, "I'll do archery and weave a basket."

"Every day's a new day, son. Every morning's a new life."

"Holy shit, optimism," Daniel said. "What's next, apologies and regrets?"

His uncle's face twitched a bit. "Things can change," Lance said. "Sometimes they do."

After a bit, Daniel said, "I'm not saying anything. I'm just saying don't sand, that's all."

"I don't mind sanding," I said. "I'd love to get it all smooth, make it right, work it clean. But how do I know... I mean Daniel showed me the lathe and the saws, I'm sure I've got that down. But," I looked from Lance to Daniel, not meaning to stutter and not wanting to get personal, "how do I, you know, how do I know how long to cut it?"

Daniel laughed and Lance winked at me like he started doing ever since the first night we arrived.

"Measure it," Daniel said, laughing and for all the world sounding like Adams' infamous cackle. "Grab that tape from the table saw drawer, drop to your knees, and measure it."

"Play nice," Lance said to Daniel. "This is about new woodworking, not old wounds."

Like they say about a car crash, I couldn't take my eyes off the two of them. I just kept watching first one face and then the other. They locked dark glares for only a moment and then looked away, but the echo of Lance's challenge, or was it an offering, hung thick in the air. Man alive, these O'Neills had a way with words. *"New woodworking, not old wounds."* Adams could talk colorful and strong to get your attention but with these O'Neills it was so much passion hidden in simple rhythms.

"Everything's about old wounds," Daniel finally said, sitting on his perch by the jointer.

"Everything's about perspective," his uncle replied.

Suddenly and thankfully the stereo up in the loft kicked in, and The Band blasted *The Weight,* a song Lance often said was one of his favorites. His squinty-eyed grin would open up just a bit whenever they'd sing about taking a load off, and open up almost into a smile when someone would put the load on me.

We all looked up and, sure enough, there was Adams, legs dangling over near the top of the ladder and a grin as large and crooked as the road to Cripple Creek cutting across his square jaw.

"A drunkard's dream, coming up next," he hollered, jabbing into and slicing off all this woodworking and wounded tension.

"Levon and the boys always welcome in this barn – straight, sober, or mad," Lance said. "Canucks, Rebs, and knuckleheads got us closed in, figured out, and delivered. Anybody care," Lance said loudly to the barn at large, "at this admitted early hour of the morning to pop cold all around and drink one clear to The Band?"

"Hell yes," Adams enthused nearly off the loft, rolling like a gymnast and almost sliding down the ladder. "About time you losers got past this 'blame your old man and piss on your kid' mutual shit kicking society and brought things back down to where they belong – beer drinking and boys' club linking, or beer chugging and boys' club loving, or something with beer, but you hosers get the idea. High past time to shift out of granny gear into five speed boys' club overdrive high. It's gotta be noon somewhere, hey?"

You could just see it. I could certainly feel how everything melted into comfortable and real and back again to being okay. We all dipped into the metal 7-Up cooler for bottles of long neck Pabst Blue Ribbon, and the sound and the smell of tops popping off spritzed and fizzed with the passing of Lance's church key and Adams' Swiss Army. After a cold sip or two, everything was back to normal – boys' club central, back to the barn, and *better than fine.*

"Don't sweat the logistics, John Gophe," Lance said, rhyming perfectly with 'soft.' "It's all finish work. It's all design work. It's just like a craft project. Pieces have all been cut to precisely twenty-three and five-eighths inches. Each and every one. A whole cradle full of twenty-three and five-eighths. Pick your piece, pick one that calls your name and you can turn it, bevel it, sand it, create it all, and by the gods of craft and severed limbs, I'll wear the son of a bitch."

"Sounds a bit like Nirvana," Adams said.

"Sounds more like indentured servitude," said Daniel O'Neill.

"Sounds kind of like fun," I managed. "I mean, I like being a part of something lasting and meaningful and real. You know?"

"Don't back down, Johnny G. Don't ever back down. You've got the groove, don't say sorry you don't. Ever."

"No," I said. "I don't mean it that way. I'm not apologizing." I looked at Adams hard, tried to let him know I wasn't a weenie, but he was already elsewhere and moved on.

"Box full of log blanks?" he said to Lance. "What the hell's up with that? Can't you find somebody out here in the middle of nowhere who can make you a permanent stick? None of my business and I won't say a word, but you ought to check into Denver or Kansas City. All kinds of new innovations made since the Civil War. 'Prosthetics' they're called. The days of Ahab are over."

"You sound just like the son of a bitch smart ass down at the Brace and Limb," Lance said. "Cocky little pimply-faced prick always talking stainless, titanium, and flesh-colored vinyl."

Daniel hooted in derision. "Isn't that Walker or Wheeler or whatever? The guy who got fired from teaching over at the grade school?"

"Damn near," Lance said. "You're thinking of Harry Wheeler, at the shoe shop, son of Herbert, or the other way around, I'm not sure. But both those damned sons a bitches are also pimply-faced, under-qualified pricks."

"Man, I remember when that happened, him getting fired," Daniel said. "Everybody was talking. I was in high school, or maybe ninth grade, but I think high school because I remember the talk in the locker room, after football practice. Man, what a pervert. Little sixth grade girl in the broom closet, or the janitor's room, or something. Shit," Daniel said, "They ought to have castrated that bastard."

"Probably lucky they didn't," Lance said, lazy and sage-like, sounding like a judge, or somebody's dad. "D.A. said no case, stood up strong and said he couldn't bring charges. They found some other reason to fire the pathetic little asshole."

"A political fix," Daniel sneered.

"More likely the son of a bitch scared the shit out of the little girl just by turning his pimply face on her," Adams said, sounding like he really believed he could possibly have a clue regarding what he was talking about. "Little girl probably hollered 'Mamma' and wouldn't talk just because he was so damn ugly."

"Sure possible," Lance said, moving a sliver of wood around and around in his teeth. "He and his boy both ugly sons a bitches."

We all laughed like you do when you're getting into the club by keeping someone else out.

"I'm surprised you remember much about it," Daniel said to his uncle. "I don't remember you being around much when it was coming down."

"Probably not," his uncle allowed, and I watched them do that O'Neill thing with their eyes.

"Anyway," Adams said, breaking into the moment, "none of this explains anything about wood versus twentieth century. None of my business and no offense, but switching out all of those pegs has got to be a bit of a cumbersome pain in the ass."

"More like a pain in the stump," I said, and immediately I couldn't believe I'd done so. "Golly, I'm sorry. That just slipped out."

I could feel my face burn even redder as they all laughed, Daniel and Adams hooting and high-fiving each other.

"Bulls eye," Adams said. "Nice freakin' shot, G."

Lance O'Neill's eye twinkled, especially when he winked at me. "Does tend to be," he said, laughing along with the others. "It does tend to be."

"So come on," Adams said, popping tops and passing a fresh round of bottles to us all. "Nobody in this day and age wears a wooden peg leg, not even out here in the middle of nowhere. No way there's not a killer story in here somewhere. I call boys' club rules. No secrets, no surrender."

"Story's nothing but old and bullshit," Lance said, smiling with warmth and smiling for real.

"Vietnam?" Adams asked.

Lance didn't say anything, but you could suddenly sure see the why of that darkness in his eyes. We were all silent, respecting and acknowledging that we had no idea what that one word could possibly mean to someone who had been there. Acknowledging that guys like us had no idea. The silence lingered and finally Daniel said, "More like the Bloody Hand."

"What's that?" I asked.

"The Bloody Hand of O'Neill. Our crest. Our heritage." Daniel looked at Lance. "Our grandfathers."

"O'Neill was the first king of Ireland," Adams said. "But I don't know the bloody hand part."

"Story is, there was a boat race to Ireland; the first man to lay a hand on shore would claim the land, would become king.

"A man named Nial, seeing that he was losing the race at the very end, unsheathed his knife, and there in his boat, he cut off his own hand and flung it to shore. Besting the others, he thus became the first king of Ireland. The Bloody Hand of O'Neill."

"Wow," I said.

"Holy shit," Adams said. "That is so cool. So what's the connection to Ahab?"

"Nothing to do with the Bloody Hand," Lance said.

I watched his fists clench. Then I watched Daniel step in and put a halter on Adams and lead him away.

"Likely a better story," he said to Adams, "is how in the hell you ended up with a name like Cib."

"I'd pay to hear that one," Lance agreed.

"You don't know the half of it. My middle name is Carkus. Cib Carkus. That's why everybody calls me Adams. Just Adams is more than fine with me."

He took a long drink from his PBR, and then he climbed ever so comfortably up and into the saddle of the storyteller.

"First part of the story is my old man's an asshole. I don't mean like a dad you don't get along with, or who won't let you take the car on a Saturday night, but a bona fide asshole. Real bastard. Always screwing with you, messing with your head, Like Trickster Coyote, 'cept for no redeeming qualities. More like Trickster Asshole.

"So once a point in time, long before I'm born, Trickster Asshole, a fancy self-important young attorney, cheats on his new bride with an uptown socialite mistress on whom he lavishes both material gifts and emotional largess. Trickster Asshole soon decides his marriage to his sweet little hometown girl was a mistake and both he and his career will shine brighter when linked legally with the uptown socialite. Uptown socialite's name is Sybil.

"But luck be damned, in the midst of rather ugly separation negotiations, somehow the hometown sweetheart finds herself with child. Actually," he said, and he smiled broad and proud to us all, "she finds herself with *this* child.

"Trickster Asshole can't divorce a pregnant young wife and maintain his affected and ever rising country club status, so he rededicates himself to screwing the uptown socialite Sybil and making her happy while screwing his hometown sweetheart and making her miserable. And then, another bit of bad luck; this child turns out to be a man-child, subsequently named Cib by Trickster Asshole to publicly honor the socialite Sybil.

"Nothing really embarrassing, no heralded family tradition. Just rather cheap. Cheap and petty and mean. And that," Adams said, "is the pathetic basis for this name. For my name, Cib."

"How in hell did you ever find all that out?"

"That's the juicy part. That's the sad, shitty part. On my twelfth birthday, Trickster Asshole gave me the present of that wonderful story. And he took particular care to ensure I understood that the ridiculous middle name – Carkus – was meant to phonetically suggest the state of his relationship with my mother. Funny joke, right? Nice guy, huh?"

"Jesus," Lance said, "with a father like that..."

"You got it," Adams interrupted, looking his way, tipping his beer and for all the world looking like the rowdy cousin who was always getting into trouble but who had finally been welcomed at the family reunion.

"Lance, Daniel, John: strong, honest, respectable names. Nattie, Becky: true, wise names. Cib and Sybil? Labels of manure rising from the human compost pit."

"Oh, come on," I managed. "It's a pretty cool name."

"Why don't you change it?" an O'Neill said. "Easy enough to do."

"Yeah, I know. The sorry-ass son-of-a-bitch wanted me to, on my 18th birthday. Bastard actually broke down and cried, sloshed on a bottle of blended scotch he'd bought and wanted us to share. See, by the time I turned 18, Trickster Asshole's testosterone levels began to subside, and he realized his legacy would most likely be blazed by his high school football star son and not by the constantly bitchy and increasingly rotund Sybil. He would have given his left nut for me to study law and join him in his practice.

"He was all over himself, apologizing about my name, about my life, and how he'd treated me. Mostly about my name. My 18th birthday present, he wants to sit down with me and come up with a new name. The son-of-a-bitch is almost pleading with me, he wants to drink scotch and reinvent me. I told him to go to hell. He cried some more. After that, he started calling me C.C.

"C.C. he calls me, strong emphasis on both syllables, like it's a mind numbing apology and an obsequious affirmation, all rolled into one."

Adams spat into the dirt floor of the barn.

"What a dick.

"After my birthday I never said a word to him until the day I graduated high school, and I said only one word to him then. He gave me a check for $5,000 and told me he'd pay for college anywhere I wanted to go. I said 'thanks.' I shook his hand, broke his little finger, and left home the next day."

Daniel squatted on his haunches, tracing circles in the dirt with a stick. "Figure you're better off without him?"

"No question. No doubt."

"You might be surprised," Daniel said. "A father's a father, asshole or no. There's something to be said for having one around. Cib, Sybil, who gives a shit. Your name's Adams, just like his."

"What's in a name," Lance repeated. "That the issue?"

"No, I don't mean it like that. A father can also be the guy who was there for you, even if he usually wasn't."

"Well anyway," Lance said. "Fathers can be there even when they don't want to be, and they can miss entirely even when they're trying their damnedest. My dad wasn't an asshole, but he could sure screw things up. He was passionate and angry and, in every way, he was all things Irish. I was born there, County Atrium, just a few months before my folks, his grandparents," he said, nodding at Daniel, "immigrated. My brother was born a year later, in Monterey, where we grew up. Danny. Every mother's dream of a name for her Irish lad. Everybody's dream of a name. My old man named me Lance as a sort of a poke in the eye to the Brits and all things British. He hated anything English, so I guess he figured by giving me this name it was like he was stealing from them for a change."

"Yeah, but even so, it's a name, and a story, to be proud of. Your name is something of a call to arms, a rally cry. My god, what a story! You've got warriors and kings and crazy passionate bastards cutting off their own hands to grab the prize. Your name is a monument to champions. It's not like you were named after your dad's mistress."

There was really nothing to say about that.

"Come on," Adams continued. "It's not like he named you Cib, for chrissakes."

"Afraid I'd have to agree with you on that one."

After that day, it became easier and easier for me to think about calling him O'Neill, instead of Daniel's uncle. He had told me to call him "O'Neill" and that was hard to do. It always felt a little like calling someone's dad by his first name. I guess formality is my calling card. I never called Daniel anything but Daniel, even though that always felt stilted and not very friendly. I liked the way it sounded when Adams called him "O'Neill" or when Nattie called him "Danny." Now that you mention it, I did call Adams "Adams" which is sort of a nickname, but then everyone called him "Adams," even Nattie and Daniel's mom, Becky Dreiling. I called him "Cib" when we first met in the dorm as roommates, and I'm a bit embarrassed about that. Not because Cib is a funny name even though it is but because it seems like something only his first grade teacher would call him.

A nickname is so powerful. It marks clearly that you're in the club, you're part of the inner circle. I guess it's pretty easy to figure out that, increasingly, as the weeks passed by and the spring meandered into summer, I felt like I could stay in the *boys' club barn* at Becky Dreiling's farm forever, because it was especially there that everyone had a name.

"Sometimes it only needs to be better than
A poke in the eye with a sharp stick."

- Nattie Sinclair

Chapter 15

"All right you brothers in boys' club arms. Listen up."

Daniel's uncle Lance didn't exactly bark when he said that, but you always perked up and paid attention when you heard it. And we heard it from him a lot because he was the captain of our *boys' club barn.*

Uncle Lance had thrown us into his pick-up truck with a bunch of pickaxes and garden shovels and driven us out after sunset into some pasture near town. We spilled out and stood around drinking beer while Daniel's Uncle Lance clomped along, pacing off the size of a buffalo waller.

"What the hell we doing out here?"

"We've got to dig a bunker," Daniel's uncle said. "Below this ridge, here in this buffalo waller, before nightfall."

"Dig a hole out in this pasture?"

"Yep. Grab shovels. That's it. Won't have to be real deep, if we keep it behind this ridge."

"That's nuts," Daniel said. "I'm not digging a hole out in a pasture."

"Hole for what?" Adams asked.

Daniel hadn't yet picked up a shovel like Adams or me, but he listened all the same while his uncle laid out the plan.

"Okay, here's the deal. You know how the other day we were trying to figure a better place for the stove in the barn?"

"Yeah," Adams said. "I still think the west corner is best, so the heat can be vented out in the summer and directed into the center when it's cold."

"Right. I agree."

Adams didn't exactly beam, but I could feel his sense of the victory, like he had scored a touchdown over Daniel, who had argued for putting it in the middle, beneath the loft. Like I say, Uncle Lance was clearly the captain, and Adams and Daniel were constantly competing to see who came next in line. More and more, Adams acted like some Johnny-on-the-spot, loud and fast and polishing up to Lance. For his part, Daniel got even more laid back, watching everything closely, saying little, always saying less.

I watched it unfold between the two of them and I could see it was beginning to change things. Change how they related to each other, change maybe even how they felt about each other. Change certainly how they treated each other. They always had this wonderful brother thing going, where they teased and competed and locked horns and such, but always in fun, like they weren't actually full bucks yet and it was all prancing for a game. Not so much anymore were they like two halves, or two buddies, or two brothers fighting for the same team.

Tense, with an undercurrent of something like danger. Daniel the real heir, the true prince, but Adams trying to be this outside knight, cozying up to the king. Turning Daniel edgy and hard, making Adams even more brazen and loud.

I just watched it play out and wondered who was going to get to be the lieutenant and who was going to have to be the sergeant, stuck bossing the privates around. It was pretty clear to all of us who was the private, so I just wanted to listen up while he gave us the plan and make sure I knew what my job was going to be.

"So here's the deal. I'm in town earlier this morning, and up at the end of Main, in front of the hardware and across from the bar, they're tearing the street up; they need to replace a busted water main. Hardware's closed, bar's closed, apparently a dozen homes up and down 5th also without water. So they're hauling ass, trying to get it finished by tomorrow."

"What's that have to do with our stove," I asked, and then immediately I could feel the red burn in my face, and my stomach dropped as if I'd just accidentally called someone's dad by his first name. "I mean your stove," I said.

Uncle Lance winked at me. "It has this to do with our stove. They've dug up a pile of old stone street pavers, six or seven tons of stone block. Just lying there right now in a pile in the street. We're going to use them for a foundation in the corner of the barn, then we'll lay a portion of the floor and parts of the two walls leading into the corner. Then we can set the stove in a little stone nook, and we can do anything we want with its heat."

"Got it!" Adams said. "Love it. Perfect idea. How many stones is six or seven tons?"

"A shitload," Daniel said. "A goddamned shitload."

"Sure is," Lance said.

"That's why we need to dig the hole out here. We'd never get them all tonight if we had to drive each load all the way back to the farm. We'll just dump them here and camouflage them; then we can come out at our leisure, picking them up as we need them."

"Why the hurry? Afraid they'll need them tomorrow to rebuild the street?"

Daniel's uncle laughed a little and said something to Daniel about being the conscience of the mission.

"Not likely," Uncle Lance said. "It'd be too expensive to re-lay the whole section of street by hand. I imagine they'll back-fill it, have the county truck in some blacktop, and call it good. It's going to be the goddamned salvage of the decade. Besides, the way I see it, we're doing them a favor, hauling the stone away."

"That why we're doing it in the middle of the night, and burying them out in a cow pasture?" It was Daniel and his uncle again – the Prince and the King, wars of the Father and of the son.

"No, we're doing that because Henderson's got his greedy eye on them. He was talking this morning about using them to expand onto the back of the hardware store. That's actually what gave me the idea. They're literally sitting in a pile on his front door step. He figures that's his payback for being shut down for a couple of days."

"Sounds fair to me," Daniel said.

"Bullshit," Adams said. "If he wants to expand his business, let him take out a loan and hire a contractor. We're making art, here.

We're honoring the stones by using them uniquely. Any idiot can build an addition; any piece of half assed plywood can be part of it. These stones are Kansas history – how long you figure they've been there?"

"Since the twenties, probably," Lance said. "Turn of the century, maybe."

"There you go, stones with history, representing a time when guys did things for themselves and did it by hand. Can you imagine how long it took to lay a street of stone by hand? Dozens of guys, working weeks, maybe, digging and cutting and laying stone. Digging up and into an ancient seabed to lay a modern street. "Jesus," Adams said, building up his typical head of steam, "This is perfect, they're so obviously meant for us and our *boys' club barn* improvement projects."

His enthusiasm, as usual, was contagious, and Lance caught the flow. "Part of the deal is we have to get them by hand, sweat our asses off over 'em."

"Exactly. Good point," Adams said. "Some guy showed up right now, with a back hoe and a bucket, I'd send him on his way, saying `No thanks, mister, we're gettin' 'em by hand.'"

Uncle Lance laughed along with him, and even Daniel grinned.

"Guess it won't hurt to take a break from the barn and bust a good sweat," Daniel said, and then he laughed out loud too. "Be a shame to see an old guy like Henderson breaking his back, moving all that stone from his front porch to his back one."

It took us until just after five in the morning to get them all. We had to make eleven trips out to our secret cache in the pasture, where we'd quickly dump the loads and then we headed back to town. Even then, we didn't get them all – dawn beat us out. But we got a bunch.

Daniel's uncle parked the pickup on the side of the hardware store, so you couldn't see it from down the street, which was pretty deserted anyway. But every now and again a car would turn up at the light. We saw several dogs running wild and nosing around.

Uncle Lance knew right away that throwing the large stones into the truck would make too much noise, so we formed like a bucket brigade and passed them one at a time. Lance worked through the pile, picked out each stone and handed it to me. I passed to Daniel, and Adams humped them into the back of the truck. The stones were all about the size of a loaf of bread, and heavy, so being the smallest, I kept at the easy job. Adams and Daniel switched off every 32 stones to give each other a breather. Every stone carefully stacked in neat rows, eight across, four deep, and four high. One hundred twenty eight stones each load, stacked over the rear axle to minimize the sway. The pick-up was old and weak, Adams said we were beating the hell out of the springs and suspension with this scavenge, but it was probably worth it. We all agreed, even Lance, whose pickup it was getting beat to heck.

"Wished we'd brought the Valiant," Adams said on our second or third trip. "She could haul forty or fifty in the trunk, easy."

The subject of the 1965 Plymouth Valiant had already come up, early on out in the barn. Adams was boasting about the great trade he had made, how happy he was with his half. I could tell that ever-present tension between Daniel and his uncle strained extra taut for a moment. They didn't say anything to each other, and then it passed. Daniel and his uncle communicated a lot just by what they didn't say to each other.

"Always had something of a soft spot for the Valiant," Daniel's uncle said in the hushed, secret-agent-man tones we were all using due to the stealth of our adventure. "Guess it goes back a ways."

"Jesus," Daniel said. "Does it ever."

Adams acted like he was oblivious to how much quiet tension erupted when Daniel's uncle found out half the Valiant now belonged to Adams. But knowing Adams like I did, I understood he wasn't oblivious at all. By ignoring it, Adams was simply taking the ownership issue off the table, regardless how that affected the O'Neill family dynamics. He made a trade for half the Valiant, and he had no intention of trading back.

"Good trade?" Uncle Lance asked in measured tones as he passed stones to me.

"Triple the money value, at least," Daniel said. "Antique Zippo. Great trade. Funny thing, too. Seems more like mine now that it's only half mine. Like I traded away all the heavy and the history and kept all the smooth. Plus, like I say, Zippo's worth a bundle."

"Maybe," Adams said, "but money isn't everything. I got half the Valiant as well as all the wisdom."

"Good wisdom?" asked Uncle Lance.

"Doubt he understands it," Daniel said.

I wanted to break in, to scream toasts of friendship and reminders of connection. I wanted to force an acknowledgement of brotherhood, of bonding, of family. That was the real trade, Valiant for Zippo. We were all family; we belonged together, we were together. We were friends. But ever since the boys' club began, Adams and Daniel were acting less like true friends and more and more often like trying to get the best of the other one, trying to beat the other one, trying to get ahead. Not like trying to bring out the best in each other, like how you'd expect true and valiant knights to act, pushing each other not with jealousy to knock the other down, but with love to build the other up so the team is better, so the brotherhood grows, so we can all be better and stronger and more honorable in the service of the queen. At first, in the beginning of the boys' club, I thought maybe that's just how boys are supposed to act when there are no girls around. Teasing and giving each other a hard time, like football teammates, or sailors chasing whales. Since I'd never been on a team and these fellows all had, I just tried to keep my mouth shut and watch and go along. But more and more, the two of them acted like they were playing on two different teams, and I didn't like it. I would have done anything to get them to treat each other like they did back when we were together in college. I knew the boys' club was a good thing, but more and more it was feeling like a trap, like something that keeps sucking you in, past the point where you can breathe in your own air. Like the exhilaration of getting on to, or off of, a roller coaster. Like looking down over the rim of a canyon. Like saying me and not we.

"Of course I understand the wisdom," Adams said. "Drink only Jack Daniel's whiskey. Drink it only one way. Lots of ice, a little

Jack, and pour it often. And also," he said, winking at Daniel, "treat the Valiant same as you'd treat a woman."

Daniel laughed. "Pretty goddamned close."

"Maybe that's always been my problem with that car," Daniel's uncle said. "Tended to treat it more like a son. Trying to strengthen it, mend it, mold it."

"Nah," Adams said. "Definitely a woman. Keep it pointed in one direction, keep the rpm's rapped up, and hold on for the ride."

"A cantankerous bucket of nuts and bolts, more like a smelly old dog needs taking out and shot," Daniel said, pretending to sound like he didn't care about the car at all.

"Love the car, myself," Adams cut in. He softly called out "thirty-two" and he and Daniel switched places as loaders. "Love my half same as I love yours," he said to Daniel. "Love the whole, Man."

"Always did too," Lance said. "Used to lie across the hood, summer times in the pasture, before we moved it into the barn. Just lie out at night staring into the Milky Way." He nodded my way. "Let's load an extra dozen or so this trip, see what happens," he said, so I kept grabbing and passing stones.

"Lying across the Valiant watching the stars. Sounds better than fine," Adams said. "Let's get a move on with this load so we can pop a beer and drink to Valiants and stars."

The stars sucked the air out of your heart. A prairie sky, beyond huge, beyond awe. The sky out in the middle of Kansas nowhere will make you cry.

"Watched a comet every night for three weeks one summer, lying there on the Valiant," Lance said. "Damnedest thing I ever saw. Made me realize, draped across the top of that little car, how screwed up we've become because we don't see the stars anymore."

He straightened up and stretched his back, bending backward and arching like some Celt warrior screaming up at the moon. He pulled his tobacco fixings from his pocket and rolled up a cigarette, even though we still needed seven more to make the extra dozen. I didn't know what to do. He rolled up the cigarette lickety-split, but instead of lighting it, he tucked it behind his ear and kept on talking about the stars. It occurred to me maybe this was a test. Maybe I was supposed to become the stone picker as well as the stone passer, but by the time I decided to scout one out and pick it up, Adams and Daniel had abandoned their posts at the tailgate. I realized everybody else figured we had a full load, so I did too.

Daniel's uncle opened the door of his pick-up and said, "Let's move out."

Adams and Daniel closed the tailgate and secured it with the hooks and chain. They vaulted over the top and sat both of them on the neatly stacked pile of stones. Adams told me to go ahead and take the shotgun and we rumbled down the deserted main street. Daniel's Uncle Lance kept talking, to me I guess, about stars and how, since we don't see them anymore, we're no longer right in our hearts and not right in our heads.

"We used to lie in the stars, every night, every year, every life. We'd climb into the great comfort of the night sky and roll around in it like newborns in fleece. It filled us, completed us, gave us heroes and movement and solace. We were there, around the fire and inside the stars, every night of our lives."

He flipped his Zippo lighter, and the blue flame danced in the darkness of the pick-up cab. I looked back through the window to see if Adams and Daniel were watching me, watching to see if I could talk with an adult about serious things.

"I never had much in the way of stars," I told him. "My house was pretty close to the city, but I remember seeing the stars on an altar boy camping trip I took once."

"I don't mean you used to live in the night sky, or that I did." He looked at me hard for a moment. "I mean we all did, as a species. Our species was born with the stars all around us. Night after night, season after season, generation and century after another, our species has sat around fire pits and looked up at the night sky. Everything we know about ourselves, everything we understand we learned in the night sky. Gravity and gallantry, heroes and hydrogen. It's all in the midnight sky – impeccably consistent, rhythmically audacious. That's where we figured it all out. That's how we started to understand. If you watch the sky, if you watch the movement and the rhythms, then you start asking questions, you start understanding spheres and circles. And then you start understanding everything. All the information we need all begins in the stars: gravity, God, physics, art and love. Every bit of it is in the stars."

As we drove, the smoke from his cigarette filled the air between us; the tension from his jaw and biceps moved the smoke and made it pulsate. I thought about little proto-people sitting around a fire pit 100,000 years ago watching the sky every night, watching it drift, watching it move across their lives. I thought about the stories they made up – Cepheus struggling to save the kingdom by chaining his daughter to the rocks, so the whale would eat her and satiate the rage of the sea nymphs, jealous and petulant about Andromeda's beauty. I thought of how frustrating it must have been for God that it took so long for people to find him and figure him out. I thought of what it must have been like when suddenly, one year or one warm summer night, something new and brilliant showed up in the sky. A comet. It must have been terrifying. They had no idea what it was, only that it didn't belong, changing position each night, racing the moon, tagging the planets. Some spindly-legged little old man squatting in front of the fire remembered some mysterious ancient story his great grandpa told about the same thing happening a long time ago. I thought of how that might have made everybody feel a little better, and then suddenly Lance flicked his cigarette toward me, and it crashed against the window next to my head. The pick-up cab exploded into sparks and commotion. I screamed out and jerked back, Lance yelled "Boom!" and his eyes turned on me and dug into my guts, and I felt tears welling up and he said "Boom!" again, and then he said, "Out of nowhere the goddamned industrial revolution lit a fire and the smoke blotted out our nighttime sky. We left the land and crushed into smoke-filled city slums where stars can't live. Like pups weaned too soon from a bitch, we were unceremoniously yanked from our cradle and thrown out onto the cold slab of modernization. Son of a bitch," he said. "We fouled our fucking nest."

***

Uncle Lance insisted on doing everything just right, which was good, because Adams would have just busted ahead and started laying stones wherever. Lance said they had to dig a foundation trench into the hard packed dirt floor of the barn. First they had to dismantle the wood stove, along with its vent, so they could move it out of the way. I helped them do that, as I had sole possession of the stove and cooking job. Because they didn't really care, I decided where the stove should be set up temporarily. The firebox itself was pretty small, about the size, actually, of a breadbox. Next to the fire box there was an oven with a fancy black cast iron door that swung open and shut on hinges. Four round holes were cut into the iron top, and the holes had round iron covers that fit neatly into grooves. You could control the heat by moving things around the top of the stove. The back of the firebox was the hottest, because that's where the air sucked the fire the fastest up and out the vent stack. By removing one of the round covers, the burners, you could expose your pan to direct fire and get a blast of intense heat.

It was a great little wood stove and, like I said before, I became very attached to it and to its cooking personality. After I had cleaned it all nicely and Adams and Daniel's uncle Lance finished the vent stack, I set up a temporary little space around the new stove location: tables and cabinets made from wooden slat boxes and broken shelving lumber and whatever. Like a campfire around a chuck wagon, or the galley buried down in the bowels of some creaky and drifting ship.

Once they were finished with moving the stove they left me alone and didn't ask for my help with digging out for the foundation; like I say, my job was cooking and tending camp.

It took them several days to make the footing wall. They cut the hard packed dirt of the barn floor with pickaxes, and then they dug and shoveled and hauled dirt and ended up with two smart trenches, both eighteen inches deep and each fifteen feet out from the inside corner of the barn. They needed a lot of concrete all at once to fill the trenches. They picked out a bunch of broken and funny-shaped stones from out back to throw in with the concrete to help fill the trench. They took some scrap 2 x 6's and some plywood and nailed together a floor pan to mix the bags of cement and sand and gulley gravel with water to make concrete. Daniel thought they were crazy not to rent a concrete mixer and he told them so.

"That's not the point, Buddy," Adams said. "If we just rent a mixer and pour bags of ready mix concrete into it and then plug it in and flip a switch, then shit, man, we've just gone along for the ride. Pushed some buttons, flipped some levers then stood back and watched it happen. But see, if we mix all the stuff ourselves, our muscles and flat shovels blending natural ingredients into liquid rock, well then by God and by the balls of a big bull, we've got a say in it cuz we've got a stake in it. It's ours. Like some heavy booted extensions of our own legs struck down into this little part of the planet taking hold probably almost forever and saying 'by God, this fucking wall's ours.' Jesus," he said, laughing and grabbing down into the old metal 7-Up ice chest for a bottle of Pabst Blue Ribbon, "I love it when I talk that way."

Daniel flicked a butt toward Adams' feet and Daniel's uncle Lance took the beer Adams offered and handed it to Daniel.

"Besides," Daniel's uncle Lance said to him. "Not a hell of a lot else going on around here. Money we save on the mixer keeps the cooler full."

"I guess so," Daniel offered, taking the bottle from his uncle and popping off the cap against the end of his workbench. "But the mixer's either a good idea or it's not; it's got nothing to do with the beer."

And then he said right to his uncle one of the meanest things I ever heard come out of his mouth. "Don't you ever have a real opinion about anything?"

There was this little silence, and I could tell just from knowing him that Adams was perched on the verge of pouncing bad and angry at Daniel.

"Saving it," Lance said after a minute, shooting a wink at me "till I find something again worth sparking off about."

Daniel didn't say anything, and thankfully, neither did Adams.

"Don't you think?" Uncle Lance asked. "One whole hell of a lot of it doesn't matter, once you get down to it."

"Maybe," Daniel finally said, "but you pick your battles forever, sooner or later the war'll have passed you by."

"Maybe so, and maybe that's the point."

"And there's a good point," Adams said. "Good fucking point. Like Shakespeare said: Do it or don't do it, but get on with it and be done."

"I'll wet one with you on that," Daniel allowed, tipping his bottle in Adams direction. "Reckon that's as good as any."

See? That's why it was so easy for me to just sit back and stir red beans and onions and sausage, or make coffee and fry eggs or whatever. It's not that there weren't any rules in our boys' club because there were a lot of them, but the rules out in the barn were safe and simple and always made sense. Say whatever you wanted, feel whatever you chose, but no residual muck, no strings hanging on. Tip a beer bottle, flash a wink, and everything was smooth again. Nobody cared if the thing was resolved or not. It was out there for everyone to take a lick at if he wanted, kick it about a bit, and then move on.

The first couple days after the salvage, the stone-building project commanded front and center attention. All our efforts focused on it. Adams and Daniel and Lance O'Neill actually building the thing, me a support services technician – food, drink, and following orders and suggestions when it was time to flip an album on the turntable. Doing whatever was needed to keep the stone-building machine greased and running well.

We cranked tunes, drank beer, and slopped mortar and stone street pavers together with a frenzied purpose that rivaled a teenage boy's desire to copulate. Adams and Uncle Lance worked well together, fit well together. They were solid, these two, like the stone pavers they worked with. You could watch their relationship grab hold like the mortar they formed into joints. Soft and unsure, maybe at first, but getting strong as it set, turning rock solid as it grew. That's a stupid metaphor, because the two of them were actually nothing like that at all. They weren't really anything like

Butch and Sundance, catapulting together, scheming against the world and falling into some kind of unlikely union. More, I guess, like Shane and that kid's dad in the book, working together on an impossible goal just for the sake of doing it. Yank the huge stump out just because the thing was there and had always been there; build an outrageous monstrosity out of stones just because you had them and because you could imagine them a new form.

The floor for the stove and the five-foot walls to catch and reflect the heat were built in just over three days. We made runs to the buffalo waller at night, so we could use daylight to build by. The cook stove heat-catching project only used up four trips of stones, so as we sat around and christened the cook stove's new place and we tried to figure out what to do with the rest of the stones.

We had an awful lot of them left over. It was curious how we hit on the idea for the new stone project – it came about while we were hanging out in the boys' club, drinking beer and talking about sex.

***

Somebody mentioned the lack of sex due to the dynamics of the *boys' club barn* and due probably to who knows what else. It didn't seem to me that Daniel's uncle and his mom liked each other in that way, plus they were related. So what with Nattie staying in the house and Adams out here with us, not much sex was happening lately.

"Just taking a break, myself," Adams said with his usual bravado. "Damn nearly blew some gaskets with the fair Nattie Sinclair over the last year; I figure this is a good time to recharge, build some new steam. I'm resting," Adams winked at me. "Just resting up."

Daniel bristled a little at the way Adams said that.

Maybe because I think both Daniel and I knew this new chaste Adams was clearly Nattie's choice, not his.

"Son, you're a damned jackrabbit, and you know it. Only thing you're resting is your ego. Woman in there's tired of bristly-ass bravado. She's re-thinking, re-looking. And you're waiting and burning."

I almost said "My ass," because I was so used to Adams saying that right about now.

But Adams didn't. He didn't say anything.

Lance popped open the top of a can of Vienna sausages. He stuck his fingers in the little can and pulled one of the little weenies out, all quivering and dripping gelatin. He grabbed a couple saltine crackers from the pack sitting on one of the shelves above my stove and made himself a quick little sandwich. He stuffed the whole thing in his mouth.

We all just sort of watched Adams, wondering what he'd say. I had learned that he might say anything. Adams had changed. He was still tough and, of course, always loud and out there, but something about the boys' club or the stones, or both had softened the edges. He was still pumped with macho, always strutting around. But, more and more, about things that mattered, he just answered what he was feeling. It kind of made me like him even more, if you know what I mean.

Finally, he just said to Daniel, "Sorry to shit-can your wet dream fantasies, Bud, but the woman's all mine. I'll agree I don't know why, but the woman's crazy about me. Can't get enough."

"Uh huh," Daniel said, biting the inside of his lip like he did when you knew he didn't believe a word of what he was hearing or saying. "She's crazy about you for sure. That why she sleeps in the house, alone, and leaves you out here roosting with pigeons and jacking off in the hay loft?"

"No," Adams said. "She does that because she's crazy enough about me to back off and let me be a full member of the boys' club."

"Must be one hell of a sacrifice for her."

"Eat shit, O'Neill. Woman's crazy about me."

"No doubt," Daniel said, both of them having fun, even though it didn't sound like it. "All signs point to it."

"Sure as shit," Adams said, "and I'll tell you what, when I first met her, I thought I was looking at a perfect carnival – great rides, a bit of mystery inside the tents, hot dogs and beer everywhere. The whole package, you know? Great sex, good times, and she's smart as a damn whip.

"I won't lie, I sure miss the sex. And I'll tell you fellas," he said, flashing a smile all around, "that's a fair amount to miss."

"Knows her way around between the sheets?" Lance said, sounding a lot like a college guy, instead of a dad.

"More than that," said Adams. "She's a woman who knows her way around her own body."

"Yep," was all Lance said. Even though I had no idea what he meant, I knew that he'd said a lot.

We all waited, hoping there was more to come. Well, I was hoping there was more to come. It had crossed my mind, living like we were in the barn, that I might never get any real first hand experience. I was starting to believe voyeurism based on the kind of graphic quips Adams and Lance traded back and forth would have to tide me over, maybe forever. Man alive. I hoped not.

Not like Nattie wasn't my friend anymore or I didn't respect her as a person or I was trying to make her into a sexual object or any of that, because of course I know better. But separated from her and Daniel O'Neill's mom like we were, and thinking about sex as much as we all were, you can kind of see how I thought a lot about them, especially at night, and about what they were doing inside the house. Taking showers, smelling nice, maybe running around wearing nothing but t-shirts. Maybe nothing but skimpy soft panties, like out in the garden. I mean even though she was Daniel O'Neill's mom, Becky was awfully pretty. And she didn't really seem all that much like Daniel's mom, or maybe it was that Daniel didn't really treat her that way, so it was easy to imagine that inside the house was the girls' dorm.

After a bit, Adams continued, and I smiled when I saw that glint in his eyes.

"Maybe I shouldn't tell you guys this," he said, "but there's something unbelievable about that woman."

I let out kind of a giggle and immediately wished I hadn't; it made me feel like they all probably thought I was nothing but a little kid. Daniel bit the inside of his lip and just listened.

"Actually, I know I shouldn't tell you guys this, but what the hell. It's the *boys' club barn*. We'll all trade stories and I'll go first.

"When you have sex with Nattie Sinclair," said Adams, beginning slowly, "you know you've slept with the gods. And I don't mean a goddess, some bitch up on a pedestal, I mean something primal, something primitive and creative. I mean the gods."

"Youthful exuberance," Lance said. "She's damn pretty, and I'm sure sweet and pure, but every young man in history's felt it every time he mounts up and shoots off. Fellas out in the western part of the state probably feel the same damn thing when they're out alone with their heifers."

Daniel laughed, but I could tell he knew, like I did, that Adams wasn't fazed or put off at all. Adams wasn't close to being finished.

"Yeah, bullshit," Adams said. "I know what you're saying, and that's not it," he told Lance. "I've been there often myself, hope to go there often again. Actually," he said, winking at Lance, "unlike some guys I know, I'm damned happy to still be of an age to go there at all. But that's not what I'm talking about. I've stalked my share of crystal stream rainbows and German Browns; hooked, played, and landed my fair share. What I'm telling you, without bragging, is it's not like this woman's my first cast ever. It's not like I'm Johnny G. here."

And then he shot a glance my way. "Sorry, Man. Didn't mean that the way it sounded," and I believed he didn't.

"I'll just out with it and tell you. She controls her own orgasms. This woman Nattie Sinclair comes in torrents. Not a little trickle, not a wetness, but a flood, a geyser, a downpour, a waterfall."

Daniel snorted. "So we're supposed to swallow the myth of the great Adams, super angler and woman killer, all rolled into one."

"Wish it were true," Adams said, not missing a beat and taking no offense. "Truth of the matter is, O'Neill, you've nailed the mystery, the point of the thing. Doesn't have a goddamned thing to do with me, nor I suspect any man she beds with.

"It's all her. She does it, it's her body, it's her orgasm, and you're just along for the ride. And somehow you know it's neither you nor another guy, nor any guy, maybe even no guy. Most times otherwise you'd get your male ego crimped and feel discarded or used or unnecessary, but you don't, and that's the part doesn't make any sense."

He looked around at each one of us. "But you sure as hell keep coming back for more."

He laughed a little, like he does, and Lance had stopped stuffing those slimy little Vienna sausage sandwiches into his mouth. It's not like Adams was nervous, but I could tell he was getting deep into something that touched him, that changed him, and maybe that frightened him some.

He laughed a little funny again. "I mean, I'm telling you guys; I'm talking an explosion here; a stream, a jet spray, an ejaculation. Soaking the bed sheets, the floor, once soaking my shirt when she was up on, well never mind, you get the idea.

"And for that moment, or those moments, you're floating with the gods, because you've sucked the sacred nectar."

"Holy Mary," I murmured.

"Shit, son," Daniel said, and then he laughed as hard as I'd ever heard him. "Woman's peeing on you."

"That's what I thought first time, too. But it's not. Not at all. I don't want to sound like some kind of pimp here, but it's unbelievable. I've had a golden shower or two, and this isn't it. Not at all the same. With Nattie, you can feel these muscles down in there, quivering and building blood full, and then her whole damn body tightens, and then whoosh, you're covered with, or lying in, or drinking nectar."

"Taste like honey?"

"Tastes like something, like something all its own. Not sweet, not sour, not bitter. Not good or bad. Tastes like dreams, or visions maybe, or, and I know this sounds like bullshit, tastes like being complete somehow. Tastes like nectar. Like being home."

"Holy Mary," I said again.

"And here's the hell of it. Like I say, I miss it, miss it a lot, but not so I feel crazy to get it. You know? Like usually when you get laid, all you want to do is get laid some more. But with this, there's a weird sort of satience. Is that a word? Doesn't matter. But an incredible sense of fulfillment. Almost like once you get the nectar, you've got enough. You can move on 'cuz it stays with you. Not a burn or a yearning, more like a leather bag filled with sacred dust. A bag you can tie to the hilt of your sword or hang around your neck and have with you always."

He laughed, and if I didn't know better, I would say self-consciously.

"So that's my story. Intend to spend a hell of a lot of my time in the future bedding beauties; but I know already I'll never have anything close to what I get from Nattie Sinclair. Miss it, sure; but more just happy I got it in the first place."

I felt stunned, and exhilarated at the same time. Right then, the boys' club moved a step closer to completion. Nattie Sinclair's Nectar, our Holy Grail, our raison d' horny.

I suddenly had this weird idea that Adams told us what he did about Nattie not to make us jealous but as a way to trade his relationship with Nattie for one with all of us. As if bringing us into the secret was somehow spreading the wealth around.

Except, like he was saying but not knowing it, without the sex. Adams got the same thing from playing around in the boys' club as he got from Nattie, buzzing on the same wavelength of not quite hyper but constant activity. Talking, moving, doing. I actually believed he really didn't miss being with Nattie all that much. I would have.

It was amazing. He was daring us, or challenging us. The buzz in my stomach flipped and flopped, and though I couldn't tell if it felt like anyone was going to mount a challenge to get the nectar, I was sure nobody thought I would.

"Sex is a slow dance
Where Creation and Destruction
Wrestle with Decay."

- Nattie Sinclair

Chapter 16

"The energy," Becky said early one evening, looking at Nattie and searching deeply, like she was trying to figure it out herself. "The energy that followed when you all arrived." She did not mean it like a compliment and Nattie didn't take it that way.

"Whatever's been in our way for so many years is waning," Becky said, knowing that Nattie knew she was talking about herself and Lance. "You can't imagine what it was like, living together here for years, but not being together. Both of us carrying resentment and love and guilt, bundling it up and giving it to each other every morning while it built and boiled, and then he'd take off for a few days, sometimes several weeks, and once for five months. Then he'd just show up, and we'd start over again, neither one of us willing to fight through it and fix it, neither one of us able to let it go."

Tears formed in Becky's heart and Nattie watched them rise like a tide and fall freely from her eyes. One splattered onto the oak wood of the kitchen table. Becky smiled at Nattie; she took Nattie's hand and cradled it into both of hers.

"And then, just a few months before you and the boys came, the gauze began to rift, and here we are, pretending we're college kids again, him sneaking into my room like on a panty raid, me watching him work and play with the boys like there's nothing more to life than having fun and doing whatever you feel like doing, whenever you feel like it. It all feels safe now, like somehow we've put the rules back together.

"Feels a little bit," she gasped a sob in a deep struggle to hold so much in, "feels almost like we might ultimately be let back in. Almost like forgiveness."

A shadow of remorse cycled erotically with her dream of tantalizing possibility, of moving past brand new into never imagined.

Becky's speech often tended toward a sweeping kind of vision, all encompassing and not missing much. She was genuinely happy that her son and his friends were at the farm. Nattie sucked in and celebrated the breath of that happiness.

Nattie swam in Becky's stream without pause, drifting into and out of her currents – swirling, floating, and bobbing every time Becky's eyes smiled or her lips pursed into a determination of finally recognizing something or anything or everything.

Nattie suddenly realized the possibility that she had fallen in love with Becky Dreiling. Not necessarily in that way, although she was beautiful and sexual and imminently touchable. In fact, spending the last few weeks at the farm, living inside the house with Becky while the testosterone bubbled and boiled out in the barn, Nattie did wonder what in the world she ever got out of sex with Adams, or with men at all, for that matter. She got a much sweeter rush just being with Becky, plus without all the mess. Can either one of us, she wondered, color within the lines of what that might mean?

Becky floated through things but she also floated deep into the heart of things, deep into the throat, everywhere, and lightly while flitting and flirting.

"Why do I suddenly wonder what's in the attic," Nattie asked.

Becky's smile was conspiratorial. "Because," she said slowly, "you sense that that's where the mystery unfolds. That's where we have stashed it all. All the answers and confusions, all the questions and clarities. In the attic," Becky said "is all the shit and all the flowers." Her smile morphed into consideration and reflection. "All our lives, everything we've salvaged and all that we've lost, all up in the attic – our altar and our vestibule."

"Nobody else is allowed up there?"

"Nobody is allowed up there."

"Just you and Lance?"

"Especially not Lance and me."

"You mean you and Lance together?"

"Never," she said.

"You don't go up there together? How can that be, you don't go up there together? I don't understand."

"Neither do I," Becky said, "not even a little, not even maybe.

"Sometimes I'll go up and I'll see clearly he's been there. I assume it's the same for him; certainly he can tell when I've been up there."

Her eyes cut into Nattie and then they cut well past her.

"I hope he can tell," she said before looking away.

The silence was enormous.

"That's an exquisite piece of something holy," Nattie finally said to her. "I can't imagine what the story could possibly be, or why the two of you don't talk about it. But I do know the gods are involved and it hurts them while they are smiling."

"Yes," Becky said quietly. "Through their tears, they might be smiling."

Nattie sat back, and Becky finished with the tea – the kettle's whistle slowly died and they let it steep for a few minutes in their cups. They both knew that it should not oversteep: too much flavor is not as good as twice as much. They drained the tea baskets on saucers and then made their way to the attic.

They climbed the narrow stairs in back of the kitchen, and the musty smells from Becky's life grew stronger as they climbed. Nattie knew they'd find important pieces of something behind the closed door at the top of the stairs. Or perhaps lost among the boxes and the barrels and the packaged memories, they'd find only the jagged spaces between the puzzle pieces already assembled elsewhere.

Becky reached above the jamb and retrieved an old skeleton key. She grabbed the doorknob hanging loosely from the skinny little door at the top of the stairs, fiddled the key, and gently pulled the door open.

When they stepped inside, Nattie gasped for breath. It was glorious.

The attic at Becky Dreiling's farm looked more than anything like a wonderfully preserved dollhouse. No junk, no boxes, no cobwebs or dust or boxes strewn haphazardly about. Rather, Nattie stepped into a Neverland; a tiny, meticulously designed nether universe, a wooden wonderland. Polished wooden planks on the floor and on the ceiling rafters. Filled with furniture and fixtures, everything polished wood and gleaming, everything one-quarter normal size, for midgets or munchkins or children. But Neverland children, who don't grow up and who never leave, and who never exist in this space to begin with. A hauntingly peaceful Neverland. One-quarter-size chairs set carefully around a small table, all wood, wooden dishes, wooden cutlery. Several tiny bed frames, wooden headboards and side rails, wooden slats but no feather mattresses, no cotton bed covers. A wooden couch frame resting on polished wooden floor planks, no cushions, no pillows. A little wooden sink carved into the top of a little wooden cabinet, a little carved wooden faucet attached to the wooden sink.

Nattie glanced outside the western gable window. It framed a waxing baby moon. Remnant rays of the setting sun reached back into evening with glorious color, as if gently cradling the infant crescent to bed.

Becky and Lance, but not together, conceived and nurtured an extraordinary fantasy. Clearly, it was never used, no one sat in these chairs, no coffee was served at this table. Wood furnishings lean and polished and unused. It was remarkable – simple and clean and unreal.

No dust in the light shafts, no cobwebs. The slight musty smell came in from the stairwell; it swirled about and mixed with the clean smell in the attic. A quiet clean, a unique peace. Nattie felt she could stay forever, and she realized immediately that a part of her always would.

It was all wood; and all of it was sanded exquisitely smooth.

***

The next morning they moved out into the sunshine past the vegetable garden and set up lawn chairs. Becky filled a bucket with dirt, and they jammed and old beach umbrella into it. They ran an extension cord from inside the barn, and the kitchen blender whirled frequently, turning out fantastic margaritas they both sipped as they sat and watched Lance and the boys turn the corner of the barn into a monstrosity of stone and open space.

Johnny said they were building more than just a stone corner for their stove. As if protecting the secret handshake, he was coy, and he hesitated to tell then exactly what was being erected, but they had taken off a dozen or more roof planks, and their stone wall was extending out the top of the barn in a shaft of controlled escape.

"*Stairway to the stars,*" is all Lance would say, then he and Adams both laughed and moved on.

They were both and each glorious to look at, physically powerful, suntanned and gleaming with sweat. Biceps bulged into tight balls as they picked up stones from a makeshift hoist coming up from the ground; Johnny worked on the ground, stacking a few stones at a time into a huge bucket and using one of Lance's angel pulleys to haul load after load up to the scaffolding. Daniel was busy at his workbench, sawing and sanding and planing. They all moved fluidly and deliberately, slopping mortar, hoisting stone, setting stone, hand over hand pulling on rope. They paused only to wipe sweat from their foreheads on the back of thick cowhide work gloves, so that a band of sweat and dirt collected around their wrists. They spoke little but remained in sync, as if generating generations of power and purpose.

It wasn't the difference in age that made the generations – though Lance was easily twice Adams' twenty-one years, they were nevertheless physically similar and exquisite. Nattie realized it was more a difference of exuberance bouncing off deliberation, or titillation compared to seduction, or always and whenever compared to now and forever.

And then she laughed loudly out loud, so much so that Becky stared at her and spilled some of her margarita. Suddenly Nattie realized it wasn't a choice between Lance and Adams, or Daniel and Adams, or each and any of them and Becky. It was a choice about nothing or having it all.

Nattie looked at Becky and then she looked at the men – even Johnny, for god's sake, with his skinny little arms and sad sack face. And then she looked back at Becky. So soft, so wise, so clear and clean and controlled. *They* slopped mortar onto stones – boys with tinker toys. *She* poured perfectly blended watermelon margaritas – a fairy-Goddess with fruited wings. Hairy and dark and dirty and mean; calm and wisdom, control and clean. Nattie saw two perfect halves of a glorious whole.

"Oh my God," Nattie said out loud. "Oh my God."

Becky glanced at her, then tipped her huge fishbowl glass in toast and agreement."Biceps and tequila," Becky said. "Better than a poke in the eye with a sharp stick."

"I'll drink to that. Johnny!" Nattie hollered over to him. "Get under this umbrella for a minute and drink like a girl!"

John Gophe had built a small fire in a pit on the ground just outside the shade of the umbrella. He ran back and forth between hoisting stone whenever they called for them and providing everybody with little shish kabobs. He cooked over the fire with all kinds of vegetables, and pieces of beef and pork and chicken and whatever else he found that morning when Becky told him to help himself and dig around the kitchen all he wanted.

Becky and Nattie lounged beneath the beach umbrella and luxuriated in the attention that wafted their way.

"Shooting stars of testosterone," Nattie giggled to Becky.

Watching Adams notice Becky gave Nattie an enormous thrill. Becky was gorgeous, and Nattie loved watching a healthy young stud strut and snort for her. His muscles flinched when she smiled at him. He loved looking at her legs; Nattie imagined his hands on her belly, on her breasts.

Becky and Nattie amused themselves whooping crude comments directed at bare, sweating torsos, drinking margaritas, and teasing Johnny.

***

Nattie laughed like hell when the boys gave them the details of their burgeoning monstrosity, first because she thought they were joking, and then even harder when she realized they were not. Adams at first pretended to be hurt at her reaction, and then he actually was, a little. Nattie didn't care about their ugly monstrosity of stone but she loved their excitement in building it. Just the fact that they were doing it at all, and then the energy of them doing it together.

Lance winked before he responded, and Nattie could see he didn't care one way or the other if she understood the why of it or not.

"That's the whole point," Lance said, and Nattie noticed the way his eyes twitched toward a twinkle. "It doesn't have to go anywhere. It goes up and out."

"That's it, see, that's the point." Adams was excited to bring Nattie along, to show her the process and make her smile. "If we were building a stairway from the barn floor to the hayloft, or even from the barn up to its own roof, well then we'd just be building any old stairway. A good one, sure," he glanced at Lance when he said this, "sturdy as hell and strong as the ages, but only a stairway. See, we're building a stairway to nowhere, a stairway up and out forever."

"To the stars," Daniel chimed in from his perch at a workbench just inside the barn door. "A *stairway to the stars*. Women aren't likely to get it."

Nattie didn't take it as a challenge or an insult, but interestingly, Adams did.

"Bullshit. Of course they do. Women get it."

"They're probably just too smart to build something like this," Johnny said, and then he turned his doe eyes to Lance and murmured, "I really like it, though."

"Too smart, maybe," Adams said. "But they get it. It's not a macho thing; it's a human thing. Think, Becky," he said to her, "of the poetry in movement going nowhere for no reason."

"When energy opens up and weaves together, you grab that synchronicity, if even for a moment," she said in that out-there sort of way she had of looking at things.

"Even if," she said again, and she couldn't help but laugh a bit herself, "the universe drops nothing but stones and mortar."

"Right. Exactly. Good point. It's all elemental, basic, molecular synergy. You either get on board and flow with it, or you get the hell out of the way."

Nattie was pleased when she heard this, pleased at Adams' uncanny ability to communicate on any level, with anyone, about anything. And she was drawn in, and drawn to him. He wasn't malicious nor manipulative. He was charming and extremely engaging. Cib Adams could talk to anyone, put anyone at ease, and make everyone part of his world. There was so much, really, of value about him.

But the recent change in him troubled her. Not obsequious so much as solicitous. She knew it was because of the sex. Or more to the point, the lack of it. She realized this was a male thing, poor bastards, but somewhere along the way she allowed herself to believe Adams was stronger, somehow immune to their gender's obsessive and pitiful need to get back from whence they came. Why don't more women understand this, she wondered, and use this?

And though he carried on with Becky, Nettie knew he was talking to her, flirting with Becky as a warm-up, to filter and fashion his communication with Nattie. But she no longer felt it was clever or witty or sly. It didn't make her want to banter or play. It no longer engaged her. Nattie suddenly felt repulsed. She realized he had gone and lost too much of himself. The silly son of a bitch climbed into the chasm, and he couldn't get all the way back out.

Of them all, right here now and over the years, Nattie believed Cib Adams might ultimately be the one who figured it out, who loved the flow like the rest but who had the good sense to get himself out of the river and back up out of the canyon and back onto his own feet. But he was not, and Nattie resolved again to remember that women don't have men for partners or soul mates, they have them around.

***

"Chicken kabobs up next," I announce with what seems like a bit too much fanfare. "Who wants what?"

"A little bob, Johnny, I want a little bob."

Nattie is teasing me, and I laugh along with Daniel, who is working just inside the huge barn door, but I have no idea what the joke means. They've both been teasing me, Nattie and Becky Dreiling, all afternoon. They've been sitting out since late morning, watching and partying as the final stones go in. Lance and Adams both swore the *stairway to the stars* would be finished today, so I decided to make an event of it – I've been cooking over an open fire pit all day, which is funny because even though it's also wood-fire cooking, it makes the wood–burning cook stove seem much more civilized. This fire pit I've dug into the ground feels more primitive, more primal. You have to pay a lot more attention, even compared to the wood-burning cook stove. So even though I sure don't want to be rude, especially to Daniel's mom, I can't talk back to them very much, or joke around, or even acknowledge the teasing. I hope they don't think it's hurting my feelings or that I'm pouting because I'm only trying to make sure I don't burn the food. Plus, they're both getting suntans; they keep moving so their legs stick out from beneath the shadow of the big beach umbrella. The short jean shorts are really short, super short on both of them, so that's another good reason for me to mostly keep my head down and concentrate on what I'm doing around the fire pit. Also, I need to be ready at a moment's notice for when I hear the call to hoist up more stones.

Adams and Daniel and his uncle are working like madmen, desperate to finish the *stairway to the stars*. The corner of the roof has been off for several days and you can see the stone walls jutting out clearly now. Daniel spent the last couple of days building a kind of sun deck on the roof surrounding the opening. Right now they're using it as a scaffold, but ultimately it will become the *stairway to the stars* observation deck. Daniel is the woodworker; he refused to do any of the stonemason work. He's now busy cutting and shaping the wooden stair treads out of a huge trunk of cedar Lance says came down in a windstorm last fall. Daniel has to measure and make each tread separately to fit into each stone pocket that's been fashioned for it. Since this is a handmade *stairway to the stars,* the dimensions aren't exact, they vary, and Daniel is intent on making each stair fit perfectly.

Nattie and Becky Dreiling haven't been up to the top yet; Adams has been insisting they have to wait until it's finished. That's been fine with them; this is the first time they've paid any attention at all in the entire week or so this project has been going on.

"Not just anybody gets it," Adams says while he mixes some water to thin out the gray sloppy mortar in his bucket. "Not just anybody gets in."

"We'll take Johnny's invite to eat as our golden ticket, our key to the stars," Becky tells him. "We get to climb on every stair because we're with the fire-tender."

"Then you're in," Adams says.

"Forever young," Nattie says. "Isn't this going to keep us forever young?"

"That would have to be a ladder," Lance says. "And you can't climb on stairs, you have to climb on every rung."

"Any moron can build a ladder," Adams snorts. "Our stone and mortar stairway will keep all women, blessed by the gods with incredible beauty," he says right to Daniel's mom without getting embarrassed at all, "forever young, and it will keep all men forever virile. What good's youth if it's all tiny and droopy, eh G?"

I could feel myself blush, but I pretended it was because I was leaning down close to the fire.

Adams cackles but good-natured and not mean and then he says something unbelievable.

"We're almost there. Johnny G., we're at the top. What say you, the true hearth and soul of us all, what say you cut the capstones?"

Man alive. We had been talking about the ceremony and symbolism of the capstones for days. The last stones that would form the top of the stairway walls had to be cut just so, to fit perfectly. All the other stones had been stacked and mortared randomly, fit in as fit can. But the capstones were like the signature of the whole piece – more important even than the cornerstone we had all selected and solemnly placed days ago.

Cutting the stone was an awfully important job. Lance kept these really old cutting tools in a drawer all by themselves. He said they belonged to Daniel's great-great granddad – his mom's great grandpa who came from Russia and homesteaded this farm. Everybody back then used tools like this to cut and split great slabs of buried limestone into usable stones and fence posts. The limestone is buried everywhere. It was the ancient seabed back from whenever ago that the Great Plains was an immense inland sea. The stones are filled with fossils of seashells and plants and underwater stuff. The people who decided to settle out here in the middle of nowhere – mostly German peasants from Russia – used the stone to make everything, since there weren't very many trees around to build with.

We had all fooled around and practiced splitting stones in the evenings, but I sure figured Lance, or maybe he and Adams together, would select and cut the capstones.

I stop what I'm doing at the fire pit, and it's one of those moments you believe you'll remember for the rest of forever. Everyone else stops, too, and I can feel all the gazes, everyone watching me. Nobody teasing, nobody talking. Man alive.

"Are you sure?" I say this mostly to Lance, but I realize I'm asking a larger question to something much bigger – as if the farm and the prairie and the dry hot wind are sagely considering me as a member. I'm filled with flashes – a memory of being lost behind the merry-go-round when I was very small; a feeling that I might cry; winning the spelling bee in fourth grade; my hamster that I accidentally dropped and she died.

When I look at Nattie and Becky Dreiling I almost do cry – the one smiling like a mom whose kid just saved a baby bird; the other like a mom whose kid might drown in swimming lessons. The O'Neill's, Lance and Daniel, like two looming statues – for some reason I think of the huge spanning legs anchoring the Colossus of Rhodes. They both watch and smoke. Daniel tapping the filter of a Winston against his thumbnail, Lance effortlessly rolling one of his own.

It feels like we're on a movie set and everything's waiting for me to deliver the scene-making line that I suddenly can't remember.

"Sign the piece, G," Adams finally says. "Sign it for us all."

I put down the fire tongs and put my hands in my pockets in case they start shaking.

"Okay," I say, and I walk into the barn and slide open the drawer that holds the splitting tools. They are wrapped in an old piece of leather and kept lightly oiled, so the bundle feels soft and fits well in my hand. I take it, along with the newly sharpened drill bit, over to the pile of remaining stone. I sit atop an over-turned bucket and I say, "okay" again.

Adams and Lance ride an angel pulley down to the floor, and we all naturally form a platoon in a production mode. Daniel begins laying in his wooden stair treads, securing them with wedges like St. Joseph did when he appeared in New Mexico and built that one church without any nails. Lance picks out stones of accommodating size and necessary smoothness and he marks a line on each at an exact five-inch depth. Adams picks up the drill and makes a straight series of four-inch holes along the mark, spaced four inches apart. I prepare to split the stones.

The splitting tools are deceptively simple – a hard metal rod, like a chisel, all pounded on the flat end and mashed down from years of being struck by a hammer, and two metal, tapered shims. It's not hard work, just delicate. The chisel rod and the shims go down into the holes. We have six sets of splitters, so Adams makes six holes along each stone. He uses a power drill, even though Lance has the old-fashioned hand drill that's shaped like a question mark. We discussed it at length, but finally voted that the immense savings in time was worth pinching a little from the traditional way.

312

I tap on the chisels, gently but most importantly, evenly, so that equal pressure is being applied along the designated line. I tap up and down the line, first one and then another until I feel the energy move from my hand to the hammer through the chisels and get packed into the stone. I pack it tighter and tighter, tighter still so I can feel the energy connect with a buzz to my stomach and then suddenly, with a slight "pop" and a rush that warms me through, the stone splits clean and straight as a fresh slice of hard-crust bread. It's beautiful, we are creating a skin of stone, cutting not only at a uniform five-inch depth but also shaping the pieces, like working on a puzzle backwards, cutting unique and interlocking shapes that fit together into a perfect whole.

It's like a dream, smooth, and it takes us no time at all, so that by seven o'clock and in more than enough time for the sunset we're carrying the 7-Up cooler to the observation deck and the women are bringing my leftover food and we all gather for the first time together on the observation deck atop the mortar and stone monstrosity that's now our *stairway to the stars*.

***

Right at sunset, Nattie felt something big, sitting atop the boys' club *stairway to the stars*. Something big suddenly shifted, finally changed. The sun set huge, bellicose and so full of itself on the prairie. It boasted and strutted; it retreated much too slowly and, like a lover you're finished with, it could not disappear soon enough. Whether a waxing moon chased it or a waning moon cringed and burned at its pursuit, the sun moved across the sky like a bully, and the relief was palpable when it finally sank and left her alone. For just a moment, Nattie felt alone with the moon.

She also felt remarkably hollow, so alone though surrounded by people, empty and sad and, though she didn't know exactly what it was, she knew it all changed, for real and for good. They all watched the sky in silence: sipping on cold beer and individual thoughts while waiting for twilight, sitting on a wooden deck newly built on top of a barn in Kansas. Nattie could still smell the not-yet-dry mortar.

"We built this stairway for you two," Adams said to Becky and Nattie, raising a bottle of beer in toast. "Women love stars."

"They always have," Nattie whispered.

God how she loved him so much only days ago. How could something so big leave so easily, and leave with so little farewell?

For just a moment she thought: Maybe just close my eyes, click my heels, and take the chance, make the dance. Take that chance, now gone, to dash back to the shade of the umbrella, grab my youth, call for Cib and run: run or drive or fly but flee. Get out. Start real somewhere far – cut free from the tentacles building slowly here like tendrils weaving in and among these people, clutching them also and binding them to me, weaving back to before being here, and back to before being anywhere. Cut free from everything I've drug along with me and built around me and drop it and run. There is a chance, for just a moment now gone, to be a real person in the real world: to climb with Adams back into space and back into time; to coddle grandkids and cuddle new puppies, take station wagon vacations and hang Christmas garland along the hallway banister.

To be normal, maybe, but then Nattie looked at Becky, who was watching Daniel, her son; and Nattie was hit by a gale of hot humid insight. Becky would always be incomplete, because in Daniel a part of her was always missing, never to be filled, never reconciled. Just like with a lover, so why go there and why risk it? Becky would always be stuck, evolving only so far, understanding only so much, because a part of her, a part of any mother, was missing. There was a hole there. That hole was where enlightenment would grow. It was where her true energy should flow. It was where her god-self would go. That hole could never fill, and who in the hell needs that? Suddenly the sadness had an edge, and for just a fleeting moment, Adams looked predictable and Becky was pathetic. Nattie's heart was falling, falling across the stone stairs and into the sunset, down and over and away. Nattie excused herself and made her way to the house.

She wandered in through the back door of the little mudroom that led into Becky's kitchen. Such a clever cleansing area. Becky kept her gardening shoes here, pink Keds caked with yellow mud. Lance's work boots thrown in a corner on the floor. Mops, brooms, bug sprays and stuff. A transition room, this mudroom. From outside to in, but more so a cleansing room. Leave the dusty male pungent hot buzzing out, come inside to softly female fragrant safe and clean. They exist and flourish outside, but always they long to come in. We train them and filter out just enough of them so we get the essence without the mess. And you've got to love them, because they'll take off their boots, wash their hands, even probably their feet if we tell them to, just to come inside.

It was ridiculously simple: keep the door open and they'll saunter in and out whenever they please, clomping their feet up on tables when they sit back to belch or belly-laugh, resting their elbows next to silverware when they eat. But lock the door and hold the key and then they're as docile as a rabbit-foot key chain you hold in your pocket and stroke when you feel like it. They'll carry your bags and your books, pick up the check, or fight dragons, just to be allowed to come inside.

Agnus Dei

No matter what others might think or even what they might say, I know it is the rocking that keeps it going. Not that Lance's truck needs the help or the extra momentum or the added energy of course. Lance's truck is just fine. But when I rock, I rock, and the truck is better. Imperceptible yet better. Just gently, just enough back and forth so Lance doesn't glare, or worse. Enough still to keep it all moving and flowing and rolling along.

Like it was with the Valiant but of course not at all the same. But the energy, like the energy that was the Valiant. Feeling it and going with it. In part it's the going with it that matters because Lance never takes the others. Not Nattie not Daniel. Only me. And even though he doesn't take me every time, he takes only me. When he takes someone he takes only me.

So those times when Lance nods to me as he walks to his truck, or when he sometimes even seeks me out in the barn or down at the cattle pond, we ride. We drive the Kansas dirt roads. Mile after mile of nowhere, straight and yellow dust and planted fields and endless sky. And like the rocking, I'm not there to change it or fix it or improve it. Just to go along.

Just to be a part of it. Again, and may God forgive me, like the Valiant – just to be a part of it. Rocking back and forth, back and forth on the long bench seat covered in an Indian print seat cover. It smells like animals and sweat, and it looks like the blanket of somebody's dad – rough and scratchy and brown and gold and mostly used up. About the rocking Lance used to yell, "Stop it!" That scared me at first and sometimes still does, but Lance didn't see the energy so of course he didn't like the rocking. Again, like I say, not to make things go faster but always to make things go well.

To quiet the rocking, to make it small so Lance will not yell, I have learned to float my hand in the wind. My arm outstretched through the open window; my hand like the wing of a hawk riding the wind. A tiny shift in my little finger and the hawk sails up or down on the wind. Soaring and searching and riding the wind. Like the rocking but backwards – the effect of it all instead of the cause.

You had to be there, the way we drove. Miles and miles of straight-ahead dirt road. Dust, like I say, always but also cultivation and irrigation. Fields high and arrogant with sunflowers in late summer. Or ready and willing with not-quite-up winter wheat in the fall, or plowed and placid in spring. Just cold and dirty white in the winter. But huge always and spreading and wind.

Carved into the land along the creek beds where cultivation was kept at bay you can see buffalo wallers. You have to look carefully to see the buffalo wallers. Or wallows. Or however you name them, but if you know where to look, they are everywhere. No matter what you call them, no matter their name, they are everywhere. In the distance an imperceptible dip, a difference in the flowing movement of the grasses: purple almost at the head, miles of grasses, and gold and green and some brown and all swaying and blowing gentle soft always in the wind.

But when you know where to look, when someone taught you and showed you, then you can see them for yourself. Off in the distance sometimes and next to the road, buffalo wallers. Years and years, a hundred years ago and more, buffalo owned this wonderment of Kansas prairie. By the millions they wandered wherever they wanted and lay down and bellowed and rolled and pawed and grooved and made commotion enough to create magnificent dents in the earth. When you look at these dents, your skin is on fire, because you know you are seeing something old and real. Because buffalo made them, but also because they made them so long ago. So long ago, and it lasted until now. The earth changed, the earth sanded smooth by buffalo. So slight, so subtle, so small, but changed certainly and changed enough that the repercussions and vibrations and that long ago rooting and wallowing are still here, impressed ever so slightly into the earth of this vast Kansas prairie.

Endless dirt roads, right in the middle of where we belong. Mile after mile of fields and pastures defined and lined by stone fence posts strung with barbwire. Fence Post Rock. Unending, unyielding. Stretching for miles, forever, silent sentinels, meticulously placed stone fence posts. Forever stretching limestone, up and out of the earth. At attention, or stone posts mile after mile at parade rest.

Trees are scarce, a few cottonwoods along the mostly dry creek beds only, but no trees really, so no lumber, only stone. Stone fence posts, stone houses, fabulous stone Catholic churches. Steeples in every small town – towering tall limestone celebrations of God.

Like the people, the lumber is an anomaly. People and lumber shipped in by rail, invaders into a land of buffalo and yellow limestone.

Lance drives the pick-up and we ride through this beautiful desolation of wind, grasses, and stone. Cold and dark when the headlights cut ahead, and you shiver and rock, and Lance keeps the window down to blow out the smoke from his hand-rolled cigarettes and throw out the butts and keep driving. When the almanac calls out for a full moon, Lance drives across a pasture to an old dead cottonwood. Its white limbs are without bark or leaves, its whiteness like bones drying into dust beneath the moonlight. We stand before it without speaking; we stand with the tree for a time, we stand and share in a portion of its death. Then Lance will say, "Play the harp, Boy." So I pull it from my pocket and blow softly a dirge laying dust to rest.

Other times he drives and he turns off the dirt road toward the tiniest little nothing of a town, but only if there is a bar, and there always is if there is a church, and there is always a church with a towering stone steeple. It either creeps up on you or it's visible next to the grain elevator for miles. Usually out by the crossroads where we travel, subtly calling to folks like us, coming from here and meandering to there, sits a bar.

And then we stop.

Because of the repetition and frequency I have learned the location of all the roadhouse bars and all the church bars. Lance in the beginning said only and always, "Don't rock and don't worry," but after a short time I learned this, so now he says nothing, only looks at me a moment and then we walk in.

318

Not dark and scary and crummy. More quiet and simple and middle of nowhere nothing. Cans of Coors and Budweiser and Lite stacked in an upright cooler with glass doors hulking behind the Formica bar. Empty tables along the wall, empty benches of red vinyl where no one sits, or maybe here and there a couple of old-guy farmers or sometimes a handful of high school kids eating hamburgers. Wanna be or maybe even used to be jocks but farmers and sons of farmers all.

We sit at the bar atop two vinyl topped barstools, each lined up in front of the bar, a straight row of chrome sentinels, each sitting on single chrome peg legs, legs anchored to the smooth wooden floor. Lance looks up and says, "Buy a couple of Coors from you, Ned?"

An old farmer sitting already at the bar turns our way and says, "Not today, Soldier. You're not buying beer in here today. Maybe tomorrow or maybe yesterday, but not today. Today, I'm buying your beer."

Lance turns slowly, and the man behind the bar sets two cans of cold beer in front of us.

"Thanks, Willie," Lance says to the old farmer. "Boy here thanks you too."

They tip cans toward each other and the old farmer says "to the bloody hand."

Several all around say "to the bloody hand," as they tip beer cans, and Lance takes a long cold swallow and I think about saying I'll drink to that.

"And then for a long time nothing happened.
Just dust settling softly into
The white space between the stars."

- John Gophe

Chapter 17

When the *Stairway to the stars* went up, somehow "No Girls Allowed" turned into "Every Night is Ladies Night." I'm not against girls, of course, but the *boys' club barn* sure changed and I wouldn't say *better than fine*. All the carousing and horsing around petered out, and more and more we spent our days just hanging out until it was time to climb the *stairway to the stars*. There, every night Nattie and Becky Dreiling would join us and we'd wait for the sunset and then watch the stars. We talked some about coming up with a new *boys' club barn* project, but nothing we hit on measured up to the *stairway to the stars,* so nothing really took hold.

Adams and Lance spent most of their time carving coats of arms into the beams and rafters at the top of the stairway. I guess that was kind of like a project but really just an excuse to hang out on the stairway. Lance, of course, was carving some version of the Bloody Hand of O'Neill, but with a stairway and a comet. At first it was hard to tell what Adams was carving but after a day or so a pretty good 1965 Plymouth Valiant began to emerge, driving through what might have been a field of Kansas sunflowers.

I kept the fire going, as usual, and still cooked most days. I could tell everyone was getting tired of the same old stews and gumbos and pots of eats.

"I'd give a shiny new nickel for a hot sausage pizza," Adams said more than once.

Daniel wasn't doing woodworking anymore, either. In fact, he wasn't in the barn during most days at all. He never said where he was going and what he was doing. It's kind of sad and disappointing to say this, but none of the rest of us even asked him about it.

When we'd sit, as I say, all together at night, the conversation became increasingly mundane and pedestrian and ordinary. Adams and Nattie especially weren't the same. They still kind of bantered back and forth, and we'd all laugh some because they were both so clever and witty, but increasingly there was so much of an edge that what they were doing was putting on a show of slowly, slyly, and cleverly destroying little pieces of each other, and much bigger pieces of themselves.

And then toward the end of the week they got into a huge fight, a ridiculous fight that didn't have anything to do with anything except them wanting to be mean to each other and wanting to redefine the world.

Adams was telling a story about our road trip in the Valiant and, without saying he was sick of my cooking, he mentioned how much he'd love to be eating a burger from that hamburger place that we saw in just about every small town. Nattie had something to say about it and Adams shot back at her.

"What the hell convinces you Mom and Pop burgers are any better than Bob's Big Boy's finest?" The tease in Adams voice was as strong as ever, but I'd been around the two of them enough to also recognize the sound of his annoyance at Nattie's near constant harp against the evils and ugliness of corporate America. "Probably not even as good," he went on. "Ma and Pa can't afford the same level of quality as Bob's; can't buy in bulk, so can't buy choosy. Mom has to buy whatever the toothless rancher, down on his luck through drought or divorce, cares to offer. Bob's gets the pick of the best cuz he can afford to buy the best. Bad for Mom but good for us."

"That's bullshit," Nattie said, not sounding all that much like she was teasing. "Take a guess how often Bob's Big Barf has put a Mom and Pop out of business. Once a month? One a week? Every day? And only because they can buy dead cows for thirty cents a pound less? Hell, it's a double dip. They're ripping off your hard-working, dental deficient rancher, and then turning around and screwing Mom and Pop. Like some giant Nazi Locust – moving from town to town devouring character and stealing individuality.

"A Bob's Big Barf on the main street corner of every town: the bloody American Dream. All of it the same, all the same, all the same."

"It's only burgers," Daniel said, sounding like he wanted to make his eyes smile.

"No, O'Neill, it's one hell of a lot more than burgers," Nattie said. "It's about a bunch of puffy white arrogant suits deciding their bottom line looks better if every small town in the world looks the same. It's about greed and it's about profit. It's a goddamn crime, and they ought to be stopped. They ought to be shot."

"Darling, that's either stupidly naïve or dangerously paranoid," Adams said. "You're not really saying that a legal corporation, engaging in legal trade and commerce, should be shut down – even though that corporation provides a product a lot of people obviously want to buy – should be shut down because you pine for the quaintness and charm of Norman Rockwell's candy store?"

"It doesn't have anything to do with charm," Nattie shot back at him, and I realized this wasn't fun anymore. Nattie was truly mad, Adams was truly annoyed, and Daniel O'Neill seemed to be enjoying the whole thing. I hated it. It felt like when your parents fight. Not that I thought of Adams and Nattie as my parents, of course, but like watching something fall apart. Something strong, like a tree, like that tree I saw growing out on the prairie, growing two huge trunks up from one, growing away from itself until it split in half and died.

"You're so missing the point," she repeated. "It's about greed, not charm. It's about the Almighty Dollar festering and rotting in corporate boardrooms, instead of food made with love and cooked by real people. Ever wonder why everybody's sick and diseased these days? It's because the food these corporate raw-raw American bastards force into every small town is killing us off. Anything you make and then eat with greed instead of love won't nourish you; it will kill you. We're being killed off by corporate greed and bottom line bullshit."

"Nobody's making anybody eat anything. Nobody's making anybody buy anything. The conspiracy grows in the liberal pack of paranoid do-gooders who smugly believe they know what's right for everybody else. Who the hell are you to say the average small town Joe should pay more for, and get less of, anything, just so you can hold onto a childish and moronic vision of a return to bartering for beads?"

"Jesus, Adams," Nattie said as she started down the stairs. "What a dick."

We all just sat there, stunned and embarrassed. Finally Daniel said, "Nice work, Cowboy. Maybe tomorrow you can tell her that she comes from a family of fat stupid people."

"Up yours, Man," Adams said.

"You two boys need to settle down, the both of you," Daniel's mom said. "All this cooped up energy and bottled testosterone's getting out of control." She threw a look at Lance, sitting back like he usually did, saying little. "Are you even paying attention here?"

She got up from her chair and followed Nattie down the stairs. She cast an eye at her son. "Mind your manners and remember you're friends."

In typical Adams fashion, he rebounded quickly.

"Women," he winked at me. "Can't live with 'em, can't shoot 'em. Don't know from one minute to the next what they think or who they want. Change like the damn weather, or like DB's scared shitless by motion and a strong arm. Doesn't mean a thing."

Holy smokes. Was he crazy? I had never, in the two years I'd known Cib Adams, heard him be dismissive of women like this. Sure he was all about macho and all about tough, but he loved women, he adored them, he protected their honor and spoke well of them. All this meanness just because he said some things he shouldn't have?

The silence there atop our *stairway to the stars* held for a while, we all three saying nothing, waiting maybe for who knows what. A bit, perhaps, of comic relief. Finally the silence moved to that place of embarrassing vulnerability.

"Jesus H, you guys, help me out here," Adams said. "Help me, hold me, tell me what I'm missing. Don't' tell me you're buying any of this 'run, Bambi, it's modern man' bullshit? This little plea for attention? C'mon, you guys. This is the boys' club, the inner fucking sanctum. We don't have secrets here. I call a council, a circle."

The O'Neill's exchanged glances, shared that non-verbal thing with their eyes.

"No doubt you're right," Lance finally said. "Whole thing'll blow over and be forgotten by tomorrow."

"She's showing your ass the door," Daniel said. "Been on to doing it for weeks now."

"Bullshit," said Adams.

"You're probably right," Daniel said. "Care to bet?"

"Fuck you, Man. Don't bet on my pain. That's an asshole bet."

"Could be," Daniel said, almost smiling. "But maybe I'm betting on my pleasure."

Man alive, did a buzz suddenly hit my stomach.

"Careful, gentlemen," Lance said. "Good time for all of us to take a break, take a breath."

"Golly," I'm pretty sure I let slip out.

"O'Neill, you're so full of shit, what the fuck's wrong with you. You don't shut up I'm going to kick your ass sideways."

"Careful, Cowboy," Daniel said. "You're in the barn of the O'Neill's. Watch your mouth."

Man alive. I looked at Lance, sitting with his peg leg dangling over the top of the stone wall. Couldn't he see it? Couldn't he stop it? Do something? Say something?

"I think we all feel grateful to have spent the summer here in the O'Neill barn," I finally said, "but it is still our boys' club, isn't it? I mean out here, we're all equal and all. Come on you guys. Knock it off."

"I'm thinking of calling in a flint," Daniel said. "Extra flints, remember?"

"What's extra flints?" Lance asked.

"Part of the trade for the Valiant. The most important part. A man's word. I can call in extra flints whenever I want." Daniel O'Neill smiled mean, and his eyes locked with Adams'. "I'm thinking your former may be my extra flint."

"That's bullshit and you know it, O'Neill. Extra flints is buying you your first shot of the night. Extra flints is helping you move when you've got a fat wife and a waterbed. Extra flints isn't my woman."

"Deal was, extra flints is whatever I say is extra flints."

"Yeah, but within reason," Adams said.

"Reasonable is whatever I say is reasonable. That was the deal, you know it. Besides," Daniel O'Neill said, "doesn't much seem like she's your woman right now."

"Fuck you, O'Neill."

"Up yours, Adams. Deal's a deal, remember? I call extra flints. That's part of the deal. You can't argue, you can't refuse, and you know it. Extra flints is my call. That's the deal."

"Yeah, but the deal was predicated on the understanding and mutual acceptance that you weren't going to turn into a total asshole. What the hell's wrong with you, O'Neill?"

Oh man, this was bad. For six or seven weeks now we had lived in a gender-clean utopian boys' club. A testosterone charged, moronic vacation of boys' stuff. Building things. Eating things. Cooking things. Drinking things. Simple rules. No dancing, no dodging, no sweetness, no games. In a word, I think, no women.

I'm not about to say women coming into our boys' club caused any of this, but clearly it did. Before, an argument like this would have been settled with a first-one-on-the-ground wrestling match, or a throw-for-cork dart tournament, or a race up and down on the loft angel pulley, or any of the many boys' club ways we had devised for settling disagreements. It was all so easy. Like no matter how bad your sin, no matter how despicable and mean, once you tough it out and go to confession, God forgives you and you're once again slapping backs with Jesus, and popping beers. But now, first with Adams and Nattie and then with Adams and Daniel

O'Neill, the *boys' club barn* stifled to suffocation with Jesus galloping in on a white stallion in Revelation, wide-eyed and take no prisoners for God. It's all done, no do-overs, no second chances. Damnation. Like that thing Nattie said about indulgences from prayer. Even if you get forgiven, you still have to atone through suffering.

It wasn't clean anymore.

When you argue over who has to get up and fetch the next round of beers, or who gets the shotgun seat and who has to ride in the bed of the truck, you're really struggling to agree on the rules of behavior. The issue is not about the beer, it's about agreeing on a code of conduct. Honorable activity. Right action. Boys' club rules. No matter the outcome, you shake it off and move on.

But when you fight over women or country or prize, the fight can never end because the prize is never won – there's always that flash of a breast and a come-on smile, and it convinces you the war must go on. More booty, more prisoners, more prize.

Dag! You know?

***

I had never gotten a hemorrhoid before, but early the next morning I woke up with a doozy.

I didn't want any of them to say anything to Nattie or Daniel's mom, mostly because it was an awfully embarrassing thing to have wrong with you but also because I didn't want to be the first one to break solidarity out in the barn. We hadn't come across a problem or situation we didn't solve ourselves. In a way, all my blood in the toilet took the edge off of Adams and Daniel being so mad at each other, and I wished I could have held up to it better, maybe like sacrificing my own blood was a way of bringing everything back to *better than fine*.

Everyone was pretty concerned after seeing the blood in the toilet (which was gross to show them but I was afraid). They all three treated it like an extremely serious mission for the boys' club. You could feel the camaraderie again, you could feel the love. I'm not saying I believe I could have saved the boys' club by staying out in the barn and bleeding to death. But the barn was never *better than fine* again.

However, my own blood in the toilet, and the pain, made me afraid. So ultimately I chickened out and decided to go inside the house and try to take care of it.

I winced with every step I took toward the back door of the house. It felt like this hemorrhoid pulsed and grew larger every time my heart beat. I wanted to lie down right there out in the yard, curl up in the dry dirt next to the strawberries, and cry. I felt like I was being a big baby, but boy did my butt hurt. I thought about my mom, and even though I didn't want her to take care of it or salve it or anything, I thought about her nonetheless. Not her being with me, but maybe just knowing I was in pain. I wanted to get by myself, out of the sun, and lie down out of sight. I considered going around the house and crawling beneath the wooden front porch, but even I knew that was ridiculous. I needed to get inside.

I had felt the thing that morning, when I used the john out in the barn. I was afraid, but I reached my hand around and slipped a finger into the crack of my butt, and then yanked my finger out when I touched it. About the size of a quarter of a grape cut longways, and really the same texture and feel as a grape. It was wedged there pretty tightly outside of, you know, the hole. No wonder it hurt. I imagined the thing could rupture at any moment, and I was terrified of bleeding to death from my butt out in the barn. That's when I resolved to get inside, back to civilization, clean my hands properly, and figure out what to do. I really hoped Nattie and Daniel's mom weren't around.

I stood for a while in the little mudroom, listening for sounds in the kitchen. Maybe they were already in town or working with plants in the early morning sun at the front of the house. I opened the kitchen door just a crack, waited a moment, and then pushed in. Empty, thank goodness. I started crying a little as I stood in the kitchen, mostly because it hurt a lot, but also because I suddenly got an image of myself lying all alone on the floor in a pool of blood, bleeding to death from my butt. The pain made me realize the thing was now as big as an apple, and I wondered how much blood could fill up in there before I'd get lightheaded. I took a long time at the sink, both to ensure my hands were super clean and because I was afraid to take whatever the next step was. I thought maybe I'd just stand there with my eyes closed the rest of the day letting the warm water run and run over my hands.

Suddenly I heard the toilet flush, and I realized the women were in the house, moving quietly, maybe just waking up or something, but certainly heading eventually into the kitchen. Oh man, I had to get out, but I couldn't go back outside. I dried my hands on a tea towel hanging from the handle of the refrigerator, and then I opened the door like you do when you're not really hungry but you just stand in front of the cold air and look at all the food. I saw a stick of butter and remembered I wanted to try making biscuits from scratch, so I snatched it and put it in my shirt pocket. I shut the refrigerator and looked around the kitchen for a place to hide. "This is dumb," I heard myself say, and I opened the pantry door.

Shelves from floor to ceiling, filled with canned goods and dry pasta and other food things. There was another doorway at the back of the pantry, and I went through it without a thought. It was dark on the other side, and I closed the door as quickly and as quietly as I could. I felt around but couldn't find a light switch anywhere on the wall, and then I noticed a little dancing glimmer above my head, something like a firefly. When I reached out for it, I felt a hard edge and realized I was holding a little glass prism hanging from a string. As my eyes opened up in the darkness, I could see a tiny shaft of light coming from beneath a door at the top of some stairs. The light shaft, comfortable with slashing through the prism, glanced nervously on the back of my hand. I pulled the string and a light came on. I was in a narrow stairwell, empty save for a light bulb with a prism on a string.

These back stairs, tucked inside the food pantry, beckoned some comforting release, like the smell of gingerbread cookies at Christmas, or the steam rising from a batch of oatmeal raisin in summer. These back stairs were cooler, felt calm, and I imagined an ice-cube shoved ever so gently up my screaming butt. The pain was the same but somehow better, I guess, because I was so hidden and secret and safe. It felt like take a breath, lie down, and heal. I kind of curled onto the bottom two steps so all the pressure was on my thighs and lower back, my butt just floating. And then I had an idea. I unpeeled the paper from the top of the butter stick and gooped it all over a finger. Then I just lay there, trying to get the courage to reach around the back and see about pushing the thing back inside.

I knew it was the size of a cantaloupe by now, continuing to fill with blood, on the verge of bursting. I felt like a baby, but I cried a little again as I imagined them finding me, butter on my finger and bled to death from my butt. I unhitched the belt from my jeans and reached around, but I just couldn't bring myself to reach inside to feel it. I didn't have the courage to touch it. I waited awhile, not for anything, just for a while to calm down and be still and stop. As I lay there I worked on building resolve, on building a plan like visualizing my finger actually doing the deal. It was just like throwing up, that first part when your stomach retches and it's terrible but you push through, and so I did. I re-gooped my finger in the softening butter stick and slowly moved it inside the crack. I was a little surprised the crack was still closed as I imagined the thing must be the size of a watermelon by now. I actually almost did throw up, and then I just pushed forward and touched it. I felt almost relief to discover the hemorrhoid was still only the size of a quarter of a grape cut longways. I resolved to think of it as a nice little green grape instead of a blood-engorged vein-colored purple grape. Or maybe artery-colored, but what did that matter?

I began rubbing it, ever so softly, just getting a feel for it and imagining the blood beginning to squeeze out of it. Man alive, this was gross. Slightly more pressure, and slightly more pressure, and then, a bit anti-climactically, my finger pushed the thing back inside me. The immediate relief was unbelievable, and I cried a little again. I slowly began removing my finger but I could feel the hemorrhoid following it back out, so I just lay there on the bottom of the attic steps behind the pantry with my finger sticking out of my butt and a stick of gnarled butter sticking out of my shirt pocket. I drifted off to a kind of sleep.

***

A kind of strange sleep where part of you stays crumpled on the attic stairs behind Becky Dreiling's kitchen pantry, and part of you listens to the incessant slam of a screen door, slamming repeatedly in the hot wind and the hot nowhere of the Kansas prairie. You hear that lonely empty screen door slam, over and over, a screen door slamming in the wind, the sound of a screen door slamming in the wind, slow and lazy and over and over.

A screen door slamming over and over in the wind, slamming over and over until it feels like you can hear a train whistle off in the distance. It's out in the middle of nowhere, nothing but hot sun, dry wind, fence post rock; and then the slamming screen door is in a little nothing farm town, and you're in a little nothing farm town that's deserted with no people, no dogs, a few houses, and empty swing sets; and the screen door slams like you're in a movie somewhere, but nothing moves except wind and dust, and then you see the church.

Huge, yellow limestone, bigger than the whole town, it towers Gothic up into the hot sun sky, a Catholic church reaching up so high your neck creaks as you look up at the three-spired stone steeples. It's a beautiful and stunning Gothic celebration and adoration rising from the hot dusty Kansas nowhere like limestone angels singing a sacred ascent. And then you see Nattie Sinclair.

You see her first walking down the street toward you and then standing right next to you in front of the church, standing close to you and looking up at the church and the spires on the steeples, standing and looking up with you and then standing and holding your hand.

You take her inside the church: fabulous, remarkable, opulent and fine, polished oak everywhere, marble columns, everything inside towering up and lifting, stained glass in the middle of Kansas nowhere and the incense smell of holy. The church is exquisitely quiet, vacant confessionals along both side walls, and like your childhood, you get more and more nervous as you walk up the main aisle and your stomach buzzes as you make your way closer, up to the Communion rail, closer and closer to the altar where Jesus is dying or dead on the cross, and of course, you're not allowed there. The altar is for priests only, and Nattie Sinclair is light and laughing and happy. She's talking and smiling and playing around, so you pull her back from the altar, away from the Holy Ghost, and you genuflect and you sit down with her in the second pew. We can't go up there, you tell her, we're not allowed. It's for priests only and the Holy Ghost. You speak quietly, the smell of incense is heavy, but Nattie Sinclair is smiling and winking and carrying on. You sit still, reverent, and then finally Nattie Sinclair also becomes quiet and, just as you begin to almost relax and you believe she will behave, she says, "We should have sex on the altar."

All the stained glass brightens and pulsates, and the Stations of the Cross vibrate, and you start to hear a choir, a Gregorian chant of the Lamentations, and she says again, "Let's make passionate love, you and I naked on the altar."

You want to hide beneath your oak pew or hit your knees and say the sign of the cross, and she says it's not erotic, it's sacred. It's pure creation. It's a welcome-home ceremony for the Goddess of Creation. We can have sex on this altar and consecrate the feminine and the divine.

She shouldn't be speaking heresy and blasphemy and breaking commandments here at the altar, and so it gets louder and louder, the chant, you hear it louder, the Signum Crucis – A plainsong almost, In the name of the Father, and of the Son...In nomine Patris, et Filii, et Spiritus Sancti... In nomine Patris, et Filii, et Spiritus Sancti... over and over in your head, and filling the church too, in nomine Patris, et Filii...The more you listen to it, the more you hear it, but the more you look at Nattie Sinclair, the more you can't help it while you hear it, In nomine Matris, et Virginis, et Sanctae Effeminatae.

Don't watch her, don't watch while she strokes the sides of her body, arches her back looking all the while into you deep – In nomine Matris, et Virginis, et Sanctae Effeminatae – but you must fight it, you must fight her – In the name of the Father, and of the Son, et Virginis, et Sanctae Effeminatae. The Holy Ghost. The

Holy Ghost, the Dove, Sancta Sophia, Sophia Sancta, Sanctae Effeminatae. In the altar and in the chant and in the church, the Holy Ghost. Spirtitus Sancti. Spiritus Sancti. But now she's unbuttoning her shirt, slowly, and smiling. In nomine Matris, et Virginis, et Sanctae Effeminatae, et Virginis, et Virginis.

You glance quickly at the wooden Confessionals, but you can't block it out, The Sign of the Cycle, In nomine Matris, and her fingers are running along the inside of your leg; you can see her fingers coming up the seam of your jeans, In the name of the Father, and of her fingers coming up to your zipper and toying with it, her other hand moving to the Son and the Holy Ghost In the name of the Father and of the Son and of her fingers pulling the zipper slowly and her other hand reaching up to the front of her bra, and she unfastens and her breasts are in there and her fingers release and your zipper is down and her breasts heave and you are on the stairs behind the pantry, crumpled and willing to sacrifice your blood.

Signum Cyclis et Signum Crucis. In nomine Patris, et Filii, et Spiritus Sancti. In the name of the Mother, and of the Maiden, and of the Sacred Crone.

***

I don't know how long I lay there; when I awoke my finger was no longer sticking out of me, and the pain was gone. Just a little itchy, and really gloppy from all the butter. I tore a piece off the tea towel with my teeth and folded it and gently pushed it in so I wouldn't get butter and whatever all over my underwear. My jeans were scrunched around my knees, and without yet standing up I was able to get myself pretty much back together.

I didn't want to go back outside, because I wasn't ready to face the fellows. I sure didn't want to face the women either, so I thought it best for me to stay where I was until I knew for certain they were out of the house. After a short while I snuck quietly up the stairs to see what was in the attic. An old skeleton key drooped out of the lock. I jiggled it quietly and then pushed open the door.

I couldn't believe my eyes. I actually thought for a moment that I was still asleep and dreaming because I stood inside the attic as if floating in a fairyland. Very clean, not dirty, no dust anywhere. A miniature wonder world set with exquisite wooden furnishings. And then as I looked more closely, I shivered and let slip out a small cry. Not only wooden furniture, but the room was filled with half a dozen little wooden people. But they didn't look like children, and they didn't look like dolls; they looked like some creepy memory or horrible dream.

And then I actually did cry when I realized these people were built from the woodworking pieces of Daniel O'Neill. They didn't really look like dolls because they weren't painted with lips and eyes so they didn't look like real people. But on the other hand, their blank faces bore right through you, like witch doctors who have those voodoo dolls they stick pins into. The voodoo dolls don't look anything like a real person, but they're creepy because you know they represent a real person. And it only took a moment for me to realize who had sewn the little pants and shirts and very short jean shorts.

***

"Shit, man, if you've been making a whole family of little wood dolls with her behind our backs, what the hell else have you been doing with her?" When Cib Adams wanted to needle someone, he'd get under their skin by verbally bopping them in the head, by "slapping them around." This time with Daniel, though, he wasn't fooling around. He was fiery mad, enraged to the point his voice was perfectly calm and controlled; no b.s., no bigger than life rowdy and loud, just controlled mean and mad. "What are we supposed to think?" Adams raged on. "Do we have to start wondering if you really are so taken by your little fucking midnight skies and morning dawns?"

"I guess you can surmise any damn thing you want to."

"How 'bout you throw us some clues? How 'bout you cut the bullshit suspense right here and cut to the chase right now? Come clean, motherfucker, and tell us what else you've been doing with Nattie. How far in does your little secret go?"

"You don't want to know, Cowboy," Daniel said to him. And then I knew, just like Adams knew, that Daniel wasn't just fooling him, and I knew even as Adams didn't, that he really didn't want to know.

Talk about a stomach buzz.

I looked up at Lance, sitting on the top landing of the *stairway to the stars*. He was working quietly and listening, chiseling on his coat of arms. I could see drops of wooden blood dripping from the wooden severed hand. I wished I had the courage to run over to him and shake him hard, to let him know this whole thing was on the verge of imploding around us; Adams and Daniel were getting awfully close to the edge, as if they were standing atop the stone staircase with sledgehammers, swinging them around, threatening to demolish everything into a crashing chaos of rubble and dust. Like another word from either one of them and all the stone and mortar and lumber would be pulverized into choking dust.

But Lance wouldn't look down, he just kept fiddling with his woodworking tools, listening I could tell, but doing nothing.

"Hey, Big Fella," Daniel finally said, "you're the stud who was strutting around in here about how fine the nectar, how enticing the honey pot. What'd you think, just because you got cut off and got your little member stung that it was off limits to the rest of us? Honey's been flowing, man, not my fault you're too busy out here dicking around with little-boy tinker toy projects to get any."

"You son-of-a-bitch," Adams said to him. "You're a fucking liar."

"Care to go knock on the back door and find out?"

Adams didn't say anything, just looked mean at Daniel without saying a thing. I was amazed that he had done it, and I was astounded that he was telling Adams he had done it.

"You and Nattie are just friends, right Daniel?" I said. "Because I think Adams thinks you're saying something else."

Then Lance looked down from carving his namesake into wood. He looked right at me and smiled a little bit. He didn't wink at me like he did a lot, but it was a smile that made me feel that this might settle down after all, it might be okay. Like somebody else's dad might smile at you after you'd just walked your friend home from school on the day he got in trouble at the principal's office, and his dad smiled at you when he sent you on your way home. A smile like maybe you're friend wasn't going to get a whupping after all. Or maybe the dad was smiling at you because you weren't going to get a whupping, and you did right by walking your friend home. Then it dawned on me that his smile was because you had no idea how bad your friend's whupping was really going to be.

I couldn't think of one good thing to say; I didn't know what to do, I just stood and looked around me.

I picked up a broom from the pile of tools beneath the loft stairs and I started to sweep. Not because the sawdust and mortar dust and the general mess we made suddenly began bothering me, but because it was a good thing to do with myself. We had allowed our boys' club to become unkempt, and it wasn't a big deal for me to sweep it up. It was easy for me to clean up the sawdust from beneath the belt sander and push piles of wood chips from beneath the lathe. Pretty soon Adams and Daniel would cool off, and I could sweep our business back to normal. Daniel would settle back down to his woodworking; Adams would sit with Lance up in their *stairway to the stars,* drinking beers out of bottles, and laughing into the night sky. I could clean a bit and then whip up a platter of some extra special appetizers – maybe use those orange and red and yellow bell peppers Becky Dreiling picked from her garden and gave me. Sweeping the barn would bring everyone back together; I could slowly and methodically move all the disjointed debris into collapsing piles of order and calm. Nobody likes dust everywhere, so I just started sweeping.

***

Well, things didn't settle down, not by a long shot. The next day Adams just stayed squinty-eyed and mean. He spent the entire morning sitting around the stove with his feet propped up on the woodbox while I cooked and cleaned and stoked and swept. It was almost funny but certainly sad, because his black cowboy boots had taken an awful beating ever since they turned into farm boots, or mortar mixing boots, or stairway building boots. Adams had come to glow with pride over the wear on his boots, much as he was proud of all that he and Lance had made – all the stone work, the walls and stairways and stars.

Adams sat all morning without saying a word. The last I'd heard from him was last night when he and Nattie were out by the stock tank, screaming at each other. He sat like that all morning, and then he started polishing his boots, just polishing those boots, making them shine like sculpted black marble. He'd pull cold bottles of beer from the metal 7-up ice chest and polish and watch the fire. Both the O'Neill's were in and out, but nobody was talking.

I couldn't stand it. All day I had wanted to throw up, so I just stayed out of the way and tended to the hearth because, no matter what else, we had to eat. Also debris had begun to filter down, ever so softly, and of course it needed sweeping. You wouldn't notice it if you couldn't see it, debris sifting from barn rafters and falling slightly from stone towers. It was easy for me to stay busy, sweeping and tending the hearth.

Finally, close to evening, he was ready to talk. I mostly listened closely because he was my friend.

"Damn, G," he started in. "Ever get that feeling you could easily kick ass in the game if the bastards'd quit chicken-shitting around, changing the rules every goddamned time it suited them?"

He was wound tight and flipping beer bottle caps all over the barn.

"I mean shit, Man, when I'm not so pissed off I could eat glass, the whole damn thing almost makes me laugh. She acts like we're still friends, and so does he. Un-fucking-believable. You know?"

It wasn't that being on the farm changed anything between Adams and me, and I don't say I was afraid of him before, but disagreeing with him somehow seemed easier whenever I was tending the cook fire.

"Maybe it's not the rules have changed," I said, "but maybe the game itself."

Just for a moment he got that look like the eyes of that kid on the playground who struggles to decide whether to punch his fist in your stomach or smack in the middle of your nose. I know Adams would never hurt or hit me, but I hesitated a moment all the same.

"I just mean the rules could still be fair but the game's maybe different."

"What the hell does that mean?"

"I don't know. It means maybe the game has changed."

"Changed how? Changed like the game is no longer about sticking with somebody?"

"I don't know," I said.

"Changed like the game is no longer about friendship? It's no longer about loyalty to those friends?"

"Cib, I don't know."

"What the hell do you mean you don't know? Either friendship is important and of value, or it's not. Which is it?"

"Of course I think friendship is important. Of course loyalty matters. But you were the one talking it up. You were the one saying we should all get some. I'm just saying maybe you changed the game, that's all."

Suddenly he was agitated, and he was livid.

"Right now, right here, no bullshit, no whimpering equivocation, no woe is me. What the fuck are you talking about? What exactly are you on about"

"You know what? Forget it. It doesn't matter and who cares. You're right. Friendship is sacrosanct."

Adams' eyes were seething now, and instead of throwing it into the red-hot fire blazing in the open stove door, I held onto the gnarled piece of mesquite, my fingers tightening to white around it.

"Listen you little weasel motherfucker," he said to me, but I knew he didn't mean it "If you don't tell me exactly what's on your mind, and right now and with no bullshit, I swear to God I'll throw your ass cross-wise into that goddamned fire."

I can say now that for just that moment I saw the other side of Cib Adams: the fire-breathing quarterback with his back stuck against a fourth down wall; the rambler needing desperately to get laid as the bartender yells his final 'last call;' the heart-cleft son clenching his anger and hurt while watching his father leave the house once again on any Friday night.

"I just mean you kind of told him to do it. You kind of told us all. With Nattie, I mean."

There, I said it, but he already knew it. But he was my friend and he needed me to say it. So I did. And it was true, so even though it was hard, he and I both knew it was true.

It's not like the wind went out of his sails or anything so silly or dramatic, but it settled him down. He just sat for a while, a long while, propped back in Lance's old hardwood Bob Cratchit chair with his boots crossed one atop the other up on the high side of my woodbox. And then he took them off. Slowly he took off his black cowboy boots and clunked them near the fire stove on the dirt floor of the barn. Not with any real anger or arrogance, and neither with resignation, but with a sort of silent determination.

"Bullshit," he finally said, shaking his head. He just sat for a long while.

"What the hell, G? You see things I don't see. You know it and I know it. Somewhere deep and often weird. But you see stuff. You see my stuff. You know? You always have. What the hell, Johnny G?"

I thought it was time to stoke the fire again, so I did. Methodically. Carefully. We made it hot, the hardwood and I. The soap water simmered almost to a boil.

"I believe I would do anything for you," I said to Adams.

"I know that," he said.

"But sometimes it feels like I'm running around below you with a net, one of those fireman nets, running frantically trying to keep up, trying to anticipate the fall. And it scares me, because... well, because it does."

"Because why? What? What is it, G? Speak."

"Well, if you fall, I'm not likely to be of much use when I catch you. I could say its because you're awfully darn big." We smiled weakly at the lame joke – the tension eased a little – but the smiles were really all about sad.

Then I had to fight against tears, and I said, "No, really, it's because sometimes, like now, I'm afraid I won't be there with the net. I'm afraid I won't get there in time."

"Our fathers have forsaken us.
But that doesn't mean
We shouldn't go into business with them."

- Cib Carkus Adams

Chapter 18

"G!" I heard Adams say. "Let's go, wake up." He whispered with so much intensity I could feel some spit spray across my face.

I was right at the best part of a really good dream and I didn't want to leave it. We were all up in the loft, all four of us sleeping naked up in the boys' club loft, and there's a barn cat up there with us, an orange tabby, lion-striped, and then there's a wooden box on the floor and inside is a whole litter of kittens. They're all squirming around each other, wrapped in this big ball of kittens, squirming and pulsing fur, when suddenly Nattie climbs up the ladder. She looks right at me and winks and laughs her approval at my immediate erection. Then she sticks her hand down into the box and squeals with delight. Oh my God you have to feel this! Have you felt this! This is the most incredible sensation I've ever felt in my life. This box is filled with pussycats. She sits down cross-legged and thrusts her entire arm into the squirming, purring litter of kittens. This feels ecstatic. All these pussycats, rubbing all over each other and all over my arm. They purr and arch their backs and nuzzle my fingers behind their ears. They arch and push and my arm is getting smothered. They lick my fingers. They're beautiful.

"G!" Adams hissed. "I mean it. Wake up! Now!"

"What's going on? What's wrong?"

"Shh," he hissed again. "We're outta here. Moving on. Now. I've already packed. I've got your stuff too. I'll meet you out by the Valiant. Hustle up."

Move on? What was he talking about? Sneak out? In the middle of the night? Why?

Adams came back up the barn loft ladder and stood looking over me.

"I mean it," he said again. "Wake up! I've already got your bag out by the Valiant. Whatever else is yours, grab it or leave it and let's go. I'll meet you out in the yard. Two minutes," he hissed again.

I pulled on my blue jeans and a sweatshirt, found my tennis shoes down next to the wood box on the hearth and slipped them on without socks. I snuck out of the barn, listening to cooing pigeons and snoring from the loft.

The sky hadn't even begun to turn gray yet, still very dark, morning chilly and end–of–summer fresh. I walked around the front of the house where Adams leaned against the trunk of the Valiant.

"This is crazy, Cib. We don't need to go anywhere. Everything will work out."

The moon had long since set, but I could see the intensity burning in his eyes even so. Rising up from behind the gable on the house, Venus hung huge, brilliant, and bright

"What the hell's wrong with you?" Adams said. "Everything will not 'work out.' Actually, everything's 'fucked up' and getting worse. There's nothing to work out. This whole deal's gotten out of control. Somebody's going to get hurt badly. It's not going to be me, and we're not going to be around when it happens. Let's go. Now."

I understood what he meant. I knew he was angry, but I couldn't leave, and I was terrified he would go without me.

"I can't go, Cib."

"Of course you can go. We're going now. I figure we'll push the Valiant out the driveway and coast 'er down the hill a ways before starting it up. I'd like to be in fucking Oklahoma before anyone realizes we're gone."

"We can't go, not yet. Cib, what's happening?"

I felt like an idiot, calling him Cib again for reasons I didn't want to imagine. I felt like a silly little kid, small and silly and like a fool. Nobody called him Cib but me, and me only when I felt silly and small and like a fool. I hated that, and I hated that the feeling was back, after so many weeks in the boys' club where I felt almost as big and as serious and as grown up as anyone else – Lance or Daniel or even Adams.

I hated that that feeling was gone, like those travelers in that movie who stumble upon a beautiful little village beneath the heather on the hill, but it only exists for one day and then is gone for one hundred years. I hated feeling small again. I hated saying Cib again. I hated being me again.

And then it fills in me, this hatred of being me and being little and silly, and it fills me, and I bite my lip, and I try to bite harder, but then it blurts out of me like some alien regurgitation.

"Well, maybe if you could have held on to your girlfriend," I tell Adams, "maybe none of this would have happened."

I can feel my chin quiver, and I fight to hold back the tears. Adams isn't at all about to cry. He looks like he's about to tear my ears off or gouge my eyes out, but slowly, and with pain. I don't look away from him, but I can't keep looking in his eyes.

They burn me hot and he says, very slowly, "What was that?"

The fear and the cool morning makes me want to pee. "You know what I said."

I can see his biceps flinching, flexing, even beneath his jean jacket. Adams doesn't move, he just looks at me.

"You want to be very careful, here."

He's looking right at me, so hot but measured and careful and frighteningly calm.

Suddenly I don't even know if I really meant it, and then just as suddenly I see him clearly – I see him again, my roommate, my buddy, my friend.

"Cib, really, please don't go. We can't go, not yet. I mean, I'm sorry for you guys, I really am, but we can't go. I heard what she said last night when you guys were fighting. I can have some too. I want to try to get some. I know that sounds ridiculous, because you think I could never have any, but I want some too."

"What are you talking about?"

I heard her. I heard her when she told you she could, you know, anyone she wants to. Maybe she wants to with me."

"Ah, G., come on, Man. This is all such bullshit. She's lost her mind, or become the queen bitch, but either way we don't want to stay around for the final act."

"I've got to try, Cib. I've got to try and get some too."

"Listen, Man, that's the problem. You probably can have some. That's why this whole thing's become such bad news. Does this make any sense to you? Do you think this kind of shit happens in real life? It's bullshit. It's crazy. Doesn't it seem a little sick to you?"

"You just don't want me to have any. You just want me to stay like I am, little and lost and empty."

"God Damn it." He doesn't yell this, we are still talking barely above a whisper, but I catch a glimpse of the air tighten and tense between us when he says it. "Get in the fucking car, and we'll argue about it on our way the hell out of here. Let's go. You steer."

He begins pushing the car. Not bending over with outstretched arms, huffing and puffing, pushing, but backwards pushing, with his butt against the low part of the trunk, grinding it out with his legs pushing. His muscular arms lift up on the back of the bumper, pushing the weight forward, lifting the Valiant and making it float. "Grab the wheel, Man."

I do, and I push against the driver's side doorjamb as I guide the car around the curve of the gravel driveway. But it is effortless. We float silent with the Valiant in the dawn; the buzz in my stomach turns the wheels and opens our motion. I could hang on and climb in and float off. I could return to our real lives, go back to college in time for the fall semester. Go back to normal where boys don't live in barns and women don't beckon and call from inside the house, smiling and silent and green eyes running deep with promise and exquisite pain. I could just climb into the Valiant with Adams at dawn, and off we'd go and it would be fine.

Back to my life.

We get the Valiant to the end of the driveway, and we hold it atop the little hill on the dirt road leading to the highway going west.

"Cool," Adams says. "Grab your stuff and get in. Let's go."

I can see he has a good hold on the car, so I let go and step back onto the gravel driveway.

"Maybe you'll just drive around a bit and then you'll come back," I tell him. "I'll just wait."

"Come on, Man. Get in the car."

"I can't, Cib. I can't leave."

"Yes you can. Get in the car."

"I can't."

"Get in now."

"I can't."

He looks at me hard for what feels like forever, and then he says, "Shit." After another long silence, he almost smiles. "Well, maybe I'm the one who's crazy," he says to me. "It's just sex, right? Maybe there's really nothing worse going on here than bullshit. Maybe it's not bad, just bullshit."

He takes in a deep breath of the air and blows it out and says, "Shit," again, and then he gets into the Valiant and it rolls down the hill. He lets it roll quite a way, and then I see the Valiant lurch and jerk, and the Slant Six jolts to life. The cold cough of exhaust kicks up a cloud of dust in the early morning almost light, and the Valiant disappears in the dust, and I stand for a very long while and listen to the day begin. I stand and watch the dust settle.

***

For the longest time I just stand there, watching the road, watching the dust settle, watching the sun rise and watching my feet, the leather tennis shoes unable to move off the crushed gravel driveway of Becky Dreiling's farm.

I say over and over Adams will be back, he will be back, but I know he won't. I know he isn't coming back. I don't feel abandoned or alone near as much as I feel lost and empty. Everyone says I'm so shy around women, but maybe I just know better, know it's best to stay away – watch them, look at them, think about them in that way at night, even, but stay away. Like go to church and pray and be reverent but don't take the Sacraments. I stand there for an awfully long time, time enough for the sun to reach around the house and then up and coming over the entire house. High enough that I take my sweatshirt off just as Daniel comes sauntering around the house and comes around the circle drive toward me standing there out at the start of the road. He's barefoot. The cuff of his blue jeans scrapes along the gravel and make tiny invisible puffs of dust. The morning sun looks good on the bare skin of his back and shoulders. He has a t-shirt tucked into the waistband of his jeans, and it hangs like the loincloth of some ancient Celt. He looks like he used to back when we all lived in the house at college – almost a part of the earth and almost a part of it all.

He walks up to stand next to me and does one of his animal-pose stretches. This one looks like a breaching whale, then turns into a cobra about to strike.

"Morning, Man," he mumbles, but clear and clean like he's right there.

Before I can wonder what he'll say about Adams is gone, he looks around and says, "Where's my Valiant?"

Oh man, I had forgotten about that part. Man alive, this is bad. I don't really know what to say to him, so I don't say anything right off.

"What happened? Cowboy got his feelings so hurt last night he drove the Valiant and drowned himself in the north pond?"

Daniel stoops to pick up a handful of gravel. "Boy never lose a woman before?"

He starts pitching stones at the telephone pole sticking up straight and strong out at the edge of the yellow dirt road. "Lots like throwing interceptions, and I know he's done more than his share of that. Learn from it, live with it, and get the hell over it."

"It's kind of strange," I finally say. "It's a really strange kind of morning." I watch my tennis shoes kick at the gravel. "Is she, you know, is she your girlfriend now?"

Daniel laughs, and he does that shadowboxing thing where he whiffs hands and air past my face, and he laughs more when I flinch and dodge.

"She's everybody's girlfriend." He actually hits me, slightly, but on my ears so I feel it. "Gophe, you know better than anyone she's no one's girlfriend." He throws the entire handful of gravel, spraying the telephone pole like with shrapnel.

"Yeah, but, you know, what about all those wooden dolls. I mean it was almost creepy, but mostly so sneaky. It kind of killed the boys' club. Not the dolls, but the sneaky." I watch him, and hope he doesn't get mad at me. "It's just that everything doesn't make sense now."

"The hell you mean, sneaky?"

My stomach buzzes from the edge in his voice.

"This isn't summer camp, Man. You don't need a hall pass to take a leak behind the barn."

My feet squirm some more, like they're trying to burrow beneath the gravel. I watch the dust rise up around my bare ankles – two fence posts set deep and solid into the earth.

"Well, I know that, but there were rules, weren't there? Boys' club rules? You know, it was our boys' club."

"Yeah, well, now the boys' club is officially a busted frat party. Girls got in, you know? It happens, Gophe."

I swallow hard and remember that he is my friend, even through the meanness. Daniel runs his long fingers through his jet-black hair, and then he shakes it out, not like a wet dog, but like a stallion.

"C'mon, Man. Where's my car?"

I run my fingers through my own hair, not like I'm copying him but more like acting like him.

"I think Adams is driving it."

"Yeah?"

"I think maybe Adams is driving it away."

"Away from where?"

"You know. Away. Away from us."

"He took my fucking car?"

"I think he was mad about last night. And you know, about Nattie and all."

"That son of a bitch."

Like I say, I hadn't even thought about this part of it, the Valiant part of it. The deal was they would share ownership forever. It couldn't be changed, couldn't be rescinded. They swore on it, although that part seems lost now, if there's no boys' club.

"Well," I finally manage to say, "maybe he figured since you got Nattie, he got the Valiant."

"For Christ's sake, Gophe. It's not like this is baseball cards. What the hell's wrong with you?"

I hear the screen door slam, and Daniel's mom is there on the front porch; I can see the steam curling up from her cup of coffee. It looks like she's warming her hands, holding the cup like it's a wounded hummingbird. I look up to the attic window and wonder whether she knows what went on up there last night. I almost start to cry and wish that she would hold me, like the mess and the anger and the hurt would dissolve if I could be that cup of coffee in her hands.

Of course, Becky Dreiling probably doesn't care if Nattie is with Adams, or with Daniel or with nobody. But it didn't feel right last night how Nattie was talking to Lance, as if she could have or do anything she wanted.

And suddenly I think maybe Adams was right, maybe this is all wrong, all twisted, all bad. I look at Daniel, who is seething and staring down the road as if by sheer desire he can bring the Valiant back. I look again at the house and watch Lance clomp around the corner. He seems unsure if to join us out at the road or go up to the porch. I look up to the gable in the attic and wonder what she's doing up there. I feel certain she's watching, she can see us and see what we're all thinking, how we're feeling, even though clearly we cannot.

"I never saw my father naked."

- John Gophe

Chapter 19

I don't know what to do, and I can't see how to spend the day. Clearly neither does his uncle nor Daniel O'Neill. It's all over, it's all fallen, it's all done but none of us have the slightest idea how to pack it up and put it away. It's not like Adams is the heart of the boys' club, not like he's the boys' club president or anything, but clearly *better than fine* is no more. I don't think Lance is actually saddened – after all, he's a grown-up and undoubtedly has better things to do with his time than hang out with a bunch of heartsick and love-starved college boys. This is Daniel's home, so I imagine he'll move into the house like a regular person with his mom and with Nattie Sinclair. Certainly Daniel O'Neill won't continue hanging out in the barn goofing off with me, and then I suddenly wonder what in the world am I going to do? I lost my ride, and it's not like I can walk home from Kansas. Man alive, Toto.

I stop myself the moment I recognize the guilt and the blame – as if I should have been able to see this coming. Dag! If you want to know, the whole thing begins making me kind of mad, in a way. Everything was going so well; better, really, than fine. Why'd these guys have to let it get away, get dirty, get stolen? Why'd they have to get Nattie involved, and involved between them? She was fine in the house, we were fine in the barn. Like my old man used to say, don't argue religion in your grandma's parlor. It mucks things up. Man alive, does it ever. At first we were all happy and innocent – not sanctified, perhaps, but pure and fine – acting like heathens, maybe, running around like savages, sure, but without malice and with no mean. Missing the Sacraments, I guess, so clearly not Baptized and not saved, but good and brotherly and like Jesus even so. And then all of a sudden His Dad barges in and tosses us out and tells us we're naked and we're doing it wrong. Cathedrals now, instead of catacombs; kitchens instead of barns.

I feel humiliated and penitent and yet I know I've broken no commandment, done nothing venal, crucified no Jew. I'd merely languished in the brotherhood, rolled mellow with the hippies, gotten along and maybe for the first time gotten it right. Dag! We didn't do anything wrong, we shouldn't have lost it all. It wasn't right. It wasn't fair. I wished I could turn it back, drag it home and force a return to *better than fine*. I wish I had the courage, or the strength, or the vision, to grab them both by the scruff of the neck, haul them both – Adams and Daniel – back into the parlor and make them sit proper in straight-backed wooden chairs perched on a braided rug covering a polished hardwood floor and then kneel and say the rosary.

I wish I could just go in the house and ask Daniel's mom to fix me a really regular meal, like the big one you have before you get on the bus or the train. I wish I could sit again with Nattie, just one more time, and watch her. Watch her throw her head back and drink whiskey and laugh, watch her eyes over the top of her coffee cup and watch her smile. I wish she didn't scare me now, and I wish she hadn't done Adams the way she did. I wish I could make it make sense.

Man alive.

I finally decide to work hard on staying out of the way, as out of sight as I can get. I realize the more everybody here sees me, the more obvious it will become that it's time for me to be on my way and, like I say, I have no idea where that is or how to get there.

The day wears on and clearly Uncle Lance has had enough. Enough of Daniel thrashing around, fiery mad about Adams and about the Valiant; enough of me, tripping overly-polite and sneaking out of sight around corners and hiding out up in the loft; enough of the whole boys' club *stairway to the stars* summertime extravaganza.

Daniel is livid, storming around the barn, throwing stuff and planning on how to get after Adams and get his car back. Suddenly his mother comes into the barn. Becky Dreiling listens to him for a short while and then asks any one of us, "What in the hell's been going on out here?"

Lance looks to her, scratching his mind about what he's going to say. And then Daniel blurts out, "You heard about the Valiant? I'm going to beat the shit out of him. I'm going to track him down, and I'm going to get my car back, and then I'm going to beat the shit out of him." He looks around at all of us. "I might even kill the son of a bitch."

Becky turns fast to Lance. "Have you lost your mind?" she demands. "Do you see what's going on here? What the hell's wrong with you? And you," she tells Daniel, "you're not going to go chase anything or kill anyone. Tomorrow's Monday. It's got a license plate. We'll get it back.

"I want you to listen to me," she says again to Lance.

I'm fascinated, and glad I'm not getting yelled at. I had never seen a mom yell at a dad before. I'm awestruck.

"This nonsense is over," she tells him. "The testosterone fest is cut off. What the hell were you thinking?"

"We made up the rules as we went along," he says, steady, not mad but not backing down, either. Calm. Resolve. "Sometimes the game hurts."

"Goddamn!" she says, and I can see tears in her eyes. "Haven't you had enough? Didn't once around satisfy you?"

Her fists kind of clench and her body looks just like right after you stomp your feet.

"Goddamn you," she says. "Not with these kids, we won't. We're not doing it to them. Goddamn you."

She storms out of the huge sliding barn door.

Before anyone can move or say a word, she comes back out of the sunshine and into the barn.

"Please," she says to him, but not like she's asking. "Move my grandmothers' cauldron back here, outside next to the barn. Put it in the ground right next to the door. There's a mess out here – all yang and destruction with no balance. That pot is calm, put it in the earth next to the barn for a while. We're going to bring balance back. Please," she says, and then she leaves the barn for good.

We all just sit, absorbing and figuring out.

Man alive.

A very short while later, Nattie appears in the wide barn doorway wearing short jean shorts and flashing a big "Hello boys" smile. She sashays across the dirt floor and, I swear, even as gorgeous as she is, I don't feel that normal groin pulse but rather I'm overcome with a sense of foreboding and dread.

Daniel sees her and his face breaks into a sly smooth smile. "I was thinking of coming and looking for you," he says.

"I'm right here," she says, looking right at Lance, ignoring Daniel and ignoring me.

Lance thinks hard with his eyes right through her. He doesn't move but his face and his fingers are tight. If Lance looked at me this way, I would pee my pants, but Nattie doesn't flinch and from all the way across the barn at my post in front of the cold wood-burning cook stove I can smell her – intoxicating and dangerous and most like a hand firmly on a scrotum – no pain yet but only because we all agree to move slowly and get along.

Her hair floats and shimmers in a soft breeze I cannot see, a subtle wind that touches nothing else. I stare at her legs as she says something to Lance about how "cool it is in the barn."

Lance watches her, and the tightness in his blood moves out of him and into Daniel.

"Cooler yet swimming in the pond," Lance finally says.

Nothing moves except Daniel's thumb; he rubs it slowly across the edge of a newly sharpened chisel. Even though he's across the barn at the router station of the workbench, I can hear his thumb scrape broadside across the metal edge, like hearing a scalpel scrape cancerous cells. I wait for him to slide his thumb lengthwise and cut a deep crimson crevice into his flesh, but he suddenly throws the chisel like a knife, sticking it deep into a wall timber. I jump with a start. Then he walks out of the side barn door. He doesn't look back; neither Nattie nor Lance turn when he leaves.

"Where's Becky?" Lance asks her, and I realize with an immediate and empty stomach buzz that I'm no longer here, no longer in the barn, no longer a part of the scene. I could be anywhere, for as much notice as they give me.

"In to town," Nattie says. "Gone till supper."

There is another long motionless silence.

"For Chrissakes, girl," Lance finally says. "I'm old enough to be your father."

Nattie smiles at him, and I'm frozen. Even the dust stops falling.

"Shit." Lance slowly creaks his muscular neck from side to side; long black hair falls and sways back and forth like the tick-tock myth of a grandfather clock.

"Shit," he says again after a long time, and then he gets up and limps slowly across the dirt floor and leaves through the same side door that took Daniel. He stops just as the sunlight hits him, and he turns. He looks at Nattie, and then he motions to me. "Boy," he calls to me. "Empty the ashes and clean the stove. Make it shine."

I look at Nattie and I don't say a thing. Her face glimmers with an effort of thought. She looks at me like a stranger, and then she turns and walks out through the big double doors as if I'll never see her again.

I ponder for a while, standing at my post. Then I build a fast small fire to heat up some water. I prepare to clean the cast iron cook stove. I recognize I've been left alone with the body, allowed to pay my respects in private. I have a big pot of hot soap water in no time and a good supply of dry rags at the ready. Opening more vents in the firebox turns the coals glowing red – the fire burns itself down with a fury. I dig yet another hole in the dirt floor of the barn and bury the ashes, hot coals and all.

I sweep the firebox extra clean with the little whiskbroom and then start in on the cooking surfaces – damp ragging and wiping dry as I go. I recognize it's the finest two hours I've ever spent in my life.

Suddenly Lance throws open the two big double doors. I finish rinsing and twisting out rags – hanging them flat to dry while Lance backs his pick-up into the barn and kills the engine. Lance rides one of the angel pulleys up along the smokestack of the cook stove and ties off near the ceiling. He begins unbolting the sections of pipe and lowers them down into the bed of the truck.

"Wrap all the burners and loose parts into those rags," he tells me. "Oil them all first."

I get the cast iron stove cleaned and oiled and wrapped in no time. When Daniel returns to the barn we've already got the thing half up the ramp and loaded into the bed of Lance's pick-up.

"Drive it around front," Lance tells Daniel. "Make sure the tailgate is backed up near the porch."

Lance throws pulleys, chains, ropes, and block and tackle into the bed and tells me to bring the extension ladder hanging by the door.

"Boys' club's closed," he tells us, as if he's telling the barn. "Last fucking call."

We move the operation into the front yard. It takes almost no effort for the three of us to slide the stove off the tailgate, down the ramps, and into the ground next to the huge black cast iron pot.

We just stand and look for a moment, these two enormous pieces together like a dance of leviathans – both are hearth, both are fire, nurture and ravage entwined.

"Load it up," Lance barks. "Let's be careful with it."

The huge black cast iron pot more than floats. It jumps. The three of us hoist, and the huge cauldron flies into the bed of the truck. I sit with it in the back of the truck. I sit holding the rim as Daniel drives, not because I fear it will tip – it weighs many times what I do – but because I feel its pulse with the earth and I want to stay down.

When Daniel begins backing up to the big sliding door of the barn, Lance tells him to back up to the house instead.

"It's going in the attic," Lance declares.

"You heard her," Daniel says. "She wants it in the ground, next to the barn."

"It belongs in the attic. If it all needs to connect, it needs to connect in the attic."

Daniel is thinking, trying to figure it out. But he can't see it, can't see that it's wrong. The balance is worse with it up there. We have to stay down, it has to stay down, it doesn't belong up, it should stay down. It's backwards, it's unbalanced, it's wrong. It needs to stay down.

"It's like earth in the sky," I say quietly, though I want to scream. "Earth in the sky."

I say again, a little louder, "It's wrong. Can't you see it? It's earth in the sky. It's wrong."

His uncle sends Daniel up the ladder to remove the gable window into the attic. Next we rig the block and tackle to the stout ridge rafter tail and we hoist the black cast iron pot up out of the truck and ultimately through the window. For a moment, as it hangs in the air, it occurs to me the huge cauldron looks like a suspended planet forced into a new orbit. Clambering into the attic through the window, we roll it on the dolly across the attic floor and off-load it along the south side. It sits here in the attic, enormous, black and metal, and out of place, earth in the sky. Ground in the air. Once maybe all about hearth and home but now weighting the beautiful and miniature wood in the attic with heavy black and with a curious and empty sorrow. We pull ourselves out, and descend to the yard.

It's dark outside by now and Lance says nothing as he looks up at the sky for a while. He looks up at the gable window and then he says, "Let's shut 'er down."

We return to what now seems like a very old barn for what I imagine will be the last time, and they open a bottle of whiskey, and we don't speak, and I drink from the bottle with them.

***

The next morning we wake early to the sound of hard rain pelting the Kansas prairie and the yellow dirt outside is mud. We trudge across the yard in the rain.

Lance opens the back door to the mudroom and we three begin to shuffle in, wet and tired kittens out of a rainstorm.

The day will likely end up dry and hot as usual, so the rain is really more like a feel of tails between our legs and a bit whupped on from the last few days. Without Adams, we're actually more like a wet and whupped three-legged kitten, stumbling into a warm dry kitchen, looking for solace or just a saucer of warm milk.

A warm dry corner where Becky might stroke us or at least give us to suckle caffeine and nicotine and leave us be.

This morning, thinking about being in the kitchen feels like coming to a safe place to crawl into, and all the rest is fantasy or fairy tale or far away.

"No coffee," Lance grunts when we all get in the mudroom at the back of the kitchen. "I can already not smell it."

We remove our wet coats and muddy boots and Lance reaches for the doorknob to the kitchen. Suddenly an enormous crash roars from inside. I jump and look at Daniel behind me, Lance says "what the hell?" and someone inside screams.

We all push into the kitchen and both of them are crumpled together on the floor in front of the sink.

A huge hole gapes in the ceiling, splintered pieces of wooden lathe hanging down and chunks of plaster and plaster dust everywhere. The cast iron pot crashed through, and I look down at both women and at the black cast iron cauldron. It's crushing one of them, grabbing hold with its hard pointed legs right in the middle of a motionless back. One's not hurt, just hugging or rocking or listening for breath. And then Nattie looks up at us and covers her mouth with her hand.

Everything is still for a moment, and then I look at both Daniel and Lance and there is nothing in their eyes. Nobody says a thing. Daniel looks hollow and yellow and gone. The air is stifled with plaster dust and debris.

It doesn't make sense, now nothing makes sense, and Nattie holds on to Becky's body, and you can see two of the three cast iron legs sticking into Becky's back.

Lance moves, clawing his way through the dust. He grabs the edge of the pot and tries to pull it off of Becky; Nattie has to hold Becky's body tightly so it will separate from the legs of the pot. The muscles in Lance's arms and back swell and quiver; he groans and then the one comes free from the other. Blood comes out and the pot thuds on the wooden floor and rolls back and forth making a bowling ball sound, and finally it comes to rest on the wooden kitchen floor.

And then there is no noise.

Lance takes Becky's body from Nattie and turns her over. He cradles her limp in his arms. He buries his face in her chest and holds her and holds on.

I stare at them, looking at a surreal Pieta. Lance sitting on the floor, holding Becky in his arms, sobbing without noise and rocking her body so slowly, back and forth slowly and holding on. Nattie Sinclair kneeling behind with her hands on his shoulders. Like marble, but moving slowly in a rhythm past sadness and past pain to just holding on, rocking slowly and just holding on.

There is no noise in the kitchen, but the air has become very thick.

Daniel O'Neill pulls a chair from the table near the window. He slowly sits down. He struggles to pull deep heavy pieces of the air into himself, then he must work to force the air back out.

And then suddenly a terrible explosion and everything crumbles and scatters and falls, stars into stairways and dust from stone walls. The air colors with tumbling stone towers, falling star chaos and explosions of dust and mortar and stone. And then fire. The wood stove spills and its angry hot coals rip into flames that leap and spread and consume. A voracious inferno. The air fills with flame jumping and burning from barn timbers and shooting from the rooftops. Fire and smoke in the kitchen everywhere.

The smoke and dust are everywhere, sucking air, and it all chokes me and blinds me and makes me burn. And then I turn and look at Nattie Sinclair.

The smoke and the dust fill the kitchen and swirl in and around her face – so smooth and pretty, not smiling now but not sad.

Then the gray smoke is in her face, and the dust is her face. Her hair is gray smoke, not auburn, now dust, now longer and swirling and dust and not pretty. The smoke hardens her face, wrinkles of smoke making it stronger, now a Crone, older, the smoke making her face mean and older and creasing her face with deep wrinkles of dust and flowing anger and calm and control. The smoke grows her hair long and colors it gray, all dust and flowing and long.

I near to retch with revulsion and fear, but, like Lot's wife, I cannot stop myself; I turn slowly and I look into the eyes of God.

I gasp in terror and then Her deep emerald reward ringed by circles of black contrition makes me crumble and cry.

Gloria In Excelsis Deo

You begin sweeping of necessity the mortar dust and stone pieces, the ash settling softly everywhere, not filth but debris needing attention. It spreads and the more you look for it the more there is needs sweeping.

Lots of activity about so you sweep around it and work around it and keep your head down, so you can concentrate on all the bits of scattered dust and debris.

Priests, for days in and out, walking about, drinking the coffee, documenting and praying, and there are some nuns, too; one who wants to know about you and who writes things down.

He leaves with a priest, or she does, or Daniel, but they come back, from Confession maybe, but your turn will come, it will come.

And then fewer priests, and no nuns, and he goes away in his truck and comes back, and goes away some more, and sometimes you go with him and sometimes you do not, and things settle down and there's still much sweeping to do in the corners and under things.

The debris and the sweeping like hags weeping the sawdust of their bones into piles before them.

***

A torrent of yellow-dirt debris churning from the back wheels of Lance O'Neill's old pick-up truck spreads and billows for a mile. The grit in your teeth remains even though the sound of the engine has already settled back into stillness.

Early morning sunlight creeps across the gravel driveway toward the wrap-around front porch here at Becky Dreiling's farm. Moments ago, shards of light glazed off the tiny rocks at obtuse angles, and then the light grazed tentatively up and into the wooden porch columns.

Dust from the distant pick-up truck settles slowly in the dead morning air and falls silently atop a morning filled already with sweeping; sweeping from the many nights before, and then sweeping again for the infinite nights to come.

Best, really, to begin before the old farmhouse stirs any further.

But the dust cloud in the distance down the road continues sifting out of the air as you sweep, and then clearly the cloud is not receding at all, and it does not come from Lance O'Neill's old pick-up truck leaving again, but comes rather from a smaller car approaching, raising dust and bringing dust with it.

Remarkably, the 1965 Plymouth Valiant pulls into the curved gravel driveway. Rocks crunch beneath the wheels of the Valiant making little explosions of dust, and then suddenly everything clears and you can no longer see the dust these wheels make.

The Valiant rolls to a stop, the door opens, and Cib Carkus Adams steps out. He looks good, clean, and no dust at all on a sharp three-piece suit. He looks grown up now, like somebody's dad. His hair is shorter and there is no dust in it. He walks up the porch steps and stops and takes your hand; Adams looks into your eyes and whispers "Johnny G," and then he looks deeper into your eyes for a long time, and then he looks away. He finally drops your hand and picks up his briefcase, opens the screen door, and goes inside.

The Valiant has been traveling out in the country, so it is dirty like you expect any car to be, but not dusty like here. You lean the broom near the screen door on the front porch and sit on the railing as near as you can get to the Valiant and you wait without sweeping.

Adams re-emerges after only a short time inside. You see the little child peering out from behind the curtain in the front room; her emerald eyes take in everything. Adams walks past you across the front porch and down the steps.

He stops and stands by the Valiant for a moment, and then he says "Lets ride, G."

He opens the shotgun door to the Valiant and holds it for you while you climb inside. It's very nice, very clean, and well cared for.

The 1965 Plymouth Valiant has all new upholstery.

Adams gets in on the driver's side and slams the door. It feels just fine to smile at him, so you do, and he smiles back. He slowly shakes his head. He looks past you, out the window and up at the house; he looks awhile and bites his lip and shakes his head some more.

He sinks the clutch pedal to the floor, turns the key, and the Slant Six starts beautifully, purrs smoothly, reliable as you could like.

Adams looks again into your face and steers around the half-circle gravel driveway. He turns the wheel and the Valiant follows the county road until it hits the highway. Adams turns west and settles back into the seat; he steers with his right wrist dangling over the large steering wheel still sporting its wooden horn cap.

You look out the window and watch the stone fence posts snap past, faster and faster until they blur into one. Then you settle back into your seat also, comfortable for a morning Valiant ride.

About the Author

A former newspaper writer and editor, Bobby Haas is a son of the Volga Germans who people the prairie featured in *Midnight Valiant*. His paternal grandfather escaped Russia before the revolution and had a hand in repairing the bell tower on The Cathedral of the Plains, one of the several magnificent Catholic churches anchoring immigrant communities in Ellis County Kansas.

As emigration is a constant, Mr. Haas feels a bit these days like a diminutive Colossus of Rhodes, each leg straddling the independent adult movement of his two daughters.

Being thus temporarily ungrounded, Haas sculpts in alabaster and frequently dreams of woodland areas, harbors, and the sea.

Feel free to visit BobbyHaas.com

CPSIA information can be obtained
at www.ICGtesting.com
Printed in the USA
LVHW01s0213030818
585752LV00005B/962/P